ORION ONE

ORION ONE

A NOVEL BY
E.D. ERKER

Orions Blackbelt, LLC

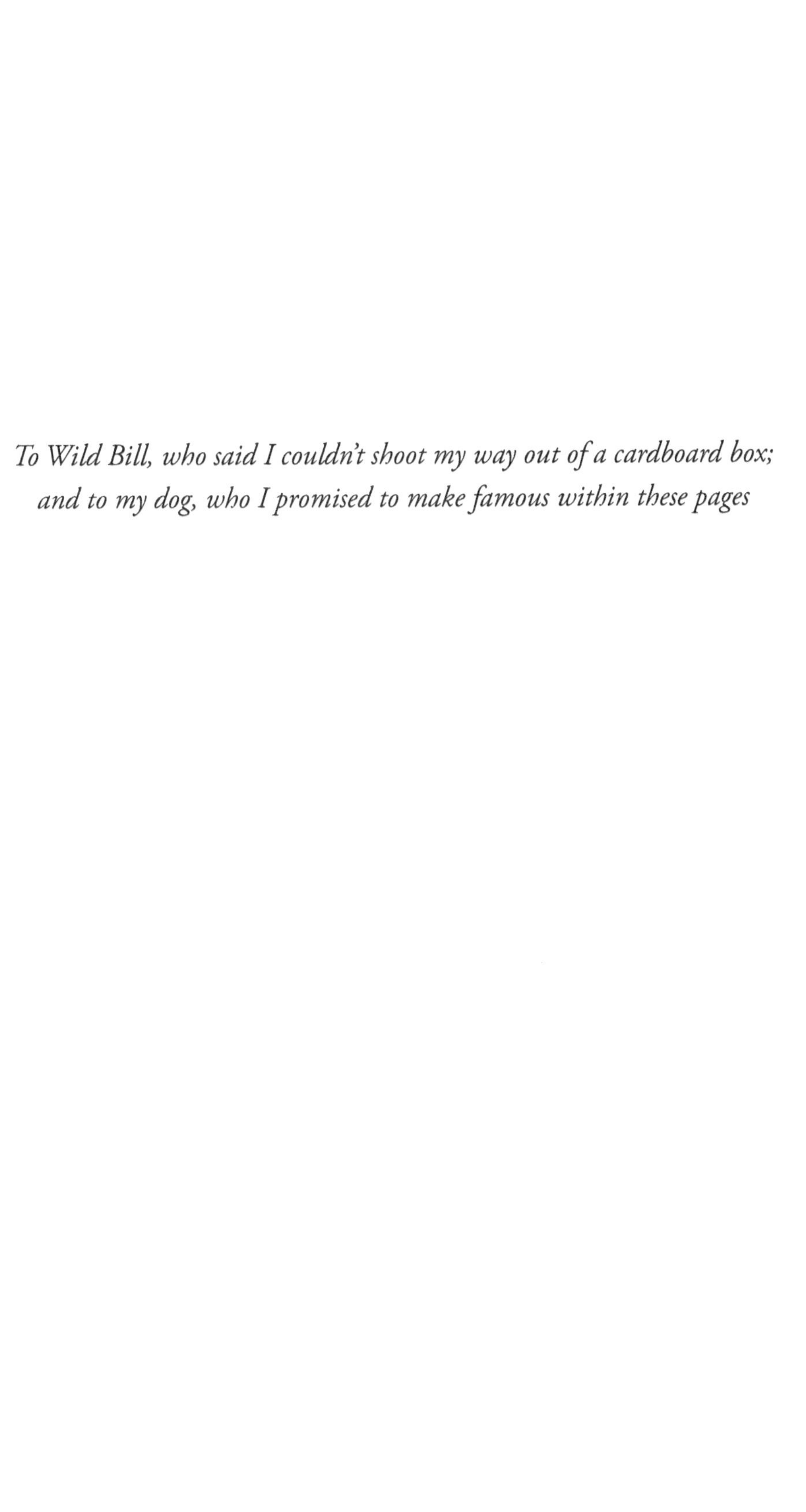

To Wild Bill, who said I couldn't shoot my way out of a cardboard box; and to my dog, who I promised to make famous within these pages

ACKNOWLEDGMENTS

First, I thank my mother, who had the patience to type my hand-written manuscript and manage not to kill me in the process. I thank my dad for making me. Without my parents, there would be no book. So, way to go, Dad! You did good.

I send a special thanks to my Krav Maga training partner, Nina Shirazi. We started out as teacher and student, and now we are more like sisters. Thank you, Nina, for supporting me emotionally through this process and keeping me strong.

There is a special brotherhood of veterans that I met while I wrote this book. These guys inspired me to push on. Some, including E-3 LCpl. Brewer, 3rd Battalion Marines 3/8 Lima Company; and Sgt. Andy Florintino; hung on every word of this book as I read it aloud to them. We laughed; we cried; we became a family. We also blew off a significant amount of steam at the MMA fights too. Love you, Brothers.

Thank you Maj. Tony Wingfield, my childhood friend who took the time to sit through interviews, making me laugh and making me proud.

Thank you Sgt. Gregory Butacan, 1st Cav. Greywolf Brigade, and the Rocky Mountain Hyperbaric Institute for connecting us. Buta, you helped me see the courage and strength it takes for veterans to heal. You inspire me to keep writing and getting the message out.

Thank you to the anonymous women of U.S. Special Forces who took the time to hang out with me on the farm and digest what it means to be a woman in the military.

Gratitude and love to Cat Ohala, my editor. Countless hours spent side-by-side, working out this complicated storyline, have led to a wonderful friendship. Without your diehard dedication and rock-star expertise, I wouldn't have this book to share with the world.

Last, I need to end by thanking my dog Susie. She didn't live to see this project launch. She is embodied in the character of Maxine, and she was my world. Without her, I couldn't have written this book.

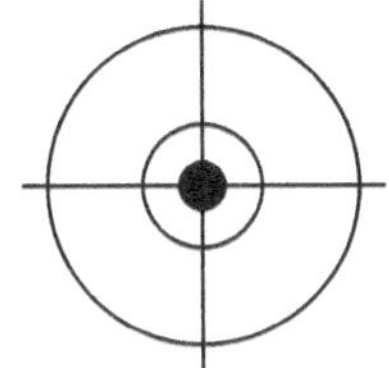

CAST OF MAJOR CHARACTERS

(in order of appearance)

Admiral John Howard	*aka Howser; Special Forces operative; later, president of Orion*
Agent Amelia DuFor	*aka The Black Widow, special assassin, wife of Howser, mother of Elizabeth*
General Elizabeth Howard	*aka G.I. Jane, aka Widowmaker; daughter of Howser and DuFor; child–soldier of Orion; later, second-in-command of Orion*
Colonel Jude Aikens	*aka Bulldog, Orion soldier, member of Jane's team*
Tom Stapelton	*Orion soldier, husband of Jane*
Dr. Mary Reid	*psychiatrist*
Marlene Stapelton	*mother of Tom Stapelton*

Sam Stapelton	*grandson of Marlene and Eugene Stapelton; nephew of Tom Stapelton*
Eugene Stapelton	*father of Tom Stapelton*
Earl Nez	*sheriff, friend of Eugene Stapelton*
Lieutenant Greg Walker	*aka Pilot, Orion soldier, member of Jane's team*
Major Brian Wright	*aka Butch, aka The Butcher, Orion soldier, member of Jane's team*
Sergeant Wilson Jared	*aka Screech, aka Professor, Orion soldier, member of Jane's team*
Robert Locke	*boyfriend of Elizabeth*

Orion soldiers are a different breed of warrior. They are influenced by the past but are futuristic in their use of weaponry and tactics. At the moment, the world isn't ready to know about Orion soldiers, so they work clandestinely—in the shadows.

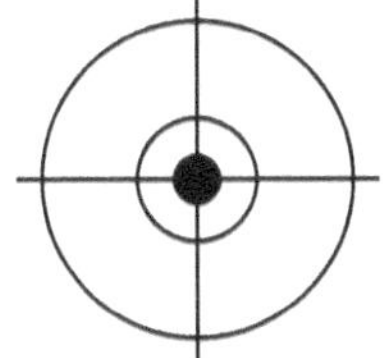

CHAPTER ONE

A team of Siberian huskies hauled the heavy sled across the snow- and ice-encrusted tundra with haste. The lead dog lathered at the mouth as he heaved at the tug line cutting into his robustly built frame. Pelting snow scorched Admiral John Howard's rough face as the burly man strapped the dogs to their limit, striking the leather whip and shouting "Gee!" and "Haw!" to keep the dogs on course. The percussion of ground explosions just yards behind him revealed his pursuers' presence.

"Faster, you goddamn mongrels! Faster!" the admiral shouted as perspiration poured off his forehead, stinging his eyes.

It was 1962. Orion, aided by a top-secret special United Nations paramilitary, was locked in an engagement with the Soviet Union and Eastern Bloc Czechoslovakia in Siberia. While at the helm of a covert operation to thwart a full-blown war, the admiral found himself dealing with another imminent matter that would alter his life permanently.

As he drove across the unforgiving terrain, Howard—also known as Howser—glanced frequently at his wife, Amelia, whose body lay in a clump in the booth of the sled. She was swathed in furs, but he could tell from her pallid face that she had lost a substantial amount of blood. In the distance, he saw chimney smoke feathering out from a few crude huts. He flogged the dogs harder, the leather strap cracking their shoulders as they charged forward. French Allied helicopters maneuvered above him firing 20mm cannons to his rear, in the path of General Boris Veldt's Soviet Army. Their anti-armor missiles annihilated the earth, effecting the admiral's escape.

"*Viva la France!*" the admiral roared as he looked skyward. British Centurian Mk3s rolled over the hill toward him, blasting their 17 pdr's at the advancing Soviet forces. "And God save the Queen!"

Howard's determination silenced the pandemonium around him. He knew time was running out. As he pushed the dogs harder, fragments of memories flashed through his mind. His thoughts took him back ten years to when he first met Agent Amelia DuFor, FSX Unit. He fought to drown out the sound of her voice as she recounted her testimony to him regarding her failed mission in Argentina.

"I am Agent Amelia DuFor. I swear these accounts of Operation OVIDA to be true to my recollection from my firsthand experience. No methods of forced coercion have been used to extract this information from me," she said, stone-faced.

Amelia was only twenty-one at the time, and she appeared in control of her emotions. She sat still in her chair, with her slender back pressed tight to its contours. She understood the importance of her recorded testimony. This account would ensure her safety and restore the newly formed CIA's confidence in her as a loyal agent.

It was as if a ghost were speaking to the admiral inside his head. He looked down at Amelia, apparently lifeless in the sled. She had the same pale, fearful look on her face the day they first met. As the dog team rushed ever forward, he recalled the events that led up to that very meeting.

On 10 JUN 50, in a briefing by CIA Director Buck Chambers, DuFor was told about a man named Martin Bormann, private secretary to Adolf Hitler, who had reportedly escaped to Argentina three months before the end of World War II. There, he fathered a son, Vestler Tiedleman Mosk, who cared for Bormann until his death. Mosk created and organized the MOSK SS leaders of the New World Order. They reportedly harbored war criminals, including Josef Mengele. DuFor was given the order to assassinate Mosk.

When MOSK SS soldiers surrounded DuFor's Jeep on 01 JUL 50, she knew her mission had been compromised. She was taken hostage and soon realized that the coordinates given to her by Chambers had been leaked to the MOSK SS. She had been intentionally led into an ambush and was being used as leverage against the MOSK SS by the United States. Openly, the CIA couldn't eradicate the MOSK SS. DuFor's death, however, would be a green light to wipe out, covertly, the Nazi presence in Argentina, which DuFor later discovered was the CIA's original objective.

Operation OVIDA forced worldwide awareness of the evil MOSK SS. DuFor's capture pushed Mosk and members of his organization to seek immunity for their war crimes along with one million dollars in restitution for what they believed to be "pain and suffering" for having to spend their lives in hiding. If their demands were met, the MOSK SS agreed to release DuFor on the condition that the President of the United States make a formal public broadcast apologizing for the mistreatment of the Nazis.

Inside the Pentagon, Chambers and his staff agreed not to negotiate with the MOSK SS, which infuriated Mosk when he was informed of the decision. On 30 JUL 50, Mosk held a formal hearing in Argentina that was broadcast over the radio. DuFor was bound and placed on a dais in the center of a round amphitheater surrounded by fifty enraged men. Mosk announced the prosecution as "Trial by Underground Associate Group." The assembly charged DuFor with the attempted kidnapping and assassination of Mosk. Mosk then proclaimed that because the United States had failed to appear to represent her, she was guilty of the charges levied against her. Following the verdict, the room erupted with boisterous shouts of "Mosk! Mosk! Mosk!" DuFor was all but forgotten in the immediate chaos. The room quieted when the punishment was read.

"Agent Amelia DuFor, you are free to go. However, before you leave, you must bear the name of the MOSK SS for the rest of your life," intoned Mosk. Once again, the amphitheater surged with shouting as the assembly began to anticipate the procedure to come. In walked a doctor, pushing a cart with rusty, blood-encrusted instruments and a red-hot branding iron. With the roaring of the crowd as background noise, Mosk ripped open DuFor's shirt and gestured for the doctor to proceed. The man approached her with a scalpel and quickly sliced open her stomach, spilling her intestines. He then reached for the branding iron and seared mosk ss onto her intestines. DuFor passed out.

A month of brutal torture ensued before DuFor was rescued by Howard. When she awoke at Womack Army Medical Center in North Carolina, she was in a hospital bed, unable to speak, with the admiral sitting beside her. She had no recollection of events subsequent to the branding.

Admiral Howard attempted to extinguish this memory as he reached the first wooden hut.

"I can't lose you, Amelia! You are stronger than this, dammit!"

He looked up to see an old man sprinting toward him to provide assistance. The villager noticed the dogs, now collapsed, frothing at the mouth, and he scowled at Howard for his harsh treatment of them. However, the admiral's concern was for Amelia; the dogs had completed their job. He snatched up his wife and brushed past the old man to enter the dwelling. The villager followed him inside the weakly lit room and directed him to place Amelia on a table in the center of the dim chamber. The admiral tenderly unwrapped his wife's unresponsive body from the blood-soaked furs that cocooned her. As his eyes scanned her lifeless body, he was consumed by an overwhelming sense of haste.

"The baby! Get the baby!" Howard shouted in the man's Turkic language as he tore through the layers of bloody clothing to expose Amelia's abdomen.

The old man drew his large hunting knife from his belt and moved in the direction of Amelia. The admiral understood there was no time to waste in rescuing the infant; he had no other choice but to allow his wife to be slashed open. The villager commenced to cut the baby free of Amelia's protective womb. With practiced expertise, he made a clean slice lengthwise across Amelia's stomach and then hastily tossed the knife to the admiral, who placed it on the table. The villager then used his muscular fingers like a skinning knife in an intricate movement to separate the layers of skin and fat. He pulled open the incision to expose the membrane sheeting. He gripped the thin but tough skin with a pair of rendering tongs and tugged the amniotic sac through the gaping incision. He then grabbed the admiral's hand and placed it on the makeshift forceps, gesturing for him to elevate the sac. With a small razor removed from his belt, the villager carefully cut through the opaque membrane. He could see the top of the child's head, wet hair swirled and mashed, blanketed in white mucus. The villager slipped his hands inside the sac and began to extract the baby.

Knowing he had to help, the admiral also slid his hands inside Amelia's womb. He expected to feel a warm sensation, but her blood had cooled as her temperature had dropped. As he began to tug gently, the baby's head emerged, then the shoulders. The old man was careful to slide the umbilical cord past the baby's shoulders. As the admiral pulled his child free, he saw she was as still and lifeless as her mother. He had hoped for a son, but that wish dissipated as he clutched his tiny new daughter.

Howard handed the child to the villager. The infant was slathered in her mother's fluids and her glossy, furrowed skin had a slight blue tinge. Yet, the baby began to twist and turn as the old man sucked the frothy mixture of embryonic fluid and blood from her airways, after which he then spit the slime forcefully onto the heated bricks in front of the fire. The watery liquid sizzled and danced in pools, bubbling until it vaporized. The steam mixed with the smoke of the fire and rose in swirls on its journey up the stone chimney and into the cold outside air. For a moment, time stood still for Admiral John Howard. Dazed, he watched the vapor rise up the fireplace flue. Then the child drew in her first lungful of existence. Her arms stretched out awkwardly and she brought her knees up to her chest then forced them out straight. The admiral felt as if he was observing an ethereal exemplification of Amelia, releasing herself into the world.

"That would be just like you, Amelia. She's not even a few minutes old and you're already giving her wings," the admiral murmured. He no longer heard the deafening rockets nor the explosions obliterating the hillsides. For a moment, he was completely at peace. As he watched the fire, a log rolled, causing it to crackle, and he shifted his gaze back to the baby. The admiral looked with wonderment into the depths of her gleaming eyes in the first moments of her new life—her wiggling body, her small fingers wrapping around his. He was utterly removed from the chaos happening around him. The admiral didn't react to the villager, who clutched his shoulder and shouted at him to sever the umbilical cord with the bloody hunting knife. He didn't register that his sergeant had entered the cabin and was informing him that choppers were landing to extract them. The admiral was, for mere seconds, entranced by his daughter's hypnotic stare. Time slowed. Although it may have only been a reflection of the dancing flames, he swore he saw Amelia's spirit slip away through the child's eyes.

A ground shudder sent an instant chill through Howard's body, as if he were suddenly drenched in ice water. Cannons shredded the village, their rockets blasting around the hut. The entire room jerked fiercely. The admiral shook his head and blinked several times to bring himself back into the moment. He watched as the villager cut the umbilical cord.

"Admiral, we have to move," advised the sergeant. "Target's at close range, sir. They're gaining ground fast. The birds have landed. We have to get to the pickup zone."

The sergeant collected the admiral's equipment and strode hurriedly about the room while trying to maintain his footing on the slick, bloody floor. As he rounded the table, his foot skated out from under him and he grabbed for the tabletop to stop himself from falling. As he did this, he unintentionally pulled away the furs that had been placed respectfully by the villager over Amelia's face. He looked straight into her cold, open eyes and quickly realized what he had done.

"I'm sorry, sir. I'm so sorry." The sergeant attempted to cover Amelia's face with the stained furs.

The admiral looked at his dead wife, then down at the child in his hands, overwhelmed with the reality of the situation. His wife was gone and he was holding their newborn child in the midst of a tumultuous firefight. He shook his head in anger at the way the op was unfolding. "I will name you Elizabeth," he announced to the child. "You will be ten times the woman your mother was, seeing as how you decided to take her place in the world."

As the admiral spoke his first words to his child, he realized they were orders, rather than the loving words he had thought he would say at that time. Elizabeth whimpered and squirmed as he held her. Howard then extended one hand to close Amelia's eyes. As he touched her face, his hand began to tremble and his grief became transparent.

"I can't put you in the dark like this. I can't do it!" Howser clenched his fist against his mouth to muffle his anguish. As he did so, he inadvertently smeared Amelia's blood across his face—much like the sign of a warrior—and tasted the metallic sweetness of her blood.

The sergeant placed his hand on the admiral's back and guided him toward the door. "Admiral, we must move." The sergeant's tone softened to show respect for Amelia, but he knew they had to get out.

The admiral leaned down and tenderly brushed Amelia's smooth, cold cheek with his torn, rugged palm. Knowing he had to leave her behind, emotions began to well up inside him. His instinct was to scream, roar, pick up his weapon, and charge ferociously into the middle of the battle raging outside. At the same time, he wanted to break down and weep. Amelia was his life, but he refused to show his passion. Not now. Not ever.

Howard took one of Amelia's furs and wrapped it around Elizabeth. He gave Amelia one last glance, then turned to head outside, where his men waited. He needed to resume his duty and lead his men home. He wanted his team to depart this battle as victors. As he slipped back into warrior mode, he felt his blood surge through his veins as adrenaline took hold. He sentenced his grief deep into the hell of his inner prison, with no chance of parole.

"Roger that!" the admiral barked to his sergeant. "Let's get the fuck out of here!"

The admiral stood tall, took a deep breath, and nodded his thanks to the villager. Howard's forehead glistened with sweat and his face was crimson from exertion. As he stepped out the door of the cabin with the small bundle in his arms, his team assembled and began the journey across the frozen countryside on their sleds to the pickup zone. A number of Huey choppers hovered over the designated retrieval site with riggings deployed. Howser's men gripped the ropes and were pulled abruptly inside the transports, two at a time.

The admiral protected the infant bundle under his coat. When he got to the back of the chopper, he drew back the fur a bit, revealing the baby.

"I need a medic!" he shouted above the din of the steel rotors.

A lieutenant questioned, "Are you wounded, sir?"

"No, but she may be."

The lieutenant recoiled with astonishment, as if he had just grasped a striking cobra. "Jesus Christ! I mean . . . sir! That's a baby! Where did that come from?"

"Son, if you don't know where babies come from by now, you'll never understand. Now get her a medic!"

The admiral leaned against the side of the craft and held back his anguish. *How the fuck am I going to explain this to President Chambers?* he pondered as he stroked his daughter's tiny finger.

He thought of his wife and felt nauseous. Suppressing the churning sensation in his stomach, he closed his eyes and envisioned grief as an enemy to be defeated, captured, and imprisoned. The admiral's tactic worked well then and throughout the coming years. If grief ever tried to escape, he took pleasure in recapturing it and torturing it. He vowed that if he was ever defeated by his own buried demons, he would shoot himself in private, rather than seek help from others and admit defeat publicly.

That was how the admiral spent his life dealing with his pain. It is also how he eventually trained Elizabeth to deal with hers. He knew that, by merely being his child, she would face many demons, significant loss, and great physical and psychological pain. He was determined to raise her as an Orion soldier—a covert warrior who could defeat the world's most dangerous enemies without anyone knowing but those within the same small elite group.

Throughout Elizabeth's life, she referred to Admiral John Howard as "Howser," like the rest of the Orion team. She hardly ever called him "Dad." They never had a loving father–daughter relationship. There were no heartfelt embraces, kisses on the head, or birthday presents. In fact, the first eight years of Elizabeth's life were spent without him. Her path was determined at birth and ingrained in her genes. Elizabeth, aka G.I. Jane, was already a child-prodigy soldier the second she took her first breath. Although it was his plan for her, Howser could not know—at the moment of her birth—that she would eventually become one of the most legendary generals in Orion's history.

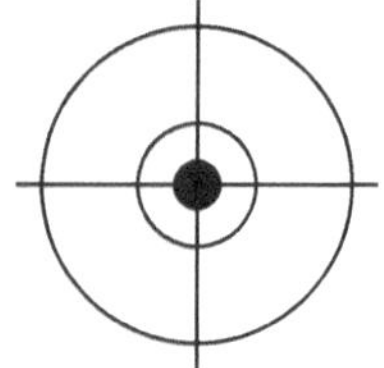

CHAPTER TWO

The admiral didn't receive a warm welcome from the President of the United States at Camp David when he arrived. Howser went to deliver the news of Amelia's death personally. The President was less pleased to discover that an infant had survived the ordeal.

"What in the hell are you talking about, John?" President Chambers asked furiously. "Did you know about this? Did you know she was pregnant and didn't tell me? Don't you know what a critical fuckup this is?" The President completely dismissed Howser's grief. It seemed as if Chambers' only concern was the outcome of the mission.

"Sir, on my honor, I promise you I didn't know Amelia was pregnant before we left for Siberia. When we realized she was pregnant, it was too late to take care of the situation."

"Situation? SITUATION! It's not a *situation*. It's a *child* we're talking about!" roared the President. He grabbed the admiral by the throat and shoved him against the wall. "I ought to have you killed right now, you son of a bitch. You think you can outsmart me? What you fail to comprehend is that the 'situation' is a human life! What the fuck is wrong with you?"

Chambers held on to the admiral's neck tightly as Howser looked at him—stunned. In one of those rare moments in his life, Howser was unaware of how he was supposed to react.

"But, but, Amelia . . . ," stammered Howser, attempting to make an excuse for himself.

The President released John, walked over to the bar, and poured himself a drink. "I *know* what goes on in this organization, John. I know who is loyal and who isn't. Before you two even deployed to Siberia, I saw the results from her physical. The fucking rabbit done died!"

"Are you telling me you *knew* about this? You let her go to Siberia when she was pregnant?" Howser squeezed his fists at his sides. He would have felt more at ease if he had a drink tumbler to fidget with. It unnerved him that Chambers hadn't offered him a drink.

"John, do you really think anything happens in Orion that I *don't* know about? You're forgetting that before I became President of this great nation, I was the director of the CIA. I have always had power, John. I have always had incredible political pull. You need to get your head out of your ass."

Chambers looked down at the ice melting in his whiskey. To Howser, it seemed like an eternity before the President lifted his head and looked him straight in the eye.

"She was a foolish woman, John. You and I both know she should've died in Argentina." Chambers shot down the rest of his whiskey and poured another, again without offering a glass to Howser. "We should've let a few more days pass before we sent you down there to clean up that mess. Operation OVIDA. What a fucked-up sham." He sat down in his chair and stared out the window at the pine trees.

Howser lowered himself into the chair across from Chambers, silently seething at the President's comments. His thoughts turned to the mission in Argentina in 1950. Chambers was the director of the newly formed CIA and he had employed Howser to assist in what he called a "covert rescue mission."

Then-CIA director Chambers was unable to get the backing he needed from the Cabinet to approve the op. So, he planned to use Howser, the first-ever Tier I command operative, and Agent DuFor to do his dirty work for him. Chambers knew Howser would slaughter all the members of the MOSK SS for killing a female CIA agent. The director had used Amelia as collateral damage and sent her deliberately into a mission at which she could not succeed. Soon thereafter, Chambers dispatched Howser to effect his "real" mission.

The admiral's primary goal was to locate the agent; secondarily, he would eliminate the MOSK SS. When he infiltrated their compound, he quietly executed the guards and found an agent bludgeoned and barely alive. He could scarcely make out the natural contours of the victim's face. When he realized she was a woman, he was astonished and infuriated. Howser couldn't comprehend why Chambers would send a woman alone on a mission. He put his face near her mouth to determine whether she was breathing. Her jaw was clearly broken and she was severely injured, but she was alive. She could wait while he went to recon the area covertly in search of the main MOSK SS facility.

Howser waited for nightfall to engage the MOSK SS soldiers. He maneuvered stealthily through the camp, killing every single soldier. When he located Mosk, Howser's rage surged through him. He couldn't refrain from tearing Mosk's throat out with his bare hands. Howser watched as the life left Mosk's terrified face, then he tossed him to the ground. He was satisfied he had taken appropriate revenge on the agent's abusers. Howser then returned to Amelia and stayed by her side for four hours, often pounding the walls in frustration, until support finally arrived.

The admiral shifted in the stiff leather chair in the dimly lit den as he thought about the Specialized Field Investigation Units from Langley Air Force Base that eventually arrived in Argentina. Agents attempted to extract information from Amelia even before they allowed her medical treatment. Howser knew they wanted to determine whether she was going to talk about the compromised mission—or whether she even recalled it. Howser watched, restraining himself, as they filmed her and bombarded her with questions. Her busted jaw hung loosely from her face while agents pummeled her with questions, reading every blink, eye twitch, and finger jerk as a response. Howser lurched to his feet as they injected Amelia with drugs to keep her conscious for six consecutive taped interviews. He tried to stop the proceedings. He railed against the agents, shouting he wouldn't allow them to make her a scapegoat for the failed mission. His words made it onto one of the films, which were never shown during the resulting congressional hearings.

After returning to the States, Amelia was sent to Womack Army Medical Center to heal, which took eight months. Howser was sent to the far corners of the earth on missions. Neither of them thought they would ever see each other again. But eventually, Howser made his way back to Amelia toward the end of her recovery.

When he arrived, Amelia still hadn't spoken; her fractured jaw was still healing. She continued to recover and, in short order, the two of them were able to piece together the events of the mission. They concluded the whole thing was a setup. It was assumed by Chambers that Amelia would never endure the torture she suffered, that Howser would find her dead and brutalized, and that he would take direct action to eliminate the MOSK SS, relieving Chambers of all responsibility. Cleanup after an agent going rogue and reacting to highly personal emotions was easier to explain to the Special UN Operations Group than the Director of the CIA defying official UN military rules of engagement.

Howser and Amelia devised a plan to use her injuries as a cover to keep her safe. They wrote their statements, kept their stories straight, and never spoke about the mission again. Howser kept Amelia by his side at all times to safeguard her further. That's how they became a team.

The President finally broke the silence. "John, dammit, why couldn't you just have followed protocol right from the beginning? You let your head, your emotions, and whatever else you were thinking with get in the way. *Now* look at us. We're two very powerful men. Did you ever think, back in those days, that you'd be calling me *President* Chambers? Hell no you didn't, or you would've shown me more respect. You thought the director of the CIA couldn't make things happen for your career. I saw how you doubted me. Well, look how far we've come. You have no choice but to listen to me now. I make all the decisions, John."

"I see," Howser said, rubbing his neck. "So, you were *hoping* she would die this time?"

"Let it go, John. She did, didn't she? No woman should be out there untrained like that. She was just a field agent, not a Tier I professional like you. You dragged her into that mess, John. Her blood is on your hands."

Chambers finally poured Howser a drink, patted his shoulder, and began to walk in a circle around him. His demeanor shifted entirely. He began swaggering in the same casual business manner John had seen many times before.

"Now let's talk about this 'situation.' It appears to me we have an opportunity on our hands here. That little baby is the offspring of two of the world's best agents."

Howser flinched, recognizing the President's contradiction in his statement. One minute he said Amelia was "just a field agent" and completely ill-prepared, and the next he referred to her as an elite agent.

The President stopped walking and looked John square in the face, grinning, and asked, "Now what do you think we should do about that?"

Howser sat motionless. Little did he know how deeply the President's words would affect him: *No woman should be out there untrained like that.* At that moment, Howser's subconscious mind began developing plans that his conscious mind would reveal to him later.

Chambers continued, "Well, I'm making arrangements for the baby to be taken care of by a devout Catholic family in the Midwest. A good conservative family. She'll remain with them until she's old enough to attend that military academy in Pretoria you're constructing. What do you think about that? You can continue to focus on your career and we can get that little shit squared away. She might make a good field agent someday. Maybe work for the Feds."

"But, sir . . ." Howser felt he needed to show some kind of protest to sound sincere, but inside he felt nothing but relief. He was sure the President would have him killed if he tried to leave with his child. Howser felt a sting when he thought of his daughter working for the Feds in a simple field agent position. His ego was larger than that.

"But nothing, you son of a bitch," crowed the President, proud of his plan. "Now get the hell out of here," flicking his hand toward the door. "I've got to clean up this mess."

Within a few weeks, Elizabeth Howard was placed in a car and driven to the Midwest. A loving family received the infant warmly and graciously into their home. They beamed at their new responsibility, yet they were also aware there would come a day when they would have to send her away.

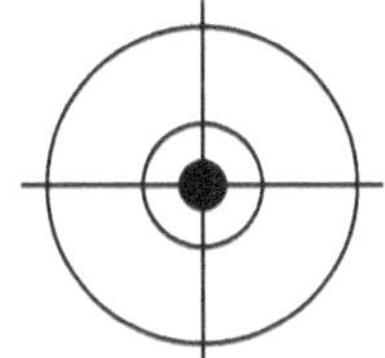

CHAPTER THREE

An unapologetic midwestern sun shone like a spotlight directly into Elizabeth's sleepy eyes. She rolled over and pulled the Batman bedsheet over her head, but then an overwhelming feeling of determination struck her nearly eight-year-old body. Jumping out of bed, she snatched up the brown- and black-spotted chicken feathers from her nightstand and secured them deftly into the top of her sandy-blonde braids, making a small Native American headdress. She stripped off her pajamas and threw them inside out in a heap on the cherry-wood floor. Fire Watch called for her Daniel Boone fringed leather coat with matching leather chaps and two silver revolver cap guns, which she strapped to each hip. Almost ready to seize the day, she slung her .22 rifle hastily across her back in a World War II sling.

Elizabeth dashed down the wooden staircase, barely glancing at her Grandma Evelyn, who was in the kitchen making biscuits and gravy, and ran out the front door. The old farmhouse was so saturated with the sweet smell of butter that it poured out the open windows. Evelyn Finn smiled and shook her head as she heard the screen door slam. She knew not to bother Elizabeth with food before she headed out to stake out her post for Fire Watch duty.

Elizabeth's innate wisdom, handed down to her by her biological parents, kicked into high gear that morning. She must have known, deep down, her life was about to shift in a very different direction. For seven and a half years, she'd had the run of the vast farmland owned by the foster family that raised her. Elizabeth was a freewheeling, down-in-the-dirt, animal-loving girl who already knew how to shoot guns. Real guns. Growing up in a big midwestern military family and hearing countless war stories from her great-grandfather, great-uncles, grandfather, and uncles had prepared her for this day in ways she couldn't yet understand. Elizabeth was enamored with all things military.

President Chambers had made a good selection when he chose her foster family. All the men had served honorably in the military, and the entire family was conservative in their political leanings as well as in their family values. Elizabeth's great-grandfather had built several farmhouses, which were nestled among elm trees off a frontage road, near the farm. She grew up wandering freely from house to house, receiving love and care from her extended family. Her foster parents' time was focused on her older stepbrother, who was born with medical conditions that required their full-time care and their attendance at near-constant hospitalizations. Elizabeth's grandmother ruled the roost; she bound the family together.

Throughout the years, Howser maintained frequent contact with the family. He believed they were good people and was pleased at how well they primed Elizabeth for the next chapter in her life. Every week

Howser carefully read the letters that Evelyn sent. He pictured his daughter going out on the farm with her war hero uncles and playing in the sprinklers while they fixed irrigation pipes. He was glad she spent three days a week in the Catholic Church, going to mass and studying the Bible. He liked that she was learning about animals and was being taught basic skills such as cooking, swimming, math, and even how to drive a tractor. Evelyn described Elizabeth as a "fiercely independent child, full of enthusiasm." Howser knew she wouldn't turn out any different.

He spent those seven-plus years preparing logistically and mentally for the day he would once again see his daughter. He imagined it would not be easy for Elizabeth's foster family to release into the custody of strangers a child they had raised, to be taken to a military school thousands of miles away. But Howser had begun to make plans for Elizabeth from the moment of her birth. He would not shelter her. He knew he could train her properly to survive as an Orion soldier. He would not let his daughter, or any other soldier who entered his organization, lack the skills necessary to survive any circumstance into which they were thrown.

The morning he was due to travel to the farm and retrieve Elizabeth for training, Howser spent several hours polishing the buttons of his dress uniform and shining his dress shoes. He hadn't spent this much time on a uniform since his days at Annapolis. He boarded the VC-137, the backup *Air Force One*—the same plane Nixon took home when he stepped down. Marine Corps Major Aikens flew in from Camp Pendleton to accompany him. The major's gold buttons blazed in the bright sun, indicating he spent just as much time on his uniform as Howser.

When they arrived at a local airport three hours later, they were escorted to a black limousine.

"For God's sake! We can't show up in a Podunk country town in a limousine! Get me a Jeep!" Howser barked at the ground crew, who scrambled and returned within a few minutes with a Jeep. "That's more like it!" he bellowed.

Evelyn rushed out to greet them as they pulled into the dirt driveway of the small farmhouse. She was a short, stout woman, dressed in a blue-flowered shirt and brown pants, and she held a lit cigarette. As she did with any guest, Evelyn made them feel like they were coming home.

"Come on in, sirs. Welcome! Come in." Howser sensed her kindness and sincerity immediately. "I bet you young men are starving," Evelyn pronounced, as she led them into the kitchen. "I'll whip up some food and get you started with a good cup of hot coffee."

Before they could say "no-thank-you," Evelyn began cluttering the red homespun tablecloth with spareribs, sauerkraut, biscuits, fish sticks, and fudge. "I didn't know if you were vegetarians, being from California and all," and she pointed encouragingly to the fish sticks.

"Ma'am, this is all too generous. Perhaps we could just have the coffee?" asked the major, holding his hat in one hand below his chest.

"My dad and my husband should be home shortly," Evelyn explained. "They went to the barbershop for haircuts. We didn't really have much time to prepare for your arrival. Now sit down and make yourselves comfortable."

Howser looked around the kitchen and at the spread on the table, and wondered what Thanksgiving was like in this house.

"Well, on second thought, some of that fudge might go real well with this coffee, ma'am." Howser couldn't resist; he hadn't had fudge since he was a kid.

Evelyn placed a healthy serving of fudge on a plate, threw some sauerkraut and ribs on the side, then winked at him as she sat the plate down in front of him.

"Where is Elizabeth, Mrs. Finn?" Howser asked, attempting to hold back his anxiety.

"Oh, she'll be in. She's on Fire Watch, so I imagine she saw you coming before you rounded the corner. She's been waiting for you."

At that moment Elizabeth blasted through the back door. She was a ragtag country urchin and looked dirty as hell. But what made the biggest impression on the guests was the .22 rifle strapped to her back. Even Howser thought she might be slightly young to be toting a real .22.

Elizabeth ran directly over to Howser and the major and saluted. She noticed the men struggling to choke back their laughter. She blushed with embarrassment when Howser told her it wasn't necessary to salute indoors. At nearly eight years old, she stood as rigid as any longtime Marine.

Just then, Elizabeth's eighty-year-old great-grandfather came through the kitchen door with Evelyn's husband. The men exchanged a few war stories while Evelyn shooed Elizabeth up the stairs to get cleaned up and change clothes.

Elizabeth loved her foster family very much. They nurtured her without being overbearing or controlling. She did her own thing, with some guidance, of course. Perhaps that was the family's way of dealing with her inevitable departure.

"I'm sorry Elizabeth's parents aren't here," Evelyn apologized. "Our grandson is very ill at Children's Hospital. We're concerned he won't make it. He's battling pneumonia." Tears welled up in Evelyn's eyes.

Howser was just about to change the subject when Elizabeth returned. She popped into the room in a little purple jumpsuit covered with monkeys, and she wore a white kerchief around her neck that belonged to her grandfather. She stood rigid at attention.

"Easy there, little soldier. This isn't a drill," Howser said.

"Actually, sir, I'm not a soldier. I'm a Marine," she said proudly, pointing to her kerchief, which was actually a Navy dress ascot.

"My apologies, little Marine!"

Elizabeth's grandfather walked over to her and hugged her shoulders as he explained to her again that she would be leaving them to attend military school. Howser expected Elizabeth to protest. She peeked around her grandpa and eyed the two strangers who were waiting to take her away, then she cracked a little smile and ran to her room and jammed clothes into her pillowcase. She was excited at the prospect of an adventure.

Evelyn burst out laughing. "Well, I guess that's the sort of enthusiasm the Marines need!"

Elizabeth spent a short time gathering her things together and saying her goodbyes. She didn't exactly understand what was happening. She didn't fully grasp how challenging it would be the next day, when she realized she wouldn't be returning home for a very long time.

The novelty of the experience wore off during the nineteen-hour plane trip to Pretoria, South Africa. Elizabeth began to get nervous. She had been escorted away by complete strangers from the only family she had ever known. She began to miss the farm. In the plane, Howser sat Elizabeth down next to him before their final descent into Pretoria. The crease in his forehead seemed more pronounced as he looked directly into her eyes. He gently took hold of both of Elizabeth's shoulders and turned her toward him.

"I have to tell you something, kid, that you may not understand just now, but later on it will make sense. I have to have all of your focus."

Elizabeth nodded at Howser in agreement.

"I know it must be hard for you to leave your family back there. Those people, the dad you have back there, they are still your family." He leaned into her and lowered his voice. "Elizabeth, I need to tell you something that's important for you to know. It's about your real family—about me."

Elizabeth leaned back a little and he took his hands off her shoulders.

"Look, I know you're young and you probably won't believe me when I tell you this, but I'm your real dad. You know, like a biological dad."

Elizabeth looked up at him, confused.

"Okay," he continued, "Let me simplify this. You are now like property, in a sense. You are an employee of the government and I'm your boss. So, you're kind of like the boss's kid. Other people might think you're getting an unfair advantage because I'm your dad. They might think you didn't have to work for your position. They might even think less of the boss. Does that make sense?"

Elizabeth nodded her head yes, yet Howser was uncertain whether she really understood, and he didn't know how to explain it to her any better. He suddenly remembered how devout the family was, so he came up with a story he thought would connect the dots. He also was beginning to regret telling her he was her biological father, because none of her peers she would meet in Pretoria could ever know about their connection. He started to backtrack.

"I believe there was some part in the Bible where a couple went in to a city. Maybe it was Joseph and Mary," Howser recounted.

"They were afraid that Joseph would be killed if people thought Mary was his wife, so they told everyone they were just brother and sister traveling together. That way, no one bothered them. *We* have to tell a bit of a lie like that so we don't get killed."

Not knowing how to speak to a child, he suddenly realized the word *killed* might be too strong.

"I . . . oh, shit. Just listen to me. Under no circumstance are you ever allowed to reveal to anyone that I'm your dad. Ever. I'll whip the shit out of you if you do, you hear me? Just call me Howser."

Elizabeth nodded in agreement, only because she was scared out of her mind. She was convinced this was her first order and she would follow it.

"Sir, yes sir," she said, trying to act brave.

Howser smiled. "Thatta girl."

He got up and walked to the back of the plane, leaving Elizabeth sitting in her seat alone and confused. All she wanted at that moment was to go back to her family at the farm, although she was beginning to internalize this was no longer an option. She had to trust a man she barely knew, who claimed to be her father.

Having never traveled outside the Midwest, Pretoria felt like—and was—a different world to Elizabeth. The most striking difference to her was the people. She was mesmerized by the beautiful, dark-skinned Africans. It was 1969 and this was her first exposure to a culture she would commit herself to, thousands of miles from her small midwestern farm. The women smiled at her with beaming, bright faces, and they wore colorful clothing and ornate jewelry. The men were lean and looked strong. She fell in love immediately with Africa. The temperature was perfect and warm, and the vastness of the land promised adventure.

Elizabeth met twelve-year-old Jude on arrival at the Orion base. Jude was Major Brad Aikens' son. Howser would do anything for Major Aikens, including covering up the fact that Jude's mother overdosed on drugs. After she died, it was easier to put Jude in the Orion program than to raise him like a father could have. Jude was the first kid to enter Howser's new military school. After two years in the program, Jude felt he had earned the right to lead. He was first on the scene to greet Elizabeth and get her settled in.

"Hey, twerp!" the tall, well-built, dark-haired boy shouted to Elizabeth halfway across the grounds of the Orion compound.

"I'm not a twerp," Elizabeth replied, then puffed up as much as she could; her body was exhausted from the flight. The boy approached her and looked her up and down.

"Oh yeah? You're pretty much a twerp. What are you? Like, six? My name is Jude. I'm supposed to show you around."

"I'm not six," Elizabeth retorted with a scowl. "I'm practically eight." She considered being mean, as a self-defense mechanism, but held back. "So, what do you do here?" she asked nervously, trying to fill the silence.

"Let's just stick to the tour," commanded Jude. "You just got here. Did you get a room yet? My room has a real arcade game unit in it and I can play anytime I want." His face lit up like a Christmas tree.

"Wow! That's cool," Elizabeth replied, not really knowing what an arcade game unit was. "Do you have chickens here?" she blurted out, placing her hand on her bony hip and cocking her head to the side. Elizabeth knew about chickens; she raised them on the farm.

"Chickens? Uh, sure; we have chickens," Jude said, confused.

"You do?" Elizabeth was anxious to see something that would remind her of home. "Could we go see them?"

"Sure. Okay." Jude shrugged.

As they headed toward the barn, Jude pointed out the dormitories, where they'd each have a room. Sidewalks meandered through the campus. Landscapers were busy unloading bushes and shrubs from trucks. Clearly, construction of the school was not yet complete.

In the back of the barn was a pen full of chickens pecking away happily at the grain on the ground.

"Oh, wow!" Elizabeth beamed as she started to climb into the pen.

"Hold on! You can't go in there. Do you want to hold one of them? I'll get you one. Pick one out."

Elizabeth pointed to a beautiful black-and-white-speckled hen. Jude climbed into the pen, deftly caught the chicken, and brought her toward Elizabeth. As she reached out to touch the hen, Jude grabbed the bird by the neck and twisted it, wringing its neck.

"Here you go," he said. "Easier to hold."

Elizabeth gasped as Jude handed her the dead chicken.

"You want another one?" Jude picked up another chicken and proceeded to kill it the same way and then tossed it to Elizabeth, who was too shocked to catch it.

"How about this one?" Then he killed another one and dropped it.

Elizabeth stood there with her mouth hanging open. She tried to scream for him to stop, but no sound would come from her mouth. She turned and, still clutching the dead hen, ran from the barn as fast as she could.

Jude entered Elizabeth's room and found her on her bed, rocking back and forth, still holding the hen and crying.

"Hey there, twerp," he said quietly.

"Get out of here!" Elizabeth yelled, clutching the hen, as if protecting her from Jude.

Jude sighed and sat beside her. He put his hand on the dead chicken and began petting it.

"Why'd you do that?" Elizabeth sniffled. "I loved her."

"Elizabeth, look. First of all, it's a chicken. You didn't even know her. I've been here two years already. You'll soon understand what I just did. This isn't kindergarten. You don't get a mat, a nap, and some cookies. You're gonna have to grow up real quick."

Elizabeth stopped crying and looked up at Jude.

"How old *are* you?" she asked.

"I'm twelve years old and I'm now your friend, okay? Now will you give me the chicken? We can bury her if you want, but just this one. Don't let Howser catch us. He would kill us if he caught us burying something we could eat."

"Okay," said Elizabeth as she stood up and gathered herself.

They put the chicken in her pillowcase and headed out to bury it. As they walked past a shooting range, Elizabeth heard someone running up behind them, so she turned around.

"Hey! Just where do you two think you're going without me?" asked a boy as he socked Jude in the shoulder.

At only eight years old, he was taller than Jude and had blond hair. He wore khaki military pants and heavy combat boots. Elizabeth thought he looked very cool and immediately developed a crush on him. She felt her chest clench up.

"Hey, Tom-rad. This is Elizabeth. We have to go bury this chicken that she slaughtered."

"Bury it?" questioned Tom.

Elizabeth noticed he had a real knife clipped to his pocket, and a big machete hung off his belt on his other side. He looked like the kid version of a real-life G.I. Joe.

"Don't you mean barbecue it?" Tom asked.

Elizabeth hadn't realized that she had let the chicken slip from the sack and drop to the ground. She was holding only a corner of the pillowcase.

"No, no," Jude explained. "Elizabeth wants to take this poor dead chicken out to the field and—"

"Barbecue it!" she interrupted. "That's what we were headed to do. Wanna come?"

Jude looked at Elizabeth closely, then punched her shoulder lightly with his fist.

"Sure! I'm Tom, by the way. Welcome to Orion. What's your name again, kid?"

Elizabeth was about to answer when Jude piped up, "Jane. We're gonna call her Jane. Calamity Jane."

"That's stupid," stated Tom. "How about G.I. Jane? 'Cause she's a tough girl, right? She's not some plain-Jane sissy," Tom replied, giving Elizabeth a wink.

"Alright," agreed Jude, "but I thought of it," he clarified as he kicked the dirt.

"So, Tom, when did you get here? Do you know Howser too?" asked Jane.

"Well, my dad and Howser are friends, so I guess you could say I got a free pass to come here. I've been here about six months, right Jude? It's pretty cool, even though it looks like crap right now. They're still building. It'll be cool when it's finished, though."

"Hey! Screw the chicken! Let's go play Duck Hunt and get this party started!" crowed Jude.

From that moment on Elizabeth began her transformation into G.I. Jane. She worked to live up to the name her new brothers in

Orion gave her. She grew to view "Elizabeth" as not only a name of her past, but also the child she no longer was. "Jane" was who she wanted to be: strong and resilient.

Jude, Tom, and Jane were all child-prodigy soldiers who trained together in Pretoria until they were ready to be deployed. As Jane grew to know and trust her peers, she had to remind herself constantly to keep the secret she shared with Howser—her lineage. Jane didn't know much about Howser, but she knew she never wanted to cross him by revealing their connection.

Jane's first hours in Pretoria in some way predicted and helped her comprehend the gravity with which her time spent as an Orion soldier-in-training would have on her life. Throughout the years, Jane slowly came to realize—experience by experience, death by death, and trauma after trauma—just how Orion defined her, set her apart from "normal" people, and made her extraordinary.

There was no escape from Orion. Jane would never play volleyball in high school, move on to college, and eventually get an office job. She'd never find a life partner and never have children. None of that was in the cards for her. Rather, she would endure unbearable torture, kill without remorse, slit the throats of bitter enemies, be shot, and put her life on the line for the very boys she met that first day at Orion.

Jude and Tom, along with the rest of the team she would meet later, became the only real confidantes she would—and could—ever have. They trained together for years and became unstoppable. They were Orion soldiers. They were crass and rude. They messed with each other constantly, cracking inappropriate jokes after a mission as their way of dealing with all the blood and killing. There was no other way to deal mentally with what they did and what they witnessed but to don skin several inches thick. However, as with any soldier who's been on the front lines, trauma can creep under that skin and wreak havoc when least expected.

In 1980, when Jane was eighteen years old, posttraumatic stress disorder, or PTSD, was just being labeled an actual psychological condition. In their line of work, being subject to PTSD was not only inevitable, but also permanent. They dealt with their horrors as best they could, in ways "normal" people might view as ludicrous. Yet, their shared experiences bonded them, and their loyalty to each other always rang through.

Jane, mistakenly, believed Howser appointed a psychiatrist to help her deal with her personal trauma as an Orion soldier. Reid informed Jane that she had served in the German military, and her means of extracting information were often interpreted as "Fuhreristic" in their brutality—from deprivation, waterboarding, and isolation to Reid's favorite: electric shock therapy. In addition, Reid managed Jane's medications. Left to her own devices, however, Reid developed her own style of therapy, which would never be condoned in civilized society. Reid was hardly someone Jane looked up to—or trusted, for that matter. But, as the only woman in Jane's life, she took on a pseudo-mother role. Yet the relationship was more abusive than nurturing. Jane did her best to make Reid aware of her hatred for her, and Reid equally despised Jane.

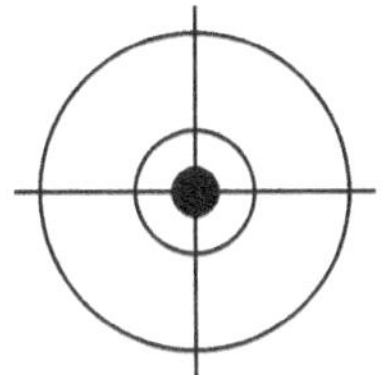

CHAPTER FOUR

Jane realized she suffered nearly as many flashbacks and traumatic episodes from her interactions with Dr. Reid as she did during the initial experiences that compelled her to see Reid in the first place. At fifty-five years old, even after Jane was long retired from Orion, her dreams were often plagued with images of Dr. Reid administering harsh medications or electric shock therapy. One late evening, well into Jane's retirement from Orion, while sequestered in her mountain home, Jane sensed a very different Dr. Reid was about to pay her a visit.

Jane popped open her medicine cabinet, as she did every night, and noticed the magnetic closure had finally given up its stronghold. Perhaps it was just old. More likely, it was overused.

"Sorry, little buddy, but if these bastards would just do their job, I wouldn't have to visit you so much," Jane murmured as she ran her finger over the worn edge of the magnet.

She scanned the neatly alphabetized pharmaceutical shelves, often wanting to throw out the useless crap like acetaminophen, codeine, Demerol, hydrocodone, ibuprofen, Motrin, and Vicodin. But if Jane did that, there would be large gaps in A, C, D, H, I, M, and V. By the time she reached into the cabinet for her daily evening reprieve, every inch of her body hurt. Jane's hand headed directly for the M-through-O shelf: morphine, naloxone, and oxycodone.

"Thank you, Dr. Reid," Jane said under her breath, as she lifted the bottles from the shelves. She tossed her meds down her throat, shuffled into her bedroom, then slid beneath the covers, waiting for the serpent to appear.

As Jane drifted in and out of sleep and into her dream, she could make out Dr. Mary Reid's white, bloodless hands clutching her Bradford number-two pencil in a death grip. Jane could hear Reid scratching notes with force into her three-ring binder as if she were carving a tree with a bread knife. Jane's eyes followed the tendons in Reid's hands as they slithered and slipped under the doctor's skin as she gripped her pencil tighter.

Reid shot Jane a scrutinizing glare over the top of her bifocals, which were perched unfailingly on the tip of her pointed Greek nose. Jane wondered why she even wore the glasses. She never looked through them, only over them. Jane supposed Reid thought they made her appear more clinical. Whenever Jane caught a glimpse of her own reflection in those glasses, it reminded her she battled Dr. Reid's demons in addition to her own.

Jane felt like she spent more than half her life tolerating a relationship with Dr. Reid. At best, it was a contemptuous, hostile, and often agonizing doctor–patient relationship that usually drove Jane into overwhelming fits of rage.

Reid appeared on occasion as Jane's less-than-feminine guide through her evolution of womanhood. When Jane needed to address puberty and menstruation, she found a movie projector to watch an explanatory film reel from the 1950s, which she thought was Reid's. In the film, a black-and-white cartoon character walked her through human anatomy. When Jane returned to her room, she saw a box of feminine products on her bed with a note that said: Follow instructions. A monkey can do this. Jane assumed they were from Reid.

This arrogant old hag had never once witnessed a day of Jane's life through Jane's eyes. Jane was sure Dr. Reid most likely obtained her knowledge within the dust-blown covers of some old clinical reference book that she held on to like the Holy Grail of Wisdom. Surely if the information is written in a book, it must be the truth.

To Jane, it seemed as if Reid went to every possible length to brainwash her and, as always, resorting to electric shock. Reid was never at a loss to find ways to make her points clear. Jane counterattacked every step of the way, usually with physical outbursts and intimidation.

Jane's body sank deeper into the bed and her dream as the medication took effect. As she entered a new state of consciousness, Jane felt a palpable tension. Suddenly, Dr. Reid appeared in front of her in her dream.

Reid initiated the session with her usual shot of Pepto Bismol and redundant inquiry.

"Jane, what was your resting heart rate this morning?"

"Forty-fucking-five, Dr. Reid," rasped Jane with a sour smirk.

"And what is your heart rate right now?" the doctor asked as her eyes shot daggers at Jane over the rims of her glasses.

Jane's heart rate began to accelerate. She placed her fingers on her pulse point and began to count the beats as she watched the clock.

"One hundred forty-eight," Jane said, grimacing.

It was as if she had just galloped to Dr. Reid's office while jumping through rings of fire and dodging mortar rounds.

"How many years has it been, Jane, and you still can't unwind around me? What are we going to do with you?"

The doctor sunk back in her chair, then took off her reprehensible glasses to let them dangle from the bejeweled chain that hung from her furrowed neck. She sighed, stood up, and sauntered over to the window with her back to Jane. The doctor's demeanor shifted from rigid to uncharacteristically casual. Reid turned halfway around and tossed her notebook onto a brown leather footrest, then rounded and continued to stare out the window. She clasped her hands together loosely and began to rub them gently, allowing the blood to flow freely, with their resulting color revealing a less skeletal appearance. As Reid moved slightly, Jane could see Reid still had her captured in her peripheral vision. The doctor casually swept a loose strand of gray hair back behind one ear and then turned her head away from the window to stare at Jane.

In Jane's dream, she couldn't be certain that this slight, paper-thin figure was the woman she often attacked physically and verbally. Reid suddenly appeared so old and puny, so shockingly nonthreatening. Jane resisted the urge to fight these new images that were overshadowing old wounds. Part of her gave in only for a moment, allowing warmth to wash over her temporarily in this altered Reid light. She even felt like apologizing to the doctor. Then Jane thought about the old Nazi war criminals they wheeled into courtrooms to stand trial—the men who appeared frail and incapable of committing heinous acts. In reality, they were atrocious demons when they served the Fuhrer.

Laszlo Csatary suddenly entered Jane's mind. At ninety-seven, he could barely walk the seventy-five feet into a Budapest courtroom, clinging to the arm of his nurse. His skeletal frame was reminiscent of the Jews during the war. Csatary had beaten them with horsewhips and forced them onto packed train cars headed for death camps. Ironically, some of the Jewish members present at the hearings sympathized with Csatary when he received a life sentence.

But like Csatary, Jane thought she knew the truth about Dr. Reid, who Jane thought was responsible for referring her to some of the most brutal punishments she ever endured, and who administered dubious medications for the management of PTSD. The meds caused Jane's kidneys to swell, resulting in such extreme pain that it felt to Jane like she was pissing glass. Other medications made her feel like she had suffered a stroke. Jane remembered quite vividly being left in a room for a week, drooling on herself, and urinating and defecating in her pants.

In other instances, it seemed to Jane that Reid brought in Catholic priests who performed exorcisms, attempting to drive "demons" from Jane. Even as she dreamed, Jane checked herself constantly to make sure she did not allow this serpent to lure her in with her deceptive measures.

"Jane, how is your retirement going so far?" Dr. Reid asked softly, gazing out the window. She spoke to Jane as if they were just a couple of regular Joes who used to work together and ran into each other years later. Inexplicably, Reid wasn't even taking notes.

When bizarre things such as the lack of note-taking transpired, Jane half expected to wake up swaddled in a straitjacket in a padded room, slobbering. She always knew there could come a time when she might just snap and slip completely from reality. Who better to lead her into insanity than Dr. Reid?

Then a liberating thought took over and Jane said to herself, *What if my madness severs me completely from any responsibility? No more traumatic flashbacks. Rather, my life replays as dreams that I watch on a reel-to-reel projector until the day I cease to exist entirely.*

"I'm not sure I like being retired, actually," Jane answered. "I'm—"

With a start, Jane realized she almost *felt* like talking to Dr. Reid. Oddly, the doctor wasn't hunkered behind her desk, threatening to push the panic button that would send her to The Room.

Maybe, Jane thought, *for the first time, I don't care.* She was retired. Most of her team members were dead or crazy. What did she have to lose in letting her guard down and talking to Reid? Some days Jane couldn't even get out of bed for fear she would shoot herself or go insane trying. *What could be worse than that?* Thus, in her dreamy, medicated state, Jane went along with the dream.

"Jane, you know what? I'm going to try something unusual today. Come with me." Dr. Reid slid open her desk drawer and removed her purse. "Please, Jane. I promise I'm not going to hurt you."

The doctor's abrupt movements snapped Jane back from her melancholic state, and she straightened up stiffly in her chair as Dr. Reid moved toward her reassuringly. Jane looked at her doubtfully; she never left willingly with Dr. Reid to go anywhere.

"I don't know, Dr. Reid," Jane quavered. "I mean, we're doing fine in here." Jane wasn't sure why, but part of her actually wanted to leave the office with Reid. The doctor motioned Jane to go out the office door.

"Scoot, Jane. You'll be fine. Think of this as a field trip."

This wasn't the Dr. Reid Jane knew—in dreams or in reality—but she complied with the doctor's wishes.

"Dr. Reid, we never take field trips. I don't need a field trip."

Jane demanded they return to the office to finish the session, but Reid had locked the door behind them. Before Jane knew it they were headed down the hall. Relief set in when they passed Elevator 23—the cold steel box that took Jane to The Room, where she was frequently brutalized. She could feel her legs moving forward, but her eyes were fixated on the large metallic doors as they walked past.

Dr. Reid noticed Jane's concern and took her arm, propelling Jane onward and toward the garage. "Come, come, come. Forget about that old thing, Jane." She waved her hand at the elevator as if to shoo it away. That action broke the spell of the steel doors and they exited the building together. Dr. Reid rooted for her keys in her purse as they reached her car. She clicked the alarm button to her new Mini Cooper convertible.

"I know you were probably imagining something a little more Cadillac," the doctor noted. "Nevertheless, get in."

Color returned to the doctor's pale cheeks as she put the car's top down. She slid in behind the wheel, her slender frame barely making a sound on the taught leather seat. Jane lingered, frozen, with the gaping door braced against her leg, and looked down into the tiny car at this woman she barely recognized.

Jane sensed Dr. Reid's impatience when she asked her to get into the car again. Jane waited to hear the click of the plastic and metal embrace of Reid's seat belt buckle, and she watched as the doctor tossed her sleek brown alligator purse into the back of the vehicle, slightly spilling its contents. Several pill bottles rattled as the purse made contact with the seat. The doctor turned the key, and the engine started, purring quietly. This was her chance! Jane slammed the door and took off running at full speed.

She blasted past the first three lines of cars and was heading for the exit ramp to the lower level when she heard the Mini Cooper squeal from its parking space. Dr. Reid pursued her, yelling her name. As Jane rounded the corner to begin her descent of the ramp, the tires of the Mini screeched around the corner and Jane felt the air of the oncoming vehicle pushing against her back. She leapt over the edge of the parking garage ramp just in time and landed on the roof of an Escalade one level below.

"I am too old for this," Jane moaned as she rolled off the car and crouched to catch her breath. "Then again, maybe not," she muttered ruefully.

Dr. Reid pulled up and opened the passenger door. Panicking, Jane found herself blocked in with a wall behind her and cars on all three sides of her. Then, as she looked around, the scene began to fade.

"Jane, are you going to get in? Jane? Hello? Earth to Jane. Are you going to get in the car or not?"

As the edge of the metal door dug into Jane's leg, she blinked her eyes and realized that, in her dream state, she had not actually taken a step since they had arrived at the doctor's car. No sweat dripped from her brow and her heartbeat was steady. She watched as Dr. Reid casually straightened her scarf.

Whoa. This is like a bad mushroom trip, Jane thought. *How is it possible to have a PTSD episode* inside *a dream? Fuck! I wish I had someone to tell this to. I wish I could wake up.*

Dr. Reid's voice startled Jane back to her dream. "Come on, dear," coaxed the doctor, patting the passenger seat with her now-supple, abnormally rosy hand.

Suddenly, unable to speak, a devastating sensation arose in Jane. It was as if her mouth had just filled with gravel. She fought back the fear of spitting out a mouthful of her teeth into her hand if she so much as uttered a sound. She willed herself to conceal her fear from Reid and reluctantly forced herself into the car. Jane's body resisted every message her brain was sending her to *move*. Her legs grew heavy and thick. Every nerve and muscle felt trapped in molasses as she climbed slowly into the car. The minute Jane's butt hit the seat, Dr. Reid raced out of the parking garage like a teenager on the last day of school.

"Oh, for God's sake! I hate that building!" Reid exclaimed. "I'm going to die in there. The atmosphere is poisonous!"

The doctor inhaled deeply and a beam of sunlight brushed across her face. Jane hadn't uttered a word since she got into Dr. Jekyll's car. *Who* is *this woman?* Jane thought to herself. She kept her jaw clenched and her tongue pressed tightly to the roof of her mouth until the mouthful-of-gravel sensation subsided and her ability to speak returned.

"Is this our Thelma and Louise moment?" Jane asked. "Have you lost your mind and are about to drive us off a cliff?"

"You know, Jane, call me Mary. And do you think for just one moment we could relate as two women? Just this once?" the doctor asked, hugging the corners and flying down the straights. Jane still didn't know whether to trust her.

"Okay, Mary," Jane said tentatively. "What are we doing?"

"Therapy, Jane," replied the doctor as she decelerated a little. "Tell me about your home. Where are you living now?" Reid looked directly at Jane, yet still managed to swerve and sweep the road expertly. Jane had the urge to tell the doctor to read her file. Orion knew everything about her, right down to the number of times she used the bathroom each day.

"Well, I just finished building a home in the mountains of Colorado. My dream home, actually," Jane began, remembering this was only a dream and it was safe to talk here. She got lost in the serene image of her secluded home surrounded by wildlife.

"I can hike, hunt, and fish on my own land." As Jane spoke, she could almost taste the water from the crystal clear river that ran through her property.

"I built myself a shooting range and I can step off my back porch and shoot my guns. Most people would consider it heaven on earth," Jane explained, looking straight ahead at the winding road, her expression softening.

In reality, the haven was not heaven for Jane; it felt more like purgatory. No matter where she went on the planet or what material items she acquired to bring peace to her life, there was always the thought that "he" would be there, attempting to take that peace from her. She could never run far enough or fast enough to escape *his* grip. Even in complete solitude, she remained perpetually tormented.

"It does sound like heaven, Jane," noted Reid, "but you speak about it with a hesitancy in your voice. What is it? What's the problem?" The doctor maneuvered the Mini into an empty parking area at the beginning of a trailhead that led into a mountain canyon. Jane was so consumed by emotion, she hadn't realized they had stopped.

"I'm not sure," Jane confessed. "I wake up so angry, with a burning hatred rising up inside of me. I head out, just me and my dog, for long hikes across my land. I try to exhaust myself, but I wake up the next day with those same feelings of utter rage. I put on a seventy-pound pack and sling my rifle on my back and climb mountains all day in an attempt to exorcise this demon, but I can't slay this beast and I can't shake this anger."

Jane eased back into the leather seat, put her head on the headrest, and looked up into the afternoon sky. She visualized the last time she stood screaming on the mountain, which was just a few days ago. She had clutched dirt in both fists and wailed out into the echoing canyon below. She had dropped to her knees and sobbed in agony. Her emotional pain had been so intensely nauseating that she had felt the world spin around her seemingly paralyzed body. No sound had escaped her mouth as her tears mingled with the spit and slobber that coated her lips. They had dangled for a moment and then dropped into the dust in languishing pools. Her lungs had felt as if they were about to explode as her chest finally rose after being denied air during her screaming fit.

Still lost in her memory, Jane had thought of the pistol tucked in the door of her truck. She had tried to convince her broken-spirited body to crawl over to the truck and grab it, but she couldn't do it. She had just fallen to the ground. She hadn't even tried to drag her arms out from under her body to push her face out of the suffocating dirt. She had just lain in the red dirt and sweltering sun for hours, until she had been awakened by the soft, gentle kisses of her dog. *If I kill myself*, she had thought, *I'll never meet the one who's caused me this agony. And I won't be able to kill him.*

"Do you know what or who you're so furious with?" Dr. Reid asked, looking at Jane sympathetically and snapping her back from her memory.

Jane wanted to tell her, but guessed that, after all these years, the good doctor was in her head enough to know why Jane wanted to kill herself and what was stopping her from doing so. Reid probably just needed to hear her say it. Jane stared back at her, hesitating for a moment. Jane actually made out a tiny yellow spark in the center of Reid's muted, grayish blue eyes. Jane had never once taken note of the doctor's eye color, let alone cared.

"Yes, Mary," Jane acknowledged. "I know *precisely* who I'm pissed at." And she did know. She was very aware. She was going to kill him as soon as she got the chance. Jane was angry most of the time. She half believed the only thing that kept her warm at this point was her boiling blood. As she thought about *him*, she had to loosen her jacket. Adrenaline started to pump through her veins, and her heart sent a message to her brain to assemble the troops and put up the shields.

Dr. Reid witnessed the obvious quickening of Jane's breath, but she remained calm and took back the reins of the conversation.

"Well, Jane, let's see if I can put my education to work here. I've seen you for almost your entire life. I'm convinced you've killed everyone you sought—aside from me, of course. So that leaves you. If that's the case, a secluded and sequestered lifestyle is not the best choice you could make. You need to get out and get a new viewpoint of the world. I propose you take a road trip—somewhere where you can meet people and have an adventure without the possibility of getting wounded."

Jane shuddered a little as Dr. Reid touched her arm as she spoke. It startled Jane to be touched by the doctor in a seemingly caring manner. Jane hated to admit it, but she almost liked the idea Reid proposed. *Maybe I do need to get away*, Jane thought.

"I don't know, Mary," Jane replied. "I'm kind of a wreck. Wait! Shouldn't you be reporting this?" She was constantly paranoid, worried that Reid would flip out and recount yet another fucked-up session to Howser. Jane thought Reid was off the mark about her wanting to kill herself. She wanted to kill *somebody*, but not necessarily herself. There was a black devil out there that she loathed like no other. Thinking of him and the monstrous crimes he committed against humanity made her skin crawl and her rage swell. Jane wanted to stalk him and kill him—and doing so was her new mission. She vowed to herself, then and there, that she would travel the world until their paths crossed, and she was convinced they would, in due course. Then she'd take action.

"To whom Jane? To whom should I report anything about you? You're retired. Orion doesn't care if you kill yourself. They'd probably prefer it if you did. Then they wouldn't have to try and figure out how to process the papers on a soldier who doesn't exist. You don't even have to see me any longer. I was actually startled when you showed up. I presume it's a force of habit. You're free to do whatever you want with your life. I recommend you find something superb to do with your sovereignty. Don't end your life when it's just beginning. That's not the Jane who emerged from The Hole after thirty days. She's much stronger than that. For shit's sake! People write books about women like you!" Reid laughed, took a flask from her purse, and offered Jane a drink. "Do something prodigious, Thelma!"

Jane took the flask. "Thanks, Louise." They sat in Reid's car, sipping gin until the sun went down.

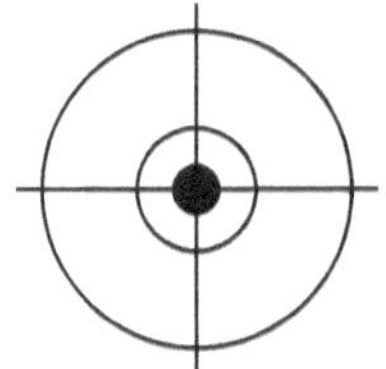

CHAPTER FIVE

Jane was awakened by gentle, wet licks on her cheek by her scrappy terrier. Morning sunbeams broke through the crack of the curtains hanging at her window. Tiny dust particles danced through the shafts of light like small fairies, catching drafts and waves of heat. As the image of Dr. Reid faded, Jane fought to recall the details of her dream in an attempt to decipher its meaning. She fell back to sleep to savor one last fleeting thought of Dr. Reid in her dream's altered light. Perhaps the figurative wall she built around her little Rocky Mountain sanctuary to keep her enemies at bay wasn't doing its job. Jane would be found no matter where she went. She suspected isolation could drive her further into her madness, but she wouldn't live in fear. She had to get out, at least for a little while. It suddenly dawned on her where she needed to go.

"Well, Maxine, Dr. Reid was right," Jane affirmed as she ruffled Max's unruly black-and-white fur. Maxine cocked her head and looked at Jane inquisitively. Jane laughed and threw off the covers with the same gusto she exhibited the day Howser came to get her at the farm and take her off to school.

She walked to her window and looked out at the clear, iridescent sky—a picture-perfect morning to pack up her old '78 Ford pickup and head southwest for a hiatus from her self-contained reality. Jane turned toward her dresser and glanced at the photo of Tom that she took with her everywhere. She paused for a moment. If she listened hard enough, Jane could still hear him talking to her at school when they were kids.

Back then, when Jane was around Tom, she forgot about everything else. She couldn't even concentrate on her schoolwork. She got flustered on "range days" if he was placed next to her. Every time he brushed passed her in the dorm, she got butterflies in her stomach. He stirred every emotion in her. The first time he kissed her, she felt a bolt of energy surge through her body.

Jane held the photograph tightly. Tom was the one person in the world she would die for. She always wanted to be near him, and she missed him desperately every time they were deployed separately.

Jane turned to Maxine and said, "Max, girl, Tom and I knew each other so well we could communicate without words. Kinda like you and me." Maxine's ears perked up. "Yeah, I know you understand, girl." Jane scratched Maxine behind the left ear as the dog leaned into her. "We'd just sit for hours in silence, simply enjoying each other's presence." Jane shook her head and smiled. "Such a good and honorable man. He loved God—hope and faith—a real all-American boy." Maxine licked Jane's hand to remind Jane she should be petting her. "I know you don't like men, Max, but you would've let this man through the door without biting him."

Jane recalled one day in Pretoria when she and Tom were about ten years old. They raced as fast as they could, rounding the corner of the Orion compound to watch the sunset from the treehouse they had built together. Tom pointed to the blazing orange sun and told her it was a miracle and that it made him want to kiss her. Then he moved in to kiss her, but pulled away quickly at the last second, probably afraid she would punch him.

They both laughed, then grew still and silent. Jane mustered up the courage to tell Tom it made her want to kiss him too. And with that, he leaned closer into her, swooping in for a fast peck on the cheek. Jane had never kissed a boy before, and she didn't close her eyes when she returned a quick kiss right on his lips. They had their first kiss in that treehouse—innocent schoolchildren as the sun set on the African horizon.

They sat there for a little while before Tom turned to Jane and said, "Jane, I think we should get married." He immediately turned his head to the side to dodge her right hook.

Jane popped back into the present to talk to her best canine friend. "Married, Max! What did we know about marriage?"

In the moment after their first kiss, Jane was overcome by an urgency to gut herself in front of Tom. That's when the truth came spewing out of her mouth before she even thought about it. She felt open and vulnerable with Tom, like she could tell him everything— and should.

"Tom," Jane blurted, "Howser's my dad. My *real* dad."

Tom gave her a sidelong look and rubbed the dimple on his chin. He then proceeded to insist Howser didn't have any kids and pointed out that Howser wasn't even married.

Jane looked at Tom, flabbergasted, then remembered how religious he was. She refrained from stating the obvious and let the silence fill the space until Tom indicated his willingness to hear her side of the story.

Jane went on to tell Tom what she knew about her life up until that point. She talked about her foster family as well as the verbal contract she had with Howser not to disclose who her father was to anyone. Ever.

"Why'd you just tell *me*, then?" Tom asked.

"Because I trust you," Jane stated simply. She *did* trust Tom. He was faster than the rest of their schoolmates, smarter than they were, and could outshoot all of them. A God-fearing person, Tom certainly didn't appreciate that Jane had just put the burden on him of keeping Jane's secret. He believed in full disclosure, but he loved Jane and he believed she told him the truth.

Tom took Jane's hand, looked her straight in the eyes, and said, "You *can* trust me, Jane."

She knew that was the truth. Tom also said she should trust her dad. He didn't like the idea of hiding his knowledge from Howser and wanted to come clean. Jane knew Howser would be furious that she told Tom their secret, so she pleaded with Tom to keep it. Finally, both Tom and Jane agreed never to tell anyone else, even Jude.

"But there was still that one caveat," Jane said smiling, coming back to the present and putting her hand on Maxine's belly. "I had to marry him one day." Maxine stretched out on her back to get a better tummy scratch.

"That's right, Max. Eight years had gone by since we first kissed. Tom was muscular and athletic. He was also crazy religious. He had a huge tattoo of Jesus on his chest. He was second-in-command at

Orion when he was only eighteen years old! He was at the top of his class in everything he set out to do. But out of every mission he ever accomplished, Tom told me that the day we got married was the biggest, most important day of his life."

Max jumped off the bed as Jane reached over to grab the card that was sitting on the bedside table. It was an invitation to their nephew's celebration that read: Sam Stapelton has joined the Marines and will be leaving for boot camp. Please join us in bidding him a loving farewell at 12:00 noon on Friday, August 10, 2017. The Stapelton Farm, Chorchata, New Mexico.

It had been years since Jane had visited the farm. She wasn't sure whether she was ready to walk the hallways of Tom's childhood home again, but she decided to give in to the impulse. After all, Tom would have done the same for her.

When she last visited the Stapelton farm, Jane had the duty and honor of laying the American flag on the lap of Marlene Stapelton, Tom's mother, while Marlene wept for Tom's brother, Colonel Elijah Stapelton. Elijah and his wife were killed in an automobile accident. They were hit head-on by a semi driver who had fallen asleep at the wheel. Elijah was a decorated Marine. Their children—Sam and his younger brother, Mackey—moved in with their grandparents, Eugene and Marlene.

Over the years, Jane stayed in touch with Sam. He reminded her a lot of Tom. He even looked like Tom, with his bright-green eyes. Like Tom, he was an upstanding citizen and was determined to serve his country. Sam and Jane had a mutual respect for one another. She knew he looked up to her, but he wasn't afraid to banter with Jane. She liked that about him. As seldom as she saw him in the flesh, Sam was still the closest thing Jane had to a son.

Jane made up her mind to attend the party. She wanted to be there for Sam in person, to see him off. And perhaps even help him wrap his mind around what it's like to be a Marine. She had stories that would probably scare the crap out of him, and she wouldn't hold back on any of the gory details.

Unlike the last time she went to the farm, this event would have an entirely different tone. Throughout the years, she prepared Sam for his departure to the military by writing letters, and sending books and videos of her martial arts training. Jane was proud Sam wanted to become a Marine like her, and like his father.

Planting her feet back on that sandy New Mexico dirt and wrapping her arms around Marlene and Eugene sounded grounding right now. It was just what she needed to remove herself from her obsession to kill the man she hated most in the world.

Jane pulled out Sam's father's Marine Corps memorabilia, which she had saved for this occasion, and laid everything on the bed. Some might think the small box contained a lot of useless junk; however, as she rubbed the surface of Elijah's worn MRE spoon, she thought about how she, and many other Marines, would agree that hope could be found from one chow to the next. Jane wrapped the utensil and tucked it in carefully next to Elijah's small journal. Although a Marine, Sam's father believed the pen was mightier than the sword, and his words were powerful and thought-provoking.

Also in the box were the standard letters and photos that inspire all Marines in battle. Their pages and edges were worn, but they had been kept safe within the confines of his journal. These objects were more precious than the rarely opened boxes of medals or letters of commendation, which often evoked substantial feelings of pain, loss, and sacrifice when viewed. Gently and meticulously, Jane wrapped each item individually, then placed all of them carefully back into the box so they wouldn't bump around. She then laid her rarely worn black suit—Jane's idea of fancy dress—over the box and carried them out to the truck.

Next, Jane flung all her camping gear, stowed in dirty canvas bags, into the truck bed. Water and food followed in short order. She packed an adequate arsenal of guns for her western journey, where all great adventures originate. Last, Maxine jumped into the passenger seat next to Jane, her tongue hanging out. Jane was practically panting right along with her. She felt exuberant and slightly anxious as they started off on that bright, clear day.

They drove south for five agonizing hours down the same straight highway lined with strip malls and fast-food chains. Jane's old truck wasn't built for modern-day excessive speeds. Road-raging commuters flew past her, many of them flipping her off. Jane laughed to herself, thinking they'd probably reconsider their actions if they knew the arsenal she was packing.

Eventually, the scenery began to shift as they neared the border of New Mexico—a seemingly mystical desert. Jane didn't mind driving at a slower pace. It gave her time to read the signs for the UFO watchtower located at the bottom of the San Luis Valley. *These might be my people*, Jane thought. She could set up camp right next to that UFO watchtower and just welcome the crazy in—especially if the "new" Dr. Reid visited her again.

Jane finally turned off onto a more pleasant, dry, flat country road. She enjoyed these roads the most, no matter what country she was in. The washboards and potholes forced her to slow down and breathe in the scents of fresh, flowering cacti and mineral deposits in cracked clay. The gently sloping hills were dotted with aromatic sage. Each time the washboards forced her tires off the road, she could smell the crushed herb wafting in the open truck windows. The assaulting heat enveloped her as it danced off the sandy hillside.

The slower speed also allowed Jane to watch for snakes. Wherever she went in the world, Jane watched for interesting serpents, then tried to kill them. She had seen nearly every species in the world. After her close encounters with mambas and puff adders in Africa, rattlesnakes and bull snakes seemed docile.

"There's one, Maxine!" Jane yelped. "I think it's a rattler. You better stay in the truck." She observed the snake as it moved stealthily from beneath the sagebrush. After Jane steered her vehicle to the side of the road, she removed her Sig P229 .357 from the door of the truck, tiptoed quietly around to the front, and pressed her butt against the bumper. As she lit her American Spirit cigarette and slowly inhaled the smoke, she sensed the sun creep across her arms. It sent a gentle charge through her whole body. The temperature still wasn't searing enough for her, though; Jane liked it torch hot.

"Fucking snake. You slithering, cunning bastard," Jane muttered under her breath.

She handled her gun easily. It felt like an extension of her own hand. Jane thought of the thousands of rounds that had passed through its chamber. Whether in countless hours of training or during live missions, she always felt safe with her trusty weapon.

Jane watched that snake sunning itself in the middle of the road in the 105-degree desert heat as she did the same. Neither one of them was perspiring. She wondered for a moment whether snakes sweat. Casually, Jane blew out the last of her smoke and twisted the cigarette under her boot heel. Suddenly, she felt her pulse accelerate, which isn't good if you're about to take a shot. She inhaled deeply, released her breath slowly, and her pulse rate decreased. She then raised her .357 and took aim from fifteen yards.

"Nah, that's not fair. Let's mix it up a little," she told Max, as she tossed the handgun into her left hand and hastily fired two shots, hitting the snake dead on. Maxine gave her two exceptionally cheerful barks of approval as Jane ambled over to inspect the snake.

"Not bad, huh, Max?" she asked, glancing back at Maxine and holding the snake up in the air. Maxine scratched at the inside of the door, trying in vain to escape the truck and shred the snake. As Jane carried the rattler back to the truck, making plans to skin it, she saw a cloud of dust move toward them like a Kansas tornado.

"Oh, shit! We must have alerted the Calvary," she griped to Max. Shooting rattlesnakes in Colorado carried a substantial fine; she could only imagine what the fee might be on an Indian reservation in New Mexico. She pitched the snake as far as she could and quickly put down her tailgate in an attempt to look casual. By the time the oncoming truck arrived, she had a nice little picnic set out, and Maxine and Jane were having a sweet time of it.

An old blue Chevy truck, just as beat-up as Jane's Ford, pulled up to face her vehicle. Two very stout, resolute old farmers, who looked to be in their eighties, stared at her for a minute. Simultaneously, both the driver-side and passenger doors swung open. As the passenger tried to exit the truck he became immediately entangled in the shoulder restraint, nearly choking himself to death. He belted out a dozen or more cuss words at the damn-fandangle-son-of-a bitch seat belt while slapping the driver with his hat. The driver was a Native American man who wore a huge bolo tie that had a chunk of turquoise on it that could choke a cow. It nearly strangled him as it swung sideways each time he dodged the other old codger's blows with the hat.

Jane kicked back on her boot heels and took in the comical scene.

The Native American started yelling at the old farmer. "Stop strugglin', you fool! You're only makin' it tighter. Relax your fat and give it a little room."

The driver attempted to wrestle the passenger from the restraint.

"Well, goddamn it," yelled the chubby farmer, "I don't know why we have to wear our seat belts when there isn't another car around for fifty miles. And who're you callin' fat? You're so full of lard that when they cremate you, you'll burn for a full year! What did you have for breakfast at the casino? Biscuits and gravy? Get me out of this damn thing!" The passenger was dripping with sweat, and the buttons on his Dickies khaki shirt were strained to the max.

"Look here, you fool! You have the strap buckled through your suspenders! That's why it won't come loose!" The Native American made a move to unbuckle his cohort's suspenders.

"Don't undo my suspenders, you idiot! My trousers will come off! Just cut the damn seat belt! I don't need it!"

The farmer reached for the bowie knife tucked into the Native American's belt, but fortunately his own large stomach got in the way. Finally, his buddy unbuckled the seat belt, freeing the stout farmer, who popped out the passenger door and skidded on the gravel, nearly losing his footing as he exited the truck. He then inhaled a cloud of New Mexico dust, adding to his misery.

Jane had been resting patiently against the blisteringly hot bumper of her truck, but when the farmer fell out of the old Chevy, holding steady was the last thing on her mind and she turned to look back at Max through the dirty windshield. Jane felt jumpy and twitchy, like a bull in the pit at a rodeo, waiting for the rider to mount. She sensed Maxine felt similarly, who looked at Jane as if to ask, "Why aren't we moving?"

Jane murmured under her breath, "Because this is more fun, Max!"

The old farmer wiped at his sweaty face with a crumpled red bandana, put on a ginormous white cowboy hat, and approached Maxine and Jane.

"Ma'am, what in the hell is a little thing like yourself doin' way the hell out here shootin' up to hell and high water, scarin' all the damn cattle?" asked Eugene, the overweight farmer, who continued to sweat like a pig in a rendering plant. He swatted at his brow again while he waited for her to answer. Jane suddenly recognized him. She knew he had a sweet demeanor and that he was a kind man with a big heart. And judging by his stomach, he had an appetite to match.

"I think you've been eating too much gravy, you old fart!" Jane said as she grinned at him.

The Native American laughed and shook his head. "So much for comin' out here and bein' hard-hittin'. I thought you were gonna be the intimidatin' rancher this time! See, Eugene? You should've let me handle the approach," he remonstrated with a scowl.

"Earl, stop that, goddammit! You look like an idiot. You couldn't scare a fly off shit with that face." Eugene looked at Jane and smirked, "Git over here, you little shit! I should've known it was you scarin' the spots off my cows like that!"

Eugene ambled toward Jane looking like Santa Claus in Farmer-Alls and suspenders, and gave her the biggest hug she'd had in years. Jane began to tear up. She knew how a bull rider felt looking for eight: pure elation and freedom!

"Would you like something to drink? I have a cooler here full of water and ice-cold lemonade," Jane offered.

Eugene's voice was abnormally dry and raspy. "Much obliged, young lady! Damn good to see you." His voice trembled at the thought of icy lemonade passing over his parched lips.

Jane tossed each of the men a drink. "Elizabeth, this two-tone, crippled, nearly obsolete Indian is the new sheriff, Eatin' Bear Coughin' Fish, but we just call him Earl."

Jane tried desperately to contain the chuckle struggling to escape her throat, thinking that could not possibly be his real name. She'd heard a lot of Native American names before, but this was a new one on her.

"That is not my name," Earl answered stoically. "He likes to say that to people who don't know me 'cause I'm a damn Indian. My name is Earl Squats When Pees."

Eugene managed to keep a straight face for about one second before the lemonade came spewing out of his mouth and they all bellowed out a laugh. After a minute or so, Eugene collected himself.

"This Indian, young lady, is the most highly respected and revered man in the West," Eugene explained, placing a dusty paw on Earl's shoulder.

"I believe that," replied Jane, "because his efforts to save you from near strangulation by seat belt clearly demonstrate his heroism." She turned to face the sheriff and said, "Earl, I apologize for the gun and the cattle. I actually didn't see any livestock. I didn't realize this was your sacred land because I didn't see any casinos on it." Jane laughed.

"Ha, Earl! Casinos! She don't even drink and she's pickin' on you. She was married to my boy Tom and he had a spicy sense of humor like that too. Look, Elizabeth, Coughin' Fish has a few tricks up his buckskin. Earl, do you want to show this little twerp what I'm talkin' about?"

"Um, I don't know, Eugene. I need to ask you—"

Eugene interrupted Earl before he could finish, "No, no, no! Go on, Earl. Show her your marksmanship. Earl here is a regular Wyatt Earp," Eugene crowed as he pointed to the pistols strapped to Earl's belt.

"Eugene, about that. We should probably . . . Can I talk to you a minute?" Earl suddenly appeared flustered.

Eugene moved to the side of the truck with Earl as he called back over his shoulder, "Excuse us for a minute. The heat must be gettin' to him. They don't make Indians like they used to."

Jane watched as Earl glanced toward her truck windshield as he spoke to Eugene. He then pointed to his left arm and his right hip. She attempted to piece together their conversation using their body language. As the two men walked back toward her, she knew she'd figured their pantomime correctly. Earl's entire demeanor had changed. He stood before her, rigid as a post.

"So, you're General Elizabeth Howard?" Earl asked almost cautiously. Eugene snickered under his breath.

"Well, Earl," Jane admitted, "I've been called worse," and she winked at Eugene.

"Holy shit, Eugene!" shouted Earl. "This is General Howard! The most decorated general in American history!"

Both men took off their hats, stood at attention, and saluted Jane. Eugene laughed, but Earl still stood at attention with a steady, level gaze.

"Easy there," Jane said. "I assure you that's not at all necessary."

"Yes it is," declared Earl, saluting her again as he spoke. "You're as legendary as the World War II war hero General Patton. CNN reported you were killed in Afghanistan!"

"Earl, stop that!" remonstrated Eugene as he donned his hat. He was done playing around. "Put your hat on, Earl. You're acting like an old fool. Elizabeth is older than shit now. What are you, girl . . . 'bout fifty-five now?"

Jane nodded as Eugene continued. "She's seen it all. She's just a regular Joe. Well," he said thoughtfully, "she's not by any means *regular*, and she's my daughter-in-law and the most wonderful woman on the planet, next to Marlene, of course. She don't like to be gawked at except by me. Isn't that right, your highness?" Eugene nudged her.

"I'm old for sure. Not dead, though. I feel like it sometimes, but that must be retirement."

Jane looked down at her boots and up again at Earl, cocking her head. "Come on, now. I'm just a general in Orion. You can't compare me with Patton. Orion is nothing like standard military. We don't even follow their rules."

Jane paused to think about that for a few seconds. She was relieved they hadn't had to follow typical military protocol. She had liked being paramilitary. She loved the freedom from government bureaucracy. Howser had called all the shots and was backed by a secret world order of government—a much more renegade "git 'er done" agency. Jane was the "queen bee."

"So, Earl, what gave me away?"

"I noticed the Post access sticker on the window of your truck," Earl explained. "There were only six of those ever issued, and they were only issued to one team of Orion. And the gun you carry, the Sig, is engraved with *Howser* on its handle. And, well, your tattoo is famous!"

Jane was caught off guard by this list of facts. "I don't understand, Earl. How do you know all this? No one knows about these things—let alone is smart enough to piece them all together that quickly."

Eugene broke the tension. "He's a spirit Indian. Goes into people's dreams and then reads their thoughts. A Windwalker." He began to laugh. "Actually, Earl spent thirty-five years working for the CIA."

Jane straightened her back and raised her eyebrows. *Well,* she thought to herself, *That explains it.*

"The CIA? No shit!" Jane exclaimed, as if she'd run into an old frenemy. "You CIA guys were either investigating our asses or trying to finagle your way into Orion."

Earl, still standing rigidly, indicated he was most likely the former. Orion recruited many of their top field agents from the CIA and the FBI when candidates showed maximum potential.

Jane smiled coyly at the two men, suddenly feeling back at the top of her game, then turned to walk to the bed of her truck. "We better pack this up. Sorry you had to run all the way over here in this heat. I was headed to the farm when that snake distracted me."

"Shootin' snakes again?" asked Eugene. "Son of a bitch. See, Earl? She's a crack shot! Well," he paused, "we better get goin'. Marlene'll have a fit if we're late." Eugene mimicked his wife by twisting the fabric of his pants with his hands the way Marlene did with her apron when she was nervous or stressed.

Jane packed up the faux picnic, hopped in the truck, and she and Maxine followed the men down the long, dusty road toward the Stapelton farm.

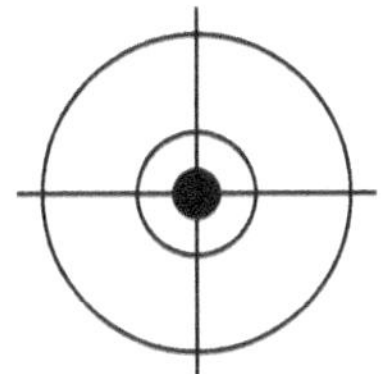

CHAPTER SIX

Jane waited in her truck for Eugene as he dropped Earl off at the sheriff's station, then continued to trail behind him as they reached the high metal gates at the entrance to the farm. Desert willows lined the driveway, welcoming them home. Free-range chickens and goats grazed within the bone-white fence that framed the yard, under the watchful eye of the family's Great Pyrenees working dog. Beyond the open doors of two red barns stood a classic, old John Deere tractor; tall piles of hay; and active livestock.

The muted-yellow farmhouse in the foreground of the panoramic view of the San Juan Mountains reminded Jane of a painting in a museum. Hot-pink bougainvillea in full bloom surrounded the massive porch, while hefty baskets of multicolor pansies hung from the rafters. In the center of the bright-green lawn stood a flagpole with Old Glory wafting lazily in the light breeze; the Marine Corps flag hung directly below it. Flowerbeds overflowed with petunias, marigolds, and daylilies. The whole property was a lush, well-manicured oasis in the middle of the desert.

Jane and Eugene parked their trucks near the house. As they, and Maxine, clambered out, they watched as a number of heavyset women rushed around the yard, spreading red-and-white-checked tablecloths on redwood picnic tables and placing multiple vases of fresh-cut sunflowers on top. Judging from the number of tables, Sam's impending party looked larger than Jane envisioned.

"Marlene," Eugene yelled across the yard to his eighty-year-old wife, "come on over here. We have a visitor."

Marlene held a bouquet of wildflowers against her cotton sundress, which was protected from splashes and spills by a brown handmade calico apron patterned in tiny orange flowers. Her slightly faded, thick blonde curls were twisted on top of her head in a loose bun. Marlene was born and raised in Texas, but she relocated to New Mexico with Eugene after the Korean War. Her Texas hospitality and Southern charm were ingrained. Eugene often referred to their little "farmette" as a mini South Fork, after the 1980s television show *Dallas*. Marlene wanted their home to appear "More Texas and less New Mexico"—from the interior design right down to the country cooking. Eugene didn't mind in the least. He preferred a hearty plate of biscuits and gravy to traditional Southwestern food.

"Eugene, you're always bringing home feral cats! It's a good thing I made extra," Marlene yelled as she placed the flowers on the nearest table and wiped her hands on her apron. She began to walk toward Jane with a pageant-winning smile, extending her hand.

Marlene realized Jane wasn't one of Eugene's strays when he announced loudly, "Marlene, presenting General Elizabeth Howard Stapelton, United States Marine Corps, Leader of Orion."

"Oh my goodness! Oh my!" Marlene yelled as she ran toward Jane. "Eugene! Does Sam know Jane's here?" Marlene burst into tears as she enveloped Jane in her arms in a big, warm hug. "I've missed you, darlin'! You made it! I hardly recognize you. You cut off all your hair!" Marlene said, her voice cracking slightly.

Jane returned Marlene's hug with equal fervor. "I hope it's okay that I brought my dog. This is Maxine," Jane said as she gestured toward her obedient companion. Max was acting unusually restrained despite the excessive amount of livestock milling around. Jane made a mental note to keep an eye on Max, who clearly was fighting the urge to bolt and chase a chicken.

"Of *course* Maxine is welcome! *Everyone* is welcome! Come in! Let me show you around. We've made some changes since you were here last. It's been such a long time! Let me show you to the ladies room and you can freshen up," Marlene directed as she gripped Jane's arm tightly. Her hold was so strong that Jane wondered whether Marlene was nervous about her arrival or because she was about to see off her beloved grandson, whom she mostly raised. Of course, Marlene was always nervous. She put a lot of effort into outward appearances and disguising her anxiety, although it came out time and again in her twisting hands.

Eugene yelled over his shoulder to one of the boys on the lawn, "Mackey, get your cousins over here to help the general with her bags!"

Remembering all the weapons she had packed, Jane turned quickly toward Eugene and said, "Sir, I better just grab my ruck and lock up the rest."

"Alright, then," Eugene agreed. He spun around and yelled, "Never mind, boys! Mackey! Go find Sam!"

Marlene directed Jane inside and led her straight to the "powder room." This time, Jane stayed slightly behind her mother-in-law to avoid the Indian arm-burn twist.

"You may want to freshen up while I get your room prepared," Marlene said. To diffuse any tension over unnecessary preparations, Jane didn't protest. Marlene had already honed in on her self-inflicted need to impress Jane. As Jane well knew, the best bedroom in the house belonged to Marlene and Eugene. Jane assumed that in the next few minutes, Marlene would gather up every female within shouting distance to transform that room into a guest bedroom—a room even Jacqueline Onassis would have admired.

Although Marlene had only a slight Texas accent left over from her youth, her sense of hospitality remained full-fledged Southern. Jane respectfully agreed to wash up, and she took her time to allow for all the fussing and switching. Max came right in the bathroom with her to avoid the impending commotion. As soon as Jane closed the door, sensible-heeled women flew up the hardwood stairs and began shifting furniture, vacuuming, shaking rugs out windows, and giggling. Jane washed the desert-red dirt vigorously from the crook of her elbows as Max drank from the cool, clean toilet bowl. Jane always overlooked her elbows, which were often caked with dirt from perching on them as she staked out a target.

As Jane stared at the russet-colored water flowing down the sides of the white porcelain sink, she felt relieved the liquid was not some kid-soldier's blood, her blood, or enemy blood. The grime from her arms and hands mixed with the running water and slithered down the drain.

Suddenly, Jane's heart began to race and her arms froze in place over the sink as the synapses in her brain began to fire rapidly, pulling a memory off the shelf marked Bloody Handwashing. Jane dusted it off, ensured the image was sealed up, and returned it to its designated place in her memory file. This was a subconscious, conditioned practice that most soldiers practiced to help them stay sane. When her brain clicked back to normal-handwashing mode, her heartbeat slowed.

Jane stayed in the bathroom until she heard the phalanx of heels trot down the creaky wooden staircase.

"Max, time to make our exit from this head," she said. *Lavatory, Jane,* she thought to herself. *Civilians have lavatories and bathrooms, not heads. Toilets, bathrooms, latrines, pissers, washrooms, water closets, johns, potties, poopers, shitters, crappers, and powder rooms.* Jane opened the door quickly before claustrophobia set in. Marlene, who was standing directly in front of the door as Jane opened it, jumped back a bit, startled.

"There! Don't you feel better?" Marlene asked, out of breath. Half of her up-do dangled over her left shoulder and her face was beet red, aside from the smudge of dirt on her cheek. Marlene looked about as frazzled as Jane felt. Jane wiped a bead of sweat from her brow. Marlene failed to notice Jane's face was also flushed.

"Let me show you to your room, where you can change," Marlene said as she led the way up the stairs. "Then come on down whenever you like. Little Sam is going to be so thrilled you made it. He reads your letters over and over."

When they reached the top of the stairs, Marlene wound her apron in her hands as she spoke without making direct eye contact with Jane. "Take your time, but try not to take a nap or anything because you'll miss the celebration. This room is exceptionally comfortable." She gestured as she smiled.

Jane assumed she was fishing for a compliment. "I'm already more comfortable than I have ever been in any room in the White House," she said, knowing Marlene wouldn't be able to wait to tell her friends what she had said. Her home was her pride and joy. Jane assumed comparing the room with one in the White House would be a high accolade for the former Texas beauty queen.

To Jane, Eugene and Marlene's home actually *was* more beautiful than the White House. Perhaps it was because Tom grew up here or because it was similar to her childhood home in the Midwest, with wood floors that squeaked, making it impossible to sneak down to look at Christmas presents early without being caught. She had distinct memories of waking up to the scent of livestock and the cackle of chickens. And here, as in her childhood bedroom, a homemade quilt sewn from precious scraps of multicolor fabric blanketed the bed.

"This place is more likely to give me a PTSD flashback than thunder, eh, Max? Maybe you should take my gun tonight." Maxine cocked her head at Jane as one ear flopped down. Jane snickered aloud, downplaying the severity of those flashbacks. Max jumped on the bed and licked Jane's face.

Jane looked around the room at the photos of Sam at various ages hanging on the walls. In his clean high school football uniform, his elbow propped on one knee, he looked like the epitome of a handsome all-American teen. There were a few pictures of Eugene and Marlene's daughters as well, but neither of their sons, Tom or Elijah. Jane could only imagine how difficult it was for a parent to lose a child, and Eugene and Marlene lost both of their sons.

Each of the few times Jane returned to the Stapelton home, she touched the walls just to feel close to Tom, and imagined him as a child in the house. She could almost hear his laughter through the walls and his footsteps in the hallway. Eugene had painted over the lines Tom and Elijah scratched on the wall, marking their growth. She pictured Eugene reluctantly covering all traces of those memories. The thought of it made her throat swell with sadness. She wished Tom were here today to give Sam words of advice. Hell, she wished Tom were here every day.

Tom and Jane might have only been seventeen when they married, and he was gone a short time afterward, but they had spent ten years as friends, military partners, and, eventually, husband and wife. Her pain never diminished, and she was certain Eugene and Marlene's hadn't either. Jane looked at the clock and realized quite a bit of time had passed while she stood lost in her memories.

"Fuck the pain," Jane said, attempting to shove it back down into the black abyss from which it came. She knew better than to let that feeling consume her. "Alright, Maxine, we better get changed and go downstairs." Maxine tilted her head again. "You know I always include you in everything," Jane explained. "You and I are *we*, silly." Maxine wagged her tail. She was Jane's only real companion now. She didn't like to let Jane out of her sight. She kept her straight.

As they made their way downstairs, Jane looked out a nearby window. It looked as if twenty more people had arrived within the past hour. The wars in Iraq and Afghanistan certainly popularized "boot camp parties" these days. In the old days, a kid just went off quietly to enlist. Now there was so much fear they were going to die or be seriously injured that people held big Irish wakes beforehand. Jane hoped, for Sam's sake, that the tone of this event didn't turn sour and that his plump country aunts held back their blubbering. She had distraction tactics to bust out if need be.

Jane avoided the kitchen, where most of the women usually congregated. She felt no obligation to be helpful or domestic. She glanced in the direction of the huddled groups of farmers smoking cigars on the porch. Likewise, she had no desire to discuss conservative Republican politics with the men, so she headed off to find the one person she came all this way to see.

Along the way, she spotted Sam's younger brother, Mackey, sitting under a tree and texting on his phone. He was fifteen years old and looked like a sheepdog. Jane couldn't even tell what color his eyes were because of the mess of hair hanging down in his face. Occasionally, Mackey would flip it out of the way to read an incoming text message.

"Hey, Mackey!" Jane yelled. "Can you tell me where Sam is?"

Without looking up, her nephew replied, "Yeah, General. Hold on one sec. I'll text him." With lightning speed he shot off a text and received an answer equally as fast. "He's in the barn," Mackey informed her.

"Which one?" Jane asked. She had always thought Mackey was gawky and a bit strange, and now she also found his inability to look at her particularly irritating. Her patience with disconnected teenagers ran pretty thin.

"Hold on," Mackey said. "Uh, the one with the pigs." He kept texting while his gangly legs twitched erratically. He seemed so detached, Jane thought for a moment he might be mentally challenged. Then she realized he had an earbud in the opposite ear so he could listen to music while he was on his phone.

Whenever Jane saw an awkward kid like Mackey, it reminded her that she was glad she didn't have boys. On the flip side, she wished for five boys whenever she watched her male recruits fling their bodies effortlessly over the wall of a confidence course or make the tough call to detonate an IED along the roadside in Iraq.

"Thanks, Mackey," Jane said. He still didn't look up at her, so she continued toward the barn. Jane decided not to cut across the lawn, where she might be seen and waylaid, so she walked around to the back of the barn and slipped in the side door, successfully avoiding having to stuff deviled eggs with the Mormon Tabernacle Choir. Jane thought she probably looked ridiculous, skulking along the sides of buildings and jogging quickly between fences, like a cop sneaking up on a criminal, but she'd go to any lengths to avoid having to stuff those damn eggs.

As soon as she entered the barn, Jane saw Sam sitting on the edge of a split-rail fence throwing vegetable scraps into the pigpen. Marlene and Eugene referred to their grandson as "little Sam," but this was a misnomer. Sam was actually a big kid, standing at least six foot three inches tall, and he was made of 190 pounds of pure farm-boy muscle. Sam was wearing a white cowboy hat like his grandpa, jeans, and a white button-down shirt, which was perfectly starched and pressed. He also sported a big silver belt buckle, with a roping award engraved on it, and a pair of slightly worn cowboy boots.

For a moment, Jane felt as if she were looking at the son she wished she'd had with Tom. Sam had acquired Tom's best features— his size, his bearing, a square jaw, and thick Irish hair. Tom and Jane would have chosen a more characteristically Irish name for their son, like Ezra, after the poet. They had discussed names before, for a dog they wanted to adopt, rather than a child. Regardless, kid or dog, they did agree the name needed to be a good, strong Irish name.

"'Let it never be misunderstood that a lone Marine is outnumbered.' Do you know who said that?" Jane asked, obviously interrupting Sam from a very deep thought; he nearly slid off the fence when he heard her voice.

Sam caught himself and planted his feet, chucking his cowboy hat to the ground and standing at attention. "Ma'am, yes ma'am! Sam Stewart Stapelton." He barked out his name as if he were her best recruit. Jane smiled to herself and remembered the day Howser came to take her to Pretoria. She saw her childlike, enthusiastic self in the young man standing before her.

"Alright, Sam. Calm down! Jesus Christ! You're still a farmer, not a Marine yet." Jane grabbed Sam and gave him a big hug, like the one Marlene had given her. "Ronald Reagan said that, by the way."

"Aunt Jane! I mean, General! I'm so glad you're here! I was beginning to think you weren't coming." He stood for a moment, smiling apprehensively and wiping his hands on his jeans.

"Sam, we have to teach you how to speak without fidgeting. You don't want to get a nickname in boot camp like Itchy or Scabs, do you?" Jane winked and jabbed his side lightly to put him at ease. She realized Sam might need to be taught how to talk to his superiors without clamming up like it was his first public-speaking gig. The idea of grooming a protégé perked up Jane instantly.

"Whatever," Sam said. "I'm not itchy, Aunt Jane. My hands are sweaty and I had pig shit on them. I suppose you want me to wipe that all over you?"

"For shit's sake, Sam! I don't see you for a few years and you get all jumpy around me? What the fuck?" Jane shoved him playfully, testing whether he could handle her crass sarcasm.

"Aaaaggghhh! Stop it!" Sam yelped as Jane continued to poke at him. "Or I *will* forget that I'm glad you're here!" Sam smiled and grabbed Jane's arm, then tightened his grip. "I warned you in my letters. I've been getting pretty good at those Krav Maga videos you sent me!" He then tried to sweep Jane's legs out from under her. Jane caught Sam's arm in a controlled hold and gently gave it an inward twist while pressing into his back. The movement allowed Jane to use Sam's own momentum against him, propelling him to the ground.

"Whoa! I thought you'd be out of practice by now!" Sam yelled from his facedown position on the barn floor. "What do I say in this situation? I can't say 'uncle,'" he griped. "Okay, okay, I give up!"

Sam struggled to lift his head to no avail. Jane held it down—rather gently by her standards. She was having fun, so she kept him there a few seconds more before offering him a hand up. Sam was covered in dust and little bits of hay, and Jane couldn't help but laugh at the sight of him. She watched, amused, as Sam brushed off the pieces of straw from his clothing. He looked young. Jane realized they needed to get down to business so this salt-of-the-earth kid could develop the backbone he needed to stand out in boot camp. Raised by his grandparents with strong family values in a small southwestern town, Sam wasn't what you'd call "worldly."

"Sam, look. You're going to run in to some fairly high-ranking officials in the next few years and I want you to make the most of it."

Sam instinctively altered his expression to match her serious tone of voice. They wandered over to a tractor, where Jane placed her hand on his shoulder to sit him down next to her.

"When I was a young girl," Jane explained, "I went to Washington with my father. He took me to dinner with one of his old friends, General Omar Nelson Bradley, one of my greatest World War II war heroes. I was in awe of him the entire night. I was so nervous I could hardly complete a sentence. I had so many questions I wanted to ask him—about his career, about the war—but his presence was so intimidating to me that I just sat through the dinner staring at him and winding my napkin in a ball. I listened to my father and the general laugh and talk about the 'old days,' but I never said a word because I was afraid of saying the wrong thing. When we were leaving the restaurant, the general took my hand and said in his big, brusque voice, 'Well, I thought for a little Marine you'd have more gumption. I suppose next time you'll find the courage to speak up.'" Jane paused for a moment, reflecting on the memory. "Then we shook hands and he left." Jane shrugged. "I never got the opportunity to speak to him again. Soon after that he had a heart attack and died. My father let me know how disappointed he was with me for remaining so quiet during dinner."

Jane didn't tell Sam the whole story. Howser actually gave her the silent treatment for two days afterward for embarrassing him. He had told the general that she was going to be quite the gifted soldier and would certainly have a lot of strategic questions for him when they met. Jane had felt sabotaged; she thought she deserved a warning of what was expected of her that night so she could have been prepared. She never wanted Sam to be that vulnerable.

"So, I guess I can tell you how I feel right now, General. I didn't think you'd actually show up. You never replied to the invitation, so I wasn't expecting you." Sam jammed his hands in his pockets, looked down, and dug the tip of his boot into the floor.

"Mackey blew in here earlier and told me you were here," Sam went on. "I didn't even clean up my room this morning. If you look in there, you won't think I'm very squared away." Sam seemed genuinely concerned about how she viewed him, which gave her a slight ego boost, her drug of choice

Sam had spent much of the week helping his grandma prepare for the party. This kid would move mountains for his grandmother.

Jane bet he remembered every minute Marlene sat with him, tending to fevers with cold washcloths and chicken soup, bandaging football injuries, and lifting his spirits when he felt hopeless about losing his parents. Jane knew Sam and his grandmother had that same healthy, strong bond some kids develop with their mother, or any other maternal figure in their lives.

Thinking about this made Jane wonder why Sam was out in the barn alone while Marlene threw a party for him up at the house. Maybe it had something to do with his young age. Or maybe it had to do with the fact that he'd been sheltered on a small farm in a tiny town and raised by elderly grandparents. Sam hadn't been exposed to too many tough, real-world experiences. He was far more polite than city kids and he seemed a bit introverted. Jane was beginning to doubt whether Sam had what it would take to finish boot camp, let alone become a Marine. Maybe he just needed to mature. *A late bloomer*, Jane thought.

"What else is on your mind, Sam? You seem a little quiet for someone who has an entire family and community here celebrating your big day. Why're you out here in the barn by yourself?" Jane tuned into her innate obligation as a general to serve as a chaplain or counselor for her fellow soldiers. Walking out of the barn and leaving Sam there to be consumed by his own thoughts was out of the question.

Sam looked Jane straight in the face and explained, "I'm *everything* to my grandparents. They count on me to make them proud and carry on the family tradition. I want to be a Marine because my grandfather was one of the first Marines. He served with Chesty Puller, you know." Sam leaned his whole body in her direction and talked expressively with his hands. It was as if the floodgates had opened. "But I don't think being a Marine is enough," Sam continued. "I have to do something distinctive. And I don't think Grandma and Grandpa have enough time left in this world to see me achieve that."

Sam let out a deep breath, like he'd been waiting to say these things to someone for a long time. Jane was glad he'd picked her to say them to. He must have sensed her maternal vibe. She doubted they'd be having this conversation if she were a male general.

"I'm not sure about this voluntary enlistment," Sam went on. "Every single male in my family has served in the military for generations. That's a lot of pressure. It's not like I can go to college instead. I *have* to do this."

"Do you think you're going to run right out and pick up a Distinguished Service Cross, a couple Silver Stars, and maybe a few Purple Hearts on your first tour?" Jane asked. "It doesn't work like that," Jane said, avoiding getting too soft with him. "Your grandparents seem pretty proud of you. Look at this celebration!"

Jane refrained from pointing out that the world does not revolve around eighteen-year-old boys, and that the prospect of having an empty nest someday might actually appeal to his elderly grandparents after raising children and grandchildren. Jane chose a higher ground, realizing that any teenage boy living in an environment such as Sam's sees his own reality through a narrow window. In Sam's mind, leaving the farm was a devastating blow to his grandparents and he needed to make it count through measurable rewards.

"General, how do I achieve what you've accomplished?"

Jane considered her answer thoughtfully. In reality, she scarcely knew this kid. She was present in his life mostly through letters and packages, and stories told to him by his grandparents. She didn't think it was appropriate, this late in the game, to be giving him a lifetime of advice, so she lightened things up and spoke in layman's terms.

"Well, Sam, it's not so hard. See, in boot camp, when you line up to load up, all you have to do is make sure you get on the *special bus*." Jane grinned. "Don't get on the bus that everyone else does to head off to the Marines."

Sam wasn't looking at Jane's face, so he took her instructions seriously. "Really? Just like that? There's a special bus? What does it look like? Does it say something on the side?"

"Sam!" Jane laughed. "Don't be stupid!" she quipped as she shoved his shoulder with the palm of her hand. "The military is the most complicated, mind-blowing, life-changing organization in the world. Right now, I wouldn't expect you to *begin* to understand how it's structured, let *alone* how to function *in* it. When you get to Parris Island, you just worry about keeping your boots on the painted yellow footprints on the ground. The drill instructors will take it from there. They'll get you sworn in, give you a nice little haircut, and issue you some gear."

Jane found herself revving up to expound excitedly about what it means to be a Marine. She nearly forgot the promise she had just made to herself to lay low and not overwhelm the kid with information. Apparently, her ego needed some management. Orion soldiers tend to have huge egos, and if they're stroked, they're as uncontrollable as a Colorado wildfire in July. Jane was aware she walked a fine line here, because she knew if she told Sam about the true workings of Orion, he'd want to try to recruit with them. Her ego was telling her to give Sam the dirt about being an Orion soldier, but logic was telling her to shut the hell up. She still wasn't sure he was tough enough to make it through boot camp, let alone Orion training.

The commotion up at the house seemed to be getting louder and Jane didn't really want to be around a lot of people. She preferred being sequestered in the barn, talking with Sam. Jane also knew someone would come looking for them very soon, but Sam was on a roll and she wasn't about to stop him from unloading.

"Aunt Jane, the last time you were here, I remember you standing in your uniform handing my grandma a folded flag. I knew right then and there I had to do this. Join up, I mean. I don't want to stand on the sidelines." Sam stood and paced slowly across the wide-plank barn floor, then turned toward Jane. "So here I am. Ready to strap on the boots." He sighed, put his hands in his pockets, and looked toward the ceiling.

Jane stood and walked toward him. "Sam, don't beat yourself up. Just because you come from military doesn't mean you have to enlist. Shit, what were you—thirteen?—when you made that decision? What the hell does a thirteen-year-old kid know about his future? You can change your mind. Just because you took an oath with a recruiting officer doesn't mean shit. It doesn't count until they swear you in at Parris Island."

"Stop saying I don't want to be a Marine!" Sam carped. "You sound like Grandma! I want to be in Orion. Like you and Uncle Tom. I'm lucky, 'cause you're standing right in front of me right now. And I can ask you . . . Hell! I don't even know what I'm asking exactly. Orion is only a name to me. I want it to be something more. I know I'm nowhere *near* where you were at my age, but I want to see inside your brain and understand what I need to get me through. Since I can't crawl in your head, I'll settle for what you're willing to tell me." Sam looked at her intensely.

"I'm not the Messiah, Sam, but I can shed some light for you so you don't feel like you're opening the door of a dark closet and stepping in with a herd of wild buffalo," Jane said reassuringly, trying to contain her self-pride. The corners of Sam's mouth turned up a bit and Jane could see the relief in his face.

"Aunt Jane, I'm jealous of you in a way because you had Uncle Tom in the thick of it with you. You guys were a team and spent all your time together. I'm not gonna have that same luxury. There're people here who I'm not sure I'll ever see again. You and Tom got to grow up together. You were a family in every sense of the word."

"What are you getting at, Sam?" Jane asked. "You got a lady friend or something?!" Sam bit his lip and looked down. Jane mimicked him and turned her head downward too. "Don't forget, Sam. I wasn't in the same position you are. I left home when I wasn't even eight years old. I didn't go to any dances, play any high school sports, or party with friends. I was too busy running obstacle courses with a rifle at the age of nine. That's all I knew."

The noise from the house grew louder the longer Jane and Sam stayed in the barn, and Jane was starting to feel antsy. "Look. I'm here for a few more days. You can ask me what you want to know. But *now*, we gotta go show our faces. Come 'ere." Jane grabbed Sam's shoulders and pulled him in for a bear hug.

"Thanks for being here, Aunt Jane."

"Now don't get too soft on me!" Jane replied. They continued to chat as they slowly made their way back up toward the house.

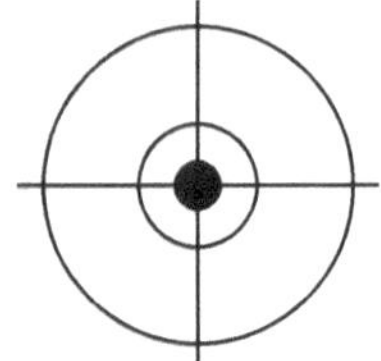

CHAPTER SEVEN

Tom used to chalk up every coincidence to "divine intervention." Jane never really bought into that "bullshit," as she put it. However, she liked to be reminded of her past every now and again. Sam's presence certainly catapulted her back in time. As they walked in silence side by side to join his family, she thought of the people in her life that eventually became family.

When Jane was fifteen years old, she had accompanied Howser to the Naval Academy in 1977. Howser was the chief operator of Orion at the time, and had unlimited jurisdiction and authority regarding all things military. He had "commissioned" her specifically to recruit Greg Walker, who later became known as Pilot. Jane had been groomed for this mission for a couple years. Howser had been assured, after her training, that Jane would be able to keep her cover at the Academy for a few months as an eighteen-year-old plebe. Sam reminded Jane of Greg. Both were good looking, tall, athletic, and overly enthusiastic. Greg had been cool, keen, and so intelligent that the Naval Academy had begun to stalk him during his sophomore year of high school. He had been commissioned unwaveringly. As the person tasked with bringing him into Orion, Jane had to attend the school as a student and try to blend in before making any moves to recruit Greg. It went without saying that no one could know her true affiliation. Although she wasn't very good at blending in, Jane had done her best.

Greg had wrestled for the Academy and Jane attended some of his matches. Watching him, she had imagined him in high school, undoubtedly the star athlete poised to wrestle for the state champion-ship. She thought she could almost hear the high-pitched shouts of a dozen cheerleaders through giant plastic cones in a gymnasium full of roaring teens and fervent parents. "Gimme an A! Gimme a C! Gimme an E! What does it spell?! *Ace! Ace! Ace!*"

Greg had been exceptional at everything, which had coined him the nickname Ace. Every girl in the place had most likely drooled over this quintessential hunky dreamboat. Jane had rolled her eyes at the thought. Greg had thick hair, straight white teeth, and a chiseled physique. All the parents adored him as well and probably used him as an assessment tool on their own children.

"Listen, Zach, if Ace Walker can get a 4.0, so can you. And if Ace Walker can play five varsity sports, then so can you."

Surely more than one kid must have replied, "If Ace Walker can have a motorcycle, then why can't I?"

At Annapolis, Greg epitomized the model plebe. His rack was textbook. He had impeccable folds in the back of his shirts and could hack the hazing. The upperclassmen respected his wrestling and football merits, and knew he would be an asset against their archrival: the Air Force Academy.

Howser wanted Greg for Orion. Period. Although he put Jane in charge of recruiting Greg, Howser couldn't help but micromanage. He ensured their lives would intersect covertly at Annapolis.

"Be subtle but convincing," Howser had coached her. "And not too much charm. Act like a girl, but not girly, because I don't think he'd like that." Howser fussed with her uniform like a fashion designer evaluating a model's attire before walking the catwalk.

"Jeezuz!" Jane complained. "You act like I'm trying to get him to go to prom with me! You know this isn't the first time I've been around a boy." Jane had shot Howser a coy look, tilting her cover downward over one eye.

Howser corner-folded her cadet blouse and tucked it tightly into the back of her skirt.

"Let me look at you," he ordered as he turned her around. "Goddamn ridiculous! Keep your grades up while you're there! And absolutely *no* fighting!"

Jane had never been a fan of Annapolis. Despite the Naval Academy's reputation as the toughest military school in the nation, she felt the school lacked discipline and was significantly less challenging than her school in Pretoria. In just ten years since Howser had established his military academy, he already had nine hundred hand-selected students. The program was run like a boot camp. Every day his recruits were put to the test. They were required to spend hours each day on the shooting range, learning to master weapons. They field-stripped and fired nearly every gun ever made to ensure no matter where they were in the world, they would be able to pick up any weapon and fire it proficiently. Some days Howser's recruits spent twelve hours on the range. All students were conditioned and trained continually to master Krav Maga as a first line of hand-to-hand combat. Some were sent to Israel for immersion programs that lasted as long as a year. While at Howser's military school, students never broke discipline. There was always a line to stand in, complete with a drill instructor barking orders. At the drop of a hat, students would fall into formation and be led to various obstacle courses for physical training. Orion students were subject to live rounds as they navigated their way through the course. The worst days for Jane and her team came when they were hauled randomly from their physical training course and subjected to torture and interrogation training.

All the physical and mental military training was coupled with an intense educational program. They studied and were tested in the classroom as well. Ten-year-old students completed college-level courses, learning several languages, physics, calculus, and engineering. Educational demands were brutal. A "hands-on program" was followed—meaning, cadre officers were allowed to punish students physically who slacked or fell behind. This training was what it took to turn out the most elite soldiers in Orion. Jane had been in the program for almost eight years when she was ordered to infiltrate the Annapolis plebes and recruit Greg.

Several uneventful weeks had passed while Jane was at the Academy before Howser instructed her to become acquainted with Greg. Jane had known it would take gumption to spark Greg's interest, and she achieved this by outshining all the other plebes in all things athletic. When she noticed Greg watching her from the sidelines, she ramped up her game, overtaking her opponents on a mock hand-to-hand training field. Jane knew he observed her fencing classes, and he timed her runs "covertly" during her physical training exercises. When Jane finally delivered an invitation to Greg to meet one-on-one, he accepted immediately.

"Hey, there! Ace, is it?" Jane walked up to him confidently at the Walter Reed Memorial Rose Garden, where they agreed to meet.

"Yes. And you are Elizabeth?" Greg asked with false uncertainty.

Jane was cocky enough to know she stood out from all the other women by leaps and bounds, so she used her assertiveness to her advantage when she recounted the words from Howser to Greg regarding the opportunities that awaited him in Orion. Jane knew how to sell that pretty boy; she made the job sound glamorous. Jane told Greg he would be allowed to graduate from Annapolis, but then he would be taken away quickly into a world of espionage and intrigue.

When Jane finished her pitch, Greg straightened his back immediately and replied, "Bond. James Bond."

She concealed her smile, struggling to keep her eyes on him rather than rolling them up toward her forehead. Not surprisingly, Greg eventually committed to becoming a recruit. He had something to prove.

After Greg had joined their team, he ended up becoming one of the most elite Special Forces agents in Orion. He acquired more "edge" the longer he was in Orion, dropping his clean-cut American façade. His more rough-and-tumble persona earned him street cred over the years, not to mention the precision and skill he displayed on missions. He and Jane had worked together for more than two decades, fighting alongside each other on nearly every op.

After they had worked together for a year, Greg confessed to Jane he had initially thought a woman like her would make a good wife for him when he became a senator or the US Secretary of Defense. He knew Jane was disciplined and could take orders. There was nothing loose about her. They had laughed together countless times over the ensuing years when Greg regurgitated his relief that he had never married her after he had figured out just how "disciplined" she was.

"Take out the goddamn garbage, you crap hole," Greg had mimicked. "The one goddamn thing I can't stand most in a trash can is trash!" They'd both bust up every time.

As Sam and Jane approached the door to the house, she paused and they both stopped walking. *Sam has the same enthusiasm as Greg when I recruited him*, she thought to herself. She knew she needed to spend more time with Sam than she envisioned.

Jane looked at Sam and said, "We may have to talk with your grandparents and see if I can inconvenience them and stay a few more days."

A genuine smile spread across Sam's youthful face, "Aunt Jane, thank you! This is awesome!" Sam extended his hand to shake hers, which Jane found a bit awkward. He did, however, have a nice strong handshake. "We'd better ask Grandma if you can stay a bit longer."

Deep down, Jane loved that Sam sought his grandma's permission over his grandpa's. Sam knew who ran that household.

During the party, Jane caught up with Sam's life since the last time she had seen him, which made her realize how much time had actually passed. He was no longer the baby-faced thirteen-year-old with scraped knees.

Jane overheard Sam's great-uncle Joe bragging to his niece as he fired off Sam's football stats. "This past year he threw the most completed passes in his high school since the record year of 1962. He's giving up a football scholarship to the University of New Mexico to join the Marines."

One of Sam's aunts piped up, boasting, "Sam is brilliant. In his high school yearbook he was voted Most Likely to Succeed, so we know that after the Marines he'll go on to college to be a doctor." She smiled at Sam across the circle of people standing around holding plates piled high with food.

Sam mingled with his family and friends, kissing all his aunts and spending a substantial amount of time playing with the younger kids. Occasionally, Jane saw him look over and smile at Marlene, who beamed with pride at her grandson.

"Hey, Grandma, can I get you another lemonade?" he asked nearly every time she emptied her glass.

"Heavens no, Sam!" Marlene replied, patting him on the back. "This is *your* party. I should be waiting on *you!*"

Sam doted exclusively on Marlene, and Jane was pleased about this. Maybe it was because Jane didn't have a mother and she enjoyed watching their exchanges vicariously from the sidelines. From what she'd heard, many sons were this way with their mothers; Jane supposed it wasn't any different with grandsons and grandmothers. Jane started to regret the decision she made after Tom died—to keep such loose ties to his family. Jane couldn't let them go altogether, but she didn't have the capacity to let them in completely either.

Marines always believe they have some innate responsibility or the power to change the outcome of a battle situation, sometimes single-handedly. Jane carried around the idea that perhaps she could have done her duty better. Thanks to survivor's guilt, she was certain—as were a few of her teammates—she should have died, not Tom. Jane often wondered whether Eugene and Marlene thought so too. Jane wasn't proud to be a decorated general in their presence, when, indeed, it should be their son parading among them at the party in full dress with a chest full of medals. Jane's regrets and longing to belong to the family began to commingle with the familiar warmth of guilt and frustration. She sat down, in her normal anxious state, and began to fiddle with the buttons on her jacket.

Periodically, Sam would come by to check on her. "How're you doing, General Howard?" he asked, deliberately calling her by her rank.

Jane got the impression he was practicing addressing a senior officer. She chuckled at how he was messing up the formality. "Boots," or "grunts," would never address a senior ranking officer unless spoken to, and in that case, the proper response would be, "Ma'am, yes ma'am!"

"Is there anything I can get for you?" Sam inquired, offering to refill her glass of juice.

"No thanks, Sam," Jane smiled. "You have a huge, delightful family who all really love you. You're a very lucky young man." She was going to say he was "blessed" instead of "lucky," but she hated it when people used that word, even though it was an equally appropriate word for the context. She sipped the last bit of juice from her tall clear glass, and the ice collected near her lips. The half-melted pieces of ice clanked as she set the glass down on the folding table next to her chair. The family knew not to offer her alcohol. She had never been a drinker.

Jane smirked at Sam's assumption that calling her by her rank intimated respect. It seemed everyone she encountered had his or her own "call sign" for her. It indicated how they perceived her. She read into it and adjusted her demeanor by the names certain people ascribed to her. She noticed that when someone wanted her to appear soft or feminine, they called her Elizabeth. When they needed the warrior to appear, as her African counterparts in the Congo did, they would call her Hatari or Baba Yaga. Her team called her Jane. The name "Jane" filled her the most with strength and courage.

"General" was often just a formal form of address or it was used by civilians who didn't understand the inner workings of Orion. Aside from the uniform, it reminded her of who she was. However, hearing the word *general* from Sam did sound overly formal. She wanted him to feel comfortable around her.

"Call me Aunt Jane," she said. "Or just—I don't know, Jane or something."

"Okay, Aunt Jane. You already know I have a lot of uncles and aunts. Remember, my mom came from a family of seven, and both my grandpa and grandma have five siblings between them, and they each have several children. I think I must have twenty-eight cousins here today!" He grinned and winked at his grandma.

Jane started to feel a little uncomfortable with all the sentiment manifesting around her. She wasn't used to it. Some of Sam's aunts were supporting each other and crying softly about Sam's impending leave-taking. She eavesdropped a bit and overheard them saying things like, "He's just gonna get blown up over there and poor Marlene's gonna die of grief." His overweight uncles, who were stressing the flimsy aluminum lawn chairs to the limit, were laughing and saying just the opposite. "Sam's gonna come home with more medals than Marlene has room for on the wall!" "He'll single-handedly kill 'em all and send the Taliban packing!" They all made machine gun noises. And Sam's little cousins launched themselves dramatically from the chairs onto the pinecones they pretended were grenades. Jane had difficulty imagining what it must be like to grow up in a huge family like this, but she made an attempt at being sympathetic.

"It must be hard for you to leave a place like this, Sam." As the words escaped her mouth, she realized just how generic the statement probably sounded. Had she known Sam better, Jane might have been able to find something more profound to say, like "Don't forget to separate the war from the warrior when the time comes or you'll never be able to come back to this."

"I suppose," Sam replied, exhaling heavily. His reaction confirmed what she was thinking: It would be hard on him to leave such a close-knit family. "Have you given any thought to what you might want to start teaching me? Maybe some of the cool crap you know? We only have a few more days before I leave." He gazed off across the farm, pretending to be casual about the question he had just asked.

Jane hesitated for a moment and her stomach seized up. She thought of Pilot's eagerness to join Orion—and what happened to him.

"I'm not sure, Sam," Jane waffled. "Maybe I better take off in the morning. You're leaving soon for boot camp and I know you'll do fine. You've had your grandpa as an advisor and there really isn't anything I could add that would better prepare you for the Marines. Besides, you'll experience your own 'cool crap.'"

Jane was certain that Sam's understanding of war consisted of what he was fed in movies. She didn't expect him to know exactly what the horrors of war really looked and felt like. The distinct smell of burning flesh after an RPG tore through one of your team members is something that can't be conveyed on film. The general public was unaware of the nightmares that consume soldiers as they experience and then reexperience mission horrors as PTSD takes hold of their lives. Sam wouldn't know this until he had his boots on the ground.

Sam turned to her and looked her in the eye. "Yes, ma'am," he said, then turned away, his face reflecting the shock and disappointment on hearing her words.

Jane expected him to question her or to plead with her to stay. She wanted to see some fight in him—the kind of fight he'd need when entering the business of war. She questioned once again whether Sam really wanted to become a Marine. Judging from his lack of protest, Jane wondered if he was sending her a signal that he really *didn't* want to enlist. Why else would he just walk away without questioning her decision to leave early? Perhaps he really wanted her to suggest he just go to college instead of enlisting. Maybe he wanted Jane to have a talk with his grandparents and explain that Sam wasn't ready to enter the military. *Whatever*, Jane thought. *I'm not his mom. He's old enough to speak up for himself. This isn't my shit.*

Jane got up from her sagging lawn chair and headed over to the barn to search for Maxine, who she'd last seen slinking around the plump chickens and skittish goats. She found her irritating the Stapelton's stoic Great Pyrenees as she attempted to coax him to play.

"Come on, Maxine," Jane said. "Let's go for a walk."

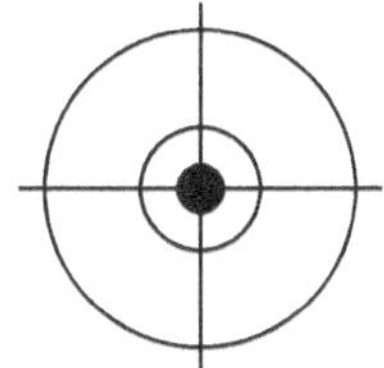

CHAPTER EIGHT

Maxine was happy to take a break. She was being run ragged by the band of small children who chased after her. Max was skeptical of nearly everyone but Jane and usually greeted people not with a wag of her tail, but with a low growl. She had, however, been more approachable on this trip than any other. She and Jane were alike in many ways, especially when it came to large groups of people. They couldn't relate to most people, so they sought solace in each other.

As they walked away from the house, Maxine zigzagged from one side of the dusty road to the other. She explored every nook, plant, bug, and crevice she could find, then peed on them to mark her territory. She was a tough cookie. If Jane hadn't found her when she did, Maxine would probably be dead.

Five years earlier, Jane's friend Raeford Jones, a member of a SWAT team, asked for her help with an unauthorized operation to retrieve his niece from a suspected meth lab. Raeford wanted to keep the operation under wraps because his niece was the daughter of a government official and the family wanted to avoid a scandal. Jane agreed to assist Raeford and quickly assembled an extraction team to move in on the lab. She had worked missions with SWAT teams before; she had also trained them.

The team headed out to a remote part of the Appalachian Mountains. As they approached a rusted-out, dilapidated trailer, they saw a dim light glowing through a small broken window. The night had reached the point when not even the bugs stirred. The team members sat behind a set of scraggly bushes in total silence, viewing the world through their night-vision goggles. They geared up, donning face masks, and crept up to the trailer, surrounding it slowly. At the team captain's unspoken signal, several SWAT members engaged from the rear while Raeford and Jane broke through the front door and moved toward the back. It was clear from their quick recon that the niece and any other adults had fled.

The trailer was a typical low-tech lab, with doors front and back. Noxious chemicals were cooking over slow-burning Bunsen burners, and the poison gas swirled through the air. From the back of the trailer, Jane heard Raeford call an alarm and she rushed to assist. There they found two children sleeping on a dirty shag carpet in an unfurnished room. Both wore torn, sagging diapers. Two slathering pit bulls guarding the kids suddenly launched themselves toward the doorway in which Raeford was standing. They couldn't shoot the dogs. Discharging a firearm in a meth lab would be like lighting a fuse to a bomb. The team had to get the kids out fast. They used their shields to block one end of the hallway, then released the dogs from the room and herded them out the back door. Once outside, officers were ready with nets to capture them. Both dogs spewed liquefied bile from their mouths, and their eyes were nearly swollen shut. The tongue of the black pit bull was swollen so profusely, that each time he barked and closed his mouth he sawed pieces of his tongue with his rotting teeth. The older white dog was missing his entire ear and diarrhea spilled down his legs as his whole body shook. Jane was horrified by what she saw, but understood why Raeford gave the orders to put the dogs down. Their suffering needed to end.

Officers had begun administering first aid to the two children and radioed for the Flight For Life chopper. The children awoke and began to cry acid tears. Yellow discharge seeped through their caked eyelids and ran down their swollen, snot-smeared faces. Jane estimated the kids to be about one year old, possibly twins. She wondered if they belonged to Raeford's niece. The team captain interrupted her thoughts when he emerged from the trailer carrying a plastic container.

"General, we have more to rescue." He held up a container, which appeared to be a dog carrier. Inside was a trembling dog. "There are more inside, General."

"Move in and retrieve, gentlemen," Jane commanded as she, too, entered the back of the trailer, passing men carrying out box after box full of dogs. She struggled to slide open two closet doors in the hallway. They were broken and falling off the tracks. She managed to open them wide enough to see a small blue dog crate sitting on top of a grimy washing machine. As she reached to grab it, the dog inside started to bark at her. She wanted to reassure the dog but couldn't take off her mask; the air was toxic. She pulled the crate through the small opening and exited the trailer.

Outside, Jane watched, stunned, as team members began sliding limp dogs from the assembled containers. Many of the dogs were no longer alive; some were so decayed they must have been dead for weeks. The team members lined up the living and dead dogs and puppies.

"Ma'am," said one team member, "it looks like just about every dog had a litter and, so far, only one mother has survived." They counted sixty dead dogs.

The burning feeling that rose up from Jane's stomach to her throat was so strong she thought her mask had malfunctioned, allowing the poison gas to wash down her lungs. She suddenly realized she was outside and not wearing a mask. Disgust, rage, and despair overcame her. She walked to the far side of the clearing to compose herself. The small dog she still carried in the crate released another fractured bark—one more fierce and protective than the last. The sound stunned her and focused her attention.

"Oh my God, little one," Jane gasped. "I nearly forgot you." The dog snarled and barked belligerently. Jane could see through the wire door that the dog was some type of terrier. She flashed her light inside the foul-smelling cage and saw what the dog was defending. Her puppies were in there with her; however, judging from the smell and their lack of movement, Jane knew the puppies were dead. This was a delicate situation and Jane wasn't certain how to handle it. Rather than force any more fear into the dog by opening the door quickly or trying to remove her from her puppies, Jane sat with her and had a conversation.

"Hey there. My name is Jane," she said calmly, removing the mask from where she had shoved it to the top of her head. "Look. You can see my face now. No more scary mask." Jane held her hand out toward the dog so the animal could sniff it. "You're a brave little dog, protecting your babies like that. I was scared to death. What a tough mother you are. You must be a natural warrior like me." The dog stopped barking. "Look. I'm going to help you, even though I know you're perfectly capable of doing this on your own, because you're so brave. I just have to help with this latch and you can do the rest. If you want to come out and attack me, that's up to you. If you want to stay in there with your babies, you can. But, sweet girl, they don't need you anymore. I'm sure they've died. I'm sorry about that. I really am. That happened to my mom when I was born, and my dad had to leave her behind to save a lot of other people. That's what we have to do now." Jane heard the distant rotor blades of the Flight For Life chopper approaching to pick up the two children. She flipped open the latch of the cage and opened the door slightly.

Jane sat down a few feet from the cage door, keeping it in her peripheral vision. She didn't want to frighten the dog as it edged slowly toward the opening. The mother dog stepped into view and stood motionless, looking at Jane. As Jane turned her head slowly to look at her, she thought, *Only a meth head would breed a mutt in a puppy mill.* The dog was ratty yet adorable. She couldn't make out one distinguishing breed. The animal appeared to have some Schnauzer, Cairn Terrier, and perhaps a little Jack Russell in her. As Jane evaluated her, one of the dog's ears slowly bent in half, and then she turned her head away from Jane.

"Oh, now *that's* cute. You're remarkable!" she said smiling. Then the grubby mutt hobbled over to her, crawled into her arms, and gingerly licked Jane's face. And that was the moment their life started together.

As the days passed, Jane watched in amazement as Maxine, as Jane decided to name her, began to come out of her shell. Initially, Max was so tentative she refused to step on grass or to walk more than a foot away from Jane. Jane realized that when Maxine sat and looked up at the sky after her first night with Jane, she was seeing it for the first time, after having lived her life cooped up in a crate in a closet.

Now, watching Maxine scamper through the scrubby grass lining the roadside and chasing after bugs as night began to fall, Jane realized how far they'd come. Nature had become Max's sanctuary as much as Jane's. Jane had immersed Maxine in the outdoors to make up for her deprivation from her early years. Maxine sensed—from the moment she was first released from her crate—that Jane had saved her. They understood each other in a way Jane had never experienced with any human companion. Even as Jane walked along the dirt road away from the farm to seek a hiatus from her inner turmoil, she looked to Maxine to be with her. Jane sat down for a moment on a fallen tree and watched the moon rise over the black silhouette of the mountains. Maxine circled her feet and eventually rested right beside them, both of them taking in deep breaths of the crisp desert air.

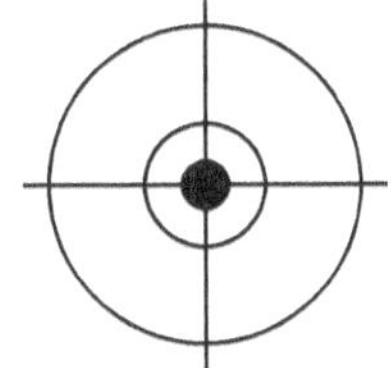

CHAPTER NINE

Max's head popped up at the sound of a car starting up. One by one, cars drove slowly away from the farm, their headlights illuminating one desert willow tree then the next. It looked like a good time to head back to the house.

As Jane walked in through the front door, Eugene's drunken voice echoed down the hallway as he rambled, "Oh, hell yes, Ben! I was still in the service when I overheard this story 'bout this little girl that just put the hammer down on old Ruggers and his boys up in Virginia."

Another man's voice chimed in, which Jane recognized as Earl's. "I told you, Charley! She was out there throwing snakes up and shooting them right out of the air—same woman Eugene is talking about. She handed Ruggers his lunch that day. I thought that was something they made up to inspire young people at the Academy!" The men all laughed.

"Hello, gentlemen," Jane said as she rounded the corner into the den, where the men congregated with glasses of whiskey on the rocks and mugs of beer. The air was thick with cigar smoke.

"General Howard! I was just talkin' about you," Eugene exclaimed. He stood up along with the rest of the men at the table. "Have a seat." He motioned to an open chair as the ice clanked in his glass. "We were talkin' about that old goat Ruggers from Virginia SWAT."

Jane hadn't thought of Ruggers in years. "Just how do you know him, Eugene?" asked Jane.

"Well, Earl was lucky enough to have gone through training with him," Eugene explained as he pointed to Earl, who dutifully tilted his hat at Jane.

"Oh yeah! That son of a bitch!" yelled one of the men. Their belly laughs indicated they had been drinking for a while. Earl's bolo tie clanked into the side of his sweating glass every time he laughed.

"Let me see that damn tie of yours, Earl. I need to stir my drink!" Eugene grabbed the sterling silver end of Earl's tie and plunged it into his whiskey. The men roared with laughter. "And this man is now the esteemed sheriff of our charming town," Eugene shouted and elevated his glass to Earl. "Let's hear it for Earl!" After the shouts and laughter died down, Jane hastened to clarify the story Earl had been telling.

"First thing, Earl, your snake-shooting story isn't true. You didn't even see me do it. And second, the world isn't that damn small. I don't believe you know Ruggers!"

"It gets smaller, General," noted Eugene. "I heard that legendary story back when I was just retiring. It hit the rumor mill like a ton of bricks. It wasn't until years later when Earl and I were talking that we realized it was true. So I was just telling these crotchety old bastards that the fabled general walks among us in my very own home. Gentlemen, may I present the woman who destroyed Commander Ruggers' ego on the battlefield, General Elizabeth Howard! Here's to a small damn world with big damn heroes!"

"Oh, I think you're overdramatizing that day with Ruggers. It surely wasn't *that* profound. I was only a kid—twenty something. How much damage could I have caused?" Jane raised both hands in the air, surrendering.

"Okay, let *me* tell the story and then you gentlemen can decide," Eugene huffed. He rustled up another round of drinks and began to set the scene for his dramatic reenactment.

"It was a dark and stormy night . . ." As everyone busted up again, one of the men nearly fell out of his chair as he threw his head back in laughter. It felt like they were in the captain's quarters of a pirate ship, celebrating the scuttling of an English flagship.

"Come on! Tell it right, you old bastard!" Earl playfully jostled Eugene.

"Okay, here goes. It was back in Virginia. One night, this little Marine and her Special Ops team climbed over the walls of the SWAT training grounds, through the razor-wire compound, and low-crawled over to the command center headquarters. They were tiger-striped in greasepaint and strapped with assault rifles." Eugene spread his arms across the table and mimicked a low crawl.

Jane shook her head. "Whoa, whoa, whoa, Eugene. I was running late and I found my team sleeping in the back of Screech's 1973 Chevy pickup outside the SWAT 'Girl Scout Camp,' as we called it. It was the middle of the *day*, not nighttime. *Most* of us weren't wearing greasepaint. Pilot had an ice pack on a swollen eye because he'd gotten in a bar fight that night."

Eugene interrupted her. "Let me finish, General. I know this story." He patted her hand condescendingly. Jane could have grabbed him and busted a move to show him just who should do the talking, but she liked Eugene, so she let him continue. "So these Special Forces guys, led by G.I. Jane," he said as he pointed at Jane, "proceeded to grab Ruggers out of his rack and drag him outside. He nearly pissed his pants when they threw a hood over his head and started to pummel him. He begged them to stop. They said they would let him go, but only if he could beat Jane on his own training course." Once again, Eugene had overdramatized the story, so Jane set him straight.

"Okay," said Jane, "I didn't *actually* touch Ruggers and we never pulled him outside. Plus, SWAT team members don't sleep at the training grounds. They're a bunch of summer camp basketball coaches with their little whistles." Jane looked around the table as she assured the men of the truth.

"See, I *told* you she was there." Eugene laughed again. "Okay, so where was I? So they lined up at the start of the course as Ruggers shook in his boots—"

"Tennis shoes. He was shaking in his tennis shoes," Jane affirmed.

"Then they fired off a round to start. Jane scrambled up to the top of the monkey bars and *ran* across them, tossed her grapple to the wall that followed, scampered over *that*, then skipped through the mud pit that Ruggers hadn't even started to cross. She ran up to the first tower, slung down her AR-15, and shot at targets on the second tower." Eugene made explosive sounds and simulated gunshots. "She was supposed to run up five flights of stairs, rescue a 'victim,' and kill anyone she encountered. Then she was supposed to go down the stairs and breech the second tower—carrying the victim, mind you—run down *those* stairs, then head for the finish line. And what did you do instead?" Eugene stopped and looked Jane dead in the eyes.

"*I* don't know! It's *your* story!" Jane took a sip of lemonade and sat back in her chair.

Earl piped in enthusiastically. "Instead, she runs up five flights of stairs to the roof, grabs hold of the support line for the jury sling—that's the basket that has the victim in it—wraps it around her wrist, cuts the support line, and flies through the air with the victim in the sling to the other tower!" Jane rolled her eyes, knowing Earl's scenario was completely untrue and impossible to boot.

Eugene took up the storytelling reins again. "She rode that basket down five flights of stairs—*with* her victim—to the bottom floor, then walked across the finish line. Meanwhile, Ruggers hadn't even made it to the first tower!" Eugene sat back in his chair and clapped his hands on the top of his head in amazement.

"Come on, General," one of the men said. "What happened next?"

As Jane started to speak, the sound of Marlene's voice interrupted her. "Ruggers was so darn infuriated, because he didn't have enough pie." Marlene walked in carrying a huge peach pie and positioned it in the center of the table. "I'm concerned that y'all aren't eatin' enough for the volume of alcohol you're consumin'." She spread some napkins and forks on the table.

"Awww, woman, we were just at the crucial part of the story!" Eugene wanted to continue talking, but he was distracted by divvying up the homemade pie.

"I know, I know," Marlene cooed, "so I'll finish it for you. Ruggers was so fired-up furious when he crossed the finish line that he spit chewing tobacco into the face of the young woman who had just humiliated him. Jane then kicked his butt in front of his own men. A helicopter landed and the Special Forces team was swept away into the night while Ruggers stood there peeing his pants. Eugene, you tell that story *all* the time. *Everyone* has heard it."

Jane chuckled at Marlene's abbreviated version of the story.

"Yeah, but Marlene, you overlooked the part where Ruggers had the gall to say to her, 'What's with the goddamn Lara Croft shit on my course?!' That's the best part!" Eugene pouted as he took another forkful of pie from his near-empty plate.

"Eugene, that was more than thirty years ago. They didn't even have *Lara Croft Tomb Raider* then. Now why would he say that to her? That's just silly." Marlene strolled out of the room. She was either sick of the noise pollution the men were causing in her home or sick of the story itself. Jane hadn't even been aware that Marlene had been listening.

"She has a point, Eugene." Earl looked at Eugene and the men began wheezing and coughing through their laughter.

"Cheer up, Eugene," Jane said. "Marlene's version is pretty close to yours. Ruggers and I *did* get into an all-out clash over an occurrence on his course. It *did* get a little out of hand. And afterward we *were* swept away in a helicopter. Then again, we were on our way to Iran to blow up the Shah's private plane and start a war. We didn't have time to babysit those pretty police officers," Jane said reassuringly.

"Blow up the Shah's *plane*?! Oh *God*, I love this woman!" Eugene crowed. "Hand me one more piece of pie, would you, Charley?"

"Thank you, gentlemen, for this boisterous entertainment at my expense. I hate to take leave, but I must excuse myself and take Maxine outside for a moment." The men stood as Jane got up to leave.

"Yes, ma'am! We wouldn't want Max spoiling Eugene's fine Factory Outlet carpet," said Earl, gesturing to the worn rug.

"Earl's just jealous because they don't make wall-to-wall teepee plush pile," Eugene shot back as he poured Earl another drink.

As Jane went to exit the back door to avoid the kitchen and possible discovery by the farm women cleaning up the dishes together, she noticed Sam standing just behind the doorway to the den. He'd probably heard the whole story. Jane motioned for him to follow her. She was in desperate search of fresh air. Although she was a habitual cigarette smoker, close-quarters cigar smoke brought up painful memories of Howser, with his teeth clamped around a noxious cigar. She felt a familiar sensation swirling inside her chest as a whirlwind of anxiety suddenly manifested. She let the feeling get as far as the back of her throat before she pushed against it and swallowed hard. Sam and Jane didn't speak as they walked outside.

Sensing her anxiety, Maxine stayed by her side, rather than bound off after a goat that appeared to be mocking her from behind a wire barrier. The anxious feeling began to decrease as Sam motioned Jane to a group of lawn chairs and sat down.

Eugene had obviously heard an inflated version of the "fabled" story. The real drama happened *after* Jane beat Ruggers on his own course. She was relieved Eugene didn't actually have all the facts. Jane collected herself after the intense wave of anxiety passed, then turned her head to look at Sam. He spoke first.

"Did all of that really happen, ma'am? I can't even imagine the training you'd have to go through to beat that guy so easily," he said in awe. Overhearing that story must have eased his disappointment of her proposed early departure from the farm. Jane found herself actually feeling torn between leaving the next day or staying longer.

"You know what, Sam? Let's walk. I'll tell you what really happened," Jane confided as she gently touched his elbow to lead him away from the house to avoid any comments from the peanut gallery. As Jane recounted the actual events, it seemed to her as if she were back standing on the SWAT training grounds. Sam listed intently.

"That morning, I was running late," Jane started. "I raced into my house and grabbed my gear—all the shit civilians don't understand, or need a glossary to explain it. Safety lanyards, rappel belt, single-point sling, ballistic helmet, multicam hat, ammo, assault hooks, collapsible halogen tool, CQB vest, and a ton of MOLLEs. I don't know of one soldier who loves the MOLLE system. I prefer the click-it-and-stick-it method; but at the time, the government seemed to believe MOLLE was 'the shit.' I don't expect you to understand all this, Sam. You'll get your own gear. I'm sure it'll be more modern and complicated than mine was at the time."

"It sounds like some pretty cool gear to me. I already know what most of that stuff is," Sam said confidently, "but it doesn't hurt to refresh my memory. Now continue, madam." Sam took off his hat and bowed facetiously toward Jane as if he were a nineteenth-century coachman.

"Okay, Sam." Jane shook her head and smiled at his stab at sophistication. "I tore into the SWAT training facility on my motorcycle. I was late; my team was already there. I looked over at the cadets and couldn't help but laugh at the sight of their perfectly slicked hair; clean, bright-white socks against tan skin; Richard Simmons basketball shorts; and matching powder-blue shirts. They were all doing regimented calisthenics—up, down, left, right, pushups, jumping jacks—as if they were in a chorus line. The scene looked like a high school athletic field, not a high-level training facility. And there stood my nemesis: Commander Ruggers." Jane paused to emphasize her loathing for the man.

"He was a conservative man, most likely from birth. He was also a devout Catholic who carried a picture of his matronly wife in his wallet next to a small card with the Ten Commandments written on it. If I'm not mistaken, one of the Commandments is 'Thou Shalt Not Kill,' which must have been a constant and agonizing reminder to this self-proclaimed warrior reduced to leading a troop of SWAT sissies. I don't know of any Commandment that says "Thou Can Only Wear Skimpy Basketball Shorts and Blow Whistles at Weenies," but I bet your ass his boss gave him a rule book that stated as much."

Jane could always sense the envy that rose up in Ruggers every time he eyed her team. He believed he could command an organization like Orion and he longed to demonstrate it. She could never respect a man who had never proved himself in battle nor taken the life of an enemy. He believed that simply by being highly disciplined and following the rules, anyone could be a leader. Ruggers' world was black and white, and Jane looked forward to throwing in a lot of gray. She knew their scheduled training session wouldn't go according to Ruggers' plan.

Old men like that beg to be brought down, Jane thought. On the surface, he appeared unyielding and collected. However, many times Jane had spotted the unauthorized chew he had camouflaged in his lip and the way he attempted to spit it covertly into the grass behind him.

"I had time to scope out the grounds as I walked from the parking lot to where my team had jumped the curb and parked the truck on the grass under a tree. I saw that most of my team, except for Jude, were laid out on the tailgate and in the bed of Screech's truck. Butch was chain-smoking his self-rolled cigarettes. Pilot looked dead."

Jane remembered how Pilot, formally known as Greg Walker—the all-American, clean-cut, preppy Annapolis athlete—proved himself to be a rough, hard-core, bloodthirsty warrior elite. That day his dirty cargo pants were half tucked into his unlaced boots and he had a hefty dagger hanging off his belt. His thick arms glistened with sweat, and one of them bore a large dragon tattoo with a vicious scar that cut through the middle—a souvenir from a knife attack in Bogota. Pilot liked the additional scar. He thought it made the dragon appear even tougher. Pilot looked like a twenty-five-year-old guy from a Coppola movie involving deranged Marines in Vietnam. He used greasepaint as an essential part of his daily wardrobe. He said it helped to fight the glare off his face so he could see well. He probably used it to look threatening. That day he had a filthy bandana tied around his forehead to hold an icepack over his swollen eye.

"My team told me Pilot had been brawling with some FORECON guys. I still can't imagine what *they* looked like the next morning, *if* they were still alive." Jane chuckled at the memory of her motley-looking crew. "Even if they wanted to clean up, their covert status prevented them from doing so. Each one had created his undercover guise to satisfy their personal fictions."

"What about your 'guise,' as you put it, Aunt Jane? What was your secret identity? You have a leather cat suit like Cat Woman? Or maybe those gold bracelets like Wonder Woman?" Sam laughed.

"Shut up, Sam! Can you imagine me parading around like that trying to do my job? Goddamn movies fuck it all up for women," Jane ranted. "I didn't need much help being different. I don't imagine a muscle-bound woman covered in tattoos in the 1980s was considered normal."

"I didn't think about that," Sam said thoughtfully. "You must have been pretty scary for a girl." Sam pointed at Jane's arms and her fading tattoos.

Jane minimized just how intimidating she had been to others. Although she was only twenty then and stood five feet four inches tall, her chiseled body was lean and strong. Her petite frame was covered artistically in tattoos and she was tanned from her last counternarcotics mission in Columbia. She lived, ate, and breathed the model of the Synergy of Discipline: the Marine warrior and the government contract killer. At that young age, only Jane knew the exact number of people she had killed. And there were many. Even the elite Spec Ops "Kentucky Boys" wouldn't mess with her.

Jane continued to describe her team for Sam. "Screech had these shit-ass dreadlocks, shabby beard, and Hawaiian shirt. He looked more like a Vietnam hippie relic than one of the world's primary special agents and a former Ranger. His puffy, bloodshot eyes told me he was short on sleep, most likely due to night terrors related to his PTSD. His body was twisted and sinewy, more like beef jerky than an elite agent. Along his forehead ran deep age furrows, despite only being in his early twenties. I don't know what aged him so rapidly, physically; but of all of us in the group, he was clearly the most immature. He had explosive, erratic, and uncontrollable behavior, but I fuckin' loved him. I can't even begin to tell you how fucking cool Screech was." Jane let out a sigh remembering her friend.

"Now Butch always looked like he just left a David Duke rally. He shaved his head and Screech tattooed it with a circle of swastikas—from his scalp to his throat. His muscles bulged out of his white, wife-beater tank top. His arms were so scarred from battle you could barely make out some of his tattoos. An eagle's wing had been scraped off in a motorcycle accident; the partial tattooed sleeve on his right arm melted off in a fire from an explosive device he was setting."

"What the hell?" Sam exclaimed. "Why did he have all that hate shit tattooed on him?"

"He didn't have a choice. Butch was working undercover, infiltrating SS Nazi bullshit compounds, seizing drugs, or stopping their little terrorist plots. Trust me; that shit bothered him."

"Oh, alright, I guess," Sam said wiping his brow.

"What I'm getting at is that these guys were tough and scary looking. Plus, they could all back it up. So could I. And I was about to prove it." Jane lit a cigarette and took a drag.

"My team eventually rallied and we gathered outside the Virginia SWAT obstacle course training grounds, which looked like it was modeled after a television show rather than a true confidence course. On *our* courses, Marines fired live rounds at us as we low-crawled through sloppy pits filled with bloody water teaming with rotting swine parts to simulate dead bodies. I'm sure Howser would've flung real bodies in there if he thought he could get away with it. We got hung up on bloody concertina wire that had pieces of pig dangling off it. Marines posing as the enemy fired earsplitting blasts into the muddy trenches around us, crept in, grabbed us, and hauled us out to endure hours of beatings and interrogations. It took *days* to get all the dried blood and mud out of every crevice of my body after finishing one of Howser's courses. The SWAT course, on the other hand, I could complete in a white T-shirt without getting it dirty." Jane looked at Sam to see if her blood-and-guts talk made him squirm. His nonreaction was a good sign.

"Monkey bars, like playground equipment, traversed mud pits," Jane continued. "SWAT had poles with ropes that were too short to use to reach the poorly constructed wooden wall. At the end stood two brick-and-concrete towers with several windows, and stairs led to the top. To my team, that course looked more like something the fire department would burn down for a training exercise."

Jane pictured her team that day as she casually sauntered across the thick grass toward them. Her guys were unique. Their situation was unique. Orion soldiers had no accountability to the US government. They were accountable to Howser. That's it. This environment allowed her team the freedom to go in and accomplish an op, doing whatever they needed to do to make that happen. Her team members all had different skills and knowledge, and their rank within the team was allocated based on what they knew and what they could do. There was a self-imposed hierarchy to give the team structure. Jane had the most experience and know-how, so she was the general, Butch was a major, and so on. And although the team members labored under and adhered to this organizational structure, which was respected by the US military, they'd never jump to attention when Jane entered a room and start kissing ass and saluting their ranks. Jane knew there was more discipline and punishment in killing than in training, which was why she respected her team, not the SWAT guys.

Jane recounted how they *hadn't* pulled Ruggers from his rack, nor had they challenged him to a match on his own course. She had been hired to demonstrate how Orion soldiers would navigate the obstacles. Jane went on to describe to Sam how she purposely took her time while assembling her gear, which she knew would infuriate Ruggers.

"Fuck *him*," Screech had said. "He's never had to wait on a woman before. He's a prick. Janie, don't forget to put on your lipstick, darling!" Screech had danced around like a flamboyant hairdresser while waving a tube of green greasepaint in her direction. "Try not to mess up your hair, Jane dear. You know how difficult it is to capture that 'feathered' look." Screech swept his hands through his rough dreadlocks.

"Bite me, Screech," Jane had replied. She slung her rifle over her shoulder and locked her P229 Sig Saur .40 cal into her warrior, a belt they each loaded up with their own instruments of destruction. "Well, boys, let's see what the adult daycare has in store for us today."

She met Ruggers at the start of the course and the race progressed, by all accounts, according to Eugene's story, minus some of the dramatic flair. She *didn't* traverse across the *top* of Ruggers' monkey bars, but she *had* severed lines on his jury slings to slow him down, crossing the finish line a full minute before he could complete his own course. He. Was. Pissed.

Ruggers finally finished as her team taunted him in front of his own men. As humiliation set in, he most likely figured he needed to intimidate Jane to regain his status. He marched directly over to her and got in her face, yelling at her. His breath was nauseating. Jane could smell the sour chew camouflaged in his lip. Suddenly the brown disgusting sludge was flung across her cheeks and into her eyes. Ruggers had spit in her face.

"What the fuck are you thinking, little girl, pulling that Nadia Comaneci gymnastics shit across my course?!"

Jane hadn't been able to help but chuckle silently as spit flew out of his mouth with each word he spoke. "Cocksucker," she said under her breath. She collected herself, trying not to laugh out loud.

"We're just having fun, sir," she said as she wiped the spit from her face. "If you didn't buy your shit from Toys R Us, maybe I'd take you more seriously. I've seen Al-Qaeda babies navigate more difficult terrain than that." Jane was really enjoying herself. The commander appeared unnerved by her confidence.

"Hold your tongue, you bitch," Ruggers snapped. Jane knew he wanted to punch her square in the face.

The word *bitch* sent a hefty dose of adrenaline into Jane's bloodstream. Her jaw tightened and her energy shifted from light to dark. For some reason, her psyche didn't react to words like *asshole*, *fucker*, and *cocksucker*—to name a few. Perhaps she'd become desensitized after years of hanging around her foul-mouthed team. *Bitch*, however, set Jane off completely, possibly because it was used deliberately to offend a woman and to segregate her personally.

"That's Bitch Actual. Step into the ring, sir," Jane announced. She assumed her stance and did not back down.

Sam interrupted Jane's train of thought by pointing out that her cigarette was about to burn her fingers. She hastily stomped it out with her boot.

"Thanks, Sam," she acknowledged and stuffed the cigarette butt in her jacket pocket. "Where was I? Oh, yes, wiping the course with Ruggers. After that, he wanted to challenge me. He got all 'up in ma grill' and things escalated. I decided I was gonna do some fucked-up, cocky bullshit to humiliate him."

"Like what?"

"Well, we had this little thing in Orion we called 'the Killing Circle.' I was gonna beat his ass in there."

"Killing Circle? That sounds horrible. Sounds like you were gonna do more than kick his ass, Aunt Jane."

"That's what Butch thought too. Butch headed toward the commander and said to him, 'Sir, you don't have to do this.' He got up in Ruggers' face to tell him seriously to back down. He really thought I might kill the guy, and Butch tried to warn him. Man, Butch was so pissed at me." Jane smiled, shaking her head. "Butch was my operative partner. He specialized in infiltrating some of the toughest meth gangs and busting them down. But he knew what I was capable of. Even *he* would never challenge me. And he didn't think it was smart for Ruggers to test me."

"I'm assuming Ruggers didn't listen to Butch," Sam remarked.

"Nope. No, he did *not*. The commander was so angered by my lack of fear that he was determined to teach me a lesson. He yelled out to his own team, 'Well, fuck me, Major! It appears the President's little attack dog is hungry to teach me some new tricks. I'm up for some training. Gentlemen, form a circle!'"

Jane had watched Ruggers' neck muscles swell as the heated, angry blood rushed through his veins. He swatted the sweat from his brow as he ground his teeth. She heard her team yelling, "Jane! Jane! Jane!"

Jane recalled to Sam how, in an impetuous and juvenile moment, after reading too many G.I. Joe comics in Panama, Screech had engraved on her arm the nickname Jude and Tom had given her years before—Jane—but his warped sense of humor prompted him to tattoo G.I. Jane on Jane's arm. There it was: G.I., for General Infantry. A tat no self-respecting Marine would *ever* tolerate. As former Army Rangers, Screech and Jude got a kick out of the idea that a Marine permanently wore an Army insignia. Jane could have cared less. "G.I. Fucking Jane" rolled off her tongue with an arrogance to match her ego. She felt as if all her beloved superheroes were rolled into that one moniker, and she was always prepared to live up to their standards.

Jane went on to tell Sam how Butch once told Jane she made the Marine Corps Martial Arts Program look like kindergarten. At that time, Jane had already endured ten years of Israeli Krav Maga training, and those were the training videos she had shared with Sam. Jane then confided that, as for grit and determination, she simply drew most of her early inspiration regarding perseverance from her favorite movies. She explained how she relished the words of Gunnery Sergeant Hartman in *Full Metal Jacket* and would often quote him, saying, "Are you quitting on me? Well, are you? Then quit, you slimy, fucking, walrus-looking piece of shit! Get the fuck off my obstacle! NOW! MOVE IT! Or I'm gonna rip your balls off so you cannot contaminate the rest of the world! I *will* motivate you, Private Pyle, *if it short-dicks every cannibal on the Congo!*"

"Sam," Jane sighed, "we were childish, conceited, brash, and resilient."

"Yeah, that's becoming more and more clear to me, Aunt Jane."

"We also had no perception of our own mortality," said Jane. "We were programmed to use coercion and force to conquer and persist. In that moment with Ruggers, I thrust all my believed self-importance and hostility toward him in a calculating game of cat and mouse." She then recounted what happened next.

"I heard Ruggers struggling to motivate his troops to join the challenge. It reminded me of this fat commander from Fort Bragg who used to bark, 'Now *git* in there and fight! Let's put some barbecue sauce on it!' What the *hell* does *that* mean? Fucking moron.

"Screech was laughing his ass off, but Butch was becoming more anxious by the minute. Butch was the one who recovered me from a Killing Circle in Pakistan. It was a bloodbath of dismembered and disemboweled desert-dwelling rapists. He and I carried that memory with us and we constantly associated it with other experiences. For Butch, the scene that was unfolding seemed to be one of those associative moments, because he switched into his caregiver role toward me. He clamped his lips together and shoved his hands deep into his pockets, which suggested surrender. Then he raised one eyebrow at me and shook his head."

Jane had managed to remain steady and calm, even though she could hear Screech mocking her, like an older brother, taunting her to up her game. That's the type of relationship Jane and Screech shared—always pushing each other to go just a little too far.

"So I upped the ante and got really cocky," Jane went on. "I said to Ruggers, 'You may find that your opponent has the advantage of a weapon,' and I threw him a four-inch knife. I'm sure he wished I'd have tossed him his 9mm. Ruggers knew that a blade would put him in the line of a sixth-degree black-belt specialist. You *never* want to be in close quarters with a close quarters specialist.

"Then I said, 'You may also find yourself in a situation where you are outmanned four to one,' and I grabbed three of Ruggers' men and shoved them toward him in the circle. None of them appeared eager to back up their leader. Then I added, 'Remember, gentlemen, dynamite comes in small packages.' Actually, I don't even know *why* I said that, because it sounds fuckin' stupid, but I was caught up in the moment.

"Last, I taunted, 'Once you have ascertained that your circumstances could *not* be any graver, you find you are now blinded by shrapnel from enemy fire.' Before I took out my bandana and put it over my eyes, I saw that Screech was absolutely cracking up at what I was doing."

Jane took out another smoke, fidgeting with her lighter. She remembered how she and Jude spent months training sightless. They called them *senseless days*. She fought every bit as proficiently blind as she did sighted in a close quarters combat situation. During training, they drew one slip of paper from a jar. Written on each piece of paper was one of the five senses. Whatever "sense" they drew, they'd have to go without it for a month. They trained to compensate for losing that sense. During one stretch of blind training, Jude went without his hearing. Getting around was terribly difficult. In live combat conditions there were plenty of times when they lost their vision or hearing as a result of explosions, flash bangs, debris, sand, or blood. Thus, they had to learn to compensate and acclimate quickly. Blind training was not an unfamiliar training method; nonetheless, Jane could tell SWAT had never practiced any comparable advanced tactics.

"What happened when you blindfolded yourself, Aunt Jane? Did he take a swing at you?"

"No, the commander unexpectedly eased up when I lost visual, gaining a false sense of confidence. 'Oh, this is fucking ludicrous!' he yelled as chew spewed from his mouth."

"Gross," Sam said in disgust.

"Then Butch leaned in and tried to warn him again. He said, 'Look, Commander, you don't have to do this. I've seen her in action. This is real. She's crazy.' Butch was generous to give this guy another chance to keep his dignity intact, but Ruggers almost shoved him out of his way. Butch was adamant. He told Ruggers, 'She'll kill all of you. That's what she does. And then a group of government suits will come in here and clean up after her.' Butch knew I had unstable moments *and* an underlying, unattended problem regarding anger. I suppose he wasn't sure when I might implode."

Jane refrained from divulging to Sam her motivation to fight. In her youth, she had gambled her own life haphazardly on the front lines—mainly to reinforce her bravery and ensure there were no weakling demons hiding under her perfectly constructed warrior veil. She continually placed herself in danger and constantly tested herself to determine whether she had the kind of courage her father told her she had. She would storm into enemy fire and take on extreme missions. She feared nothing, choosing to live on the precipice of death. Often, Screech and Jane jazzed themselves up on adrenaline so much that they thought they were immortal before a battle. And sometimes—like on this day with Ruggers—she abused her power, knowing Howser would clean up her mess.

"Commander Ruggers swallowed hard," Jane continued. "I heard the tumor of chew he'd stashed in his lip get sucked down his dry, swollen throat. Then he said, 'Holy fucking shit.' All of a sudden, a cloud of dirt began churning around us and we were pelted with loose stones and other debris. Two choppers swarmed in above the training grounds, hovered, then swiftly released several ropes. I ripped off my blindfold and stared at Ruggers through the dust, then I patted his rough cheek, gave him a smart-ass grin, and said, 'Lucky bastard.' Then I ran toward the rope, grabbed it, and was hoisted up into the sky. Butch, Pilot, Screech, and I were gone in an instant."

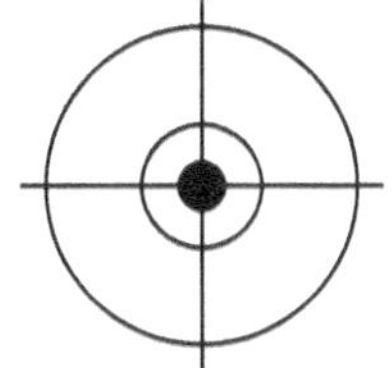

CHAPTER TEN

"Wow, you showed him!" Sam said in awe as he simulated amateur Krav Maga moves. "Now I know why your team named you G.I. Jane."

"Well, Sam," Jane explained, "Orion trained me thoroughly to give the smackdown to people far more dangerous than Ruggers. He just happened to be in my way that day." Sam stopped moving and looked at Jane with his hands on his hips.

"Could you teach me some more of your moves, general? I want to go into boot camp ready to kick some ass." He jumped around, jabbing at the air with his fists. Jane quickly swept his legs out from under him with one swift kick and he fell to the ground stunned. He lay there for a couple seconds before they both cracked up.

Jane smirked. "Sure, I can teach you a few things. And remember, don't call me general." Sam sat up and wrapped his arms around his knees.

Jane looked at Sam and lowered her tone. "First, you're gonna need to understand a few things about Orion. Yes, it's military, but it's a small subset, like a secret society within a larger organization. It's not where you're headed, but it's important to know the difference. You may be working with these people throughout your career without even knowing it. My goal is to help you know more than you think you need to know to stay alive."

"Yes, ma'am. I appreciate that. I'd like to stay alive."

"Our training," Jane went on, "your Uncle Tom's and mine, was more intense for a reason, but we'll get to that. This is a celebration. There are still a few people here we need to entertain," Jane said, pulling him up off the ground.

They walked slowly back to the house, which was still abuzz with a few straggling partygoers. Jane hoped Sam was fully aware of how much he meant to his large and very proud family.

When they entered the house, they saw that Marlene was busy making sure everyone was having a good time as she piled fried chicken, which was just a light late-night snack in her eyes, onto Dixie paper plates. She was always pushing food at people, especially Eugene, who really didn't need the extra grease in his diet. That's how some women of her generation coped with stress—especially with regard to war. They just beetled around the kitchen, cooking and plying everyone with food. Back in Marlene's day, when the subject of war came up, it was always met with pride and patriotism. Women gladly partook in the wartime rationing programs. They made sacrifices at home while their men made them overseas. Marlene was one of those girls who had used a marker to draw a line down the back of her legs to simulate stockings when the government rationed stockings. Everyone knew the materials were being used for military supplies such as parachutes, which might save some young man's life.

Marlene continued to squash her own stress while maintaining an outward appearance of joy. She still felt she needed to "rally the troops," but inside she felt every emotion. She felt overwhelmed at the thought of losing Sam in a war. She carried the pain of losing two sons already and she wasn't about to let Eugene or any of her friends know her feelings. There was no way she would let them know she slipped off secretly to have a smoke on occasion. Or that sometimes, when Eugene went into town, she would stay back and pour herself a stiff drink and cry unconsolably while looking at her sons' photos. Eugene never knew how Marlene punished herself. Her anxiety showed outwardly only by her constant twisting of her hands in whatever piece of fabric she wore. She always pretended to be wiping something onto her apron or wringing out a cloth, but her hands gave her away.

As the party wound down, Eugene still sat in the den and recited every war story he had compiled for the past fifty years. Dramatic sound effects could be heard throughout the house. Jane crouched down outside the den door to listen. Eugene captured the attention of every young boy as they sat in a semicircle in front of him. He narrated stories of blazing kamikaze pilots colliding with the decks of their ships while terrified young sailors bailed thirty-five feet overboard into black, shark-infested waters.

As Jane stood up, her knees ached as the imprisoned synovial fluid froze in her joints. She remembered how every morning she had fed her sentries—her body's defenses—their morning meds to enable them to defend the front lines against one of her enemies: Major Pain. Yet as night crept in, Major Pain usually managed to infiltrate and attack her system, swelling old wounds, stiffening joints, and cracking bones like a deconstruction crew. Every pin and plate grated across strained tendons, reminding Jane of the day she received each and every injury. Her body was exhausted; Jane was ready to retire for the evening.

"Come on, Maxine," sighed Jane, "let's make a hasty retreat to that splendid Neverland upstairs." Before she slipped into bed, she downed a few pills to safeguard her sleep. With Maxine tucked beside her, Jane fell into a dream state.

"Nighty night, Jane." Dr. Reid's ghostly voice echoed in her head.

Jane slept hard for the first time in years. When she awoke, the golden morning sun spread across her comfortable bed like warm honey. Maxine apparently slept as well as Jane. Her dog was curled up like a cat and snoring as loud as a freight train.

"Hey, lazy bones," murmured Jane. "Good morning. Rise and shine, good dog; we have things to do today." Maxine roused slowly, stretched, then pounced on Jane and covered her with morning kisses. Jane showered and dressed. She liked that she had cut her hair very short. It made getting ready for the day much easier.

Jane grabbed her rucksack before she and Maxine wound down the stairs and through the house to the outdoor porch. It was as warm outside as it appeared from her window; the air stirred with the slightest cool morning breeze. At 6 am it was already seventy-two degrees. The unforgiving desert heat would kick in around midday.

"Mornin', General. How'd you sleep?" Eugene asked as Jane plopped her rucksack on the floor. He was lounging on the porch, drinking black coffee and smoking a thin cigar. The sight of the rising smoke compelled Jane to check her jacket pocket for her cigarettes. She felt the box inside and her body relaxed.

"I slept fine, Eugene. And I'm not a general anymore," Jane replied as she looked away and swatted the air dismissively with her hand.

"You aren't a general any *less*, either," he noted, and Jane's eyes softened. "Marlene's cookin' up some breakfast," Eugene went on. "Should be ready in half an hour. The usual biscuits and gravy."

"Thank you, but—"

"Pancakes, sausage, toast, eggs—"

"Eugene, thank you," said Jane, trying to stem the tide. "However, I—"

"Fried ham, country fried steak, and hash browns. *You* know. Nothin' fancy."

"Eugene, no disrespect, sir, but I can't really eat regular food anymore. When I was wounded, my system became compromised. I never told you because I didn't want to make a big deal out of it. I love all the foods you just mentioned; but, as much as I wish I could, I just can't eat 'em anymore." Of all the meals she missed the most, Eugene just recounted her favorite: breakfast.

"I'm sorry, General. I wasn't aware," Eugene apologized in a low voice. "Well, what *can* Marlene make for you?"

"Nothing, sir. I brought some things. I can have juice and coffee, and Max can have bacon and a scrambled egg. It's not a big deal, really. I just don't want to offend Marlene. It sounds like she went to an awful lot of trouble over breakfast."

"Oh, hell no! She cooks like that every mornin' of the week. That's why I'm so damn fat. Doc says my nitroglycerides and my cholerterum levels and my heartburn are through the roof. If those numbers were my stock portfolio, I'd be sitting on South Fork Ranch right now!"

Jane appreciated how Eugene made her laugh. She was sure he intended to say *triglycerides* and *cholesterol,* but she wasn't going to correct him.

"Eugene, have you seen Sam this morning?"

"He had to drive to town real quick to adjust his work schedule, since you're sticking around a few more days to mentor him."

"I was going to speak with you about that, Eugene. First off, I probably should've asked your permission to stay for a few extra days. I certainly don't need to take up space in your bedroom. I'll move to another room. Second, I don't want to step on your toes. If you don't want me speaking to Sam about this stuff, then I'll just pack up and head out."

Jane didn't want to undo what the family had worked so hard to accomplish in urging Sam to join the military, but she knew her discussions with Sam might open a Pandora's Box for him. What she planned to tell him could at least help him understand how to deal with some of the situations he'd eventually face. As with any soldier she'd trained or mentored, she had a responsibility to time the delivery of critical information appropriately so her soldiers didn't run off the rails. Jane always talked about Suzuki Roshi's quote: "In discipline there is freedom." With Sam, Jane intended first to cite the importance of discipline and then bring to the surface what lay beneath. She knew Sam needed to walk before he could run; otherwise, she feared he'd end up getting in over his head.

Eugene reassured her. "Your stayin' on is a sign from the good Lord Himself and we aren't about to take that for granted around here. We want you to stay for as long as it takes to guide Sam in any way you see fit. We've given him as many opportunities as we could, but we aren't modern, that's for damn sure. You can tell him how things have progressed and help him prepare for what's really to come."

"Well, I'll make an attempt, but things are shifting faster than you or I can imagine. The world is incredibly different than when I was working—and that was just a short time ago. I'll lead him to the present, but he'll have to take it from there."

"That's all a parent can do with any child," Eugene said, patting her hand gently. "That's all *anyone* can do. Then we just hope for the best."

Marlene bustled out to the porch carrying a cup of coffee for Jane and a plate of food for Maxine. "Breakfast is practically ready, you two." She looked as fresh as a daisy and ready to greet the day. Her hair was already up in a bun and she wore a stunning pale-blue sundress with an impressively clean white apron over it, despite the fact that she'd been cooking all morning. At nearly eighty years old, Marlene was still a classic beauty.

"Marlene, the general is just going to enjoy your delicious coffee this morning. She and Sam are going to be out all day and don't need a big meal weighing them down. Miss Maxine is going to share some of my bacon and eggs," noting that the dish of food Marlene put down on the floor for Max wasn't nearly adequate.

Jane thought Marlene might be disappointed on hearing this arrangement, but instead she looked at her husband and declared, "That's even better for you, Eugene! You'll have more bacon to eat. You know the doctor wants you to keep your strength up and your cholesterol down," she reminded him as she handed him a handful of bacon to tide him over until breakfast was ready.

"Doesn't that seem counterintuitive to you, Maxine?" Jane whispered to Max, as Maxine swiped a piece of glistening bacon from

Eugene's generous hand. Both Eugene and Jane appreciated a few more minutes of morning sun in silence. She smoked a couple cigarettes and watched as Maxine took off to distract the Great Pyrenees from protecting the rollicking goats, but the working dog wasn't about to give up his post.

Not long thereafter, Sam rolled up the long tree-lined drive. When he saw Jane sitting on the porch, he nearly jumped out of the truck before he switched off the ignition.

"Good morning, General! I hope I didn't keep you waiting." Sam was close to panting with excitement. Although he'd been driving, he was out of breath, like he had just sprinted all the way down the driveway.

"Nope, Sam. Just finishing my coffee. I'll be right with you." Jane turned to Eugene and asked, "What the hell's gotten into *him*? He's pretty peppy."

"Oh, he's just a kid," explained Eugene. "They get all excited about the dumbest crap. I think he was in town talkin' to his girl. *That* get's him all flustered like that. You two have a good day," Eugene said, smiling broadly. "And remember, Sam's like a sponge. Just soak him with information, wring him out periodically, and then soak him again." Eugene twisted an imaginary sponge between his rugged hands. Unfortunately, it looked more like he was wringing a chicken's neck.

"Yes, sir. But I think I'll try to be a bit more gentle. Thanks for the coffee and for Max's breakfast." Jane grabbed her rucksack, which held her water, juice, and extra smokes, and headed out with Sam.

"I thought we'd approach this a different way today," Sam explained as he angled toward the barn. "You ride?" Sam pointed to the strong quarter horses outside the stables.

"I love to ride, but I don't think Maxine does."

"No problem," Sam declared and let out a loud whistle. In less than a minute, Mackey appeared. "Hey, Mackey! Can you take care of the general's dog today? It's a very important job. Actually, it's the most important job you'll do today and I'll never forget it as long as I live." Sam patted Mackey on the shoulder.

"Oh my God, Sam. Of course I will!" exclaimed Mackey. "I'll *never* let you down. You can count on me as long as you live. Semper Fi, brother! OORAH!" Mackey stood at attention, flipped his long hair out of his face, and saluted Sam, then he picked up Maxine and carried her to the house like a baby, talking to her the whole time.

"What the hell just happened?" Jane asked, dumbfounded. "I've never seen that kid so attentive. How'd you do that?" She hadn't heard Mackey utter more than a few words. He was usually less than enthusiastic about everything. Clearly, he admired Sam. She wondered why he wasn't around much.

"Mackey's just a nerdy kid. He wants to be a Marine too. Truth is, he'll probably end up being a better Marine than me. He's a real computer whiz. That phone he's always texting on? He rigged that up himself, and it's faster and holds more data than the fastest iPhone currently on the market. He just needs to get older, that's all."

"Well, I'll be damned," Jane said stunned. She didn't know anything about Mackey, really. She suspected with the new soldiers "on the market" these days, he could end up joining the Air Force. She thought that with his technical skills hc could fly drones, provided he had perfect eyesight. Jane just didn't see Mackey as a Marine.

Mackey must have gotten the horses ready as well, because Jane noted they were already saddled when she and Sam reached the barn. They mounted up on two very large, sleek horses and headed out.

"I figured you might want to get out of the house to experience the landscape," explained Sam. "I get a little antsy just sitting in one place."

"Me too," Jane replied, without engaging much. She enjoyed riding in silence for a bit, observing the beautiful terrain. The cloudless sky was quintessential to New Mexico—so blue it appeared purple. The soft desert breeze kept her thoughts moving freely through her mind. For the first time in a long time, her head cleared.

Sam broke the silence. "Aunt Jane, did you ever have any fun in Orion?" Sam knew Jane was a serious Marine, and with that came a heavy responsibility. He wasn't sure if he was up to the same task. Jane looked over at him and then returned her gaze to the horizon. She had to think about her answer. Being willing to die for your country and your team carried an unimaginable burden. She needed to ponder how fun played into the life of an Orion solider.

"I need to think about that, Sam."

After an hour, Sam reined in his horse and dismounted. Jane followed his lead and slipped off her horse as well. It felt good to stand up and feel the blood return to her thighs.

"You want a drink? I brought water and lemonade," Sam offered. He had obviously put a lot of forethought into their outing. Jane took him up on the lemonade, lit a cigarette, and sat down on a rock.

"From all the stories I've heard about Orion soldiers, those guys seem like a bunch of cocky jerks." Sam smiled as he adjusted the brim of his hat. "I mean, probably not *you*, ma'am. I didn't mean *you* were a jerk. God that sounded bad! I'm sorry." Sam backpedaled, worried he may have offended her. Actually, Jane admired his honesty.

"We *were* cocky. You're right. *And* a bunch of assholes," Jane replied. "I'm sure, though, that the stories you've heard being passed around are a bit out of context. We earned our right to be a little arrogant. We could back up everything people heard about us. We underwent some of the most callous and grueling training, then we took it to the streets and accomplished some of the most challenging and important work of the times. It's not like we just walked out of an Air Force recruiting office and said, 'We're here to kick your photocopier's ass! Hand over your stapler or be damned!'"

"Yeah, Air Force sucks! Bunch of pencil pushers!" Sam agreed. But Jane knew that those in the Air Force had the best chance for a future—at the very least, hot meals and clean clothes.

"General, can I ask you a question?"

"Yeah, Sam. That's what this is about. I talk a little and bore the shit out of you, then you ask questions, and then I smoke cigarettes while making fun of you."

"Shut up," teased Sam. "I'm serious."

"Okay, what is it?"

"I was just wondering why you smoke. You did all this training and were in such great shape. I mean, you're still in really great shape, but you smoke." Sam motioned to the pack of American Spirits beside her.

"Really Sam? That's your question? Not something like: Why'd you choose to use a .357 over a 9mm? Or: Why'd you choose to become a Marine? You ask why I goddamn smoke? Really? Are you some kind of health nut?"

"No, I mean that as a serious question. The reason I ask is because I wondered if you started smoking in the Marines because it was so stressful. Ma'am, I don't smoke or drink alcohol. And I've never done drugs. I was kind of hoping to keep it that way." Jane thought Sam might be joking, but judging by his serious tone, she realized he was speaking the truth.

"Sam, I really can't remember why I started smoking. I'm certain you'll be fine. It just takes discipline not to begin something like smoking or drinking. Wanna drag?" She held out her cigarette to him. It wasn't her job to shelter this kid.

"No way. It's not my thing. I tried it once and it made me cough."

He was so straight-laced. Jane speculated that wouldn't last long when he entered the military. As she lit another cigarette, she made a mental note not to smoke so much around Sam. Usually Jane didn't care what others thought of her, yet when someone mentioned her smoking habit, she sometimes felt guilty.

Jane inhaled the smoke while thinking about why she did it. *Stress relief*, she surmised. Perhaps Sam might begin smoking if he didn't address his stress earlier than she had. She decided to turn the tables on Sam.

"Sam, why don't you tell me how *you* are. Have you talked to anyone about the car accident that killed your parents? It's been more than five years and, according to your grandpa, you haven't opened up much about it." Jane knew that bringing up the question might prompt Sam to shut down. She also knew that talking about a traumatic experience helps people process it better, allowing them to move on. She didn't do a great job of that herself, and she didn't want Sam to suffer like she had.

"I don't think that's really going to help me with my training," Sam answered curtly. "I mean, that happened quite a while back and we've all just moved on." His expression was emotionless. It was clear to Jane they weren't going to talk about his parents.

"Alright. Fair enough. I don't have to tell you why I smoke and you don't have to tell me about your parents." Jane looked away and took another drag. "You asked if my life was ever fun. Let me tell you, getting revenge on Ruggers and Virginia SWAT—*that* was fun."

"I loved hearing what really happened that day. You're such a badass!" Sam crowed, which fed Jane's ego. "It's obvious your training in Orion proved superior to some of these other organizations. You probably think boot camp is for sissies." Jane noticed Sam puff up a bit as he continued. "I don't think I'm really gonna have much trouble in boot camp. I'm in great shape and I've heard all about it. I think as long as I just pay attention and follow orders, it's a piece of cake." Jane, knowing how tough training and boot camp really are, simply ignored his comment—and his cockiness. He'd learn soon enough.

"I really enjoyed your grandma's ending of my story last night. She sure shut your grandpa up fast." Jane twisted the butt of her cigarette under her boot, wondering if he caught on to the fact that she had switched topics.

"Well, then, you should hear her tell the *whole* version of the story. It's a riot! She's the funniest lady I know." Sam glowed as he spoke about Marlene. Jane's tactic had worked.

"It's pretty obvious you love your grandma, Sam. That's awesome," Jane said sincerely.

"Yeah, well, it's no secret that you like her too. Grandma is an extraordinary woman. She's what keeps this family bonded, and I am not bothered about saying that. Grandma's our glue."

"Why would it bother you to say that, Sam?" The comment didn't seem unusual to Jane. *She* was the one who kept her team together all those years. Jane wasn't sure if Sam was referring to some gender-equality issue with his statement.

"Oh, I don't know. I suppose, around here, everyone assumes my grandpa shoulders all the decision-making and keeps things working smoothly. You know, being a man and all. I know the truth is that a strong woman is usually really running the show. I want to marry a girl like my grandma someday. She is heaven-sent." Sam gave a little grin and blushed.

"I don't think God is producing girls like your grandma anymore, Sam."

"Oh, I can think of one." And with those six words, Sam was lost in a daydream, clearly thinking about one special girl.

"Hey, lover boy! Are you a hippie or are you a Marine? Shall we return to the business at hand or would you rather dream about stuffing flowers in the barrels of my guns with your pretty lady?" Jane teased. She was reassured he was interested in a girl. The Marines can be a mighty hard place for men who aren't.

"Jeez, ease up! I was only saying that . . ." As Sam trailed off, Jane could tell he had started thinking about his girl again, given the love-stricken look on his face. Jane had to reel him in fast.

"Sam, your Uncle Tom was a crucial part of Orion. It's important that you understand your family history. People buy in to all sorts of conspiracy theories and propaganda about Orion. There's an overabundance of misleading information floating around out there."

"Sam, do you know how the Central Intelligence Agency was established?" He snapped out of his daze and looked at her.

"A history lesson? Really?" Sam let out a groan. "Yes, Aunt Jane, I do. It was established during World War II and was kept top secret, even though the public actually knew the agency existed. That's not unlike today. The best way to hide something is in plain sight," Sam replied with confidence. "You see that shit in movies and TV shows all the time."

"Very good, Sam, you egghead. What most people *don't* know was that at that same time, another cell was under construction. This one was a deeper and more impenetrable division of the government. This agency was newly formed specifically to seek a world order of government. The goal was to create a controllable, unified world government."

"Come on! They actually were doing that way back then?"

"Yep. No shit. A man named Jim DeClaire was working as an advisor to the President," Jane explained. "He persuaded our President, along with the leaders of the British Commonwealth and the USSR to begin the process of training Orion soldiers. Soon, France, Belgium, South Africa, Greece, Czechoslovakia, and Brazil had their own cells of Orion. It was a big undertaking. Most of the agents were compromised, lost, or killed. DeClaire wanted too much power too quickly and the entire program was compromised."

Sam leaned in toward Jane. "That doesn't sound too good. How'd they fix it?"

"Fix it! They just fired the fucker. Our President decided that establishing order was necessary, so he took back the power. He designated Buck Chambers as director of the CIA and head of Orion."

"Let me get this straight," Sam said pensively. "Our President designated Chambers as the leader of a top-secret organization that had powers beyond the League of Nations and was designed to seek a world order of government using super-soldiers?" Sam stood up and frowned, wrinkling his forehead.

"Hold on. I'm telling you about an organization that was structured to be the 'good guys'—member forces focusing on counter-terrorism and ending smuggling, communism, and genocide. You're thinking more twenty-first century when you think of super-soldiers.

This organization trained *super-agents*—elite infiltrators, spies, and extreme-reconnaissance soldiers. It built super-allies, corridors, and trade agreements, and conducted missions covertly. It didn't want to involve respective military agencies publicly because of the damage it would cause their countries' economies and infrastructures."

Jane stood up, stretched, and continued. "Chambers recruited two elite agents to help redesign the program from the bottom up: my father, John Howard, and my mother, Amelia DuFor. All Orion missions from that day forward, throughout the world, were based on their training and missions."

"So, basically, your parents were the father and mother of the entire worldwide Orion organization?" Sam asked, appearing a little overwhelmed. "That's some cool-ass shit, Aunt Jane."

"Yeah," Jane sighed, taking a deep breath and lighting a cigarette. "It's a little tough being this cool." She smiled and flexed her bicep.

"You really *did* get on the special bus!" Sam exclaimed as he dropped back down to sit on the ground. "But how was it that nobody knew this was going on? Why didn't anyone try to stop this from happening? Nowadays when shit like that happens, everybody's throwing up protest signs and marching."

Jane squatted next to him. "Well, you have to remember there was a war going on. The public was entirely distracted by Hitler's advancing army. And heroes like General Patton were all over the press. It was easy for groups of men to gather secretly in Washington, unnoticed, and formulate plans. It wasn't until 1977 that the Operative Force, or Professionals, as we call ourselves, became a super-force recruited from the world's elite Special Forces."

"Wait. 1977? You were, like, what? Forty?"

"I was only fifteen. Jeezuz! How old do you think I *am?*"

"I'm just shittin' you," replied Sam, rolling a pebble back and forth between his palms. "But I don't see what all this has to do with helping me. I mean, I think I know what to expect."

Jane realized Sam was, indeed, just a know-it-all eighteen-year-old kid. All kids seem to think they know what real life is about—until they get into it.

"Back then, the United States contributed two cells, with an initial investment of five hundred operatives. There are only six surviving US operatives, and they make up part of my team. Today, throughout the world, twelve hundred planted, specialized teams of six-member units are deep under cover as one of the world's best-kept secrets and most dangerous weapon: Orion."

"I *knew* it!" Sam jumped up and shouted, "I *knew* there was something bigger than SEALs, bigger than Delta, and super-secret! There was just too much getting done. I *knew* that some of the things that are going on can't possibly be happening unless we're actually partners with some of the countries we're at war with." Sam stood up and ran his fingers through his hair.

"Chill out, Sam." Jane remonstrated. "You need to separate what's real from fucking social media." Jane thought it was time to change the subject.

"Hey, Screech once told me he wanted to die getting eaten alive by a tiger," recounted Jane. Sam's head snapped back in her direction.

"What the—? I *love* this guy!" Sam laughed. "He sounds *insane!* Who'd want to get eaten by a tiger?"

"Well, Screech *is* insane. He wanted to get eaten feet first so he could see if the tiger enjoyed the way he tasted."

"Ugh. That's awesome and messed up at the same time," said Sam, shaking his head.

"I know. Sounds like you just described Orion. 'Awesome and messed up at the same time.'"

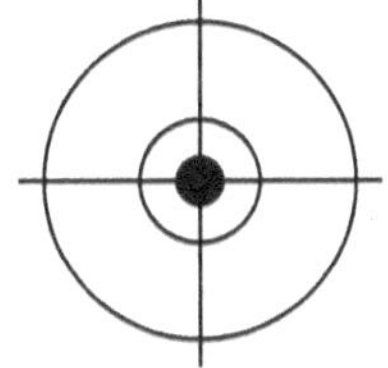

CHAPTER ELEVEN

Many Orion soldiers experienced trauma during their childhood, hardening their emotional core as a self-defense mechanism—a learned tactic essential for a successful secret soldier. Bryan Wright, aka Butch, was no exception. He was an American-born son of a decorated Vietnam Army captain. His father died overseas and, not long after his death, Bryan's mother committed suicide. Bryan was only seven years old when he discovered her purple, swollen corpse hanging lifelessly in his closet in the center of what used to be his favorite playthings. His Hot Wheels collection was a jumble of crashed cars beneath the tipped chair onto which she had climbed to reach the noose. His G.I. Joe plastic soldiers did not save her. They had amassed themselves around the bookcase, just where Bryan had left them, on security watch. The cord she used to suspend her body from the shelving unit had been coiled in the center of a tire that

Bryan planned to make into a swing. Had he not been too lazy to put up the swing, perhaps she never would have had the means to hang herself—or so he thought. Bryan relived the moment he opened the closet door over and over again, torturing himself until the trauma finally rendered him utterly speechless. He was placed in foster care.

After Bryan found his mother, he bashed his head repeatedly on the closet wall, causing damage to the right hemisphere of his brain. He found out much later that the left hemisphere compensated for this, giving him amazing skills in mathematics, yet his vocabulary was limited. Not only was Bryan sequestered in what appeared to be a self-imposed prison of silence, he was often held hostage by a newly developed compulsive urge to sort and count nearly everything he encountered. It began on a macro level as he gazed out the window of his classroom, sorting and counting the cars in the parking lot, and brick buildings versus wooden ones. Then he began to narrow his focus and count the number of bricks on the courtyard below the window. He sorted their size, color, and position. He determined which were laid first. He went outside and lay facedown on the courtyard, counting each minuscule grain of rock in the brick so he could extrapolate how many grains in total made up the entire courtyard. Often he would stay in the courtyard for hours. He would leave his self-appointed tasks only when he was fully satisfied he had definitively counted and sorted every leaf on a particular tree, for example. He did this while shutting out the entire world completely. He heard none of the taunting and teasing of his classmates or the imploring voices of doctors and teachers. He reacted to no one. Eventually, Bryan refused to return to school. His severely unusual behavior eventually drove doctors to discontinue his treatment and label him a lost cause.

After six months of demonstrating this behavior, his foster parents also gave up on him, Bryan was sent to live with his frail grandmother in a small Greek fishing village. The elderly Greek woman was the only family member willing to take responsibility for him. She welcomed the company and never pressured him to speak. Eventually, he suppressed the trauma that silenced him, and found his voice again.

Bryan spent most of his early teens fishing and working the docks, hauling in massive nets and cleaning barnacles off boats. Enamored with water, his daily swims sculpted his muscles like a professional athlete. He and his friends secured ropes to the bottom of the cove and dove down deep, pulling their lean bodies beneath the sea, holding their breath for a remarkable three to five minutes per dive. They hunted for pearls and scavenged for mussels. Often they would just sit still at the bottom of the ocean with their knives in their mouths, challenging each other to stay down the longest. Bryan almost always triumphed.

He frequently made the long trek to the south side of the cove to seek out the largest overhangs. Repeatedly, he would climb the steep, white rocky cliffs and jump off, sailing down like a seagull, one hundred feet below into the turquoise water, deftly avoiding the protruding, jagged rocks. Bryan thrived on any added element of danger.

In addition to his physical prowess, Bryan triumphed in school. He spent a lot of time alone in his room solving complex math equations. Eventually, he held the title as the nation's second leading mathematician while he developed manuals for aquatic survival concomitantly for the Navy.

Howser heard of Bryan's exceptional mathematical skills and his athleticism through the Navy. He also knew Bryan was a loner—a prime candidate for Orion. Howser approached Bryan in Greece and offered him a slot at Orion. Although Bryan was intrigued, he turned down the job, telling Howser his obligation was to his grandmother. Years later, when he was a part of Jane's team, Bryan mocked Howser's reaction to his decision not to join Orion.

"You want to talk about obligations, son? You have an obligation to get your ass back to the States and use that God-given talent you have for something more than scraping barnacles off fishing boats. It's a goddamn shame to waste your talents when your country needs you!"

He mimicked Howser perfectly, right down to the yelling, spitting, and pointing of his finger. According to Bryan, he almost laughed out loud right in front of Howser. Bryan didn't remember reading about any American war or catastrophe in the States that needed rescuing by an eighteen-year-old ocean-obsessed brainiac. He told Howser it wasn't the right time to leave, then gestured to his grandmother, who was hanging the wash on a clothesline. Howser looked at her and told Bryan there was only so much energy left in the old woman and not to waste time trying to keep her from dying. Bryan disagreed, speculating that his grandmother's good health might keep her around another ten to fifteen years.

Ironically, Bryan ended up on a plane headed for Quantico only a few months after he delivered his decision to Howser. His grandmother had taken a steep fall down the steps of the terrace and died instantly. Sometimes Jane wondered if Orion wanted Bryan enough to create such a mishap. Howser never told her what had actually occurred, just that she was about to get a new partner to train.

Howser took Bryan to a training facility in the bowels of Quantico and gave him the call sign "Butcher," which the team later shortened to "Butch." Soon after his arrival, the military became his life and high-tech equipment became his passion.

Like Butch, Screech had also dealt with childhood trauma that fueled his fury. Ironically, Screech's anger and possible psychosis—combined with fearlessness—helped him become an exceptional soldier.

Jane met Screech on her first day of "regular" school outside of Washington, DC. Howser enrolled Tom and Jane in a public school when they were thirteen because he had four months of work to do in DC, and he figured Tom and Jane could learn something from public school with regard to civilian life.

Tom and Jane stood together in the schoolyard when they heard a kid shout, "Give me that sandwich, Jarhead!" The other kids gathered around a boy named Jim Peters as he struck down a smaller boy with pop-bottle-lens safety glasses.

"No way! My mom made this for me! It's mine," Wilson Jared said to Jim in a moderately raised voice that cracked slightly. Wilson wore perfectly starched, ironed clothes and he kept his hair in a tight crew cut.

"Turd-eatin' mamma's boy!" yelled Jim, who then proceeded to kick dirt on Wilson and grab his sandwich out of his hand. The other kids cheered Jim on as he raised Wilson's lunch high over his head. They cheered not because they were proud of Jim—they just preferred he take Wilson's sandwich instead of their own. Jim opened the sandwich and smeared it onto Wilson's face and clothing, then turned and walked into his classroom.

Wilson didn't cry. Apparently, he never cried when others made fun of him. His schoolmates watched him walk calmly into the school. Tom and Jane looked at each other and followed him to the restroom. Tom entered the bathroom a minute later and found Wilson scrubbing the stains obsessively from his clothing. Jane waited outside, eavesdropping with her ear to the door.

"Need a hand with that?" Tom asked, pretending not to notice how unusual the scene might appear to most kids. Tom always tried to make things better. Plus, he must have seen some potential in this unusually thin kid standing there in black socks with sock garters that only middle-aged fathers from the '50s wore. Wilson's white undershirt was tucked into his white briefs, shielding a very freckled, pale body.

"I don't believe this is your concern, new kid," Wilson replied. "You may end up making this worse for me. I suggest you relieve yourself and then be on your way. I have a stain to fight." Wilson continued to scrub the mustard off his clothes until his hands were chapped and raw. He paused only long enough to watch as some of the blood from his hands pooled, then mixed with water and ran down the drain. If Tom hadn't been there, he may have even smiled.

"I just came in to let you know that my friend Jane and I—my name is Tom, by the way—want to be your friends. We thought you were very impressive. We also heard you're one of the smartest kids in this school and we need another kid with a big brain to be in our club."

"Club? Why would I want to be in a club?" Wilson still hadn't taken his eyes off of his task, not once glancing in Tom's direction. "Who told you I was smart?"

"Everybody," said Tom, trying to use flattery to win Wilson's trust. It didn't work. Jane heard a thud through the door when Wilson suddenly turned toward Tom and pinned him to the bathroom floor.

"Liar! Your name is Tom Stapelton. Today is your first day of school. You arrived from a secret military school in Pretoria with your little friend. You don't have one friend here besides her and no one has ever spoken to you about me. Why are you lying to me?" Wilson pushed his thumb into Tom's throat, preventing him from answering.

Tom recognized the wild look in Wilson's eyes. Choking and gesturing him to stop, Tom struggled to get the kid off him. Then, just as suddenly as he attacked Tom, Wilson released him and resumed washing his clothing.

"What the hell, Wilson? Why'd you attack me? You're crazy!" Tom rubbed his throat.

"Screech. Call me Screech. Yes, I'll be in your club."

"And you attacked me because . . . ?"

"I'm not weak. Or crazy. Nevertheless, if you make your enemy think you are, then that becomes *their* weakness. *You* let your guard down; you made an assumption about me. You aren't much of a special military school soldier. You just got your ass handed to you by a half-naked, featherweight nerd. You're an asshole," Wilson said, laughing a little, then returned to his cleaning.

"Okay, man. Well, I have to go to class. We'll see you later." Tom left, shaking his head as he came out of the bathroom. Jane looked at him, eyes wide in disbelief.

As it turned out, nothing Wilson had said to Tom was untrue. When that day had long passed and they were a team, Screech reminisced with them about what had happened after their first encounter, disclosing information they never knew and would never repeat to anyone.

When the final bell rang that day, Wilson stayed behind, inside the school. He hung his damp, and now perfectly spotless, clothing in the restroom. He hid in the dark school, pressing his clothes with the weight of heavy library books as they dried, not once thinking of Jim, the bully. The morning bell rang and Wilson went to class without so much as an hour of rest.

When he arrived home that afternoon, his parents were waiting for him in the kitchen with stern looks on their faces. His mother's hands were clamped so tightly they were bloodless and white. He knew they were not upset about him not coming home the previous night. They probably hadn't even noticed. Mr. and Mrs. Jared were upset because the school had notified them of the fight. Fighting was against school policy. Violation of that policy could tarnish Mrs. Jared's reputation with the PTA.

"So, my boy, you think you're a tough guy," his dad said grimly. Wilson's father was tall and slender, and sported a tight crew cut and glasses. He wore a perfectly tailored gray suit and his straight white teeth complemented an iron jaw. His mother wore a pressed dress that fell just below the knee and cinched at the waist, pumps, and, when she left the house, white gloves. Although it was 1975, their house could have been featured in a 1950s edition of *Better Homes & Gardens*.

"Bob, I think you need to take Mr. Wilson to the back bedroom and teach him a lesson about disgracing this family," Wilson's mother said with disgust as she turned toward her son. She grabbed her martini shaker, screwed the top down tightly, and rattled the contents viciously. Wilson watched as each shake disturbed the streams of smoke curling through the air from the cigarette that hung from her bright-red lips.

She set the shaker on the kitchen counter and, smiling, handed her husband a long, black leather belt. Bob then dragged his son to the back room for a beating. Wilson never uttered a sound nor shed a single tear as he was struck repeatedly with the belt. Afterward, he simply walked back to the living room, kissed his mother's hand, and made his way quietly to his bedroom.

Later that night, Wilson awoke suddenly, breathing hard. He shot out of bed. It was a starless night and the east coast breeze blew through the open window and into his room. He went to the bathroom and looked at himself in the mirror. He rubbed his jaw and turned his head from side to side, slowly running his fingers through his tight crew cut.

Wilson went back to his room and opened the drawer of his nightstand. He took out a book and flipped open the cover. The center had been hollowed out. Inside rested a Jack Field hunting knife. He got dressed and slipped quietly out his bedroom window.

Wilson made his way to Jim Peterson's house, which was only a mile away. He found an open window, removed the screen, and fit his thin body through the gap. Moonlight filtered down the hallway, guiding him to Jim's room. Jim lay belly down on his bed, head turned to the side, asleep. Wilson crossed the room silently, like a ghost, and slit Jim's throat.

For weeks and years following the murder, no suspects were found for the ghastly crime. Although it stayed on the books for decades, it finally fell into urban myth. Wilson continued to take beatings from his father. At eighteen, he left his family and headed to North Carolina. He quickly became the most recognized soldier at Fort Bragg, with the fewest friends.

Of all the team members, Tom was the only one who hadn't suffered severe trauma during his childhood. His entry into Orion began November, 3 1969. Eugene, his father, had just turned on the old tan box radio that sat on the kitchen counter. His mother,

Marlene, was dishing up some after-dinner pie. Eugene tuned in just as President Nixon was making his address.

"Good evening, my fellow Americans. Tonight I want to talk to you on a subject of deep concern to all Americans and to many people in all parts of the world—the war in Vietnam."

"Ohhhhhh, doesn't he sound *good*? He sounds so *strong*, Eugene. Do you think he's finally gonna end this war?"

"Well, *hell*, woman! Why don't you pipe down and let's hear what he has to say. If you keep talkin', we're gonna miss the whole damn thing!"

Nixon continued to talk about what he had encountered when he was inaugurated on January 20: The Vietnam War had been going on for four years, a total of 31,000 Americans had been killed in action, the training program for the South Vietnamese was behind schedule, and 540,000 Americans were in Vietnam and there were no plans to reduce that number.

"Oh my goodness, Eugene! Did you hear that? *Thirty-one thousand* of our boys killed over there. That's just so *sad*. I can't even imagine what their mothers are going through. Do you think we're *ever* gonna get out of there? I swear, if I was a soldier I'd just leave that miserable place and head home."

"Marlene, for Pete's sake, will you just let the man *speak*?"

"Oh. Sorry. What did he just say about Americans and peace?"

Nixon's voice echoed from the radio, "Well, let us turn now to the fundamental issue. Why and how did the United States become involved in Vietnam in the first place? Fifteen years ago, North Vietnam, with the logistical support of communist China and the Soviet Union, launched a campaign to impose a communist government on South Vietnam by instigating and supporting a revolution."

Eight-year-old Tom wandered into the kitchen, drawn by the smell of peach pie, fresh and hot from the oven. "What're you guys listening to?"

"Thomas, you do not need to be listening to this program. It's all too upsettin' for a little boy," lectured Marlene as she tried to usher Tom from the room.

"Mom! I'm *not* a little kid! I know all about this war. See, I listen to the news programs on this." Tom held up a small transistor radio.

"Thomas Stapelton, where on earth did you get that?"

"Would you two take it outside, please? I'm *tryin'* to listen to the President," Eugene said loudly.

"Eugene, look at this." Marlene held up the transistor radio. "Do you see what our son is up to?"

"Where'd you get that, son?" Eugene turned the small radio over in his hands, noticing that it appeared homemade rather than purchased.

"It's just something I put together with some scrap stuff in the shop." Tom took the radio from his father.

"Eugene, we can't encourage this. He's already different from the other kids. He's not gonna fit in if he keeps—"

"What, Mom? 'Keeps getting smart?' I can't help it if I just know this stuff. I just know things. I like numbers and gadgets and science. So what?"

"Eugene, are you just gonna let him talk to me like that?"

Eugene attempted to dial into Nixon's last statement: "For the future of peace, precipitate withdrawal would thus be a disaster of immense magnitude. A nation cannot remain great if it betrays its allies and lets down its friends. Our defeat and humiliation in South Vietnam *without question* would promote recklessness in the councils of those great powers who have not yet abandoned their goals of world conquest."

"Eugene Stapelton, you will address this now!" Marlene twisted the knob and shut off the radio. "I want you to call your friend. John Howard. Is that who I mean? I want you to see if he can get Thomas into that school you mentioned. I think what Thomas needs is a real-world lesson in respect. It's embarrassin' what the other mothers are sayin' about him. Sorry, Thomas. I didn't mean to say that in front of you. Go on up to your room and let your father and I discuss this. Shoo now." Marlene gently pushed Tom out of the kitchen.

"Marlene, first off, John Howard isn't my friend like you think. We just crossed paths in Korea. That's all. And second, I don't know if he was serious about that school in Pretoria. That might've just been somethin' people say in that situation."

"For goodness sakes, Eugene! It wasn't a situation! You saved his *life*. Of course you're friends now. He said he owes you. I think you should give him a call."

"What's he gonna tell me that we already don't know? We *know* Thomas is different. I can't do *half* the math that kid can. He sees the world in numbers. I don't understand it either, Marlene, but we just have to work with what we have: the New Mexico school system."

"You don't care about me, do you? You don't appreciate the sacrifices I made for this family. I left my home, my life, my family in Texas—"

"I know! I know! Just to be with me. I took you away from the 'only happiness you ever had' and plunked you 'in the middle of the desert.' I'm just a good-for-nothin' unappreciative oaf. You poor thing."

"Oh, stop it. Now y'all are being dramatic. Finish your pie. In the morning, I hope you reconsider and call your friend."

"He isn't my friend. I haven't spoken to him in twenty years," Eugene scoffed.

"Eat your pie!" Marlene's words shot out of her mouth in one swift, angry breath, then she stalked out of the kitchen.

Eugene switched the radio back on.

"As President, I hold the responsibility for choosing the best path to that goal and then leading the Nation along it. I pledge to you tonight that I shall meet this responsibility with all of the strength and wisdom I can command in accordance with your hopes, mindful of your concerns, sustained by your prayers. Thank you and goodnight."

"Awww, dammit! I missed the whole damn thing."

Several days passed before Eugene finally opened up his old address book from his service in the Korean War. He skimmed past most of the names until he saw John Howard's in his own handwriting.

"Good Lord," Eugene murmured. "John Howard. Howser. I haven't thought much about you since I pulled you from that ditch all shot to shit."

This wasn't exactly the truth. Eugene often thought about Howser. Every time he saw him on a news reel or read about him in the papers, he wondered if Howser considered how different his life would be if Eugene hadn't stumbled upon him in that pit.

"Here goes nothin'," muttered Eugene, and he dialed the number. Surprisingly, Howser answered.

"Howard here."

"Uh, is this *John* Howard?"

"Speaking. Who is this?"

"John . . . Howser . . . this is Eugene Stapelton. You know, from Korea?"

"Well, holy hell, Eugene! How the hell are you?"

"I'm fine; I'm fine. I was just callin' to see how you're doin'."

"Awww, horseshit. A man doesn't telephone another man just to shoot the shit, Eugene. What're you calling about? Do you need a job? I can find something important for you to do."

"Oh, good Lord no! I'm enjoyin' my retirement from the military. I have a farm to manage, a wife, twin baby girls, and two growin' boys. As a matter of fact, that's what I'm callin' about."

"You need some money, Eugene, for the farm? Is your wife sick? I'll send you any amount you need. You damn saved my life. If it weren't for you, I'd be lying dead over there. I owe you, Eugene."

"Oh, Jesus. Come on now. It wasn't like that. You would've saved yourself, dug out your own bullets, and killed everyone on your way back to camp. I just happened to get lost from my platoon. I was damn stupid."

"We both know that's not how the story goes. Why don't you just tell me why you're calling."

"Well, it's about my oldest boy. Thomas. I was wonderin' if you ever opened up that school. That military school you were talkin' about?"

"I did. We broke ground in '63. We don't have any students yet. Well, we got one boy, but he's Major Aikens' kid. Aikens' wife just passed and I took Jude in as my ward while Aikens' is taking some time off. We've just been training the staff so far."

"Oh, that's too bad. Aikens is a good guy. Well, I was hopin' you were admittin' students. My son Thomas? Well, he's a bit different; doesn't really fit in with the other kids. I was thinkin' he might need a little time in a more *sophisticated* school."

"Different how? We don't take mentally handicapped kids, Eugene. Or troublemakers."

"Oh, he's not like that. He's just unusually gifted with numbers. It seems like that's how he sees the world. In numbers. It kinda sets him apart from the other kids his age; but as far as his teachers go, well, he's doin' things with math they can't even comprehend."

"Hmmm. That's interesting, Eugene. I've heard of kids like that before."

"That's not all he can do. I mean, maybe if you take a look at him, you'll see what I mean. Well, I mean, you probably have your hands full with our boys in Nam. I'm sorry even to have bothered you with this."

"Nam, hell, Eugene! We're gonna be there for *years*. I have time for this."

"Years? But I thought Nixon was gonna pull out our troops. You know, 'Johnson's war isn't gonna become Nixon's war?'"

"Oh, that's horseshit, Eugene! War makes presidents popular. That's our business. I'll tell you what. When I come stateside next month, I'll give you a call and see if I can evaluate that kid of yours. 'Til then, you take care."

"Alright, I appreciate that."

Howser made good on his promise and flew in to meet with the Stapeltons the following month. It didn't take him long to discover that Eugene was downplaying Tom's gifts. He appeared to be remarkably intelligent. "Off the charts," as Howser put it. He offered to fly Tom to Washington, DC, to undergo testing with professional scientists.

Eugene agreed to let Howser take Tom for further evaluation at the Advanced Study for Intelligence Institute in Washington, DC. A team of scientists and doctors bombarded Tom with mind challenges, mathematical equations, cognitive tests, and an assortment of problem-solving scenarios. After a full week, they met with Howser to deliver their findings.

"Admiral, we haven't seen intelligence like this in a child before. In some areas we don't even have an appropriate measurement standard for him. He's a true genius."

"He seems like a normal kid. Are you sure about this?"

"Normal? Somewhat. He has excellent social skills and is not mentally unstable. Outwardly, he appears like any other eight-year-old boy. But his brain? Well, that's extraordinary."

"Send him in here."

Tom entered Howser's temporary office at the institute and slowly glanced around before Howser offered him a seat.

"How'd I do? Did I pass?" Tom questioned Howser.

"I'm afraid so. It appears you're pretty smart."

"Oh, I don't know. I liked the tests, though."

"Son, tell me about this room." Howser waved his arm around the space. "What do you see?"

Without hesitation, Tom began rattling off facts.

"It has four hundred round objects and twenty-two spheres. There are three thousand items that are square, not including the 1152 floor tiles. You have seven ink pens on your desk. There are sixteen furniture items and it took forty cows to make all the leather products in here, including your belt and shoes. Your suit has six buttons and one is three shades lighter than the others. Judging by your sandwich, you like ham and cheese on rye, and—"

"Okay, okay, okay. That's good for now. Thank you." Howser turned to the study team and asked, "Can you take him to get some lunch? And send in Mitch for me."

Howser's assistant entered a few minutes later. "What's up, John?"

"How many floor tiles are in this room?"

"Sir?"

"Just count them, Mitch."

The following day Howser called Eugene.

"I think we can work something out with Tom. You're right. The boy has some gifts."

"You think he can attend that military prep school? Do you think that might help him? Marlene and I just think he really needs some teachers who can give him a proper education and keep him out of trouble. What do you think? A couple years there and he can return home. If we can just get him ready for high school, I think we can take it from there."

Howser cleared his throat. "Yeah, a couple years oughta do it. High school, huh? I think he's meant for bigger things, Eugene, but we can cross that bridge when we come to it." Howser had already made up his mind how he was going to begin Tom's training in Orion. His plan didn't include Tom going to high school in New Mexico.

Jude's path to Orion was as heart-wrenching as that of Butch and Screech. Jude was the first student to be placed at the school in Pretoria, and his arrival and transition were not smooth.

"Thanks for seeing me, John," said Major Aikens. "And thanks for cleaning up that mess quietly. It would've wrecked my career if The Brass found out about it."

"No problem, Aikens. It wasn't your fault she went sideways like that. Sometimes wives just snap. There's a lot of pressure on these dames to keep up a good front and maintain a respectable home. Some of the other wives can be pretty hard on one of their own."

"I don't know, John. I think she might've been predisposed to some sort of sickness. Her aunt hung herself back in Missouri a few years ago. Maybe that family has a weakness."

"What happened, Aikens? How did Janet end up so far in the gutter without anyone knowing?"

"I guess she didn't have many friends and I suppose I just stopped caring. Janet ousted me from our bedroom years ago, after I got into that mix-up with Carol, Ben Brewer's wife. Janet bought into those rumors. John, I swear to this day I never touched that woman. Carol was as crazy as they come."

"Not any more so than Janet. Sounds like you married a hot one, Brad."

"Yeah, well, I don't have to worry about that now, do I? I just appreciate you making it look like an accident."

"It *was* an accident."

"John, no one *accidentally* overdoses on drugs, do they? In any case, I appreciate the car-wreck coverup."

"I don't know what you're talking about." Howser winked at Aikens as he walked to the bar in his office and poured drinks for both of them. "Now we gotta figure out what to do with this kid of yours. You want me to take him, huh? I told you the school won't be up and running for at least another year. We aren't even staffed yet."

"I know, but Jude's a handful right now. He isn't taking his mother's death very well. I can't keep an eye on him and I can't afford to pay someone to come in and look after him while I work. I figure we have at least two more years before we pull out of Nam, maybe longer."

"I'm not a goddamn nanny, Brad. *I* don't know what to do with the kid."

"Put him to work. He's eleven years old. Practically a man already. Have him push a broom or clean up the construction yard. He's a good kid; he just needs to stay busy 'til you get that school operational, then he'll be a good cadet."

"We're going to have *students* there, not cadets. Cadets are for Annapolis and West Point. I'm going to turn out some big-brained, well-trained soldiers, but first they have to get an education."

"Okay. Alright. He'll make a good student. He likes school. I promise he won't be any trouble. I really need this, John."

"Alright, let's ship him over next week and I'll take it from there."

"Thank you, John."

"Oh, don't *thank* me. I'll probably be calling in a favor from you in the future."

"You got it. Anything you need." Aikens shook Howser's hand and left to tell Jude the news.

The major wasted no time in getting his son on a plane to Johannesburg. In two short weeks, Jude had arrived.

Howser waited on the other side of Customs in the Johannesburg airport. He held a sign that read Aikens.

Jude passed through the doors, read the sign, then proceeded to brush into Howser's arm, knocking him out of the way.

"Come on," said Jude gruffly.

Perturbed, Howser reached around and grabbed Jude by the arm, turning Jude to face him.

"Hold on there one minute, mister. I don't want to have to whoop your scrawny butt in front of all these people, but I will if you don't show me some respect."

"Respect? You're just my *driver*. Take me to see this Howser chump. Let's go."

"Alright, yeah. Let's go see this Howser fella." Howser played along.

When they had traveled out of Joburg and were on the road toward Pretoria, Howser pulled the vehicle over.

"Get out, kid," he ordered, reaching across Jude to tug on the door handle and open the door.

"*What?* No! I'm not getting out here. We have to go to the school in Pretoria."

"You're a tough kid. You'll find it. Good luck."

"Hey! You can't do this! I'm gonna report this to Howser. He'll have you fired."

"Get the fuck out, kid. You have about forty-eight kilometers to go. You better get moving. You don't want to be on this road at night, you know, with the thieves and all." Howser shoved Jude out of the vehicle. "Oh, you *do* know what a kilometer is, don't you?" Howser laughed. *Dumb little shit*, he thought as he drove toward Pretoria.

Seven hours later, and well into the middle of the night, Jude arrived at the school in the back of an old Toyota truck bed. The African man who had finally picked him up tossed his bags out of the cab.

"You really should not be wandering around like dat alone. Get inside de gates and stay dere."

Jude was exhausted from nineteen hours of flight travel and seven hours of walking in the dark. It was one o'clock in the morning and there was only one guard at the school that he could find who was awake.

"Hey, mister," said Jude slowly and tentatively, "can you tell me where I'm supposed to go? My name is Jude Aikens. I'm supposed to see Howser."

"You do not need to call me 'mister.' My name is Gadfrey and dere is no one dat can help you tonight. De admiral, he is sleeping.

Like everyone else here." The guard smiled at Jude then turned and began to walk away.

"Um, hey. I'm supposed to be here. I need a room. You know, a place to sleep," explained Jude as he followed Gadfrey.

"I know what a room is and we do not haff one for you. Go sleep by dat wall. Someone will find you in de morning."

Jude slunk over to the wall and sat on top of his duffle bag. Eventually, he fell asleep.

In the morning, a cheerful African woman in her thirties nudged Jude awake with her foot. "Get up, boy. You are working with me today. Here. Take dese boxes and follow me."

"But I have to go see Howser," pleaded Jude. "I'm a student here."

"A student? We don't haff any students. You are working for me today. Now get de boxes and move it."

Jude worked all day hauling boxes into empty classrooms. He was hungry and he hoped there was some sort of lunch break. It never came. Dinner passed as well. He could barely move a muscle, but he still kept working.

Gadfrey approached him and ordered, "Get in de truck, boy. I haff another job for you."

"But what about *dinner*? And when am I gonna get to see Howser?"

"Howser? Oh, de admiral? He left today for Washington, DC. He will not be back for a week at least."

Each day, Jude was tasked with moving and unpacking boxes, sweeping up debris, and whitewashing walls. Every evening he went back to the wall and slept on the ground, curled around his still-unpacked bag. Occasionally, a woman named Goodness would bring him a small plate of food.

"You haff to keep a little meat on dese tiny bones of yours. Even a raven would not want to eat you. You are so small."

Jude knit his eyebrows and looked at Goodness. "I'm not *that* small." But he was. At barely seventy-five pounds, his eleven-year-old frame was scrawny.

At the end of the week, Jude was directed to the campus showers, where he was handed soap and a towel and was told to get cleaned up.

"You haff a job in town today," Gadfrey told him. "You should put on some fresh trousers and comb your hair." Jude was so disheartened at this point that he didn't argue with the man.

A half hour later, Gadfrey picked Jude up and they headed back to Joburg. "I recognize this place," said Jude as they neared the airport. "Are you sending me home?"

"No, boy. You may not be going home for a very long time. Today I will park de car and you are going to go to meet a man, den carry his bags back to de car for me."

Gadfrey pulled into the temporary pickup point and Jude got out of the car. "Here," he motioned to Jude, "take dis." He handed Jude a piece of cardboard with a name written on it. "Dat is so he can find you. Wait outside Customs."

Jude took the sign and tucked it under his arm without reading the name. He stood outside Customs, holding the unread sign. Then he saw his driver from the previous week heading toward him. He looked at the man, then flipped over the sign and read Howser.

"Oh, crap," moaned Jude.

Howser stood before Jude and gave him a stern look.

"So, boy, how do you like school so far?" Howser brushed passed Jude and dropped his bags at Jude's feet. "I'll meet you at the car."

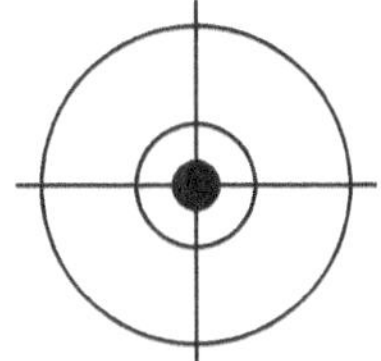

CHAPTER TWELVE

"Come on, Max," called Jane as Maxine ran up to her, tail wagging while she dodged horse hooves, as Jane and Sam returned to the farm. Jane dismounted from the horse and put her hand on her lower back. "Sam, I have to go take a rest. My fifty-five-year-old body feels about eighty right now, after that ride."

"No problem, Aunt Jane. Mackey and I'll take care of the horses. Go rest your old ass."

Jane turned to Maxine. "Lets go lie down for a while. My knees are killing me." They walked up the creaky staircase to Jane's room. "Maybe Dr. Reid has something in the medicine cabinet for me, eh Max?" Jane fumbled through her bottles, finally finding an anti-inflammatory and a Klonopen. "Like this shit's gonna work," she griped to Max. Jane swallowed the pills in one gulp, kicked off her boots, and climbed onto the bed. Maxine curled up next to her as

Jane lay down and drifted off to July 1986 and Virginia SWAT. Her team was just exiting the SWAT training grounds, where she left Commander Ruggers standing in the dirt.

As they scrambled inside the CH-47 Chinook and became airborne, she could barely make out Ruggers and his team in the cloud of dust below. Adrenaline, her drug of choice, burned hell fire with every breath she inhaled. She imagined it dripping down from her sinuses and heightening her senses like cocaine. As the zing settled in next to her anxiety, her imaginary pusher hooked her, like warm milk to kittens, with the illusion that using was helpful and harmless. Adrenaline committed her body to accomplishing what her mind could not comprehend to be moral. Or possible.

Oh, fuck yeah, buddy, Jane thought as she exhaled calmly when she realized she was safely among her brothers. The pounding in her chest returned to a dull thud that beat in unison with the rotors as she quickly scanned the craft for Screech, Pilot, Butch, and Jude. All present.

"Nice to see you could make it, Jude," Jane snarked. Jude had remained behind, choosing not to watch the exhibition at the SWAT grounds. Judging from his protruding black eye, she assumed he had served as Pilot's backup in the bar fight. Certainly those FORECON guys were dead now.

Butch heaved Jude out of the way and proceeded to lecture Jane en route to their ultimate destination: Iran. Butch's thick, scarred arms bulged as he pounded one fist into the other as he spoke. Over the din of the helicopter, he growled at her like an attack dog.

"You are such a tyrant, Jane! What you did back there to Ruggers was egotistical and irresponsible. What were you gonna do? Beat him up in front of his own *men*? How do you explain *that* one?"

Jane knew deep down that Butch respected either her bravado or her insanity. They'd been on many missions together and they worked in tandem seamlessly. It suddenly occurred to Jane that the way she acted with Ruggers might have brought up some emotions for Butch that sent him to his own personal dungeon. She guessed, by his reaction, it had something to do with the day he carried her out of the filth of blood and body parts of the Killing Circle. That was the first time Jane actually had to put her Killing Circle training into action. Her team had killed many and could never extinguish the fires of certain horrors of that op in Pakistan.   "Whoa! Back down, Major Daddy. Let's get on task here." Jane quickly redirected his anger. "What's with the Army chopper?" she asked sarcastically. Orion's hodgepodge of soldiers from different branches of the armed services made them unique. The teams consisted of Rangers, Marines, and SEALs—all directed by an admiral. Although they were specialized across the board, that didn't necessarily guarantee they got along. Jane held a personal bias against Army aviators after they busted in on a captain who had flown with them in Africa. He was a big, burly man, yet they caught him dressed in women's underwear while surfing porn magazines. The experience made her forever question what those guys were wearing under their flight suits.

"Come on, Jane! Live a little!" Screech bellowed from the back. "This is the Army aviators' paramount combat deployment. Besides, they're just dropping us off at Ja'b Bhudi airport." Screech could always be counted on for an opinion.

"Good God!" Jane yelled back. "I hope they aren't taking us all the way to the airport and dropping us in front of the target! They *do* know this is a covert operation, right?" she questioned, with increasing concern.

"Are you kidding?" answered Screech. "These fucknuggets would take forever to get there. We're bringing in the big birds for this op. I was pulling your leg. These boys aren't dropping us off in Iran."

Screech climbed into her lap and then wrapped his arms around her. He snuggled his head into her shoulder like a small child. "There, there, now, General Cranky Pants. If you need to hold me, I'm right here."

Jane squeezed him, laughing. "Ugh, you stink like crap, Screech. Get off me. What the fuck, dude?"

"Relax! It's my lucky rabbit's foot," explained Screech as he pulled a large, severed, half-rotten jackrabbit foot from inside his coat, which caused those watching to gag at the sight. *And* the stench.

"Good God! You sick bastard!" Butch snarled. He snatched the rabbit foot and tossed it up front onto the aviators, who lurched, stomped on it, then kicked it back in their direction. The severed foot remained generally intact.

Screech snatched it up. "Hey, fuckshit! That was lucky!" He chucked the foot toward Butch's shoulder then leaned over to retrieve it.

"Not for the rabbit, you douche," yelled Butch. "Leave it. Leeeeeave it . . . Leave it," Butch instructed, as if he were a dog trainer. Screech sat down, disheartened.

Pilot looked back and motioned for Jane to come up to the front of the cramped craft.

"Hey, princess!" yelled Pilot. "It's time for your weekly call-in." Pilot handed Jane a headset.

"Who we got here? The commander-in-chief?" Jane asked. She had to bend over to slip on the headset because the curled cord twisted over itself several times, shortening its length by half.

"Hardly," Jude yelled from the seat next to Pilot. "It's your boyfriend Biff!"

Jane had a tough time coping after Tom died; she wasn't ready to move on to another relationship for several years. Robert Locke was her choice of boyfriend. He was the undersized, nerdy kid in high school who won all the science fairs but never made the wrestling team. As a young boy, he was picked on and tormented for his unusually large ears, small body, and goofy smile. Nevertheless, he was smart. His degree earned him a position as the city manager of a small municipality. He then went on to pursue his dream job with the city fire department, where he protected two square miles of Virginia as if he were the fire chief of Chicago. His paramedic skills landed him a position with SWAT as their medic. Jane knew he wouldn't have lasted one day in the US Marine Corps School of Advanced Warfare, but she sure appreciated his enthusiasm. After all, Mayberry needed a police force too. His naiveté allowed her to pursue her covert operations without having to explain what she was really doing when she traveled. He believed she sold technology for a newly developing international computer company.

Jane supposed this is what she got for requesting that she be allowed to live in the "civilian sector," as they called it in Orion. She could have a somewhat normal life, as long as Howser dictated where she lived and who her friends were. She had to ask for permission before attending any event that was not regulated by Orion. At least it beat living at Quantico full time. Jane was surprised Robert met Howser's approval, but Howser had vetted Robert's file and pronounced him "suitable."

"Shut up, cockmunchers! His name isn't Biff! It's Huge-Cock-Keep-Me-Up-All-Night!" slammed Jane.

"In your dreams, princess," Jude sneered. Jude had earned his rank through sweat and blood. Because he was the first student to arrive at the school in Pretoria, he thought that gave him the right to be second-in-command. He griped constantly about his lower place in the team's ranks; he bore this grudge openly. Although he loved Jane like a sister, he grew more and more angry at having to make allowances for her. Because of her elite agent status, and the amount of money and training time invested in her, Howser treated her like a rare and precious treasure. An Orion mission never engaged without her final authorization. Sometimes this meant waiting for her to emerge from an appointment with a tailor for a fitting for a sari, a spa treatment, or a haircut. These delays set Jude on fire.

Jane was Orion's only female commodity and was often deployed into situations based solely on her gender-biased technical prowess. Sometimes her role was to lure marks further than they meant to go, keep them longer than they meant to stay, and cost them more than they intended to pay. Orion often required intel to be extracted by violent means. Other times Jane merely guarded officials and ambassadors by being on their arm during an event, making it easier for her to secure their safety. Her covert presence in those situations was in stark contrast to the obvious Secret Service members, who looked like bankers with earpieces and who sported monkey suits. Jane often wore burkas, saris, kimonos, and evening gowns with elegance and ease as a result of years of grooming and special training. Although Howser was her father, Jane proved time and again that she had earned her rank without question, and she was prepared to fight to the death anyone who *did* question her.

Jude shoved his way angrily to the back of the congested chopper and began to inscribe his call sign on his boots in black Magic Marker: Bulldog, it read.

As he watched Jude, Screech probed, "Isn't that a little superstitious? Aren't you tempting death by writing your name on your boots right before a mission?"

"That's not what I'm doing. I'm just making sure you keep your grubby mitts off my stuff. I'm *labeling* them. There's a difference."

"Here. Carve Widowmaker on *mine*, so I can fuck with Jane. I've been fancying her boots all morning!"

Jane's mother, Amelia, was known as The Black Widow. Jane, the second female professional in Orion's history, presumed Howser liked the theme and coined Jane's call sign. The correlation to her mother turned out to be so symbolic for Jane that she had several black widow spiders tattooed on her body. She enjoyed the fact that female black widows are so isolated from the males that they use them only for mating, then kill them. After a black widow spider gives birth, she casts her babies off her web immediately and eats the ones that straggle.

Preoccupied by the boyish banter around her, Jane had overlooked Robert, who was waiting on the headset. Thankfully, she hadn't yet switched on the communicator.

"Hey, you! What's up?" she asked Robert over her headset. Robert spoke hesitantly. Jane could tell he felt awkward calling her "at work." Her number was always rerouted and screened by Tully, their communications specialist back in Virginia. Tully decided when a call was worth sending through to Jane. This setup allowed Jane to remain covert when necessary. Robert thought she had a male receptionist at her technology firm.

"Oh, you know. Just work," Robert replied, "and thinking about you all day. Are you coming over this weekend? Or do you want to come over for a romantic dinner tonight?"

"I'm not sure I can make it this weekend," Jane responded. "And, unfortunately, tonight is out. I'm working late. We have a project that we haven't even started yet." Jane tried to use an apologetic tone. She had completely forgotten about her plans to go with him to a barbecue that weekend. In reality, she didn't know if she would *live* through the weekend.

"You really are working too much," admonished Robert. "I mean, I know we both agreed that work takes precedence, but it just seems like you bust your ass for that company and you get no respect."

"Robert, you have to command respect. If I'm going to show these guys that I, as a woman, am more than capable of kicking some ass—I mean, selling more accounts—I have to stay on top of my game."

"Then maybe you need to be a little more assertive. Draw a line in the sand."

Jude, who was listening in on the other headset, put his hand over the comm and said sotto voce, "Oh *fuck* no! If you were any more assertive I'd have to shoot myself!"

Jane hushed Jude by waving a knife at him, then pretending to cut her throat with it, indicating she'd slit *his* throat if he didn't stop with the commentary.

"I'll call you when I'm finished, Robert. I'm getting ready to go into a big meeting and I have to freshen my makeup." Jane tiger-swiped sticky black greasepaint across her already solid green face.

"Okay. I'm sure you look ravishing!" Jane could picture the huge smile that likely spread across his face. Meanwhile, Jude had dipped his finger into the greasepaint and had drawn a circus ringleader mustache across his lip to distract Jane, who was trying to remain focused on what Robert was saying.

"Hey," Robert continued, "be careful leaving the parking lot. Those underground garages worry me. I wish you would take that self-defense class." Robert always got freaked out in those garages; he watched too many horror movies. He once confided to Jane that he often pictured chainsaw-wielding killers hiding under his car, who then proceeded to cut his Achilles tendons.

By now, Jude had painted two Groucho Marx eyebrows on his face. Jane seized him by the throat as he continued to taunt her through a muffled gurgle.

"I wrote it on my list of things to do," Jane replied to Robert, struggling to hold Jude in place while lying to Robert.

"Why that's the most ridiculous thing I ever hoid, Jane, dear!" gargled Jude in his best Marx Brothers' voice.

Frustrated by Jane's lack of enthusiasm regarding his suggestion, Robert said, "Okay. At least think about it. I'll talk to you later."

Hours later, the team geared up for their switch to the Marine helicopters. Once onboard, Jude began making some last-minute modifications to the sights in his laser rangefinder as he and Jane settled in at the rear of the chopper.

"You know, I ought to kill you!" Jane fumed. "Don't fuck this up for me, Jude!"

"Jane, do you think the targets will be running *toward* us or *away* from us? That's going to make a difference in how I program this, darling." Jude spoke in the condescending tone he knew Jane despised. "You know you're messed up for even dating this guy, Jane. You don't have to have some big-shit relationship just to get laid."

"Yeah, I have sex with myself all the time," Screech said, looking at his hand, "and we hate each other." He then slapped himself across the face. "What the fuck are you doing?" Screech yelled at his hand.

"Oh, is that it? You're going for makeup sex? Well, you're just going to have to wait 'til we get home, mister!" He paused and looked at his team. "Oh, that didn't come out right."

"Professor, nothing you *ever* say comes out right. You are *so* weird." Jude patted Screech on the back.

Although Jane's relationship with Screech was loving and tolerant, her link to Jude was a lot more complex. She had spent many satisfying years working as Jude's partner, but she also endured as many equally painful years seeing him through drug rehab. As a result of his extended clandestine deployments to Columbia, where he had planted himself deeply into the operations of the most cold-blooded drug lords, he battled inexorable addictions to heroin and cocaine. Jude had succumbed to the demons he was sent to seize. The team had frequently recovered him among lifeless cartel members, along with hundreds of kilos of product. Once, they found him huddled in a corner, pulsating, seizing, and nearly dead. Jane spent months by his side as he recovered. Doctors resurrected him to fight another day. Unfortunately, Jude never managed to shake his urges completely, so she monitored him, which agitated him even further.

Born with a brilliant mind, Jude's aptitude for mathematics and complex scientific equations created an opportunity for him to act as her indispensable sniper-spotter. He possessed the skill to program air density, land speed, frequency, range, and weather quickly. He could redirect within seconds for even the most subtle changes. As long as they could temper his ego—and his drug use—Jude was dazzling and exceptional at his craft. He existed on a high note. He pursued women, but hardly ever caught them. Once they got past his shockingly white smile, jet-black hair, bottomless blue eyes, and brawny physique, the insensitive, ill-mannered, self-interested warrior burst through like a captive animal set free. His assets certainly backed his gigantic ego. He was the second leading martial arts expert in the world. He once spent sixteen hours a day for an entire year training in Krav Maga in Israel. He was a master swordsman and a sharpshooter, and his intelligence matched his brawn.

Despite Jude's impressive credentials, he never failed to exasperate Jane with his foolhardiness. He used to recite John F. Kennedy quotes at the most inappropriate times. "Forgive your enemies, but never forget their names," he once told the hysterical queen of Zanzibar as she clutched her dead husband, who had his assassin's knife still sticking out of his chest. He initiated brawls that Jane had to finish and he had unquestionable discipline problems. And although Jude was the first child–soldier in Orion, Howser never deemed him responsible enough to promote him to second-in-command.

"Alright, ladies," Lieutenant Pilot spoke up, "We're gonna load onto the C-130. Once onboard, we're gonna cut comm in T-twenty. Is your gear ready?"

"Hey, Pilot! You *do* realize that it's just me and Jude dropping down there, don't you?" Jane asked.

"Yeah, why?" Pilot turned to look at Jane. His face was covered in greasepaint. He was strapped to the gills with weapons and appeared ready to rumble. Jane eyed the greasepaint and shrugged her shoulders.

"Uh, nothing. Never mind."

Jane began to look through her gear. She grabbed her M16A2 and tossed it aside, opting instead for her H&K rifle that could toggle between black-hot and white-hot imaging. "Holy shit, sir! Is this thang loaded?" she said with a Southern drawl, sounding like Darrell Waltrip announcing a NASCAR race. She loaded the long-range sniper rifle with low-drag bullets. The ambient air density was much lower than she was used to. With these bullets, she could fire from a great distance if needed.

Pilot continued to rattle off logistics as Jane and Jude donned their small oxygen tanks. "Locked into Joint Special Operations Task Force and we are live, ladies. Task Force Commander Mundy, you have the theater."

Commander Mundy piped in over the radio, "Widowmaker, you are such a dork!"

Mundy was an Annapolis graduate and a close, longtime friend of Jane's. She immediately felt at ease on hearing his voice through her headset. If anyone could lead her home in one piece, Mundy would. She thought of the way he mentored the young plebes at the Academy; he created excellent officers, ready to serve. Jane respected his command and cherished his friendship.

"Nice you could join us, Mundy. I appreciate the jab. I was beginning to think I was High Command." They both laughed. "I'm going to take Sammy boy with me," she said, grabbing some small SAM packs and setting them up for the jump. "By the way," Jane turned to Screech, "nice job modifying these surface-to-air missiles! They're so *cute* and compact!"

"Careful there, girlie," Screech warned. "They may be small, but they'll blow the shit outta you! Oh. That didn't come out right."

"Nothing you *ever* say does."

"Bulldog and I are gonna run down in silent check mode in less than thirteen. We're locked and loaded and looking for goose, sir!" Jane grabbed the MANPADS and strapped it into the joint compartment of her harness. She then hitched a SAM on her back, feeling the natural rush of adrenaline when she did so as she prepared to jump willingly from the aircraft. Although they rarely used SAMs on burst missions, she always felt an irrational sense of false security when she had one on hand.

Jane's heart started to pound as she tightened her harness straps. The veins in her arms swelled from the increased blood pulsing through them. She wasn't sweating like Jude, though. His greasepaint was already smearing into one color across his face and he looked black. *Thank God I don't sweat like that*, she thought. *I'd freeze HALO jumping from an altitude of 15,000 feet with any bare skin exposed.* She felt slightly concerned for Jude, but wasn't overly worried.

They sealed their helmets and respirators, then secured their packs for the third time, decreasing any chances for a failed chute. Jane and Jude hitched their pulleys to the jump line and waited for the jump master to green-light them. Pilot then released the hatch at the rear of the craft. The seemingly bottomless black pit looming below them was their only visual.

Jane heard Commander Mundy give the GO order. "Widow-maker Actual, prepare to engage CT op. You kids are about to punctuate in fifteen minutes what has taken two years to plan! Five, four, three, two, engage CT! Repeat, engage!"

Listening to the whirr of the pulley clipped to her back, Jane spit out of the hatch and into darkness. Initially, her guts churned with the rush from bailing out into black oblivion, then her senses caught up with her imagination. Jane felt the force of the freezing air pressing against her cheeks and chest as her body careened through the atmosphere. She remembered to keep her body planed, with only a slight bend to her feet. Even through her helmet, the wind was deafening as her body reached terminal velocity. The cold penetrated even the smallest crevice of her jumpsuit.

The freefall ended when she threw her chute. As she sailed gently to the drop zone, she took the last few seconds to scan the heavens for Jude. She noticed him floating effortlessly. Hanging in the air felt like the moment between dreaming and waking—when absolutely nothing happens in your mind but silence. Then BAM! Their feet touched the ground. Jane and Jude swiftly severed the ropes from their chutes and sprinted to the objective, all while receiving codes and directives from Mundy, who was observing their thermal movements via satellite. Jane's dual-purpose thermal-vision goggles served as her computer screen of sequencers, quadrangles, and codes.

"Five minutes to target," Mundy calmly reassured her.

Bulldog and Widowmaker threaded through a maze of rocks, hills, and fallen trees. Running felt like breathing to them. They ran every day of their lives as part of their training, and they approached training with mindfulness. They transcended their bodies when they ran, never feeling pain. This mind-set allowed them to navigate all sorts of terrain efficiently and swiftly. They compensated for obstacles almost as quickly as a computer.

Jane was grateful for the countless years she spent training for these situations and was happy that Jude was beside her. Thousands of miles away, Mundy continued to track along with them via satellite from the command center in DC. She vaguely heard Command Colonel Jenkins speak to Mundy as she reached a wall—the coordinates given to her and Jude. The colonel was a very serious man, unlike Commander Mundy. Jude joined her within seconds and they both began to scan the area ahead.

"How close are they? Go to visual," the colonel ordered abruptly. A successful mission would guarantee him an immediate promotion to general.

Mundy viewed the satellite image. "Five minutes from the target, sir," he reported.

"This is our only chance. Tell them the targets are making the exchange! We should send in the SEALs now! Forget Orion!" Jenkins barked as he watched the command center screen. For a moment, it sounded as if the colonel questioned their ability to accomplish the task.

"Whoa, whoa, whoa," Mundy replied. "She's got this. We're on task. The SEALs are ready to insert after Orion has been extracted, per mission protocol."

"Widowmaker," Mundy continued, "it looks like the tea party has already begun. We are awaiting visual confirmation of the White Rabbit. Can you confirm?"

Jane and Jude watched through their goggles as one man opened the passenger door of a Jeep while another stood guard. A third figure exited the vehicle. Jane recognized Habib Abadi immediately, known as the "Mad Hatter" on this mission. He was not their primary objective; he was the mark with whom the "White Rabbit" was to exchange money, heroin, and one massive arsenal of weapons.

"Negative, Command," Jane replied. Then a Lincoln Town Car pulled into view. She exhaled, squinting slightly through her lenses as she peered around the side of the wall.

"I require a better position, sir. Stand by."

Jane's adrenaline surged when she realized Command had miscalculated their location. They were too far away for her to make the shot.

"She'd better hurry up," Jane heard the colonel say worriedly.

She secured her grapple to the top of the formidable wall before her and scaled it. After she scrambled to the top, she wrapped the rope around her wrist and ankle, removed her rifle from her back sling, and waited for Bulldog to sight her in.

"Fuck, Bulldog! It's gotta be 900 meters! What the fuck?"

Jude sighted in, sounding somewhat worried. "Correction. It's 1280 meters. You have to fire, Widowmaker. If you don't make it, I might as well shoot us both. *Take it!*"

Jude confirmed the target to Command. "Affirmative, Command. We have eyes on White Rabbit. Sighting in. Yellow," Jude lied to Command. He was not equipped to sight in at 1280 meters and they didn't have time to maneuver closer. Jane placed her now-useless H&K rifle on the wall and moved quickly to drop the pack from her back.

"What the fuck are you *doing?*" Jude whispered stridently at her.

Jane continued to remove items from her bag. She began assembling steel parts until she held a prototype XM8 future assault rifle with a long-range sniper variant. Screech had designed it for her. They hadn't field-tested it yet, but Screech had assured Jane it would save her ass one day. The XM8 had the range and accuracy of a .50 cal, thanks to Burroughs' Cal Force engineering, yet it was lighter than an M4, thanks to the genius of Heckler & Koch and, of course, Screech. She hoped she'd soon be calling him a wizard to his face.

"Widowmaker! Are you out of your goddamn mind? I can't sight you in on that! I don't have the equipment! You're gonna get us killed!" Jude began stripping down his equipment and preparing for plan B.

Jane calmed herself and whispered under her breath, "Shit, shit, shit. This is my rifle. There are many like it, but this one is mine. Without my rifle, I am nothing. Breathe deep." She knew a lot of marksmen make the error of holding their breath when sighting in a target and they miss because their heartbeat gets in the way. "Take the shot at the bottom of a calm exhale and you can't miss," she whispered to herself.

Jane heard the puzzled colonel ask Mundy, "What did she say? Why is she talking?" He could hear Jane over the comm, but the words were barely audible because she spoke so quietly.

Mundy had steadfast confidence in her abilities and did not dare interrupt her thoughts. Jane thought that, by now, Mundy must be aware they weren't in range to fire. Perhaps he had gunmetal backup for them that she was unaware of.

Jane sighted in and continued her mantra. "Without me . . ." then she took the shot, ". . . my *rifle* is nothing!" She watched the man she targeted crumple to the ground as the top of his scalp splattered against the window of the Lincoln Town Car. Direct hit. The surrounding men dropped to the ground in panic. Jane swung around, slung her new rifle over her shoulder, grabbed her H&K, and BASE-jumped off the wall, yelling, "No mercy!" Jane had just made a direct headshot from 1280 meters with a prototype rifle. Her body was ablaze with adrenaline. One shot, one man down.

At the target zone, both parties were in a frenzy, ducking behind their vehicles for cover. White Rabbit's men began shooting at the first vehicle as they placed the body of their dead leader in their car and raced off. The Mad Hatter and his two men dove for the Jeep. Jane took off in a full sprint, with the Rolling Stones' "Paint It Black" blaring in her head as she maneuvered to the pickup zone. She could feel her warm blood pulsing through her body. She moved with the speed and agility of an antelope, jumping over fallen trees, and sliding down embankments like a downhill skier. Jude copied her every move and stayed right with her. They navigated the mountainous terrain quickly, moving like a symbiotic being.

Jane stayed focused on the pickup zone and was not distracted by the men in the Jeep hunting her and Jude. She spied a tree ahead, signaled to Jude, then took her grapple from her warrior. At a full run, Jane swung the grapple up into the tree. The sharp flukes dug immediately into a protruding branch, sending a shower of moss and wooden shrapnel raining down on her. She scaled the tree swiftly, like a monkey. Jude, calculatingly, dropped to the ground, feigning injury. The men in the Jeep advanced with caution, weapons drawn. From her higher vantage point, Jane fired with her Sig, killing all three men in seconds. Jude jumped up, Jane jumped down, and they continued running to the pickup zone.

Commander Mundy broke in over her headset, "Widowmaker, 275 meters to retrieval."

"Widowmaker Actual, 10-40. Roger that. We have visual on the pickup zone." As soon as the SEALs had visual confirmation on Jude and Jane, they lifted off for their insertion, leaving one chopper behind for Jane and Jude's extraction.

The SEAL Team 4 pilot responded, "Roger. Engage mission."

As Jude and Jane were extracted, Jane felt proud to have been given the honor to pave the path for the SEALs that day. Unfortunately, there was a high casualty rate among SEAL teams as they laid the groundwork for subsequent covert invasions against major weapons routing and Enemy Alliance Activity in the Middle East. Good men died, some whose names would be engraved on The Wall in Virginia—a place of honor. Missions like these made it hard for veterans to realign in society, to appear normal and untouched. These soldiers couldn't tell their friends or family that select locations around the world were saved from a global attack. These men, and Jane, could not say they had stopped a nuclear war. Their friends and families wouldn't be able to comprehend or even believe it.

"Goddamn! What a rush! Twelve hundred eighty meters! His chunky motherfucking scalp flew off! BLAM!" Jane yelled, throwing her arms in the air. She then crept around inside the hull of the chopper like a gangster. This is how they behaved after a mission. Reflecting on it later, she realized this "peacocking" desensitized the reality of the situation.

Jude shoved her down in her seat. "Yeah, what're you gonna do now? Go home and bake cookies, Susie-fucking-homemaker?"

"You're just jealous, ball licker!" retorted Jane. "Give me one of those!" Jude tossed her a bag of food. She started searching for that juicy Quarter Pounder she'd been craving.

Jude removed the top bun from his burger, which was slathered with ketchup, and propelled it against the window of the helicopter. It stuck, then slowly slid off, leaving behind a slimy ketchup trail on the glass.

"Jane, look! It's that dude's scalp!" He grabbed the bun and licked the ketchup, groaning loudly.

"Hate to break up you two love birds," said Screech as he tossed Jane her headset and motioned her over. He turned to Jude. "Did she really scalp the fucker? That is so fucking cool!"

"Shut up, you assholes!" Jane yelled. She seized the headset and inhaled deeply. Robert's soft, submissive voice broke through.

"Hey," Robert cooed, "sorry to bother you at work. Big Dog is having the guy's over tomorrow. Throwing some meat on the grill. Okay, I know you don't do the meat thing—"

Pilot, who was listening in over the headset, just about pissed himself as he watched Jane shove half the burger in her mouth. At home, Jane was strictly vegetarian, but the adrenaline of an op made her crave junk food. She had developed a special need to eat red meat immediately after a mission.

"But," Robert went on, "there'll be a bunch of SWAT guys there, some firefighters, and their wives. I thought you told me you wanted to meet them." He posed this almost in the form of a question, as if he couldn't remember if she'd ever expressed an interest in meeting his friends.

"You can go, sweetie," Jane replied. "I've had a pretty big day. Besides, I still have to meet with the president." Jane was riding pretty high and, for a moment, forgot who she was talking to.

"The president of your company? That's awesome! Did you get a promotion?" Robert loved to praise and please Jane, yet his overenthusiasm made her feel nauseous. She wasn't used to that kind of genuine sweetness toward her in a relationship.

"Hardly! Um, I'm pretty sure I'm going to be reprimanded for wearing tennis shoes. You know how these companies are. Strictly business."

"I'll wait for you to get home. I really want you to come. The guys are beginning to think I made you up."

"Listen, Robert, I have to call you back. I have to call my boss to see if I can get out of the meeting." Jane sensed his excitement at the possibility. She pushed her way to the back of the hull, through her sprawled-out team, and grabbed a personal communicator.

She punched in her objective and within minutes she heard Tully's voice on the other end of the line. She didn't know if he was overweight because she'd never met him, but he sounded like he wore a tight collar that strangled his thick neck. He wheezed into the receiver, swallowing thirty times every three minutes, on average—an indication he was a mouth-breather.

"Foxtrot Charlie Delta," Tully panted over the communicator.

"Charlie A-T twenty-nine," Jane responded.

"Comeback."

"Forty-four, ninety-nine, forty-four, forty-four, twenty-one." Jane spewed out numbers like a quarterback.

"Voice identified and recognized. Hey, Jane, what's your favorite movie?" Tully asked, slobbering into the communicator. "Would you like to catch a flick with me sometime?"

"My favorite movie is *Slumber Party Massacre II*." Jane was pretty sure Tully was Mormon, so she enjoyed being lewd with him.

"Jane, why do you always do that? You're a mean girl."

"Because I'm peeved!" she barked. "Look, Tully, we are *not* friends, okay?"

"*I* think we are," Tully replied enthusiastically.

"Tully, why don't you patch us through to NORAD and see if hell finally froze over. Get me the president of Orion!"

Clearly hurt, Tully barked back, "Sir, yes, sir!"

"Funny," snarked Jane. "Hey, Tully! When're you gonna go back to the WHCA?" Jane's comment probably made Tully feel degraded. She bet he didn't like to be reminded that he still hosted radio broadcasts for the White House. Thankfully, Howser picked up the line.

"G.I. Elizabeth!" he said, sounding like a jovial TV announcer. There were times when this tone of voice reminded Jane more of Bob Barker, rather than the commander of Orion. She half expected him to shout, "Come on *down*!" Jane always knew that when he used this upbeat timbre, there were most likely other people in the room with him. He always put on this friendly demeanor while among colleagues.

"Jane, sir," she replied as she rolled her eyes. She didn't like it when he called her Elizabeth because it feminized her. Howser had done that her whole life; she'd been trying to get him to call her Jane for just as long.

"Elizabeth, that was amazing! I watched it all! You . . . What can I say? We couldn't do this without you," he said enthusiastically, ignoring her previous request. Jane knew this wasn't true; she knew she was expendable. If she were to be shot or taken hostage, Orion, as well as the President of the United States, would deny her existence.

"Glad to be of service, sir. Look, sir, I have to ask you a favor."

"Elizabeth, anything," he said with unusual eagerness. Jane didn't generally dare make a request of Howser because he could be as volatile as nitroglycerine. He could be breezy and fun loving, but if she crossed the line, she might find herself in a death grip fighting for her last breath. None of the members of Orion knew exactly where "the line" existed in Howser's world. They usually just obeyed orders and asked for nothing in return. There were instances, though, when Jane remembered he was still her father. When she could, she'd nab the rare opportunity to approach him as his daughter. This was one of those times.

"Robert wants me to go to a friendly barbecue tomorrow. Would it be possible for us to debrief afterward, on Monday? I have to keep my cover, sir. Plus, I really want to go." Jane could sense the tone of her voice elevating and thought, *Damn! Why did I do that?* Rather than making a statement about wanting to attend the barbeque, she had asked a question. It would be easier for him to deny her request.

"Shit, Elizabeth. I thought you were going to ask me something big. Get the hell outta there! Go have fun, kiddo. See you on Monday," he responded without wavering. He must have been truly pleased at the outcome of the mission. She had expected at least some resistance for asking to delay a debriefing. Government protocol insists on retrieving information from teams immediately, before they leave their sight, in the event they get hit by a bus or kidnapped before they have the opportunity to report. Although Jane was surprised by Howser's decision to let her go, she didn't question it.

"Thank you, sir."

Jane was about to sign off when Howser whispered, "Dad."

"Excuse me?" Jane said, unsure she had heard him correctly.

"You know," Howser replied, muffling his voice, "it wouldn't hurt to call me Dad once in a while. No more 'Sir, OORAH! This is my rifle; there are many like it.' I admire you G.I. Jane, even though you are a leatherneck Marine!"

Jane laughed. "Leatherneck *or* Marine! You can't mix up the two! That just sounds stupid," she responded lightheartedly. "And thank you, sir—I mean, Howser," Jane said, ignoring his previous request like he did hers.

Although she wouldn't admit it to anyone else, she deeply appreciated Howser. Just about every action she took in her life was aimed to prove her grit to him. In the back of her mind, she always speculated whether he would make a decision similar to hers. Did she secretly desire to carve out a path equivalent to his? He was the most daring, audacious man she knew, with more battle scars than any warrior she'd encountered. He was intellectual and precise. He had earned the respect of almost every leader in the nation. Those were the shoes she attempted to fill and the man she sought to impress. She wanted to earn her star and officially become second-in-command at Orion. Jane knew she would have to endure impossible things to accomplish that.

Howser could also be foul and aggressive. He always chomped on a cigar, spewed profanities, used intimidation, and even resorted to violence to get what he wanted. He was flashy and kept his back overly straight in public, literally puffing his chest out.

She supposed that was what America wanted as a military figurehead standing next to the President of the United States. Howser evoked strong, charismatic leadership—a modern-day John Wayne. Once, during a press conference, he waved to the cameras while standing next to the President. Howser was a poster boy for the press and he loved the attention. He soothed the public, yet remained sharp, hard, and cunning behind closed doors. He could convince any country to buy oil at two hundred dollars a barrel simply because they believed his propaganda. His persuasive negotiation skills made him indispensable to the United Nations—and to Orion.

What the American public did not know was how harsh he actually was in private. Despite being family, Jane was never excused from penalties and beatings. Often he would administer them personally. There were no words to describe the training Howser forced on his soldiers. Any normal person would view it as utterly inhumane. Jane believed her father got some kind of satisfaction from gaining optimal control over each of them, using fear as a motivator. She forever carried with her the indescribable pain and shock she felt when she first realized the one person in this world who possessed an unwavering duty to protect her would hurt her to make her stronger.

Jane remained forever on her guard since the day she lost trust in him. Howser had dragged her out of bed in the middle of the night, thrown a black hood over her head, then pitched her, handcuffed, into the back of a van. Laying on the floor of the vehicle, Jane felt the pressure of a boot heel on her soft throat tissue, and the punches to her face and kicks to her ribs at the same time. She struggled to press her chin tightly to her chest to avoid suffocation. Howser's men tightened the hood back over her mouth, tipped her head back, and poured water down her swelling throat. To keep from drowning, Jane thrashed and attempted to close off her breathing, not knowing how long each waterboarding was going to last. This torture went on all night—as part of her combat pressure training—to which the whole team was subject for years. There was no six-week boot camp and graduation for Orion soldiers. At any point in time, on Howser's whim, they were hauled away for a "refresher course."

Jane often thought about how her experience reflected a special kind of hell—a truly vicious cycle of torture and trauma. Orion soldiers spent their lives in that cycle, until every bone in their body was compromised, every relationship was ended, and every friend they had was lost. Howser was no exception to this separation. His loss of Amelia hardened him to the core and allowed him to perpetuate the trend of isolation for the next generation of Orion soldiers.

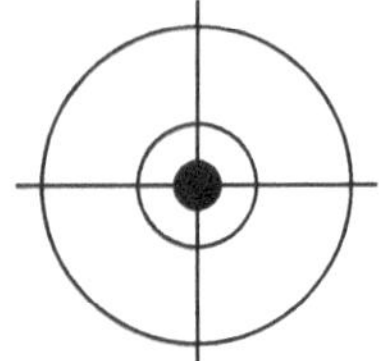

CHAPTER THIRTEEN

Jane ambled down the stairs with Max and headed outside in the late-afternoon sunlight, feeling refreshed after her nap. Sam walked toward them holding a bouquet of lilies wrapped in a purple ribbon. His hair was still wet from his recent shower. His short-sleeve red-and-white-plaid shirt was tucked into his clean Wrangler jeans. As he approached Jane, he took out one of the lilies and handed it to her.

"Afternoon, Aunt Jane," he said, with a wide, sparkling smile. Sam seemed older to Jane that morning; he held his chin up slightly and made solid eye contact with her. Sam put other people first. After he lost his parents, Marlene and Eugene became his world. Jane had begun to notice the little things he did for Marlene. She knew the rest of the flowers were for Sam's grandmother, and that he bought them for no other reason than to let his grandma know what she meant to him.

"Sam, you'd do anything for your grandma, wouldn't you?" Jane asked, already knowing the answer.

"Of course!" He paused for a moment and looked down at the bright-yellow lilies in his hand. "I'm not getting soft or anything," Sam explained, "but I feel a little bad leaving her. She raised me, you know. Grandma was nothing like your dad. After hearing about the Killing Circle, I can see that parents would do anything to keep their child out of harm's way—even going to such lengths as Howser did."

"No parent wants to lose a child, and I suppose that was Howser's twisted way of preparing and protecting me, given my unique circumstances."

"Yeah. And no child wants to lose a parent," Sam said thoughtfully, looking at Jane. She caught a glimpse of a yellow spark in his green eyes, reflected in the afternoon sunlight. They both knew what it was like to lose a parent and, in Sam's case, two. Although Sam never talked about how it affected him, Jane knew he must also suffer from his own form of PTSD.

"Sam, sit down for a second." Jane felt the need to explain the significance of the Killing Circle and Howser's motivation for putting her in one. She wanted Sam to understand how different people grieve and how they take action against the fear of losing someone else. Perhaps it would help him begin to fathom his own grieving, rather than continue to push it to the back burner.

"Alright, I'm all ears," Sam complied, carefully placing the bouquet of flowers on the grass next to him as he plopped down on the ground alongside Jane.

"Back when my mom got the crap beat out of her by the MOSK SS, Howser internalized why it happened. My mother was completely ill-prepared to protect herself going into that situation. She had no combat skills. My father spent years afterward asking her to relive that experience and taking notes. He devised a training method so that if she, or any other agent, was faced with the same situation, she could kill her captors and escape. He never wanted any of his team to have to endure what my mom went through. Ever. He became obsessed with the Killing Circle when I came along. Now you can see why. I suppose if there were any human on the planet he wanted to teach that shit to, it would be me."

"He saw her in you," Sam noted.

"Exactly. Every time I returned from a mission broken or damaged physically in any way, my training became more intense. He took every scar, every abrasion as a personal affront to Orion training. He always felt he had failed me, and I know his feelings went as far back as the day he found my mother in a cell."

"I can see, now, the value in the Killing Circle training—and why Howser was so brutal on you—but I still don't understand why he put you in the Orion program to begin with." Sam looked down and began to tear out some of the surrounding grass while he waited for a response from Jane. A reply that never came. Jane knew better than to try and fill the silence.

Sam stopped tearing at the grass and looked at Jane. "Aunt Jane, I feel guilty sometimes. Or, I don't know. Selfish, I guess. Since my parents died, my grandparents have had to do *everything* for Mackey and me. One minute I'm frickin' sad that my dad isn't here throwing the football around with me or that my mom isn't yelling at me to get to school on time, and then the next minute I'm pissed off at God for letting them get killed. Why didn't anyone send *me* off to the Orion school when my parents died, instead of burdening my grandparents? When I have the most strength and determination to do something, it's when I think about that. My parents dying, I mean." Sam paused. "I gotta get these over to Grandma. She'll probably want to put them on the table tonight."

Jane nodded at Sam and lit up a cigarette, trying not to blow the smoke in his direction. She glanced toward Marlene, who had just come out to set up the picnic table.

"It looks like Grandma is serving us supper outside tonight," Sam said.

Jane put her hand on his shoulder. "Thanks, Sam, for a great day today," she said. Sam smiled, picked up the flowers, and jumped to his feet. He brushed off his jeans and started walking toward Marlene. Jane watched Marlene as her face lit up when Sam handed her the bouquet.

Jane got up to stretch her legs. After that long morning ride with Sam, moving seemed to take slightly more effort on Jane's aging body. She ambled across the lawn as best as her sore body would allow. Good ol' Major Pain had hunkered down in her spine and hips, and took random shots at her legs. *That fucker*, she thought. Ol' Major Pain was a sneaky bastard, launching his attack on her body. And like most good resistance fighters, she didn't feel the aches until she moved. Jane had done fine up on that horse, but once she gave up her position, that bastard let loose, placing a stronghold on her knees, detonating mini roadside bombs in her joints, and fast-roping her tendons with sharp, stabbing pricks. As Major Pain's minions went to regroup, Jane called in for backup—meaning, she headed for her bedroom and her kit, searching for her meds. She downed a handful of pharmaceutical soldiers to strengthen her front line so she could enjoy the night.

When Jane went back outside, she lowered herself onto the porch swing. It had probably been hanging on the porch since the day the house was constructed in the early 1900s. It was likely made from the weathered leftover slats of decking. The extra length of swinging loose chain rapped gently against the taught metallic cuffs that held the rickety, splintered seat. The clanking sound bothered her as she swayed back and forth, waiting for her meds to kick in. *Why doesn't anyone ever cut off those extra lengths of clinking fetters?* she thought, irritated. They sounded like prison chains to Jane. Like many soldiers and Marines, she was easily distracted and annoyed by everyday things most people wouldn't notice. The rhythmic *rap-tap, rap-tap* made it difficult for her to ponder her situation on the Stapelton farm. Her simple trip to attend a going-away party had turned into a protracted visit. *Fucking swing,* she said to herself.

Maxine must have sensed Jane's mood shift because she trotted happily through the grass toward Jane, making a few pee stops along the way. Once on the porch, Max jumped onto Jane's lap. Jane scrunched her fingers deep down into Max's coarse gray hair, which instinctively made Max stretch out her hind leg.

"Maxine, I'm always either in some messed-up situation or the cause of a situation. Have you ever noticed that?" Unconsciously, Jane started chewing around her fingernails, gnawing at the tough skin and ripping it until she could taste the metallic blood in her mouth. She tore the skin off, chewed it between her front teeth, and spit it out. Some of the spit sprayed onto Maxine's fur, making her flinch. "Sorry, girl," Jane said as she wiped her bleeding fingers onto Max's furry neck.

Jane sat up slightly as they watched Sam approach. The aroma of savory herbs of oregano, rosemary, and basil trailed out from the kitchen in a thick cloud of sweet butter, past their noses and into the warm New Mexico breeze.

Sam took off his white cowboy hat, and a bead of sweat dripped from his hair onto his shirt. "I hope there's mashed potatoes involved tonight," Sam said, rubbing his stomach.

"Do you even doubt that?" Jane asked, raising an eyebrow.

"Come on, you two cowpokes," Eugene said, shoving his head out of an open window. "You know your grandma doesn't like to serve cold food. Come on in and get washed up so we can eat outside. And hurry. I'm starvin' to death. I'm likely to waste away."

Marlene hustled back from the picnic table and scooted inside; Sam and Jane followed. Maxine rushed over to Marlene, who was placing a small plate of fried chicken cut into cubes, mashed potatoes, and corn off the cob—all covered in gravy—onto a placemat on the floor.

"Marlene, she shouldn't eat that. She's a dog," Jane said.

"Yes. She *is* a dog," Marlene replied, "which is *exactly* why she should eat that. It's chicken. Plus, it makes her feel like she's a wild coyote. Look at her tearing up that chicken. She's happy. A happy, wild dog." Marlene looked at Maxine proudly and wiped her hands on her apron.

"It has gravy on it, Marlene. And buttered corn." Jane paused, "Okay, okay, you're right. She's completely wild." There were some battles Jane knew not to fight with Marlene, and many of them involved food. Jane proceeded to the bathroom to wash up for dinner.

As she made her way back into the kitchen to mix up her protein drink, Marlene whisked past Jane toward the front door with a large dish of hot, sweet yams with the butter still sizzling.

"Oh, Lord," Jane groaned. She couldn't imagine what kind of dinner spread awaited them after hearing the breakfast menu that morning. Eugene had managed to dodge the subject that morning, but Jane felt Marlene should know she couldn't physically digest solid food.

"Wait, Marlene. Ma'am, there's something I should tell you."

Marlene jerked to a halt. "General, I have to get these on the table before they cool off." She proudly held up the yams to Jane so she couldn't fail to notice them. Jane could still hear them popping like a hot fajita skillet coming off a grill. The yams certainly weren't going to cool off any time soon. "Come on, General. Soup's on."

Reluctantly, Jane followed Marlene outside, clutching her bottle of shaken, liquefied protein. Her eyes widened as she neared the picnic table; she was utterly amazed at the colorful banquet gracing the rough-hewn planks of wood. There was scarcely room for silverware among the heaps of mashed potatoes, boats of gravy, platters of fried chicken, towers of corn, stacks of biscuits, and, of course, flaming hot yams.

Eugene seated himself at the end of the long table and tied a big white-linen towel around his neck like a bib. He commenced dishing up mashed potatoes with one hand while pouring gravy with the other. Marlene slathered butter on biscuits like a mason troweling mortar on bricks.

Excitedly, Marlene dragged Jane to the other end of the table and gestured with her arm, hand splayed like the models from *The Price Is Right* when they showcased prizes. Jane couldn't believe her eyes. There must have been twenty different glasses and cups of juice, milk, tea, soda, pudding, applesauce, creamed soup, and ice cream.

Speechless, Jane looked at Eugene, who just gave her a wink. She turned to Marlene, who had the biggest smile on her face, and said, "Marlene, you are a remarkable lady."

The older woman clutched her apron and replied, "Oh come on, now! I'm not half the woman you are, General. Now drink your dinner before it gets cold." Jane laughed as Marlene put Jane's anxiety to rest.

"So, Grandpa, the General and I had an excellent day today. She told me about some missions they did. There was this one guy who wanted to get eaten by a tiger while he was still alive," Sam said, getting the dinner conversation going.

"We don't have to talk about that at dinner, Sam," chided Eugene as he motioned toward Marlene.

"Oh, really, Eugene?" teased Marlene. "But we can talk about war and invasions? I'm not a schoolmarm. For goodness sake, I talk about all kinds of nasty things when you're not around." Marlene turned to Jane and whispered loudly, "I even cuss up a storm sometimes." She swooshed her napkin at Eugene.

"Really, Grandma? You? Cussing?" Sam was curious.

"Okay, well, just the other day, I called Emma Smith a frumpy ass. She was *pissed*," Marlene chortled.

Eugene, Sam, and Jane all sat there quietly for a minute and thought about what Marlene had just said. Almost in unison, they sputtered, "We should talk about military stuff after dinner."

"What? Come on! That was some tough, mean talk comin' from me! Emma was really upset." Marlene laughed and placed another ear of corn onto Eugene's plate. Jane sensed Marlene was putting on an innocent front.

Just then, a car pulled up and parked. "I wonder if Mackey is finally coming up for air and joining us for dinner." Eugene laughed, his smile sporting bits of corn.

A deep voice answered from across the yard. "No, no. Don't get your pacemaker all de-fiber-lated you, old fart. It's just me." Earl sauntered across the grass, dusting off his hat and wiping his hands on his jeans. He placed his tan leather jacket on a picnic bench, further exposing his impressive turquoise belt buckle. Earl was also wearing his infamous, clinking bolo tie.

"I don't have a de-fiba-lator pace-paker, you fool. Who invited you? Or did you just smell the corn from the road?" Eugene asked as he motioned for Sam to scoot over to make room on the bench, then handed Earl a plate and an ear of corn.

"I just come over to give the general some top-secret CIA documents regarding national security, for your information," Earl proclaimed as he cleared his throat and straightened his posture, alluding to his self-importance. He captured the family's undivided attention as he leaned over and pulled an envelope from his jacket pocket. No one appeared more intrigued than Sam. "I still have my connections," said Earl, winking at Sam.

"What in hell's shitbag are you up to, Earl?" asked Eugene as he attempted to grab the envelope.

"Nothing. I just have some information for the general that I happen to know has been suppressed. I thought she might like to have it, that's all. Can I have some of that gravy? And some mashed potatoes and chicken?"

"Earl, you don't work for the CIA anymore and the general is our guest. She doesn't need Tonto pokin' around in secret documents. Now get your hands off that gravy boat 'til I'm through talkin'!" chided Eugene, slapping at Earl's hands.

Jane interrupted, "Eugene, I'm sure it's fine. I'd like to see what Earl went to the trouble to get me." She reached over the table and took the envelope from Earl, who huffed at Eugene. As she scanned through the papers, the rest of the family clanged their silverware into their plates and continued eating, trying very hard not to ask her about the contents of the envelope. Sam scanned Jane's poker face hard for any kind of sign while Eugene eyed Earl suspiciously until Jane scooted back on the bench slightly and relaxed. She felt them all exhale as a group.

"Thank you for taking the time to find this, Earl," she said at last. "I'm sure you had to dig pretty deep to get this information."

"Well, what *is* it?" Sam finally burst out.

"Nothing, really. It's just some stuff about my mom, my dad, and me. I did know about this, Earl," Jane confided.

"You *did?*" Earl looked a bit deflated. Jane supposed it was somewhat thrilling for him to use his "connections" and uncover what he believed to be a dark secret. He did a good job; Jane liked Earl. "I thought it might've been some sort of burden or something you'd been carrying around," Earl continued.

"Would you two Mata Haris like to enlighten the group or should we talk about the weather or Mrs. Baumstetter at the post office?" Eugene asked.

"Sorry," replied Jane. "I suppose back in 1961 this would have been top-secret classified information. Now it's just . . . it's just what it is." Jane proceeded to fill in Tom's family on the details of the story regarding her mom and Howser in Argentina and Operation OVIDA. And about how her mother had been used by the President as a sacrificial lamb and subsequently became a security risk.

"I imagine the President was worried my mother would have a change of heart and expose the operation. He watched her and my father diligently. Before they left for their mission in Siberia, during her standard medical exam, the doctor discovered she was pregnant. A report detailing her condition was sent to the President," Jane said, holding up the medical report. "They didn't tell my mom or Howser."

"How do you not know you're pregnant?!" Sam interjected.

Marlene took over the conversation. "Are you kiddin'? I think I was nearly halfway through my pregnancy with your Aunt Betty before we even had a notion. Back in those days, we didn't have home pregnancy tests or ultrasonic machines like they have now. You just kept workin', cookin', and cleanin' right up to the day you gave birth. If y'all really wanna know, the doctor used a rabbit and injected it with . . . hmmm. I don't remember if it was blood or urine from the woman. Anyhow, that indicated, some way, that you were pregnant. I think they had to kill the rabbit or somethin' to find out the results."

"Seriously? That's the weirdest thing I ever heard," Sam blurted out.

"I can also tell you," Jane chimed in, "that as a female agent, you're always under duress. Nothing in your body is regular. You're nauseous and weak one moment and strong the next. If my parents hadn't planned the pregnancy, they wouldn't have known about it."

"And then, back in those days, there were no other options for women," Marlene went on. "I don't imagine secret female agents could just slip off quietly to a distant relative's house, have a child, give it up for adoption, then continue her spy life."

"What about abortion?" Sam asked.

"Sam!" Marlene said, raising her voice. "Perhaps you've forgotten that the baby we are talkin' about is your Aunt Jane. Thank the Lord that *wasn't* an option."

Eugene stepped in, shaking his head at Sam. "There wasn't such a thing then, Sam. Well, maybe for some, somewhere, as an experiment. But it was illegal and dangerous."

"It wouldn't have mattered," Jane broke in. "This is a key piece of classified intelligence," Jane said, holding up another document. "Chambers saw this as an opportunity. He believed sending my mother on a dangerous mission in Siberia would get her out of the way. He wouldn't have to kill her personally. His plan worked, except that my father returned with me, alive."

"Oh, Christ!" Sam edged forward and put his head in his hands.

"Sam, watch your mouth," Marlene scolded gently.

"However, Chambers, as opportunistic as he was, suggested to Howser that I might possess certain genetic skills, being the offspring of two elite agents. He used Howser's vulnerable frame of mind to convince him it would be best to have me placed with a foster family until I was old enough to enter Orion. Then, in 1961, they conceived the plan to construct the training school in Pretoria."

"How did Uncle Tom get into that school?" asked Sam. Jane looked at Eugene to see whether he would answer Sam's question.

"Alright," began Eugene, "since we're spilling family secrets—"

"That was a long time ago," Marlene interrupted as she started clearing the dishes from the table. "We have hot cobbler to eat."

"Come on, Marlene," Eugene wheedled. "It's my fault. We know it's my fault. If I hadn't gotten Tom into that school, he might still be alive."

"Oh, cool it," said Marlene, clamping down on the story. "We've had enough spy talk for one night. Let's eat some cobbler. You mentioned Mrs. Baumstetter down at the post office. What was she saying anyway? She's always pokin' around about that Monsanto business. She started a thing called a 'blog' about it. Do you know what a blog is, Sam?" Marlene succeeded. They weren't going to talk about Tom.

After dinner, Jane stepped away to enjoy a smoke. She wandered over to where Maxine was pestering the Great Pyrenees. Despite Maxine's efforts to get the farm dog to play, he still refused to abandon his post near the goats. Jane sat on the ground to watch. Entertained by this spectacle, Jane hadn't noticed that Marlene had come up and sat down beside her.

"Would you mind if I had one of those, General?" Marlene asked, rubbing her hands on her apron and motioning to Jane's cigarette.

"No, heck no! But I didn't know you smoked," Jane declared. Jane knew Eugene enjoyed an occasional cigar, but Marlene didn't strike Jane as a smoker.

"Oh, I haven't smoked since Sam and Mackey arrived for good. I didn't want to be a bad example for the boys, as they were so young."

Jane lit a cigarette for Marlene and handed it to her. Marlene took a long, slow drag. Jane could see the immense satisfaction Marlene got from the inhale. As she exhaled, Jane watched the smoke drift through the air and disappear.

"Thank you for my special liquid dinner tonight. That was very thoughtful," Jane said, trying not to disturb Marlene's interlude with too much dialog.

"I just want you to be comfortable," Marlene said.

Jane admired her sincerity. "Marlene, I can't even tell you how comfortable I feel here. I love this place. This farm is incredible. Before I left for military school, I lived on a farm like this, so this place feels like home to me."

"We never knew much about your life before you met Tom," Marlene said quietly. "We knew that you lived in Africa most of the time and spent many years in Virginia and Washington, DC."

"Howser kept a pretty tight lid on my childhood. Well, he kept a tight lid on just about everything."

They sat in silence for a moment, smoking their cigarettes. Jane looked around the vast land in front of her. "Like I said, I grew up on a farm like this one. My foster parents were the kindest, most loving people in the world," Jane reminisced.

"Oh, my. That must've been a wonderful childhood," noted Marlene, placing her hand on Jane's shoulder. "There's nothing like the bounty of God's earth to ground a child," she said, sounding just like Tom. He had talked about God a lot.

"It was breathtaking at times," Jane went on. "I had the best foster parents, grandparents, great-grandparents, and even a brother. All my great-uncles were war heroes, so I grew up listening to their stories. I had so many animals there—from cows to barn cats. I truly loved that place." Jane took a drag of her cigarette and pictured her treehouse in her grandma's backyard. She couldn't even remember how many times she and her brother had rebuilt that treehouse, adding levels and windows.

"How long were you there before you went to Africa?" Marlene asked curiously. She looked sad that she had finished her cigarette, and she put it out in the grass. For the first time since Jane arrived, Marlene had stopped twisting her hands in her apron.

"When I was almost eight, Howser showed up with a major to pick me up."

"Oh, honey!" cried Marlene. "You must've been devastated to have to leave your family like that."

Jane suddenly realized Marlene had stopped calling her "General" and was now calling her "honey." Jane thought that, perhaps, she had finally connected with Marlene and could relate to her on the same level, rather than having Marlene wait on her. Marlene was always overly nice to Jane, but Jane never felt close to her.

"It was tough leaving," Jane explained, "but I think it must've been in my blood to move on. I was ready to leave the day my foster parents told me about my future. I had always wanted to go to military school. I loved everything about the military from the time I was a small child. My brother and I watched old John Wayne movies and played anything military that had to do with guns. Howser promised me I'd be able to see my family again if I did well in my training."

Jane offered Marlene another cigarette and let her smoke it in silence, watching her savor it. "Marlene, do you think it would be possible for you to call me Jane instead of General? I'd feel more comfortable."

Marlene paused a long time before answering. "You know what, General?" she said as she stood up, "I think I'm gonna take a little walk and have some quiet time, if you don't mind." She held up her cigarette like it was a Fourth of July sparkler. Jane had never seen someone relish smoking so much. "I have to go clear my head," Marlene explained.

"Is everything okay?" Jane asked. Jane noticed Marlene's use of "General" and sensed a subtle change in her tone of voice.

"You know, General," Marlene responded, "you should be thankful you have that family to go home to if you want. At least they know you aren't dead."

With a start, Jane realized Marlene was thinking about her sons, Tom and Elijah. Jane felt comfortable talking earlier to Sam about his uncles, but she didn't feel that way with Marlene. Jane just felt flat-out shitty that Marlene would never see Tom again. Survivor's guilt again. Jane didn't want the topic to come up in conversation and then feel the blame.

Jane got up and started walking across the grass in a different direction than Marlene when she heard Sam yell from across the yard, "General! Wait up!"

"Hey, Sam! That was quite a meal, wasn't it? Your grandma is quite a lady."

"Yeah, but she's probably going to kill Grandpa the way she's feeding him," Sam acknowledged. Sam pointed at Eugene, who had fallen asleep in his rocking chair on the porch, with his hands resting on his round belly. "Let's go for a little walk."

"Sure," agreed Jane. "Is it okay if I go find Maxine first? She wandered off while I was talking to your grandma and I feel like I've been neglecting her. She'd probably like a good walk. We're usually no more than three feet apart," Jane said laughing. She was actually surprised Max felt so comfortable at the farm. Usually she would be more anxious in unfamiliar surroundings.

Jane and Sam headed back toward the barns and split up, looking for Maxine. Jane figured the best place to look for Max would be by the goats and chickens—anywhere the Pyrenees hung out. Max appeared to enjoy bugging that dog.

"Found her!" Sam yelled, coming around the corner of the pig barn. "You are *not* going to believe this," Sam said as he doubled back to the barn.

When they arrived, they saw Maxine in a game of tug-of-war over a piece of rope with the farm dog. The big dog flung her to the ground as she growled at him, then he tossed the rope in the air and ran away from her. Maxine took off after him, barking as he turned and rolled playfully in the hay. Max had finally gotten him to abandon his post.

"Well, I'll be damned," Jane exclaimed. "This is like a magical farm. I guess Maxine is fine! Let's go."

They wandered down the long dirt drive. Jane was glad she'd grabbed her coat. Even on the hottest days in the New Mexico desert, the nights could reach temperatures as low as forty or fifty degrees when the sun went down.

Sam shuffled alongside Jane. He walked with his head down but kept looking over at Jane until she finally asked him, "What is it you want to ask me, Sam?"

Sam laughed and stopped walking. "How did you know?"

"Oh, wild guess, I suppose," Jane said as she nudged him.

"Were you ever able to have a normal relationship after Uncle Tom passed? I'm sorry if that's a loaded question. I haven't heard of anyone in your life since, and maybe there wasn't room for that, but, well, I just wondered and . . ."

"It's okay, Sam," Jane said, smiling. "I'll tell you. Yes. His name was Robert. And he was a civilian. I made an attempt to do normal things with him, like go to barbecues with people I didn't know or like." Jane continued smiling. "Robert was a total wuss."

Sam busted up laughing. "You were going out with a *wuss*? I can't imagine that. How'd *that* work out for you?" Jane shoved Sam toward the side of the road, nearly knocking him over.

"Good Lord! You are *tiny* but you just about laid me out!" Sam said, looking shocked.

"Jeezuz, Sam! That was just a little shove! You better toughen up," Jane laughed. She began to tell him about Robert and the barbecue as they continued down the dusty road as the sun set, leaving only a silhouette of the mountains in the distance.

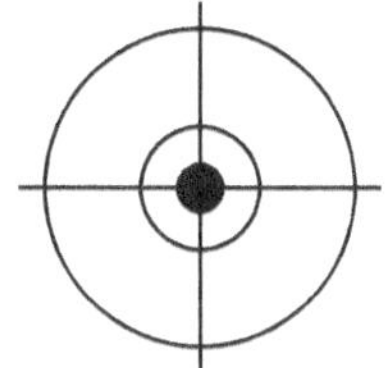

CHAPTER FOURTEEN

"How'd you convince anyone at the barbecue that you were just a regular person?" Sam asked as he kicked up dirt on the road with the tip of his worn cowboy boot.

"Well, that barbecue was sort of a disaster because I assumed I knew what I was getting myself into. I thought that a casual gathering with a bunch of people throwing burgers and steaks on a grill and hanging out would be no big deal. I'd done that with my team plenty of times, so I didn't put much forethought into it. I put on my favorite tank top and jeans and drove over to the address Robert had given me."

Sam chewed on a piece of sweetgrass he had plucked from the roadside as he imagined the scene. "When I got there," Jane went on, "I realized pretty quickly that I wouldn't make very many female friends at that gathering. I stayed in my truck for a bit and watched a few women wobble up the front steps in clunky high-heeled shoes and wispy, flowered sundresses. It was as if they were going to a New York City fashion show rather than a backyard barbecue with a bunch of SWAT guys and firefighters. Their attire was certainly unfitting for a Podunk, rural Virginia town of about eighteen hundred people. I sat there laughing to myself as they adjusted the straps on their dresses, put on lipstick, and twirled their hair into perfect ringlets before walking through the door. And the goddamn shoes! They looked like newborn giraffes attempting their first unsteady steps, and they swarmed into the house carrying casseroles, cakes, and neon green Jell-O molds. Ugh."

"And you were wearing jeans and a tank top! I bet you didn't even comb your hair," Sam laughed.

"I also didn't bring a goddamn Jell-O mold," Jane groused. "Shit! And why do girls need to wear all that stuff? It can't be comfortable. What if someone starts up a softball game or flag football? No one would pick them to play!"

"Um, Aunt Jane, girls like that don't play flag football at parties," Sam explained as he scratched his head. "They sit around and look pretty and let the guys play the sports. They aren't supposed to get dirty." He was obviously proud to be informing *Jane* of something this time.

"Good Christ, that pisses me off," Jane shot back. "They have no idea how much fun they're missing. They're forfeiting most of life sitting on the sidelines, afraid to get dirty. At least those women certainly were."

"You didn't just stay in your truck and gawk at the Stepford Wives, did you?"

"Nah. I eventually went inside, regardless of my first impressions. Robert introduced me first to his foul-mouthed, weekend-warrior fire department captain. This guy apparently spent most of his time in his office surfing Internet porn, rather than investigating fires and setting up fire inspections for the whole two-mile radius he was in charge of. Robert hoped to remove that 'stain' from the department by vying for his position."

"Sounds like a real winner," Sam snorted.

"After Robert introduced me, the captain put Robert in a headlock and forced his body in my direction and said, 'Holy shit, bro! Who the fuck is this hot chick? She's four-alarm! She looks like SWAT. I tell you, she can sure swat me!' All the time he talked, he was hacking and wheezing, trying to force down a giant ball of phlegm that was stuck in his throat."

"Robert must have been pissed!"

"Ohhhhh yeah. I could see Robert cringing physically at the thought of the captain pawing at me. He choked out, 'What makes you think a girl like that would want anything to do with a fat, old, bald fire captain, bro?'

"Robert knew the captain was already drunk and told him to watch his language in front of me. He kept apologizing to me for the fact that the captain 'cussed like a Marine.' If he only knew!" Jane said laughing. "Smith then held out his gross, plump hand with these short, stubby Vienna sausage fingers. I gave him a weak handshake as I looked him up and down and wondered if this guy had *any* self-respect."

"Clearly not!" Sam said. "Gross."

"As we walked away, Robert said to me, 'You gotta excuse the captain. He's a small-town guy who doesn't get out much. I'm doing my best to get him stationed somewhere more appropriate.' Robert tried to protect me, which I really didn't need, but I thought it was sweet and went along with it."

"I can't see you holding anything back. You just seem to tell it like it is. That must've been frickin' hard for you to stay cool."

"I just found a spot to sit and watch while Robert mingled. I avoided talking too much. I watched the manicured women as they scurried to cater to their out-of-shape, beer-guzzling husbands, who all sat around boasting about the glory days. The wives probably believed the party wouldn't have been possible without them. Those women thought of everything—from the placement of the food to the Mason jars filled with white flowers to the deviled eggs sprinkled with paprika and topped with a minuscule sprig of parsley. These ladies carefully considered each and every detail, all of which were missed entirely by their drunken spouses. I kind of felt bad for them. Those women actually thought coasters, beer cozies, and cork-heel platform shoes mattered, and that people cared. Who were they trying to impress? Each other, I guess.

"You're being mean, Aunt Jane. Some women like that stuff. I see them do that all the time."

"I don't think they really enjoy it," Jane continued. "I think they do it to get attention, knowing full well they aren't *ever* going to get that affirmation. Then they feel unappreciated and it gives them something to complain about. The problem is, most women won't admit they do this or aren't even aware they're doing it. Being the 'pretty girl,' making everything pretty, and strutting around in ridiculous, painful shoes because they are pretty makes them feel validated. Oh! And for Christ's sake! They don't ever put on a fucking coat when it's cold because men can't see their fucking body!" Jane said, raising her voice.

"What are you talking about?"

"Sam, how many girls do you see running around freezing their asses off, prancing around in their supposed high-fashion attire?

They're just trying to look good for some bozo dude in his leather Armani jacket and high-thread-count scarf, all fucking warm, while the trophy girls die of pneumonia and look like hookers!" Jane ranted as she turned to look Sam in the face.

"I don't really see that around here. I like my girl in a nice flannel shirt, good jeans, and some riding boots, actually," Sam said, blushing slightly. "I mean, a dress is nice too, but with some nice boots. I want her to be able to go dancing or for a walk," he said. Jane liked that Sam was down-to-earth and unimpressed by flashy women.

"Exactly," Jane affirmed. "I think a real pretty girl is far more natural, takes less time to get ready, and is a lot more comfortable in her own skin." She could tell Sam wanted her to ask him about the girl, but she held back from asking any questions. She knew they'd get to that sooner or later.

"Well, I eventually got tired of watching the hoity-toity scene unfolding in front of me, so I strolled across the lawn and played commando games with some of the kids. We tossed rocks like grenades and fired sticks as if they were rifles. A few of Robert's SWAT buddies egged him on as they watched me play with the kids. Jake was particularly interested and asked Robert if I was military. He had seen my G.I. tats."

"Uh-oh. That must've given you away."

"It may have. Robert had to explain that 'Elizabeth' is just one of those unconventional chicks who *appears* to be tough, and that the closest I ever got to the military was my ROTC high school boyfriend," she said laughing. "He told Jake I was just 'one smokin'-hot sales rep.' Later, I saw Robert speaking to Jake, who had this thick handlebar mustache and deeply creased brow. He made me uneasy. I saw Robert shove Jake and puff himself up to appear larger than his five-foot seven-inch height. I felt like I'd seen Jake before but couldn't place him. Jake then nudged another guy in the group, causing him to choke on a lip full of chewing tobacco. I overheard him say, 'Listen to her call signs! I swear she just told your kid to circle the goose! And called him *stinger*! She sure looks more like Special Forces than Special Sales Rep.' That's when I started to get a little worried.

"Robert said to Jake, 'Get out, man! She reads *Guns & Ammo* instead of *Good Housekeeping* and she loves those tough-guy movies, but she's not a soldier. Plus, buddy, she watches *me*—the ultimate warrior.' He flexed his rather unimpressive right bicep and I held back my smile."

"Wow. So what happened, next?"

"Jake turned to his friends and told them to challenge me, asking for a coin for a toss-up on who was going to do it. They all reached into their pockets at the same time to pull out handfuls of SWAT challenge coins. Their coins are oversized meritorious rounds engraved with a seal of merit on one side and the year and location of issue on the other. Fortunately, to these guys, a challenge consists of arm wrestling or grappling, and the winner gets a beer and the coin. Little did they realize that, to an Orion soldier, a challenge is an ultimate one, such as the Killing Circle, where the winner reigns supreme and the loser dies."

"No way!" Sam exclaimed as he rubbed his forehead.

"Yes way!" Jane retorted. "Jake flexed his stubby arms and shouted over to me, 'Hey! G.I. Jane!' And I said, 'Excuse me? What did you say?' I realized my confrontational tone may have blown my cover. Jake pointed to my G.I. Jane tattoo and snarked, 'What. Are you *antimilitary?*'

"I explained to him the tattoo 'keeps me motivated' and if I tattoo my arms, I have to keep them in shape. You know, no one would want to see a tattoo if it were on a big fat arm like his. I tried to talk my way out of the situation."

"He wasn't buying it?"

"Not really. The guy was a relentless meathead. Then I wondered, *Who would tattoo G.I. Jane on her arm if she was antimilitary?* Then he said, 'You must be pretty tough,' sounding disgusted. Jake was probably one of those typical wife beaters hiding behind the badge. Keep the wife oppressed."

"Really? You think he was one of *those* guys?

"Women with confidence scare guys like that," Jane explained. "The man was so weak that his only tools were violence and barbarism. His thinking came from a reptilian brain. If a woman stood strong by his side, he'd probably beat the shit out of her." Jane felt Sam should know how to spot guys like this. He was sure to encounter some. Maybe he could get through to one or two of them along the way. Sam was one of the good guys—honest and respectful toward women—having been raised by Marlene.

"Did you kick his ass?" Sam asked as he punched the air in front of him.

"Robert tried to redirect the situation by telling Jake I'd never even taken a self-defense class." Sam covered his mouth, muffling his laughter.

"Sam, at that point, I couldn't imagine myself stepping down. I wanted to go for his guts and emasculate the guy on the spot. But I knew I needed to keep my cover as a sales rep who had never taken a self-defense class. My inner ego screamed at me to punch him in the sternum while landing a blow to the throat, but I didn't kill him and I let my better judgment guide me. Unfortunately, he came at me."

"Oh my God! What'd you do?"

"I really detested his knuckle-dragging display of machismo. I let that chauvinistic jerk-off spew his Barney Fife, Mayberry, bullshit for ten minutes. Then he started displaying his hometown, self-taught, grab-my-shirt attack tactics. I let him hit me in the nose, which immediately began spewing blood. I dropped to the ground, shedding fake tears, which ensured my cover would remain intact in case anyone was suspicions about G.I. Jane. No Special Forces soldier would *ever* be dropped by a punch from Barney—and they certainly wouldn't cry over it."

"Whew! Saved!" yelled Sam, throwing his arms in the air.

"Of course I knew, as I sat on the ground, pretending to be hurting, that in *my* world I could have taken on ten of those jerk-offs and fought them right to the death. But I had to suck it up. If I wanted to walk among civilians and go to barbecues and talk with SWAT wives about the weather, I'd better cry at an accidental bloody nose. Pretending to be vulnerable upset me almost as much as realizing I was never going to be able to live a regular life as long as I was in Orion."

"Did anyone *help* you? You were *bleeding*, for God's sake!"

"Well, Sam, I sat on the ground bleeding and not one woman stepped in to help me. A few of them even turned away when Jake punched me. Those were the women I was certain were being beaten at home by these assholes. Robert ended up running to my side with a towel. He turned to Jake and yelled, 'Jesus Christ, you moron! You hit a girl!'"

"And Jake? What did he do?"

"Jake stammered and told Robert he thought I was a Navy SEAL. Robert was clearly mortified and he just knelt beside me and wiped the blood gently from my face. Any other girl might've been cooing at this treatment, but I was mad and just grabbed the towel from him. I wanted Robert to turn on Jake and pound him into the ground, defend my honor! My dad would've done that for me. My team definitely would have. Shit! *Women* even back each other up. I see that all the time. Robert just rolled over and exposed his belly in submission. Loser."

"So you didn't just pummel the guy?"

"No, Sam. I couldn't. But when I was certain no one was paying attention, I locked eyes with Jake and shot him a steely-eyed stare. It hit him like daggers. It read: 'Later I will kill you and feed you your balls for dinner, you cocksucker.' He certainly got my point. As a matter of fact, he came closer to me; I thought he was going to apologize. Instead, he whispered, 'I know who you are . . . General.'"

"*What*?!" Sam yelled. "What'd you say?"

"I just whispered, 'Fuck if you do, asshole. If you say *anything* you'll be dead by morning. I promise you that.' Turns out his dad was Commander Ruggers. Jake said he 'wouldn't say shit,' then reached out and shook my hand. I felt sorry for him. Ruggers' kid. No wonder he was such a prick. And a dumb prick too. *Just* like Ruggers. Who the *hell* tells an undercover covert operative they know you're an undercover covert operative, but don't worry because they won't tell anyone?" Jane let Sam ponder what she had just told him and held back from disclosing aloud what happened later.

After her encounter with Jake ended, Jane waited a few minutes before slipping inside to page Howser with code F2460 to inform him of the security breech. He responded with the affirmative P2269, then dispatched Screech. Before long, he arrived covertly in the alley behind the house. As Jake left for a beer run, Screech pursued him, forced Jake's car off the road, jumped out, grabbed him from his ride, and hauled him into the van.

"Hellooooo, lover boy!" Screech announced gleefully, "Got something for you!" He landed a knockout blow to Jake's face, then drove him to an abandoned lot. Jude, Pilot, and Butch were waiting to assist.

"You suppose we should've just had him sign some sort of waiver stating he won't tell anyone what he knows?" Pilot asked, laughing a little at his flippant suggestion.

"Nah, I think he might need a little more sugar than that, boys. Not sure he can sign a piece of paper with this broken hand." Jude proceeded to crush Jake's hand as Butch covered Jake's mouth to muffle his scream.

"I *am* worried, though. It appears he has pretty sharp vision. Looks like he might have seen us all now," Screech observed. Screech wasn't convinced Jake would keep his mouth shut. He forced open one of Jake's eyelids as Jake struggled against the team holding him. Screech held up his infamous Jack Field hunting knife, waved it in front of Jake's eye, and said, "Seems like I could just pluck these out and then we wouldn't have to worry about that." Jake panicked and struggled to pinch his eyes shut.

"I don't know, brother," Butch chimed in. "I gotta pretty good grip on his head. I could probably just give it a *little* twist. Just enough to paralyze him for life. 'Course, if I get it wrong, I might just snap his neck."

By that time, Jake had pissed his pants, but the shock and fright of the latest threat caused him to pass out.

"Oh, shit. You win," groused Screech as he took out five dollars and handed it to Butch. Jude was already digging in his pockets for a five-spot.

"Son of a bitch! That's not *fair*!" Pilot piped up, looking at Jake's limp body on the ground. "I didn't even *get* my chance with him."

"Yes, you did," Jude noted. "You asked him if he wanted to sign a waiver. Ooooo, now that's scary."

"I didn't know that was my *turn*! Wait a minute! I didn't know we had already started!"

"Too bad, so sad," chuckled Butch as he counted his money.

They waited for another ten minutes before a van showed up with some agents to collect Jake for his debriefing with Howser. After Howser finished with him, there was *no way* Jake was going to talk.

Jane didn't think Sam could fully comprehend the measures they needed to take to protect her. Jake had been a security threat and the team had followed Howser's orders, as they always did. Well, sometimes they added their own pizzazz.

"Okay, so you don't do well around civilians," Sam said, jolting Jane back to the present.

"The point I'm trying to make, Sam, is that sometimes you mess up and crave a regular life. You see people having barbecues and being with family, and you start to think you're missing something, so you try to function in both worlds. When you do this, the worlds start to bleed into each other. You can't help who you are. Bottom line: You can't be in an organization like Orion and have feelings for friends and family and lovers. You have to turn the outside world off and accept that you'll never get to have that."

"But you can't turn *everything* off. That's impossible. You have to have bonds with people, right?" Sam stopped and looked Jane directly in the eyes. "A human being can't live without love," he said passionately. She admired his conviction; he wasn't aware of her internal struggle over the years.

"Sam, I have loved more deeply than you can imagine, for longer than I can remember. The greatest pain I have *ever* endured was the loss of your uncle. If I had one day of my life to change, it would be the day Tom was killed saving my life. That should've never happened."

Sam dropped down and sat in the middle of the dirt road. He cupped his face in his hands and swallowed hard. Jane just stood there. She felt a burning inside her chest and her heart rate began to increase; she knew she was headed for a PTSD episode. She gritted her teeth to fight back tears. As she fought the grief swelling inside her, she knew she had to clamp down on it. This was not the time for her to lose control.

Sam looked up at her and said sternly, "If you think I don't know what it's like to lose someone you love more than anything, you can go fuck yourself, General." He got up and turned away from Jane without saying another word. They walked back to the house in silence, then went in different directions.

After a while, Jane headed down the hallway toward her room. She noticed a sliver of light peeking out from beneath the door that led to Tom's room when he was a boy. Jane thought Sam might be in there, needing comfort, so she cautiously opened the door a bit. She saw Marlene sitting on the bed in her bathrobe, with her long hair released from its usual captive bun. Marlene held a cigarette in one hand and a photograph in the other. Then she stood up and let the cigarette hang from her lips as she taped a picture of Tom to the dresser mirror. Marlene took a long drag from the dangling cigarette and reached into a cigar box to pull out another photograph. She picked up a pair of scissors that rested on the dresser and began to cut the photo. Jane recognized the picture of her and Tom. Marlene taped another photo of Tom to the mirror. She picked up another and applied the scissors to it surgically. Jane continued to watch as images of herself fell away from Tom's onto the floor.

"There, there, General," Marlene said quietly as she spoke to the fractured picture of Jane she held in her hand. "Men make sacrifices for their countries. And mothers—well, mothers make sacrifices for their sons." She leaned over and picked the pieces up off the floor, then tossed the scraps of Jane's images back into the box, twisting out her cigarette on them.

Jane closed the door quietly, without saying a word, and continued down the hallway to her room. Visions of Tom flooded her mind as she lay down on her bed. Jane couldn't blame Marlene for her feelings toward her. If she were a regular person like Marlene, she'd probably feel the same way, given the situation. But there was nothing regular about Jane. Born into this life, she knew all too well how and when to shut down her emotions, blocking them from getting the better of her.

Maxine jumped up on the bed and curled up by Jane's side. As Jane ran her fingers through Maxine's coarse fur, she thought about how Sam wanted to make his grandparents proud by carrying on his family's military legacy. Jane now had confidence in Sam as a Marine, but she still didn't think he fit the mold for Orion. Sam was attached to relationships and he had a lot to lose. The perfect Orion candidate most likely had a pretty severe detachment disorder and, often, displayed psychotic tendencies. Even though Tom and Sam came from the same bloodline, Sam was much more malleable, agreeable, and too "normal" for Orion. Jane and her team, they were a different breed of warrior altogether.

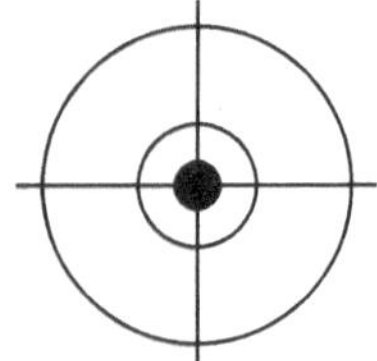

CHAPTER FIFTEEN

Jane lay on the bed beneath the red and ivory hand-sewn quilt that Marlene had placed there, and Maxine snuggled up closer to her. Max had a way of making Jane feel settled when she felt vulnerable.

"Maxine, all my brothers are dead or crazy now, so that means you're stuck with me. You're my best and only friend, my sweetie girl," Jane crooned, scratching Max's scruffy face, in between her eyes, and around her ears. "You have to stay strong and healthy, okay? Nothing can ever happen to you. You know I need you in my life."

Jane grabbed Max's face with both hands and leaned in even closer to her. Maxine looked at her with wide brown eyes as if she understood every word Jane said; Jane had no doubt she did. Jane could feel emotion welling up inside her. She was not only attached to Maxine, she was dependent on her. She never felt loneliness or fear as long as Max was by her side. Jane assumed Maxine would be with her years longer than the normal dog life span, and chose to remain in denial that Max wouldn't. Jane would never have rescued her if she hadn't felt so compelled to do so. Everyone Jane ever loved had died. She couldn't bear the thought of losing Maxine too. Jane looked at Max a while longer, then placed her head on Maxine's side to feel her breathe for a while, knowing it would calm her own nerves and help lull her to sleep.

As Jane started to drift off, she heard a noise outside her door and saw a slip of paper slide underneath it. She kicked off her covers and opened the door quickly to confront the writer of the note. Her instinctive self-defense mode kicked in as she opened the door abruptly and grabbed at any body part she could get her hands on.

"Good God!" Sam squeaked. "You scared the heck out of me! I thought you were sound asleep." Jane pressed him into the doorframe, twisting his body up sideways as she gripped his shoulders.

"Sam, you know better than to sneak up on a Marine." Jane let him go, picked up the note, and read it aloud: "Dear Aunt Jane, I'm sorry for my harsh words earlier. We both lost important people in our lives. I'm looking for guidance on how to be strong, like you, and just how to handle relationships and the possibility of losing them during my time as a Marine. I greatly respect your take on matters such as these and I appreciate any input you're willing to give. Yours, Sam." Jane put the letter on the dresser and looked at Sam.

"Sam, I know it's not easy for you, growing up without your mom and dad. And I do understand how it feels to lose someone close to you. Rebounding from that isn't as easy as you may think, even for me. Well, especially for me." Jane looked at the floor. She could feel her blood begin to churn in her veins as memories began to flood her conscious mind.

"Aunt Jane, I know you understand. I just don't talk about this stuff much and it's easier that way."

"Yeah, I get that." Jane had her own way of burying the past.

"Grandma and Grandpa always say you and Uncle Tom had a special bond even though your marriage was short."

"Yeah, that's true. Sam, the girl you've mentioned—are you serious about her or something?"

Sam blushed. "Well, yes, there *is* a girl I really like, but I'm leaving soon and I can't take her with me, obviously." He laughed awkwardly and leaned back against the dresser. It gave way slightly under his body weight and scooted closer to the wall.

The sound of the dresser legs scraping the wooden planks sent an intense chill through Jane. For a moment, she stopped breathing. It was the same sound the chair had made—the one Tom was seated on—when Sharik made the video. Jane's mind flashed to an image of Tom struggling against his captors. His chair scratched the floor just as the blade slashed across his throat.

Jane began to breathe faster and her heart started pounding as fleeting images of Tom continued to rip through her brain. Sam froze, noticing Jane's breathing had changed. She was looking past him instead of right at him. As Sam went to reach out to touch Jane's shoulder and ask if she was all right, Maxine jumped off the bed and positioned herself between Sam and Jane. Maxine always sensed the exact moment when something triggered Jane's PTSD. It was as if Maxine was trying to tell Jane to shut the door, with Sam safely on the other side.

Jane didn't see Maxine. She began to feel the blood heating up her body and face. Her jaw clenched tightly as she detected an all-too-familiar metallic taste in her mouth. Her mind amplified the scraping sound she'd just heard, drowning out Sam's words. Her body suddenly felt as if it were on fire.

Maxine barked and growled at Sam, warning him to leave. Jane saw Sam's lips moving but couldn't hear his voice over the sound of her own heart beating in her head. Suddenly, she felt herself falling backward, as if she had just stepped out of a plane, her body freefalling at 125 miles per hour. Trauma took hold as Jane's world went black.

Jane woke up in her truck several hours later in the middle of nowhere, covered in blood. When she was fully aware, she turned on the overhead light to do a complete body check to try to figure out where all the blood came from: her or someone else. She felt no pain and found no injuries. She searched the truck cab and truck bed for the source of the blood. She was alone, barefoot, and had none of her possessions.

These episodes had happened a few times before and Jane knew it was useless to try and recall what had occurred. She'd never been able to dig up events that happened during a flashback or blackout. Jane realized she needed to return to the farm as quickly as possible to assess the damage and see if she'd hurt anyone. She started the truck and drove off, leaving a wake of dust on the dirt road behind her. Using the stars as her navigation system, she concluded she was at least forty miles from the farm. As her surroundings began to look more familiar, she picked up speed. When she approached the farmhouse, her stomach sank.

"Oh, shit," she muttered under her breath, as she drove up the driveway and spotted three police cars and a fire truck—all with lights blazing—in front of the house. Marlene, wrapped in a quilt, was sitting on the porch and talking to a deputy sheriff. Her hair had escaped her usual neat bun; it hung all the way to her waist in loose coils. She wiped her nose and her eyes with a tissue.

"Oh, fuck! What did I *do*?" Jane parked the truck, stepped out, placed her hands on her head, and moved in front of the vehicle's headlights.

"Officer!" Jane shouted to the nearest sheriff's deputy. He ran over to her while calling for two paramedics to assist. She expected to be thrown to the ground, handcuffed, and arrested. Instead, a man and a woman escorted her very gently to the fire truck and placed her on a gurney.

"General!" she heard Marlene yell as she leapt off the front porch and ran toward her. Jane cringed and put her arm up to block a punch that was surely coming.

"General, my God! Are you okay? We were worried sick! Where did you go? There's blood on you! Are you hurt?" Marlene blurted out rapid-fire questions as she attempted to hug Jane.

Overwhelmed and surprised, Jane asked, "Did I hurt anyone? Is Sam alright? What about Eugene? Where are they?" The last memory she had of Marlene was watching her cut out Jane's picture from all the photos of Jane and Tom.

Marlene calmly edged in close to her and put her arms around her. "Sweetheart," she whispered, "they're both out looking for you and Maxine."

Jane jumped up and threw the blanket off her shoulders. One of the paramedics attempted to get her to sit back down, but Jane shoved him aside and took off running for the house like a charging bull. She barreled past two officers who tried to stop her and raced down the hallway to the room where she'd been staying. The door lay canted in the hallway, completely off its hinges. The inside of the room looked like it had been hit by a tornado. The contents of the overturned dresser were strewn across the floor. The mirror was shattered and the window panes were broken.

"Jesus! *Fuck!*" Jane said as she stood there assessing the disaster. She had no memory of what had occurred. She walked over the broken bits of mirror carefully and put her boots on. There was no sign of Maxine. As Jane headed back outside, she passed the officers she'd bowled over as she ran into the house. One held a QuikClot on his nose.

"I'm so sorry, officer. I—" Jane threw up her hands and went to find Marlene to ask her what had happened.

"I think it might be best if you let Ryan take care of you until the boys get back," Marlene said as she motioned to a paramedic. "You need to calm down and get your head together." Marlene looked exhausted, showing her age for the first time Jane could remember. Jane felt miserable. She wrecked Tom's family's home, and her best friend was missing.

"*Maxine!*" Jane sobbed and buried her face in her hands. "What did I *do*, Marlene? *Where's Maxine?*"

Marlene put her arms around Jane and rocked her like a child. Perhaps Marlene didn't dislike her as much as Jane thought.

The sun was just starting to crest the horizon when Sam's truck approached the farm. Marlene excused herself to go brew fresh coffee and make breakfast for the emergency responders who remained, in order to keep the focus off Jane and to keep her from getting into trouble, by serving any kind of food and beverage she could whip up.

Eugene got out of the truck with Sam and walked straight toward Jane. As he got closer, she noticed his eyes were red and puffy. She stood up, expecting the worst. Eugene grabbed her in a bear hug and began to weep. She wrapped her arms around him as she fought back tears. He took a step back and wiped his nose on his sleeve.

"I'm sorry, honey," Eugene apologized. "I got emotional just then. I thought I might have lost you. I'm real fond of you. You're like my daughter. I can't have anything happen to you," he said as he rested one of his hands lightly on her head.

"I am so sorry, Eugene. I can't . . ." Jane struggled to find the words to explain her inexcusable actions. "Did you find Maxine?" she asked desperately.

"No, sweetie. We looked everywhere. I don't want to scare you, but Maxine hurt herself going after you. She was cut up pretty bad. There was a lot of blood. I'm afraid the coyotes may have been attracted to the smell and, well, she may not have been able to fight them off."

"*Jesus Christ*! How could I have *done* something like that? She's my whole life! She's all I have left!" Jane sank onto the grass. Agony whirled inside her. She wanted to start screaming and throwing things, but she had to hold it together and force herself to push her feelings down deep. She couldn't afford another emotional outburst.

"*You* didn't hurt that little dog, General. She hurt herself trying to go after you when you left. You took off after you destroyed every-thing in your room, then you broke the window and jumped out. Maxine ran after you and slipped on pieces of broken mirror. Sam tried to help her, but she bit him pretty hard and took off running into the desert after you. We tried to track her but couldn't find a thing. I'm afraid some predator picked her up and carried her off. I don't know where all the blood came from that's on you. You weren't bleeding when you left here," Eugene said, puzzled.

"Eugene—" Jane began as the deputy sheriff walked up and interrupted her to talk to Eugene.

"We're gonna eat some breakfast here, then head on back into town. Marlene says the general will be fine staying here. You'll have to keep an eye on her. And we still have to figure out where all that blood came from that's on her," he said, taking his hat off and rubbing his shiny bald head.

"She'll be fine right here, Bill," said Eugene reassuringly. "I'll look after her."

"Bill, I think you better collect my clothes," noted Jane, "just in case they become evidence in a crime." She knew she could have slaughtered someone that night.

"Yeah, I guess I probably *should* do that, if you don't mind," he replied, clearly more concerned about getting another helping of Marlene's biscuits and gravy than about her bloody clothing.

Jane went inside to change. She slipped her garments into a plastic Ziploc bag and labeled them herself.

Shortly after the responders left the farm, Eugene and Sam began cleaning her room to restore some semblance of normalcy. Marlene led Jane to Eugene's big chair by the fireplace, covered her with her warmest comforter, and made Jane drink a cup of her secret sleeping potion. It worked like a charm, because Jane fell into a deep sleep, waking up hours later to find Sam and Eugene by her side.

As Marlene walked into the room to join the family, Jane was saying, "I am so sorry about last night. I'll get someone to fix everything right away. I'll also be leaving so I don't cause any more trouble for your family, but I have to find Maxine first." With that last comment, Jane tried to stand up; tears filled her eyes. Her legs started to buckle, but Marlene caught her quickly.

"Jane, honey, come look here," said Marlene softly as she half-carried Jane to the porch and opened the screen door. Eugene and Sam followed closely behind them. Marlene continued, "Shep came back with Maxine while you were sleeping. He was out all night looking for her. Poor little critter dragged herself home, with Shep leading the way, probably warding off predators."

Jane walked through the door and saw Maxine. Her midsection was bandaged and she was snuggled into a pile of quilts. Shep—that huge, loving farm dog—had curled himself around her. Both dogs were sound asleep.

"We called the vet and she came out and dressed her wounds. She also gave her some antibiotics and sedatives. She's going to be fine, honey," said Marlene as Jane leaned against her and let the tears flow.

"Thank you, all of you." Jane sighed as she settled down in a chair next to Maxine to keep an eye on her. Sam sat down across from Jane as Marlene and Eugene wandered back into the house.

"Are you okay, Aunt Jane? Last night was pretty scary. I'm sorry if I—"

"Sam, I'm never really okay. It's just that some days are harder than others and some sounds trigger PTSD episodes for me, like what happened last night. Honestly, some have been worse than what happened last night. That's why I don't usually stay with other people. I'm safer being alone."

"Do you have any idea why you have those, um, why you react like that? I mean, I've read some stuff about PTSD, but I've never seen anything like that. Do you know a lot of veterans who go through what you do?"

"Yes, Sam. It's seriously contagious. As a matter of fact, after what you saw last night, you may have been exposed. You better get your shots," Jane quipped, trying to inject some humor into the situation. She knew she probably shouldn't be a smart-ass after everything she'd put the family through, but she couldn't continue to apologize either.

Jane was an expert in self-recrimination. She'd killed thousands of people. She had a journal in which she'd listed the names of the people she could recall, along with the location of the kill. She made up names for the unknown victims, trying hard not to forget a single person. She kept her sins close by. She forced herself to remember what she'd done. Her demons haunted her day and night.

"Aunt Jane, I know PTSD isn't contagious. What I meant to ask is, is it common in the military? Will I suffer from something like this too? Will I subject my family to this?"

"I guess it depends on the type of person you are and what you do in the military. Maybe if you sit in a cubicle all day, blowing up buildings with remote-controlled drones and then go home each night to your wife and comfortable bed, you might not."

In Jane's line of work, PTSD was pretty much guaranteed. She flashed back to one horrific episode and thought sarcastically, *Well, if you lie in a muddy culvert for ten days, pissing and shitting yourself while waiting for a foot patrol of rebel soldiers to pass and then you spring up and shatter one soldier's skull with the butt of your rifle, sending pieces of his brain into your mouth, yeah, you might suffer from a little PTSD. When you have to turn around and rip out the throat of another soldier and disembowel him with your blade, then strangle the next one until his eyes burst out of his sockets, then shoot the rest of the patrol, awash in their blood, that might haunt you. If you dive back into the culvert to avoid more soldiers and a grenade is tossed in front of you and you're forced to haul ass backward into oncoming enemy fire, you might suffer a bit of angst. When you're praying gunmetal is on the way before you die, and you poke your head out of the culvert and spot Apaches lighting up the hillside as a grenade detonates behind you, you might have a bad dream or two. If this is the case, day after day, year after year, yes, you'll have PTSD.* She spared Sam the gory details that ran through her mind. After all, he was more likely to end up flying a drone from a cubicle. *The modern-day soldier*, Jane huffed to herself.

"I don't know if I could do that to my family," Sam went on. "What if I hurt them? Last night, your strength was triple that of a normal person's. And you said . . . Your words were incredibly hurtful." Sam placed his elbows on his knees, then used two fingers to massage his right temple. Jane didn't want to ask what she'd said to Sam. She was keenly aware that the emotional and verbal abuse she suffered from Howser and Dr. Reid often carried on down the line. It hurt Jane to know she had upset Sam in that way, but she didn't have the wherewithal to deal with the situation at that moment. All she could do was put her hand on Sam's forearm. She closed her eyes and took a deep breath.

"Regular people don't understand what veterans go through, Sam. No one does but another vet who's seen action. No matter how hard you try to make both worlds work, and hope your partner understands, it never works. What I had with Tom was different because we were both in the program, both in active combat. We knew exactly what that life asked of us. After he died, I was never able to fit in with anyone outside of Orion. I tried because I craved both worlds. I wanted a relationship where no one got hurt."

Jane took her hand off Sam's forearm, sensing his sudden discomfort. He folded his arms and tilted his head back. She knew she'd just squelched his idealistic vision of having a normal relationship as a member of Orion. And although many soldiers had seemingly healthy relationships, she still wasn't convinced they'd truly work out. There were just too many demons.

"Aunt Jane, I know you've seen a lot. I can't begin to imagine just how much. But I'm not sure I believe you when you say that. Maybe I don't want to believe it." Sam smiled bleakly. Despite the fact that he'd experienced so much loss at such a young age, Sam still held an optimistic view of life and a teenage idealism that Jane couldn't help but find fascinating.

"You and Uncle Tom may have not been 'regular' people," he continued, "but love doesn't know the difference now, does it?" Jane smiled and pointed her finger at him, allowing him to one-up her. Perhaps he had a point. Perhaps Sam had his own way of smoothing out Jane's sharp, jaded edges, intentional or not.

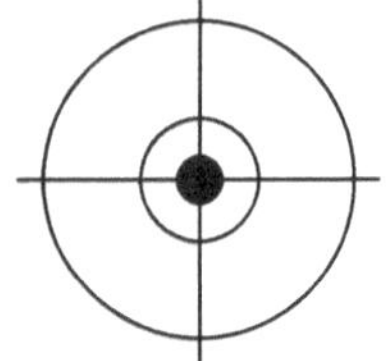

CHAPTER SIXTEEN

Marlene walked up and sat in a chair next to Jane.

"You mind if I join you two?" she asked as she sat down.

"No, not at all," Jane replied.

"Aunt Jane, were you and Uncle Tom able to have a proper wedding?"

"Oh, I was so sad we never got to see that," Marlene remarked. "Tom just called one day and said you two got married. I never heard any details about it." Frankly, Marlene couldn't bear to hear the details and she'd never asked Jane. She resented Jane because Jane replaced Tom as general after he was killed. However, seeing Jane covered in blood the day before, as a result of her PTSD episode, Marlene had gotten a glimpse of the depth of Jane's mental struggles. She also realized Jane probably hurt as much as she did from Tom's death. She felt a sudden empathy for Jane that she'd never felt toward her before.

Jane smiled. "Well, by Orion standards, I suppose we had a proper wedding. We were actually about to jump on a plane to deploy to a yearlong mission in the Congo the day we got married. We didn't have a big ceremony or anything."

"What did that look like? You in a white dress and Tom in a tux—with both of you wearing your combat boots?" Marlene chuckled. She finally wanted to know about the events of that day. She sat back and listened intently as Jane described the scene.

"Not exactly," laughed Jane, "but I'll paint you a picture, Marlene." Jane leaned forward in her chair.

"That morning, we'd assembled in the hangar. The doors were open and sunlight poured in. The glare was almost blinding because it was reflecting off the giant puddles left on the deck from the morning power wash. Screech and Pilot had gone into a small room in the hangar where we kept a bunch of 'toys' to play with while we waited for the plane to be flight ready. You gotta remember that we were still kids, really—only seventeen years old. The guys started a game of basketball but then switched to pelting each other with racquetballs as they hid behind fifty-five-gallon drums. Butch found a Big Wheel buried in the back room. It must've been really old because one wheel was bent out of shape, but that didn't matter to Butch. He scrunched himself into the seat while dodging a flurry of incoming balls. Tom hopped on a kid's scooter and tried to ram him."

Marlene and Sam snickered, imagining the spectacle.

"Then Jude came out of the back room with a huge smile on his face. He was holding a pair of black roller skates in one hand and a Nerf gun in the other. He tried to squeeze his foot into one of the skates, but of course it didn't fit. He was about to cut the toe open with his Ka-Bar so he could jam his foot into the skate when I called him a dumb ass. *I* wanted to try on the skates. I shoved my feet into them and they fit. I stood up and hollered at Tom. He stopped chasing Butch and looked at me. He motioned me to skate over to him."

"So you were an expert at martial arts *and* a roller skater?" Marlene asked.

"Um, not really. I tried to make myself go forward and nearly fell about ten times trying to get to Tom. The guys just busted up laughing at me. Tom walked over, turned his back to me, and told me to put my hands on his shoulders, which I did. Then he walked around the hangar, dragging me around on those darn skates."

Sam snorted. "That's hilarious!"

"Yeah, it was quite the show. Jude laughed and punched Screech on the shoulder and said to him, 'She can kill a man in less than five seconds but she can't roller-skate!'

"As Tom and I rounded a corner, Howser entered the building. I nearly lost my balance and fell—again—but Tom caught my arm. Howser just looked at us and shook his head, then gave Tom a wink and said, 'Alright, let's get started.' His voice sounded like he'd just swallowed a bunch of gravel. I figured they were the first words he'd spoken all morning. In any case, the words sent chills down my spine. Tom and I knew what Howser was about to say—and do—and we couldn't believe he was actually going to keep the promise he made to us the previous night. We'd asked him a dozen times if he'd marry us, and just as many times, he'd refused. That night, however, he said he'd seriously consider it. Tom and I never thought he'd do it. I think we were as caught off guard as the rest of our team."

"*Howser* married you?" Marlene asked.

"Indeed he did." Jane puffed her chest up and lowered her voice to mimic Howser. "'So here we are, in the presence of God and a

C-130 transport. Elizabeth and Tom would like the blessing of God to become man and wife. Today, we honor that commitment. I wish we had more time to do this proper; you both know I'm strongly in favor of this. Now kiss 'er and let's get the hell out of here!'"

"Howser could have done that for you at any time, right? Was he a minister or something?" questioned Marlene.

"Yes *and* no, to answer both of your questions. And we never knew for certain if the marriage was even legitimate or legal. Tom and I took it seriously; we were married. But, looking back, you never really knew what was 'real' in Orion."

"Huh. Okay. Well, I know Tom took it seriously. I could feel him through the phone. He was so full of joy," Marlene said, scratching her hand. "Thanks for telling me this. I've always wondered." She stood up and straightened her skirt, trying to hold back the wave of emotion that suddenly came over her. Ladies like Marlene always held it together in front of others. She turned to Jane. "Can I get you anything, honey?" Jane was relieved she hadn't called her "General."

"No thank you. I'm just fine to sit here a while."

Marlene motioned to Sam. It took him a moment to realize she wanted him to get up and follow her. "Oh, yeah," said Sam as he stood up. "You probably want to rest." Sam and Marlene retreated into the house, leaving Jane with thoughts of the day she married Tom.

It was the best they could do for a wedding, given where they were headed. After the ceremony, Tom kissed her quickly and they all grabbed their rucks and boarded the plane. With a thunderous roar the craft taxied down the runway, bound for the Congo. Jane wanted to run to the back of the plane and cry because she was so happy, but she couldn't allow herself to do that. She was visible from any point in the aircraft and she didn't want to appear "soft" in front of her team. They strapped themselves in along the wall for the long journey. Jane chose to sit across from Tom so she could smile at him. She barely took her eyes off him for the entire trip.

At one point she noticed Screech running his hands over his bearded jaw while he looked at a photo. Jane knew the picture was of his father. Screech wasn't aware of how often he looked at the picture then rubbed his jaw. Jane knew Screech despised his dad. She also knew he grew his scraggly beard to cover up his own "iron jaw." Screech hated the fact that he resembled his father. He grew his hair long to hide the likeness even further. While Screech sat with his own thoughts, Jude and Butch sat together and sorted out sleeping pills.

"Hey Tom-rad!" yelled Jude, rattling a bottle of pills at Tom. "You want some of these? We have human, horse, or elephant strength." Tom rolled his eyes at Jude. Screech held up a rag and quickly put it over Jude's face. Jude slammed into the side of the aircraft—unconscious. Screech held up a vial labeled Chloroform.

"That'll fuckin' do the trick," noted Screech. "Won't have to listen to that bastard for the rest of the flight."

Concerned, Tom unbuckled his harness and headed toward Jude.

"Jude! Wake up!" He loosened Jude's collar and slapped his face to try to wake him, then he took off Jude's harness to allow him to breathe easier. "Screech, you idiot! Seriously? You *had* to do this?"

Screech started laughing as Jude opened his eyes and kissed Tom right on the lips. Surprised, Tom looked at Screech, who drank the contents of the vial. It held plain old water.

"Awww, Tommy! I didn't know you cared about me so much," Jude quipped. "Careful, Jane, I just might steal your man-bride." That time they *all* busted up with laughter.

The plane ride to South Africa was brutally long—about twenty-three hours, with all the stops and transfers. For long trips, Jane usually tossed back a few valium, which could knock out a water buffalo for hours. This time, however, she stayed awake. She wanted to spend some quiet time with Tom. Butch, Jude, Screech, and Pilot were all asleep, so Jane and Tom didn't have to worry about the guys seeing them hold hands or kiss. The two of them never demonstrated their affections in public, and certainly never around the team. Tom lived by rigorous military standards. As second-in-command, he had to remain in constant check of himself. However, that night he allowed Jane to tussle his hair and run her fingers through his beard without fighting her off.

"Maybe you should shave that beard off," murmured Jane. "We *are* going into the Congo. I think it's gonna be a little warm."

"No way! I like it that it bothers you. Plus, I look like Jesus," Tom joked as he splayed out his arms.

"Oh no you fucking *don't!* Jesus was thin and tall."

"Don't make me show you!" Tom started to lift up his T-shirt to reveal the tattoo of Christ on his chest. He knew Jane was crazy about his muscular, chiseled body; it was her weakness, her kryptonite.

"*Stop* that!" Jane whispered, swatting at his hands. "Jesus! You're gonna wake the guys!"

"See? You even *call* me Jesus."

"Oh God," Jane said, exasperated.

"No, that would be my dad," laughed Tom.

"*You* are a shit."

Tom always tried to get Jane riled up—in any way he could. He knew she didn't like his beard. Special Ops junkies loved the fact that they got to grow facial hair; conventional military men were not allowed to do so. However, Tom had such a handsome face that Jane missed seeing all of it.

"Do you think we'll ever have a family, Tom?" Jane knew the answer. No member of Orion was ever allowed to have children. Jane thought that Tom, a devout Catholic, would want kids. She was on the fence about the whole thing. She wasn't certain she could have a child *and* keep her career. It didn't matter anyway. Orion wasn't going to let them have children.

"We have a family, Jane. Right over there." Tom pointed to the front of the plane and their fellow team members stretched out on the benches.

"I suppose so. I'm so proud of *all* our little boys. Look how they've grown! I hope little Screech is able to make some friends in his new school. We've had such a hard time with him."

"I think it's because you didn't breastfeed him. You *didn't* breastfeed him, did you?" Tom tried to twist her nipple between his fingers.

"Shut up, jackass! I wouldn't breastfeed Screech with *your* boob!"

"Good answer, Widowmaker."

Tom and Jane spent a good deal of that flight kissing and touching each other's face.

"Oh my God, Jane! Do you know what I just realized?"

"What?"

"We *both* have to survive this mission—no matter what. You have to *promise* me you won't die," Tom said desperately.

"Okay, okay, I won't die. Why the sudden concern? You aren't gonna do this every time we go on a mission now, just because I'm your wife, are you?"

"No. Just this once. Now that we're married, we can finally have sex." Jane had never seen him smile so big and blush at the same time.

"Oh, Jeezuz! You're *right*! You better not get killed. And for God's sake, do *not* get your junk blown off!" Jane started to laugh. She was slightly nervous at the thought of losing her virginity. She didn't have a clue what sex might be like, other than listening to Screech brag about his conquests. He seemed to be the only one who was getting laid. Jane shuddered at the thought of losing her virginity to Screech. She loved him, but he was truly nuts.

"Janie? Jane, Jane, Jane. Are you thinkin' 'bout my dick again?" Screech sat up and grabbed his crotch.

"What the hell? You're supposed to be sleeping!" yelled Tom.

"I've been awake this whole time, you fuckin' horn' dogs. Get a room!"

"Get a *room*? When we get back, we're getting a whole *house*. We can live in a house now," said Tom excitedly.

"Yeah, but did you see the paper? You probably won't ever get to live there. We have too much work to do," Screech pointed out.

"What're you talking about?"

"Idi Amin finally got the ax. His dictatorship ended."

"No shit? Well that's *good*," Tom replied.

"Nope. They're like cockroaches. You get rid of one, then another one comes along. Seems there's a new kid on the block already—and I mean 'kid'; he's *our* age. Guy's name is Kony. Crazy motherfucker. I imagine we'll be called on to handle that shitbag." Screech pulled his blanket over his face and feigned sleep.

Jane stood up to check on Maxine, who still lay coiled up asleep within the warm confines of Shep. Jane needed to shake off her gloom, so she decided to take a walk. As she crossed the lawn, she thought about the home she and Tom finally got when they returned from the Congo. It was a small country cottage in Virginia, with a tiny front yard full of fragrant magnolia trees. Usually, they'd only be there for a twenty-five-day stretch. They were away on missions for six to twelve months a year, many of which required them to work in separate locations. They adored their little home and loved all the work that came with having an older house. They closed with their realtor and moved in three days before shipping out again. They were excited about owning their own home and wanted to do *some* type of home improvement project together during those three days. They didn't have enough time to tackle anything bigger than painting, so paint they did. The front door. Jane paused, thinking about that damn door. *That* was their big house project.

The only thing they could afford back then was enough paint to cover a door—and even that was a stretch. Tom went to the local hardware store, picked a can of Cove White paint out of the bargain bin, and returned home to paint with Jane. When they opened the can, Cove White turned out to be Cranberry Red. Shocked and disappointed, Tom asked Jane if they could take it back, but Jane knew all items in the bargain bin were final sale. So Tom happily slopped the bright-red paint onto the door before Jane could stop him.

"*This* will keep your dad from visiting," teased Tom, "*especially* if I do a shitty job."

The little task reminded Jane of one of the stories in Tom's Bible. "Isn't there a part in the Bible where everyone was told to paint their doors red to avoid a plague sent by your bloody, vicious God? If the door had lamb's blood on it, then God would 'pass over' it and not slaughter the first-born son, right? Isn't that what Passover is all about?"

Jane teased Tom constantly about his religion. She'd say things like, "Ooooo, Angel of Death, no sinners here! Move along; move along. Nothing to see. You might want to check out Bob next door. He's the guy with the white door."

Tom just shoved her hard and said, "Ease up there, heathen. And I was only kidding about your daddy. I love your father."

It worked out fine that Tom and Jane had their differences regarding religion. They'd just make fun of each other. Tom asked her if she'd been reading his Bible secretly, because she seemed to know a lot more about it than he thought she did. He was proud of her for knowing there was a part about slaughtered goat's blood, not Cranberry Red paint, being splashed on doors in Exodus 12.

"You know," Jane went on, "the color of that door is pretty disgusting. The neighbors might think we're crazy. Why don't we paint the Marine Corps globe and anchor symbol in the center of it?"

"Nope. It's gonna stay red. Besides, we don't have any money to buy more paint. Plus, if we paint the insignia, we might scare the crap out of our neighbors. What would they think if they knew a couple of Marines moved into the neighborhood?"

Tom and Jane were never home together for any extended period of time after they had bought the house. The red door became a focal point in their relationship. Jane pulled up once after a deployment to find a paintbrush taped to the door with a five-dollar bill wrapped around the handle and a note attached that simply said: "Love, Tom." In retaliation, Jane left Tom an entire gallon of paint with a note attached that said: "You two have fun." When Jane returned next, she found a note and a Polaroid snapshot stuck to the red door. In the picture, Tom was asleep on a lounge chair in front of the door. The paint can was curled in his arms. The note said: "The paint and

I got too drunk last night. Sorry." This bantering went on between them until they got to the point that they would never, ever consider painting that beloved red door.

That project ended up being the only thing they ever did together around the house. After Tom died, Jane couldn't bear to part with their home. It was her refuge, if only for a few days or weeks at a time between deployments. She found serenity there.

Jane saw the irony in Tom's fervent belief in religion and accidental choice of color for the door. No amount of red paint saved Marlene's first-born son—or even her second-born son—from the wrath of mankind, which infuriated Jane every time she thought about it. She was so incredibly angry with God.

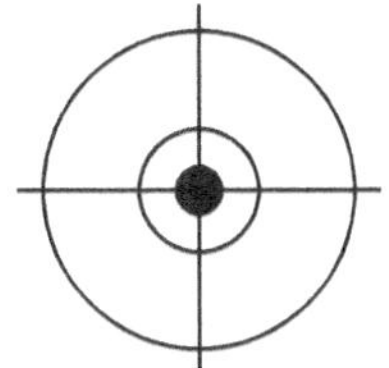

CHAPTER SEVENTEEN

Robert had been the only other man in that house besides Tom. Jane allowed Robert to enter her life slowly. She was especially wary of getting involved with a civilian. She withheld things from Robert. Big things. Including her true identity, her job, and, most of all, her feelings. She opened up only slightly and was protective of her emotions. She felt certain she had everything under control; but, ultimately, Howser controlled everything in Orion, including her life.

After Tom died, Jane was still able to have some peaceful days in her house. One morning in particular, she lounged on her overstuffed cream divan in her white cotton robe as the sun streamed in through the open window. A steaming cup of milky coffee sat on the maple end table to her right. She'd become addicted to café con leche while vacationing in Mexico and couldn't start her morning without it. As she sipped, she perused her mother's weathered journal. Jane had read it a hundred times and always found the words comforting, knowing her mother had written them. Pachelbel's *Canon in D Major* played in the background and Quill Gordon, her twenty-pound gray tabby, rested by her feet at the foot of the sofa. Her parakeet, Pudgy the Budgie, serenaded her from his wrought-iron cage. Easy-to-maintain pets such as cats and small birds fit her sporadic schedule. Jane never knew when she'd need to leave at the drop of a hat, or for how long. Thankfully, Jane had a trustworthy sixteen-year-old girl, who lived next door with her parents, who took care of her little family. Jane always imagined that, while she was away, Quill and Pudgy acted like Sylvester and Tweetie. That particular morning, however, the three of them were able to enjoy the sunshine and peaceful comfort of her cozy sunroom, which was a rarity for Jane.

Jane heard a car door slam outside, then she heard her red front door open. Robert walked down the hall to join her.

"Good morning, sunshine!"

Jane was glad to see him. Robert entered the room and crouched next to the couch and rested his head in her lap as she reclined with the morning newspaper. Jane ran her fingers through his thick, dark hair. She constantly bugged him to cut it high-and-tight, telling him it would make him look younger, but really she just liked the look. Robert gazed up at her with his brown puppy-dog eyes.

"Hey, baby, have I told you that you're the most beautiful girl in the world?"

For some odd reason, Jane didn't mind him saying things like this. Robert brought out her softer, feminine side, which she had buried for most of her life. When she was with Robert, Jane allowed herself to be everything an Orion soldier was not. She never cursed around him, and he was the only person who called her Elizabeth without it bothering her. Jane let him shower her with presents and open doors for her. She wore fluffy pajamas and soft bathrobes. She even cried openly in front of him once. Jane had structured the relationship so she could be feminine—a woman—and not be compromised. She had never acted this way around anyone. Even Tom. She was always a soldier. If she had ever behaved like a stereotypical "girl," another team member would have teased her endlessly.

Her own father had tried to cleanse the girl out of her by ordering additional training and sending her on extra, particularly gruesome missions to toughen her up. Robert was a safe haven for her—a dream place where she could expand and strengthen her femininity, which actually made her a better agent. She tapped into her female intuition; demonstrated enviable multitasking skills; and developed self-confidence and an ability to nurture, show empathy, and be loved.

Because Jane was not allowed to explore her feminine nature at a young age, she was not adept at understanding the nuances of a romantic relationship. She forgot anniversaries and birthdays; she generally labeled herself a horrible girlfriend. Robert made candlelit dinners and brought her stunning bouquets of red roses. But as much as Jane relished having a seemingly normal relationship with Robert, she knew she couldn't let herself fall in love with him because of her secret life. She always kept him at arm's length.

"You *still* think I'm beautiful? We've been together for two years! You're silly. Come here," Jane joked as she opened her arms for a hug.

"Look what I have for youuuuu," sang Robert. "Cherry Garcia ice cream!" he exclaimed, holding up the frozen pint.

"Robert! You know I can't eat that! I'll get fat and I can't afford new clothes! Grrrrrr! Get over here!"

They spent most of the afternoon and well into the evening making love and cuddling in each other's arms. Jane lay on her side, facing Robert, satiated, lightly tracing the contours of his body with her fingertips. Mesmerized by his scent, she wanted to breathe him in so she wouldn't forget this moment. She touched the dragon tattoo on his arm and wondered if he cried when he got it, then laughed quietly as she pictured that. He grabbed her, threw her on her back, and climbed on top of her, kissing her neck and breathing into her ear.

When they weren't in bed, Robert came across as dorky and submissive. Yet, intimately, he knew how to take control. Their sex was mind-blowing. There were times when Jane wondered whether she kept seeing him just for the physical satisfaction he afforded her. Never in her life had Jane done anything just because it felt good, and she got angry at herself when she felt bad about feeling good.

Jane reached toward the nightstand and grabbed the carton of Cherry Garcia. She shoveled the half-melted ice cream into her mouth, then traced her nipples with the cold spoon as Robert watched.

"Mmmmmm. Come here!" he said, reaching for her.

"Just a sec. I'll be right back. I have to pee." Jane slipped out from under him and sauntered to the bathroom, not bothering to cover her body. She enjoyed being naked. As she walked down the hall, past her front door, her intuition made her pause. Something wasn't right. She couldn't pin down what she felt, so she continued toward the bathroom. As she washed her face, she felt a chill run down her spine and she raced back to her room.

"Get up! Get dressed! Fuck, fuck, fuck!"

Robert was half asleep, waiting for her. "Elizabeth, what is it? You're freaking me out!"

Seconds later, the front door was kicked in and a black-masked Special Ops team began to sweep through her house. They grabbed Robert, dragged him outside, and threw him into the back of their van. He resisted, but was overpowered. Jane snagged her deuce gear as she followed Robert out of the house. She threw it into the open side door and jumped in naked after Robert as they peeled away from the curb.

Screech eyed her body, which he had seen countless times before in the showers, and smirked, "Hey, Jane, nice to *see* you." Jane smacked him in the head and began to dress out in her full tactical gear.

"Where's Jude?" Jane demanded. "And who are these yahoos?" she asked, pointing at the other men jammed into the back of the van, as she continued to strap on her gear. "What the *hell* were you guys *thinking*, busting in my door like that? Fucking idiots! You could've called!"

"We were just messing with you," Pilot quipped. "It was Jude's idea. He thought it would be funny."

"We didn't know you had company. Since when are you into chicks?" Screech asked as he motioned to Robert, who lay huddled on the floor of the van.

"Where the *fuck* is Jude?" yelled Jane.

"Right here, Jane." Jude bellowed from the front seat. "These guys are Nazul Tech Op Team 20."

"Who called in DAOS?" she asked, irritated that no one informed her they were working an op—and with the French, no less. Secretly, Jane was glad they accompanied them; Captain Feraud had the best Special Forces team in Europe. The French were kick-ass elite operatives. She grew certain of the success of their upcoming mission because they were allied with such a strong team.

"Comprendez-vous la mission? Et qui est responsable?" Jane asked the DAOS team, making sure they understood the mission and that she was in charge of the op. Having been raised in Africa, she spoke French, although she was told she spoke French like a German, likely because of the heavy German influence in South Africa.

At that moment, Robert sat up in the back of the van. "Jane? Jude? Twenty Tech Nazul? What the *hell* is going on here? You speak German?" Evidently, Jane's French was not improving.

"Uh, Widowmaker, they speak English, you show-off," Jude teased.

"I *know* that," replied Jane, even though she didn't. "I can't believe you asshole cocksuckers came to my *home*! Son of a *bitch*!" she fumed. Jane looked over at Robert and knew he had to be in shock over the language spewing from her mouth and the inconceivable situation in which he found himself.

Pilot tried to calm her down. "Well, *now* what do we do? We don't have time to take him in," he noted, pointing at Robert.

"We could throw him out of the van," Screech suggested enthusiastically. "Nah. He's gotta come with us. Well, at least on the plane. I've gotta call Howser and see what he wants us to do with him."

Jane wasn't sure what to do. The secrets she kept from Robert were clearly out in the open now. And her immature team had evidently defied standard operating procedures by snatching the two of them from her home.

Butch eyed Robert and said, "Well, then, dearie, you'd better put these on." He threw some fatigues, a T-shirt, and boots at Robert. "You can't come to the party in your birthday suit." For the first time, Robert realized he was naked. He got dressed quickly.

Butch then handed Jane her headset. "Jane, I've got the president."

She grabbed the headset and started yelling. "You *son of a bitch!* Why did you come to my *house?* We had an *agreement!*" Jane knew her home was now compromised and she probably wouldn't be allowed to return. She no longer flew under the radar in her neighborhood; there'd be too many questions she wouldn't be able to answer.

"Did you just call the President a *son of a bitch?*" Robert asked horrified.

"The president of Orion, numb-nuts," Screech explained condescendingly. He was opposed to all outsiders—especially weaklings—which is how he saw Robert.

"Elizabeth," boomed Howser, "my apologies about the house. We had no choice. We have the target pinpointed and we only have a T-thirty window. That's it. Kid, this is our only opportunity. We've waited six years for this."

"No pressure, sir!" Jane knew her smart-ass tone was uncalled for, but the words escaped her mouth before she could rein them in. "But my *house*, sir?"

In his deeply authoritative tenor, Howser ordered, "Do it, Jane, dammit! Or don't come home!"

Jane was rarely on the receiving end of Howser's if-you-don't-do-this-you-might-as-well-kill-yourself speech. She understood his directive loud and clear. He meant business. She knew that, as the A team, if she and Jude didn't fulfill this mission, her entire team would be unable to come home. Howser would abandon them, and the US government would deny any knowledge of their existence.

While Jane talked to Howser, Robert peppered her team with questions, which they studiously ignored. The entire mess was beginning to make Jane's blood boil. She was humiliated at being caught by her team members in such a vulnerable position, who would undoubtedly tease her about it mercilessly for years to come. *And* she had lost control over her carefully structured relationship with Robert. Her rage continued to build as Robert persisted in questioning her team.

"Roger that!" Jane barked at Howser, ending their communication. Then, without knowing what she was doing, she snapped and hit Robert across the face with the headset. "Shut the fuck *up!*" she screamed at him.

She handed the headset back to Butch and began to prepare for their ten-hour flight. When they arrived at the aircraft, the team members boarded. Screech hauled Robert up the ramp by the back of his shirt and pushed him into a seat. Jane's team began going over maps and their prelaid plans. Because of Jane's tension, the flight seemed shorter to her than she expected. Before she knew it, ten hours had passed.

Red Leader Command came through the team's headsets, initiating the mission. "Tac op in three. Roger. Operation Red Badger to commence. Awaiting instruction."

Jane turned immediately to look at Jude and ask him if he was ready. When she looked closely, Jane noticed a change in his usually cocky demeanor. Jude seemed unnerved, even vulnerable.

"Fuck . . . shit . . . fuck!" Jude swore as he struggled to zip his jumpsuit with slightly trembling hands. He knew the consequences of a failed mission and, clearly, it was eating at him. No matter how many years a soldier prepared for a mission, and how perfect it looked on paper, fear tended to rise up when the moment actually arrived. Soldiers had to master compartmentalizing that fear or it would compromise the op.

Jane offered Jude support while they secured their goggles. "Jude, I can't do this without you. You *know* that. This is why we're here. Now get your shit together!"

She knew he had better pull it together—and fast. Jane watched Jude as he continued to fumble with his gear.

"*Wait* a minute! What the hell, Jude? Are you *high*?" Jane grabbed his face to look into his eyes. Jude's pupils gave him away. "Are you fucking *kidding* me? Butch! You're on deck! Jude is out of commission! Sit *down*, Jude."

Jane was furious with Jude. She'd been by his side through countless rehab stints for his heroin addiction and she tried to watch over him to make sure he didn't fall off the wagon. Jane felt responsible for Jude and she was livid that he was using again, *especially* before a mission.

"Jane, I don't have to sit this out," he insisted. "I'm fine. I need to be there. I have your back."

"Like *fuck* you do. Butch is gonna have to do this. You fucked up, Jude. You always do." Jane didn't mean her last comment; she realized this as soon as it left her mouth. Still, she didn't retract the stinger. Jude shoved her out of the way angrily and sat down in the hull of the aircraft.

Jane looked over at Robert, who still had no concept of what was happening. He had sat nearly motionless and completely speechless for most of the flight. When he saw Jane looking at him, Robert stood up.

"Elizabeth, what's happening? Are you in danger? Are we being taken hostage?" At that moment, Jane knew her soft feminine side and her caring, sweet boyfriend Robert never belonged anywhere in her world of Orion.

Butch shoved Robert back down to the floor of the plane and said, "You'll have to remain silent or we'll have to sedate you." Butch then made his way toward Jane and got ready to take Jude's position for the jump.

Screech, in his usual half-crazy state, interjected, "That's his way of saying, 'You'll have to be quiet or we'll have to shoot you.'"

Jane didn't doubt that Screech would think twice about shooting and killing Robert. Screech got a huge high from killing. He reminded her of a modern-day Billy the Kid, only slightly more insane. Even under the threat of death, Robert proceeded to question her.

"Elizabeth?"

"They aren't gonna shoot you," Jane said reassuringly. She felt bad for smacking him in the face.

"Thank God!"

"More than likely, they'll just throw you out of the plane." Jane wasn't serious, but Robert's presence was beginning to annoy her. She didn't want her team to see how weak he was. Robert spent the next half hour sitting completely still and silent.

Jane locked into Command, setting the diameters of her lenses.

"Code Force twenty, go to visual. Lock left. Turn lock twenty degrees. Copy. Right forty-five. Download. Running programs. Audio tap-time, gear sequence, check."

Jane turned to Butch and asked him to wrap her wrist. Butch had broken her wrist during a training operation, which almost cost Jane her career. He tended to her constantly because he felt bad about it.

Jane looked at Butch. "Time, Butch? *Butch*? Fucking time?" Jane's frustration grew as Butch fiddled with his lenses.

"T-fifteen," Butch finally replied. "Jeezuz, Widowmaker! Give a guy a break! I was setting my lenses up. I had to hear Command."

Jane yelled to her team inside the aircraft as the hatch slid open. "Widowmaker to silent transmission. Let's rock and roll, ball lickers!" she shouted, trying to hype them all up. The entire team, with the exception of Jude, was secured in the jump lineup. They were hooked and harnessed and awaiting the GO signal. When it was given, Jane jumped out of the plane first, with Butch right behind her, followed by the rest of the team.

On the ground, Jane's tech op teams dispersed quickly to a set of low hills to set up a command center. Butch, Pilot, and Jane went three hundred yards to the left and secured themselves near a hill opposite from the command center. The three of them were fully covered and well protected from the desert elements until a dust devil formed unexpectedly before them. It slammed into them like a sandblaster. Any exposed skin was pelted with high-velocity sand grains that felt electrically charged.

"Pilot! Take the cave!" Jane shouted as she pointed to a shallow indentation in the side of one of the hills.

"*Hell* no, sister! I am *not* going in there. It's full of skaggers!"

"Hold your position! Butch and I'll split the goose and circle," Jane commanded, refusing to argue over Pilot's phobias.

Butch and Jane split up around the hill, with Butch taking the high ground and Jane staying low in the sand. Two hours later, all of Jane's team members had established their positions and Jane radioed Red Leader Command.

"Command, Widowmaker. Report."

"Widowmaker, what's your status?"

"Nothing, sir. The cow's gone dry."

"Widowmaker, move in. Juke right five kilometers. Sit tight."

"Roger. Widowmaker out."

Jane ran the five kilometers across the Afghan desert, found a secure position, and waited for several hours.

"Command to Widowmaker."

"Copy Command."

"The horse is in the barn." And with that communication, Jane realized there would be no mission that night. Their mark had stayed home.

Jane had waited six years for this mission—pumping herself up, visualizing, training, preparing to run full speed into a firefight and slaughter the enemy. Yet she now sat completely still. No mark, no mission. As her adrenaline rush let go, it poured out of her body like blood from an open wound.

The morning sun broke across the cold desert landscape and the wind kicked up. Jane tied her bandana around her face, pulled her cap down tight, and secured her goggles. The sun was piercing, but she welcomed the warmth as it seeped through her clothing and calmed her aching body. Grains of fine sand ripped across the high dunes, strafing her relentlessly despite her protective gear. Jane opened her rucksack and pulled out the topographical map tucked inside so she could scan it and survey the area for important landmarks. She lay the map on the sand, took out her Ka-Bar, and began to slice through the map, cutting it up to make it more manageable to view while battling the winds that whipped around her. Jane gripped the knife handle tighter with each cut and she felt her pulse start to quicken as sand bombarded her face. A familiar metallic taste entered her mouth and she began to stab the map, driving her blade through it and deep into the sand. She could hear her heart pounding in her head.

Why the fuck now, Jane? Why a flash now? Everything's fine, she thought to herself as she tried to keep herself connected to reality.

Butch had lost communication with Jane two hours earlier and had headed out to find her. He spotted her in the distance, not moving. When he looked through his binoculars, he couldn't believe what he saw. He dropped his gear and raced toward her. Jane was sitting upright—covered in blood. When Butch finally stood in front of her, she wouldn't look at him.

"Jane," Butch pleaded, "it's not real. There's no one here but us. Shit! You gotta get some help, sister! Hey, sis? Look at me! Come back, sis. I'm right here. It's not real! You aren't in Pakistan! This is Afghanistan! I got you," he said, recognizing the terror in her eyes.

During her flashbacks, Jane saw herself from a third-person perspective. She could see herself undergoing torture and trauma, but she couldn't feel pain. She wasn't aware of what her body did during these fugues. This time, she had cut her hands repeatedly because she held her knife tightly by the blade, then swiped sporadically at the sweat and sand that covered her body. When Jane finally became aware of Butch's presence, she dropped her knife and sank farther into the sand.

"Hey. Hey, Jane. Come here. It's okay. I'm your brother and I'm not gonna leave you. I do this shit all the time. We all do. We're just working too much. We never get a break! You're just a little shell-shocked," babbled Butch, trying to snap Jane out of her trance. "Look. This was just an accident. You blacked out when you were holding your blade. You didn't cut yourself on purpose. Don't worry about it."

Jane could hear Butch, but she couldn't shake the overwhelming feeling of despair that seeped through her. To pull herself together, she thought of Tom and used her memories of the two of them to snap out of her flashback. When she became fully aware, Butch helped her trudge through the shifting sand to the makeshift command center. As she walked, Jane pressed Tom's photo to her chest—the one she always carried with her—and fought back the urge to sob. Maybe it was the sand or maybe it was the desert solitude that had sent her down the rabbit hole.

Earlier that month, Jane had endured a gruesome attack in Pakistan and had never received any treatment afterward. Not even time off. Had it not been for the skills Howser had taught them in the Killing Circle, Jane wouldn't have survived the encounter—although surviving and living with the consequences of what she did for a living were two different things. Howser never prepared them for that. He also couldn't seem to comprehend that they needed a break every once in a while.

Homebound in the cargo plane, Jude looked over at Jane and saw her staring at Tom's picture. Jane could tell he was irritated when he sniped, "You're chasing ghosts, Jane!"

She tried to ignore him by cranking up Led Zeppelin's "Black Dog" on her Walkman and setting up her chute. As she buckled into her harness, she replied, "I don't know what you're talking about."

Jane really *did* know what Jude was talking about. She wished she could go back and have more time with Tom. Some days, she wished she had the courage to shoot herself—to end the torment she felt by what she had done, what she still did, and what she would continue to do. Jane could feel a burning sensation rising in her chest and up into her throat. *Good God*, she thought, *I'm about to cry*.

Jude continued to yell at her. "Robert is *not* Tom. Did you *see* him? The guy has no balls! Face it, Jane! Whatever you had with Tom is *gone*. He's *dead!* You have to let that go, sister! We can't have some scrawny coward in your life trying to replace one of Orion's greatest soldiers!"

Listening to Jude, Jane realized Robert had likely already been taken back home. She started to get pissed. Jane pushed the release button for the hatch, grabbed a line, hooked it to her harness, and ran out the back of the plane.

"Fuck *ooooooooooooooooff*! she shouted as she jumped.

She soared behind the plane and watched it disappear. As she sailed toward the ground, she finally let her emotions rip.

"You left me alone, damn you!" Jane hollered at the sky, hoping Tom's spirit could hear her.

When she touched down, she let her legs crumple beneath her, then she threw her arms into the air and, with all the force of her soul, began to scream. Jane screamed until it seemed as if no more sound could pass through her larynx. Then, she fell face first into the dirt and sobbed. Tears coursed down her muddy cheeks, and slobber and spit spewed from her mouth as she continued to rant.

"*Why*? Fucking *why*? Fucking God! Fuck you, God!" This was the same God to whom Tom had prayed every day of his life. *That* God let those men sever Tom's head from his body.

"Fuck you, God! My Tom! My husband! Oh, how I hurt!" Jane cried so hard her throat began to swell, her head pounded, and her eyes became red and puffy. It seemed as if her heart would burst and she felt as if she was being kicked in the chest.

"*Please*, God! Give him *back*! I'll do *anything*!" she pleaded. "Oh, *God*! *Why* did you take Tom? I *hate* you! I'll kill you! I will meet you and then I will kill you!"

Eventually, Jane exhausted herself. No more words could issue from her aching throat. She lay on her back, chest heaving as she clutched handfuls of earth and mud. She listened to the fluttering of her parachute and looked up at the black sky. Jane lay there motionless and wished she were dead. She couldn't even blink. All she *could* do was listen to the pounding of her own heart in her head. *Maybe next time*, she thought, *I'll cut my chute.*

Forty days later she sat in a chair in her living room, where she never thought she'd be again. Her home didn't seem as sunny anymore. As she sat there looking at the houseplants that hadn't survived her last deployment, Robert walked in through the front door.

"Hey! I missed you! I couldn't get here any sooner. I had to be debriefed. Boy, that was weird! But then you know all about that! Holy cow, that was cool!" gushed Robert. His mood certainly didn't match Jane's.

"Mmmm," Jane responded, looking down at her hands.

"What's wrong? You're like a military superhero! I bet you're *still* exhausted."

Although Jane was a little put off by what was, to her, a strange compliment, she did feel compelled to apologize to him.

"Look, Robert, I'm sorry I didn't tell you what I do. I couldn't. And I'm *really* sorry I clobbered you. I know we agreed to be honest in our relationship."

"Are you *kidding*? That was the coolest thing ever to happen to me in my life! Even you clocking me like that was cool. I mean, don't do it again. But it was cool. Did you see how I pushed that one guy when he grabbed me and tried to throw me into the van? That was *awesome*! He was like a Navy SEAL guy and I gave him a shove like I was gonna kick his ass," Robert exclaimed as he pounded one of his fists into the other one.

"Okaaaaaay," responded Jane. "Okay, I don't feel good about this. Maybe I should quit. I liked having separate lives. I liked having a quiet, comfortable home. I feel like my worlds have collided and I can't breathe."

Jane wasn't sure why she threw out the choice to quit her job. She knew she couldn't leave Orion. Leaving Orion was like trying to leave The Mob. *No one* left.

Jane was certain Robert didn't want her to leave Orion. Although he was surely given strict orders during the debriefing to keep his mouth shut, and probably was threatened with death if he told anything to anyone, he obviously couldn't wait to spill his guts to his friends. Knowing Robert, he'd want his buddies to know they were right about her.

"Jane, we'll be fine."

"*What* did you say?"

"What, that we'll be fine?"

"You called me *Jane*. *They* call me Jane! G.I. fucking Jane!" She got up, went to the bathroom, and locked the door.

"I'm sorry, Elizabeth," Robert whispered softly through the door. "I thought . . . I just thought we were a team."

As Jane sat alone on the other side of the door, she realized she'd never live her fairytale dream in her house. With *anyone*. She lay down on the cold bathroom floor and let herself drift off.

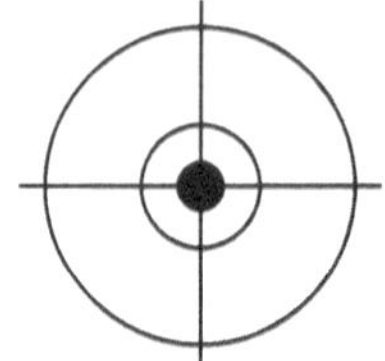

CHAPTER EIGHTEEN

After a PTSD episode like the one Jane had at the farm, she was always disturbed for several days. Although she felt safe at the Stapelton's farm, her dreams after the incident there were the opposite of peaceful. That night she revisited a place to which she never wanted to return.

As she fell asleep beneath another one of Marlene's brightly colored handmade quilts, images of the beige desert sands of Pakistan slowly became visible. Night had fallen and extreme cold set in as Jane began making a fire. She expected her team to arrive the next morning, but she was on her own until then. Jane loved recon because it gave her some desperately needed solitude. Up until that point in time, she wasn't afraid of very much at all.

As she sat there in silence, she thought she heard voices in the distance. She quickly doused her fire and began to trek away from her camp. She took out her thermal mini monocular and scanned in the direction of the voices. In the desert, sound can be deceiving. As she reached for her communicator, someone struck her from behind and her world went dark.

Jane awoke naked and bound, feeling the sweaty shank of a huge man pounding his dick inside of her. Two or more men restrained her by her hair. Her head was covered by a hood, so she couldn't ascertain how many men were there. Jane calmed herself while the behemoth jerked inside of her. She had to figure out how to kill him. Fast.

She determined that her hands were bound behind her by some sort of tape, but she could move her body. Jane began to rock with the man's motion to try and shove sand into the exposed tape. By twisting her wrists, she was able to line the tape with sand, freeing them. As she carefully removed her wrists from their confinement, Jane felt an unmistakable object grinding into her side. The man was strapped with a blade or sword. Continuing to move in tandem with him, she slipped her hand from behind her back, under his robe, and inched the blade about three quarters of the way out of its sheath. Jane knew he wasn't the only man who wanted to have a turn at raping her, so she waited for him to finish.

As he rose, she tore his sword from its sheath and rolled in the direction from which the least amount of cheering emanated. She jumped to her feet and began, tactically and swiftly, to cut down the bodies—all while still wearing the hood. She felt the blade drive across each of the men who had been grouped in a circle around her. That configuration made it easy to slash out at them and bring them down, one by one, without seeing them. Their moans of agony grew then faded as she continued to hack into their bodies and kill them. Finally, she plunged the sword into the gut of the last man standing, ripping it upward and jerking it from side to side, disemboweling him. Jane tore the hood from her face and saw six men and her rapist dead on the ground. As she looked at the dead men, a brief moment of utter gratitude for Howser's Killing Circle training washed over her. Jane found her gear quickly and radioed in for backup. Adrenaline surged through her, fueling her rage.

Butch arrived first at the scene. The image of Jane sitting in the middle of a circle of bloody, decapitated bodies was certainly one he'd never forget. He always wondered whether Jane cut their heads off *after* killing them, because the way the corpses were positioned didn't make sense. Jane couldn't remember the exact details of the attack to relay what really happened. Her naked body was covered in dirt and blood and she wouldn't look at Butch. He took off his jacket and wrapped it around her.

"Butch . . ." Jane began. He knew instinctively what Jane wanted to ask of him—without her having to say it. She wanted to preserve her integrity and her dignity.

"No worries, Elizabeth. I won't say a thing. This one is all yours."

Somehow, just the very act of using her Christian name created a bond between them that could never be severed. Butch and Jane had crossed a bridge together, transitioning from soldiers to siblings. They were a family before, but even more so at that moment.

"Look, kid, you did everything right here. It's gonna be okay." Butch took his time comforting Jane before he escorted her back to camp a few miles away.

When they returned, Jude was waiting for them and he was furious.

"What were you *thinking*?" Jude stormed toward Jane and handed her a blanket so she could cover up. "Do you really think it was a smart move to leave me behind, Jane? I could have protected you. I should've *been* there with you," Jude raged. Wrapped up in his own self-punishment for taking drugs before a mission yet again, he didn't even acknowledge that Jane had been compromised.

"Jude, you're not consistent," Jane said wearily. "I never know when you're gonna be fucked up on heroin. You weren't reliable backup for this mission. You're using again. Do you *really* think you could have helped me? What are *you* thinking? You disappoint me." She shoved him aside and began to walk past him.

Jude felt the verbal slap and softened his tone. "Jane, I'm sorry. I'm having a hard time. I've got a lot on my plate. I don't know what I was thinking," he explained, trailing after her. Jane turned around and faced him.

"You abandoned me either way, Jude. I can't count on you. I needed you and you didn't take that seriously," she countered while struggling to secure the blanket that covered her.

Butch stepped between them. "Is everything okay, you two? What's going on?"

"Get the hell out of here, dude," snarled Jude. "This is between me and Jane."

"Hey, whoa there, Colonel. I don't know who the hell you think you are, but now is not the time to be getting shit fired up. Come on, Jane; let's get you inside." Butch shielded Jane and directed her toward a tent.

"No, it's okay, Butch. Jude and I have to figure this out. I'm fine. I'll be there in a minute," Jane reassured Butch as Jude stood there seething.

"Alright," agreed Butch, "but holler if you need me."

"She *doesn't* need you," Jude said firmly to Butch.

Jane sat down on the sand, her body aching from the attack. Jude squatted next to her. "Shit, Jane. Good God, I'm sorry. I should've been there. Haven't I always been there for you? I was your first friend in this shit-hole program!"

"Yeah, but Tom—"

"Tom is *dead*, Jane! Even when he was alive . . . Look, he couldn't possibly have protected you like I can. He wasn't the big-ass leader everyone gives him credit for, Jane. He was Howser's favorite. *That's* how he got that position. *I* was the first one recruited into Orion. *I* should've been leading. I'm *glad* he's gone."

"What the hell did you just say that for, you sick bastard! Tom was *everything* to this team."

"No, Jane. He wasn't everything to this team. He was everything to *you*. To me, he was just an arrogant dude that preyed on you. And fucking Howser . . . Shit! Jane, why won't Howser recognize that it's *me* that needs to lead this team? I want to *kill* him sometimes."

"Jude! Jeezuz! What the fuck are you *saying*? I can't listen to any more of this." Jane stood and started to walk away.

"Jane, stop letting everyone come between us! It's making me crazy!"

"Jude! Shut. The. Fuck. Up. There is no *us*! Get a grip!" Jane snarled as she stormed into the tent.

When Jane woke up she was eye to nose with Maxine on the hardwood floor, back on the farm. *Fucking nightmares*, she thought. Jane could feel Maxine's warm breath swirling from her nostrils onto her half-closed eyelids. Jane kicked the quilt off her sweaty body and reassured herself she was no longer in Pakistan—and that her dream was no longer her reality, despite how vividly real it seemed.

"Hey, lady," Jane murmured to Max, kissing her on the nose and scratching behind her left ear. Maxine opened her eyes and started licking the sweat from Jane's face, but she didn't move from her side. Jane could tell she was in pain.

"I am *so* sorry, sweetheart. You are such a brave dog for what you did for me. I can't ever repay you. *Thank you*," Jane whispered, tearing up again when she thought of Maxine out in the New Mexico desert alone, injured, and scared.

"How is she?"

Jane jerked upright. She didn't realize anyone was in the bedroom with her. She saw that Sam had spent the night on the floor too, sleeping beside Shep.

"She's pretty sore, I think," Jane replied while she got up to stretch. "What're you doing? You didn't have to sleep in here with us; we would've been fine." She was surprised at Sam's deep concern for Maxine.

"I just wanted to be here with all of you. I'll get you a cup of coffee so you can stay with Maxine."

"I can get it, Sam. Plus, I want a smoke." Jane hobbled down the stairs to the kitchen, where she poured herself a steaming cup of coffee, then she went outside to the porch, where she found Earl and Eugene with their caffeine fix.

"Mornin', General. How'd you sleep with that quilt on that knotty floor? Must've felt like boot camp." Earl chuckled, wheezing as he laughed.

"I slept alright," she answered, sparing him a description of the nightmare she'd relived in her sleep. "I just feel bad that Sam slept there too. That's sweet of him to be so concerned for Max." Jane sat with the two men and gulped her brew in comfortable silence.

After a while, Eugene stood up. "You want another cup of coffee, kid?" he asked, motioning to her cup.

"Sure. Thanks!"

"A little FYI. Sam was worried about *you*, not the *dog*." Eugene leaned down and kissed the top of her head, then went inside to get more coffee.

Jane sat there for a moment and reflected on that gentle act of affection. She wondered whether that was what real dads did for their daughters. She thought about Howser and how tormented his life had been since the moment she entered it. From the very beginning, he never really wanted her. Jane had killed his wife—the love of his life and his partner. She could have ruined his career. He only kept her because of the President. She could only imagine what that must've been like for Howser.

She thought of her father pouring his nightly glass of whiskey and sitting down with Amelia's journal. She imagined him wanting to throw the book into the fire. Maybe that would release him from his anguish. Jane knew, however, that Howser would never destroy Amelia's writings. His connection to Amelia was as intoxicating to him as his whiskey. Jane hoped Howser felt some torment throughout his life for how he treated his daughter. He never once kissed her on the top of the head, like Eugene had just done. As Eugene came back out to the porch with a fresh cup of coffee, Jane couldn't help but think of how lucky Tom was to have had him as a father. He was probably a big reason why Tom was such a good man.

"Sam'll understand if you need to take some time off to be with Maxine," Eugene commented, handing her a steaming cup.

"Oh, she looks to be in pretty capable hands," Jane said, thinking of how Shep had curled up around Max when she and Sam left the bedroom. As she was speaking, Sam burst through the screen door with boundless teenage energy and plopped down beside her. Jane began to feed off his enthusiasm to perk her up, although part of her still felt shredded from the events of the previous night.

"How're you feeling this morning, Aunt Jane?" Sam asked with genuine concern for her well-being. "You've been through some tough stuff."

"Yeah, I guess I have, Sam. And I still pay for it."

"What got you through the hard times? You must've taken some heavy meds."

While Jane contemplated briefly whether Sam was serious, Eugene interjected, "We'll get out of here and let you two talk shop. Come on, Earl. We probably have a stack of pancakes to eat."

As Eugene and Earl started to rise from their chairs, Sam grabbed Eugene's arm. "Come on, Grandpa. Stay here. It may help you with your own PTSD," he said, half joking. Then Sam turned to Jane. "Is that alright with you, Aunt Jane?"

"Of course, Sam! We're all family," Jane replied, sensing their warm presence and desire to have her there.

"Alright, then, Sam. Your grandma can feed us out here, I suppose." Eugene smiled.

Jane hadn't yet told Sam about the infamous Dr. Reid and her ironically pivotal role in her PTSD.

"Well, there was someone I saw after every mission, although I'm not sure if she helped me get through much at all. Dr. Reid was an uptight, crabby bitch." Jane shook her head and lit a cigarette.

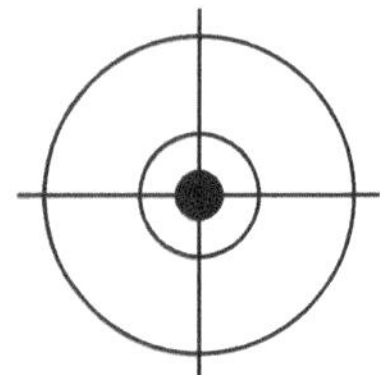

CHAPTER NINETEEN

"Well, well, well! Look who's come to shit on my parade," Dr. Reid groused as she exhaled cigarette smoke through one corner of her pursed lips.

Jane said nothing. She simply sat back in her chair and eyed the tender, half-healed cuts on her hands. She wondered if they'd scar.

"You're pathetic, Jane. You let your demons impregnate you," Reid said with disgust while scratching in her notebook. *Skritch, skritch, skritch.*

Jane looked down at her own hands again, thinking it would be cool and intimidating if they scarred like Pilot's.

"Listen to me, Jane! You're a disappointment to Orion—*especially* to your father."

Jane's head snapped up and she watched the doctor closely as she scratched even harder in her notebook. Reid stopped only briefly to peer over the top of her glasses at Jane. "He wants to get rid of you, you know," the doctor said derisively. "He *should* have gotten rid of you. But . . . well, he didn't. Did he? Even your own team members have their doubts. Jude was just in here talking to me. He thinks you're plotting against Orion and are working as a double agent. Is that true, Jane? Is Jude on to you? Do you want Howser's position bad enough to betray your whole team?"

"That's a lie!" Jane knew none of her team would ever talk about each other to the doctor. "What's the matter, Mary? Are you out of wizard tricks? Have your textbooks let you down?"

"Shut up, Jane! You don't have any power here!"

"Ohhhh, thaaaaat's right. According to this month's copy of *Rules of Engagement of the Spanish Inquisition*, this dividing tactic is supposed to work! How *frustrating* for you! But there's always electric shock therapy, exorcism, drugs, isolation, and reverse psychology." Jane stood up and got in Dr. Reid's face. "You're a fucking piece of shit, Mary."

The doctor stood abruptly, picked up a heavy psychotherapy book from her desk, shot Jane a look of disdain, and threw the book at Jane's head. "This shit works!" Reid yelled, and she grabbed another book. She slammed it repeatedly on her desk and her voice raised to a cackling screech. "This is fucking *science*! What is *wrong* with you people? You're *monsters*! These treatments work on *normal* people!

As suddenly as she lost control, the doctor calmed down. A smile slowly engulfed her face as she straightened her glasses.

"Fuck you, Jane," Reid intoned, and she pressed the panic button.

"No, no, no!" Jane yelled. "Dr. Reid! No!" Jane stood up and raced around the room, looking for a way out, but she knew she was trapped. She jumped onto Reid's desk and slammed a book into the doctor's face, who ran quickly out of the room. Jane proceeded to take the room apart, ripping up folders, smashing furniture, and knocking pictures off the wall.

Suddenly, Howser burst through the door. The anger on his face cut into her psyche like a dagger. Both his fists were clenched, as if he intended to walk straight into the office and punch Jane in the face. She could see he was trying to control his breathing, and his lips were clamped shut.

Fuck this, Jane thought. *I'm the one who gets to be angry here.* However, she knew she had to obey Howser. Without receiving any verbal instruction, Jane followed him out the door and down to The Room.

Howser and Jane passed through the door and sat opposite one another at a gray metal table. Her father placed a pair of handcuffs in front of her. They both sat there for a few seconds, looking at them, until Jane surrendered. She put her arms behind her back and Howser rose, walked behind her, and locked the cuffs down tight on her wrists.

Anyone can do anything for thirty days, Jane thought. *It should be easy. One, stay on a diet; two, quit smoking; three, house-sit. Some might think that it's downright torture to cut red meat from their diet. But, if a doctor says it might save you from a massive coronary someday, you might be inspired to give it a try.* Torture. *Now there's a word that's widely used and largely misunderstood. Everyone has a different impression of what is torturous. One person might believe it's torture to be in gridlocked rush-hour traffic for two hours; another might feel tortured sitting through a Sunday sermon. But I know that's bullshit, because I know what torture is. And it happens in The Room.*

On her first day of thirty, Jane was dragged to a cold concrete room. It was small—about seven feet by ten. The men who surrounded her were dressed in nondescript black uniforms and all of them wore black ski masks to make identification impossible. For all she knew, they could be her own teammates. Jane was then forced to kneel on a broomstick that was secured to a wooden pallet. Another broomstick was placed and tied down directly behind her knees, compressing her tendons. Any pressure placed on the sticks would send searing pain from her knees to her feet. Her handcuffs were removed and her hands bound behind her back. Next, a rope was tied around her neck and was secured to the bindings on her hands. Last, her hands were then tied to her feet. Any movement was impossible. If she tried to move, she'd choke herself to death. As pain began to set in, Jane knew she had to conjure up memories that would help her endure what was to come.

She thought about how she used to run through the giant walking sprinklers on the farm where she spent her younger years, hearing their *swish-swish* as the machines went through their revolutions. She saw so clearly the fertile fields with gently swaying acres of corn. She smelled the pungent earthiness of sugar beets after they'd been harvested. She remembered how the four two-story farmhouses stood close together, nestled in a valley off the winding, sloping frontage road. Large Dutch elms encircled the structures, protecting them from the sudden, fierce prairie winds—winds that could sometimes carry two-foot drifts of topsoil from the open fields and dust the yards like snow. Her grandfather had toiled to build these simple homes and, as her external torture began, Jane longed to be back there.

Her second day in The Room was no more pleasant than the first. Her mouth was gagged with a saltwater rag, and Jane's thirst began to build as she watched water drip from a spigot just inches away from her. She still remained on the pallet, kneeling and strapped in the same position she was placed twenty-four hours earlier. The pain in her knees was finally past the agonizing burn; it had shifted into a disassociated loss-of-limb feeling. Jane focused on her combat pressure training to get her through her second day.

Jane thought of her grandma back in the Midwest, whose small kitchen was always thick with the smell of biscuits and gravy, home-made bread, and slabs of meat atop freshly picked vegetables roasting in the oven. Jane's kitchen job was always to knead bread, folding and pushing it into just the right consistency. She'd let it rise, then knead it again; let it rest, then put it in the pan. Just like the song. *Pat-a-cake, pat-a-cake, baker's man*, she thought as she struggled to keep herself removed mentally from the torture.

"You ready yet, you coward?" The harsh tone of the punisher-in-charge broke through her meditation. Jane heard the instrument he carried as he scraped the handle against one of the walls. The man stopped behind her and slashed at her back swiftly and repeatedly with a riding crop. A separate part of Jane's brain noted he had attached a steel tip to the end that tore through her skin.

"Are you getting thirsty?" he taunted when he stopped splitting her back open. "Too bad I can only spare a drop of water." Although Jane was somewhat delirious from thirst, she couldn't help but think her punisher sounded like Colonel Klink from *Hogan's Heroes*.

The corners of Jane's mouth had begun to crack and bleed as the salt gag cut into her cheeks. The leader ordered a few of the men to get her a drink. She didn't expect she'd get water to drink so soon, and that certainly was not what she got. Instead, the men hung a bucket of ice-cold water directly above her head. Ever so slowly, it released its contents one tiny drip at a time. A bead of water dropped onto Jane's forehead and ran off her brow. She found it impossible to direct the droplet into her bleeding mouth. Her head was still tied to her legs. She believed the success of this torture method was based on the randomness of the water dropping and, certainly, the temperature. On this second day, her excruciating thirst made the torture effective. Jane felt a small—very small—amount of satisfaction knowing her interrogators had to smell the stench of her piss when they entered the room. To escape her raging thirst and searing pain, she had to drive herself deep into some other memory.

Jane's Uncle Fred was a large man. He wasn't fat; he was just a stout farmer. And he always smelled like Old Spice aftershave. Uncle Fred used to drive her over to the farm fields in his truck—American made, of course. All the while, they listened to AM talk radio. He took the washboard dirt road to the pumphouse, which was full of spiders, snakes, and gophers. Some days, he'd turn on the massive, twisting, walking steel sprinklers. The sprinklers . . . *Water. I need water*, Jane moaned to herself. With that one thought she was jolted back into her body and the physical reality of her torture.

On the fourth day, Jane was given a freshwater rag to chew on. It felt as if heaven rained down the very tears of God and delivered them directly into her swollen mouth. Her "captors" released her from her hog-tied position and placed her immediately in wooden stocks. Suddenly, a black hood was jammed over her head and they dragged her *and* the stocks outside. Jane wondered how many of her teammates had their own head in this very same bag at one time or another. It smelled like oil and, she assumed, it was soaked in some type of creosote. The vapors fostered her nausea. If she had had anything in her stomach, she surely would have vomited into the bag, further complicating her situation. *Get your mind out of here, Jane. Think of something else,* she urged herself.

Her nausea made her think about the first time she drank too much—and it certainly wasn't alcohol. She had stolen a bag of sugar from her foster grandma's pantry and tore down the road to a rendezvous with her foster brother and his friends. They met in their fort: a bunker they had carved out of the side of an irrigation ditch. Each one of them spilled their booty. Her brother, Mike, had a plastic pitcher from their mom's house; Beau brought cups; Craig had sixteen packets of cherry Kool-Aid; and, of course, Jane brought the sugar. The four of them pretended they were in a MASH unit as they stood at their makeshift bar, mixing drinks and downing them like Hawkeye and McIntyre. They had a chugging contest and told made-up war stories. Her brother was the best at acting drunk. He sauntered out of the MASH bunker and pretended to step on a land mine, blowing himself to bits. They dragged him back into the enclave and pretended to amputate his legs. Before "operating," Jane chugged three pitchers of the super-sweet Kool-Aid and promptly barfed right in the middle of their camp. She couldn't stop throwing up bright-red liquid. It looked like blood. Jane didn't know whether to think her puking was disgusting or cool. Her brother and his friends didn't think it was cool, and they promptly abandoned her. Jane remembered thinking that if they were real soldiers, like her grandpa's hero, Audie Murphy, they never would have left her side.

Jane moved inadvertently and suddenly felt the wooden stocks dig into her outstretched arms and bite into her throat. Jane's mind wasn't strong enough to maintain her distracting meditation. The pain of the torture was too great. She tried to stand on the tips of her toes to relieve the pressure on her throat, but the muscles in her legs felt like they were on fire and they could barely hold her weight. The removal of the broomstick and the fact that she wasn't kneeling on the pallet should have brought her some relief, but excruciating pins and needles coursed through her nerves. The oiled hood was removed and Jane instinctively inhaled deeply, hoping to taste fresh air. Instead, she gagged. She opened her eyes and found herself staring into a literal shit hole. A barrel of brown, soupy feces, buzzing with hundreds of flies, had been placed directly below her head. The insects stopped their ravenous feasting on diarrhea momentarily to swarm her freshly exposed eyes, looking for moisture. Jane blinked and tried to shake her head to throw them off, but each time she moved her head she felt the wooden stock choke down on her. *Oh, not fair*, she thought to herself. *Not fair*. And she took her mind back to the farm.

Vince Breckner was bigger than all of them. Jane didn't know how old he was. She just knew he didn't ride the bus to school with them, so he must have been about sixteen. Jane was seven. Every day after school, Jane, her brother, and his friends walked across the uneven fields to Vince's house where they usually worked together on some project, like a minibike or a muffler that needed welding. That day, they all sat on the top rung of the wooden corral and watched Vince work. He told them war stories he had picked up from his brother, Grant. Grant had been in Vietnam and he had told Vince gruesome stories about encountering Vietnamese tunnel rats and cutting off their heads with his knife, or about guys being blown to bits and having brains splattered in his face. They never saw Grant. He usually stayed in his dark bedroom and drank. That day, however, was different.

"Hey," Vince said nonchalantly, keeping his eyes shielded under his welding hood, "wanna go see Grant? I think he's gonna shoot himself."

Of course they did! They didn't really know what that *meant*, and Jane couldn't understand why he'd do such a thing. When you're a little kid, you don't really understand that death isn't like a cartoon. When you see Wile E. Coyote fall off a cliff and then get back up a thousand times, you don't comprehend death.

Vince took off his welding gear and the kids followed him into the dark house. The windows were covered with Rebel flags instead of curtains. A plastic-covered green velvet couch sat in the entryway and the house smelled like bacon grease and stale beer. They walked up the stairs toward Grant's room, which was located at the end of a long brown-paneled hallway. The boys stopped at the top of the stairs.

"Heck no! I'm going home!" Jane's brother whispered to Vince, copping out. "Your brother's gonna *kill* us!" He and his buddies flew back down the stairs and out of the house.

"You aren't gonna quit on me, are you, soldier?" Vince asked Jane as he took her hand and squeezed it. "You're my first sergeant and you have to lead the mission. See, I'm wounded and I can't get Grant out of the jungle without you. Hear me, Sergeant?"

"Aye, aye, Captain." Jane had heard that phrase on *McHale's Navy* and thought it was the right one to say. There was no way she was going to let Grant stay in the jungle alone. She liked this game Vince was playing with her.

They walked slowly down the hall and peeked into Grant's room. Vince gave her the "silence signal" by dropping on one knee, raising his arm, and making a fist. They sat tight. Jane could see Grant sitting at his desk, drinking booze directly from the bottle. He looked scary. Then he put the bottle down, picked up a gun, placed it in his mouth, and pulled the trigger. Jane heard his brains splatter against the half-open door. She tried to run, but Vince grabbed her hand and jerked her to her feet, dragging her into Grant's stale room.

"Jesus! He fucking did it!" Vince yelled, finally letting go of her hand so he could touch the pooling blood of his brother.

Jane took off. Vince turned around and chased her. She was just about over the corral fence when he grabbed her and threw her to the ground. He placed his hand over her mouth and pushed hard.

"You don't tell *no one* about this, y' hear?"

Jane tried to shake her head yes, but Vince was pushing downward so hard she couldn't nod. He removed his hand, grabbed both sides of her face, pressed his mouth on hers, and shoved his tongue in her mouth.

As he pulled away, Vince growled, "Now git home and never come back here again."

That afternoon, Jane heard a fire engine race toward the Breckner farm. Word about Grant had already reached her foster family. From her room, Jane could hear her mom on the phone with her grandma saying, "It's not fair. That's just not fair."

On her fifth day, Jane was repositioned yet again. The men released her from the stocks and dragged her toward a nearby river. There, her ankle was chained to a pallet. Her arms were stretched outward toward her sides and were tied to a bamboo pole placed across her back. She felt like Christ waiting to be crucified. Her blistered, bloodied body ached and her split, dry lips cracked painfully with any slight movement.

As they moved to cross the river, Jane splashed water clumsily up onto her face. Despite her struggle to haul the wooden pallet with one leg, she was able to consume some water. When they reached the other side, she was left to stand in the blazing hot sun. Her dry skin began to burn and Jane could feel the layers peeling off her shoulders and hanging from her back where she had been whipped. Flies gathered on the open wounds, irritating them further.

Well, at least they're not snakes, Jane thought. *Flies, I can handle. Snakes? No fucking way.*

As her thoughts drifted, Jane realized how thankful she was that Howser went to extraordinary lengths to make sure Orion soldiers were trained to deal expertly with any circumstance that could possibly arise on any mission. The child–soldiers had had the luxury of training in a facility Howser built to prepare them specifically for jungle invasions. He resurrected an old airplane hangar they lovingly referred to as "Montezuma's Revenge," mostly because it was guaranteed they would crap their pants if they got hung up on one of the electrical wires Howser used to simulate stinging jungle creatures. The temperature in the hangar was cranked up to a balmy one hundred degrees Fahrenheit, along with one-hundred-percent humidity, making maneuvering in combat fatigues exhausting.

"Aaaah-eeee-ah!" bellowed Screech as he swung through the fifty-foot-tall trees. He rappelled to the ground, landed softly at Jane's feet, and said, "Me, Tarzan. You, Jane. Kill, kill, kill!" Then he released his carabiner and bolted through the jungle, yelling "Tag! You're it!"

Jane rocketed after him in an attempt to capture the flag he had secured to his belt, which was worth ten points in their mock training. Jane was careful to avoid the clever traps and hidden tripwires Howser had installed.

Butch, Tom, Jude, and Screech were far more proficient in Montezuma's Revenge than Jane. Screech could survive in almost any situation, like a cockroach, but he excelled in the jungle. Jane had never seen another person more self-reliant. Although he complained the most, Jane speculated that he, like Butch, feared nothing about the jungle. Jane, on the other hand, was often "captured" or "killed" inside the hangar. Usually it was because she allowed herself to become preoccupied with the extraordinary size of the plants. She always stopped to feel their leaves, certain that Howser must have created them from some synthetic material.

The animals they encountered were equally overwhelming. Once, when Jane was clearing a path, a giant rodent—larger than a sheepdog—startled her and she fired at it. Had her weapon been loaded with live rounds, a very docile capybara would have been splattered to bits. There were ghostly sounding howler monkeys no larger than house cats, yet they scared the shit out of Jane in the dark. And then there were the snakes. "Fucking snakes," as Jane called them. Most of the reptiles Howser released into the facility were nonvenomous and were supposed to keep the rodent population at bay. Regardless, Screech told her one day that he had spotted a highly venomous fer-de-lance, which was equally as deadly as a mamba. Jane asked Screech why Howser would do that to them.

"I don't know. Maybe to keep us on our toes. But make sure you keep a lookout in the trees. They hunt from the trees but live on the ground," Screech informed her, moving his body up and down from a crouched position.

"So I guess I'm not safe *anywhere* in here? Jesus Christ!"

Screech shook his scruffy head. "Safe? You think Howser wants you to feel *safe*? Jane, this is a deadly killing simulator. You're fucked up. Speaking of which, shouldn't *I* be killing *you*?" He smiled, smacked her in the leg with a billy stick, and sprinted off, only to return a few seconds later. "By the way, the snake I saw has a nest right behind you under that tree," he whispered in her ear. Jane jumped and turned around, firing her dummy rounds at the base of the tree behind her.

Jane's memories helped her through the torture as it continued until the seventh day, when she was stripped of all clothing and taken to The Hole—damp, solitary confinement. There, Jane crawled to the blackest corner and began to rub her ankle, where the metal chain had gouged into her skin.

Is this real? Am I gonna die? Is this training? This is training. This is training, she repeated over and over. *It can't be punishment for what I did to Reid and her office. This has to be training.*

Jane tried to focus and conserve her energy as the days passed. Each day brought another challenge: having to eat food soaked in piss, warding off swarms of cockroaches, being doused with a water hose. She kept track of the days up until day ten. After that, despair set in. She was cold, weak, and delusional. Her body temperature had plummeted from being hosed down consistently in the freezing cement cell. She grew too weak to jump around to keep warm. Jane huddled in the fetal position most of the time, breathing warmth into her cupped hands and rubbing them over her sore body.

At one point Jane was dragged from The Hole and shoved into a room, where she was tied to a wooden chair and given an intravenous line that delivered fluid.

Oh God! Does that feel good, Jane thought. The solution coursed through her veins and Jane reveled in the knowledge that she had made it through Survival, Evasion, Resistance, and Escape training. Or so she thought.

Suddenly, she felt a solid "thwap" across her shoulders and then her shins. A rubber hose whipped her across her inner thighs. She tried to yell, but her dry, swollen throat couldn't produce noise. Jane hadn't spoken for weeks. She had to escape quickly, mentally, to survive what came next. *Meditate, Jane! Get your mind out of here or you're gonna die.*

Jane raced into her grandma's house from the bus stop—her usual routine. As an after-school snack, her grandmother made her hobo pie: a homemade biscuit smeared with butter and sugar, then doused with hot coffee. After Jane scarfed down the treat, she left the house and walked down the pathway to her great-grandpa's house, where she was given a tall glass of ice-cold milk mixed with Nestle Quick. Then he and Jane rocked in his chair for a while, and her great-grandpa filled her head with interesting World War II stories about sinking submarines and kamikaze pilots crashing into his sons' Merchant Marine ship, sinking it.

"Those young sailors were so damn terrified, they couldn't make themselves jump off the side of those ships that were about to sink! Your grandpa threw a life vest around their necks and tossed as many of them as he could off that burning ship. He was a hero, I tell you. *Three times* his ships were sunk in shark-infested waters," he reminisced. Jane knew that her uncle was a hero too, although he never talked about it. Jane found his medals stashed out in his work shed. He spanked her once for wearing his Navy Cross when playing in the field.

After her visit with her great-grandfather, Jane moseyed back to her grandmother's house. When she walked in, her grandma asked her to hop up on the kitchen counter so she could talk to her while she prepared dinner. Holding a half-peeled potato in one hand and a paring knife in the other, she looked at Jane with concern showing in her lovely brown eyes.

"Elizabeth, you'll be staying here for the next week or so. Your brother is in the hospital again and he's very sick. Your parents are staying there with him."

Jane loved her brother, although she rarely got to see him. He was constantly in the hospital, quarantined inside oxygen tents. Everything seemed to give him pneumonia or allergy attacks. They'd play together for a few weeks and then he'd be gone again, back to the hospital.

As a little girl at that time, Jane didn't quite understand what was going on, so she agreed to behave and stay with her grandparents. The farm was her utopia. She had chickens, horses, cows, and geese, and two rusted-out Army Jeeps that her uncle had dumped in the backyard for her to play in. She shot everything in sight—birds, squirrels, rabbits, even snakes and rats—with the single-shot .22 rifle her grandpa had given to her. Truth be told, Jane preferred playing alone.

Jane had no idea how long she had lain naked in The Hole. Eventually her "punisher" came in and threw her uniform at her. She welcomed the sensation of the rough cotton against her skin. To her, it felt like silk.

"Put these on, Marine!"

Jane donned her uniform as best she could. She had no strength to tuck in her blouse or tie her boots, and she could barely button her top. Two men then dragged her out into the blazing sun, where she felt like a vampire burning to cinders.

Jane slumped over and covered her eyes from the blinding light. Then she heard a familiar voice shouting at her. It was Howser's.

"Marine! You *will* have bearing! The manner in which you carry yourself will reflect alertness, confidence, and competence!" Howser cleared his throat before continuing, and Jane's eyes began to adjust slowly to the light.

"Marine! You *will* have courage to remain calm while recognizing fear. You *will* have moral courage to stand up for what is right and to accept blame when something is your fault." Jane tried to listen to Howser's words, but her head pounded from severe dehydration.

"Marine! You *will* have decisiveness to make good decisions without delay. You *will* announce your decision in a clear, firm professional manner," Howser shouted.

As her mental fog cleared, Jane realized that her team members were standing before her. She saw Howser standing on a wooden platform. It may have been the bright sun, but she thought she saw his eyes water.

"Marine! You *will* have physical endurance and mental stamina, which will be measured by your ability to withstand pain, fatigue, stress, and hardships." As Howser continued, Jane began to understand what was happening and her own eyes filled with tears. The saltwater burned as it ran down her battered face and into the blood-encrusted cracks in her lips.

"Marine! You *will* have enthusiasm and a sincere interest in the performance of your duties." Jane straightened her posture slightly and stood without assistance, awash with pride. She vividly remembered watching Tom struggling to stand in the exact same spot several years ago.

"Marine! You *will* have initiative to take action even though you have not been given orders! You *will* meet new and unexpected situations with prompt action!" Howser's eyes gleamed at her achievement.

"Marine! You *will* have judgment and justice to be fair and consistent!"

Butch, Screech, and Pilot stood at attention as Jude hoisted the American flag, one notch at a time, as if in slow motion.

"Marine! You *will* have tact to deal with people in a manner that will maintain good relations and avoid problems."

A young major stepped forward and placed his arm beneath Jane's to help her stand taller.

"Marine! You will do this with *integrity*!" Howser continued.

"Marine! Your loyalties will lie in the devotion to your country; your corps; your seniors, peers, and subordinates. The motto of our corps is *Semper Fidelis*—Always Faithful. You owe unwavering loyalty up and down the chain of command. *You* are a United States Marine!" Howser approached Jane and shook her hand with a firm grip. She even noticed a slight smile on his face.

As Howser pinned on her star, Jane watched the American flag continue its slow rise up the pole in front of her wounded body. Twenty Marines stood at attention and saluted her while a bugler played "The Marines' Hymn." She had just earned her rank in Orion; she filled Tom's boots as second-in-command. Howser was the president and commanding officer of Orion; Jane was now the new general.

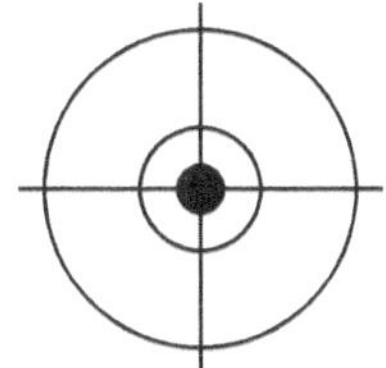

CHAPTER TWENTY

Jane took out her American Spirits and lit up a smoke. She thought about the courage and endurance it took to be an Orion soldier. She thought about Sam. If he survived an experience like The Hole, he'd exist in the world differently too. Jane knew Sam's military path wouldn't be the same as hers, and Sam wasn't nearly as hardened or gritty as she had been at his age. At eighteen, she'd already killed an estimated eight hundred men, either by direct assassination or in bombings and explosions. Sam lived his sheltered, safe life on the farm, awaiting his next chapter.

Removed from her foster family at an early age and thrown directly into the lion's den, Jane was forced to detach to survive. This strategy allowed her to become an effective assassin. Her early training in Pretoria prepared her to conquer any future situation into which she might be thrown, at any cost. One mission to Africa in 1979 and

1980, when she was only seventeen, challenged her the most as an Orion soldier and also exposed her to some of life's greatest lessons.

Jane entered the home she shared with Tom and flung her exhausted body across the bed. Her cat jumped up and joined her.

"You know, Quill Gordon," she murmured, as she stroked the silky fur on his back, "I don't even like cats." Quill snuggled into her and kneaded her arm softly with his paws. Tom entered the bedroom and fell backward onto the bed.

"Is that a piece of *brain* on your jacket? Yuck!" he teased, flicking her sleeve.

Although the two of them were just teenagers, they both felt like they were forty after returning from their equally grueling, separate deployments.

"Remember when you asked Howser if we could take roller-skating lessons?" Tom asked as he turned onto his side. His blonde, scruffy teenage beard was starting to take hold on his handsome face.

"Oh God! We were terrible!" she laughed, remembering the scene. "What was I *thinking*?"

"*You* were terrible. Jude and I were *awesome*! You looked like you were skating on rusty tuna fish cans!"

"I didn't know they were gonna make a big spectacle of that," Jane protested, holding her hand over her eyes. Through their laughter, they heard a knock on the front door.

"That's Jude. I told him he could crash here," Tom informed her as he got up to answer the door.

"Hey, Tom-rad!" Tom and Jude man-hugged, patting each other on the back. Jude then dropped his gear in the living room, went straight to the bedroom, pounced on Jane, and kissed her hard on the cheek.

"Your Holiness!" Jude exclaimed as he lay on top of her. "You survived! Me too! My group took out three cartels. What was your body count?" Jude asked, referring to his deployment to South America.

"Stop it! You *stink*! Cooties!" Jane yelled as she squirmed away.

"We were just talking about our skating lessons. Remember those?" Tom asked Jude.

"Yes! We divided up—boys on one side and girls on the other. Then when the music started, we had to skate as fast as we could to the opposite side of the rink," Jude reminisced. "Then *scratch, screech, scratch*. Here comes little Janie-poo, walking in her skates across the center of the rink! We had to wait, like, twenty minutes before she made it to the other side!" Jude and Tom busted up laughing and they both started to tickle Jane.

"Stop it! That's not true! It was more like *five* minutes. The longest five minutes of my *life*! I'd never been on roller skates before! I grew up in the *country*! With dirt roads! And, what, just like that I should know how to skate? I thought that's what lessons were for—to *teach* you!"

"Yeah, and you were the cutest little girl out there," Tom said kissing her cheek.

"Nerdiest, don't you mean?" laughed Jude. "I even remember her outfit!"

"Hey! I worked hard on that skating outfit. I saw something like it on an ABBA record—tube socks, satin shorts, and a yellow shirt with a star on it."

"Don't forget the headband! That was the clincher!" Tom crowed, tickling her again.

"*I* was awesome," grinned Jude. "I think the teacher wanted me."

"You were awesome because you were so much older than the rest of us. You were practically an adult! What were you? Eleven? Of *course* she wanted you," Jane teased.

There was another knock at the door.

"Oh. I told Screech and Pilot they could sleep here too," Jude said, shrugging his shoulders.

"What *is* this? A slumber party? Maybe Jane and I want to be alone, if you know what I mean," grumbled Tom while Jane sat on the bed, blushing.

"That's okay," Screech said as he skidded into the room. "We can watch wrestling or something. Go ahead. Where's the TV?"

"We don't have a TV. When would we ever watch TV?" Tom asked, perplexed, as they all moved into the living room.

Pilot looked around. "You don't have a couch? Or a chair?" He went into the kitchen and opened the cupboards. "Or plates, cups, bowls?" He continued rummaging. "Where are we supposed to sleep?" he demanded.

Everyone turned and watched as the closet door swung open. From the inside.

"You'll just have to figure it out," Butch advised, kneeling on the makeshift bed he had constructed in the closet. "Now will you ladies keep it down?! I'm trying to sleep."

Tom and Jane just looked at one another, rolled their eyes, and headed for the bedroom. The others had to make do on the floor or wherever they could find space. They didn't bother to change out of their combat BDUs because they only had a couple hours to rest.

In the middle of the night they arose, bleary-eyed, and made their way to the airport to catch their private plane to Africa for a yearlong deployment. As they walked through the terminal, Jane spotted a gold necklace on the ground. It had two large circles affixed to the bottom of a cross, and the words *Saint Anthony, Pray for us* were inscribed on the back. She picked up the piece of jewelry, dropped it into her boot, and continued to the plane. Once seated, Jane took it out and put it around her neck without thinking much of its meaning. She proceeded to pull out her language book and cram Swahili. She discovered that *jambo* meant a formal hello and *mambo* meant an informal hello. *It's all mambo-jambo to me*, she laughed to herself.

The flight was uneventful until the last thirty seconds before they were to land at their destination. Just before touching down on the runway, the plane suddenly rocked violently from side to side and then pulled up drastically, skyward. Jane looked out the window and saw they had a near miss with another plane sitting on the runway. She felt the blood rush to her head as she realized what had just happened. When they finally landed, after circling for a few minutes, a feeling of relief washed over her. She glanced down at the necklace hanging from her neck. *Thanks*, she said to herself.

When they were on the ground, Jane discovered that the African MONUC leaders requested that she command the operation rather than Tom. He would be her second-in-command. Jane had spent several years, off and on, training some of their members and developing Orion's relationship with them, so they preferred she lead the mission.

"There you go, stealing my thunder, Jane," Tom said, feigning disappointment as they loaded their Jeeps for the drive to Angola.

"Awww, don't worry about it, Tom-a-llama. Jane just wants your extra poop patrol," Butch chimed in.

"What do you mean by 'poop patrol,' Butcher?" Jane asked.

"You get to take care of all the extra shit. Like a big boss." Butch saluted her. "Would you like some ass-wipe, General Aggressive, ma'am?"

"I take *enough* shit from you guys. I don't need any more. Hey! Actually, I do need that. Give it to me, Major Britches." Jane tried to grab the roll of toilet paper from Butch.

"No *way*, General Heinie! Get your own." Butch tucked the roll into his deuce bag and grabbed his mission notebook.

As Jane scanned her notebook, she looked at each of the guys. She hoped to be tethered to Butch on this op. He had a greater understanding of Africa and certainly a better understanding of her quirks. Plus, he was older than her; Jane looked up to him like an older brother. Pilot and Screech would most likely be teamed together, yet Screech would rather be with Jane. Ever since Tom, Jane, and Screech had formed their small club during their brief stint in public grade school, Screech took his relationship with Jane very seriously. He had formed a brotherly attachment to her that no one could separate. They had spent countless hours talking about and dissecting the purpose of life and death. Screech allowed himself to be vulnerable only around Jane. He knew she would never violate his trust. There was never a moment that Jane doubted his skills, brotherhood, or insanity—and she loved him, regardless of the latter.

Although Screech saw Jane as his sister, he was certain Pilot was his best friend. They shared many common interests in weapons and they loved to modify them for specific purposes. Screech thought Pilot reciprocated their best-friend relationship; but, in reality, Pilot and Jude were closer. They were nearly inseparable outside of deployments. Jude and Pilot enjoyed instigating fights and proving to themselves that, together, they could fight their way out of any situation. They were also great wingmen for each other. They were both good-looking and fit, and had no problem picking up girls. They rarely let Stinky Screech come along to pick up chicks. Pilot and Jude bunked together at Quantico, leaving Butch to bunk with Screech. Butch was oblivious to the subtle friend bonds. He just assumed every person on the team was his family and best friend.

The intricacies of their relationships didn't matter to Jane. She was with the boys she loved and respected, and they were headed deep into her favorite place on the planet. To Jane, Africa was her home away from home, and she returned time after time in the years that followed. It was said that Africa had *onguma*, which meant it's so beautiful you'd never want to leave. Now that she was back, she couldn't imagine why she'd ever left.

Jude didn't share Jane's love for Africa. He'd never recovered from the trauma of being hauled away from his mother the night she overdosed, then being taken to Howser's school in Pretoria. Tom witnessed the manifestation of Jude's resentment toward Africa in many subtle—and not so subtle—ways. He once caught Jude deliberately torching villages in Sudan, along with livestock. Tom had to tackle him to stop his crazed behavior. Reluctantly, Tom kept their secret.

As Jane stood outside the airplane hangar, a strong wind swept through the valley and focused her attention. She drank in the overwhelming beauty of the expanse before her. The desert scene washed over the plains like a raging ocean wave. Whenever fear and stress seeped into her head like a mist through a crack, she simply paused and pulled from her memory the scenes of surreal African grace. As soon as her feet hit the hot soil, her body warmed to the perfect temperature. She never felt cold here. Whether in the thick central jungles of the Congo or the dry Namibian deserts, Africa cradled her like a baby in her mother's arms.

Just as the team finished packing the Jeeps with equipment to head to the game reserve in Angola—a welcome refuge before they began the nauseating Cessna flight to Uganda—Howser barreled toward them in a Land Rover in a swirl of dust. They were surprised to see him; the team didn't expect him to show up until much later.

As Howser's boots hit the ground, he bellowed, "Jude! Get your gear and get your ass in the truck. You're coming with me. A spot's opened in the Ranger training program and you're in."

Jude opened his mouth to reply and Howser snapped, "You got somethin' to say? Get your *ass* in the car."

Jude looked at him in disbelief. "Are you kidding—"

"Wait a minute, Howser!" protested Jane. "We need him on this op."

"To do what? Babysit you? Carry your bags?" Turning to Jude he yelled, "Why're you still standing there? Grab your shit and get in!"

Jane shook her head in frustration and ordered the rest of the team into the Jeeps. As they headed for the reserve, Jane realized Howser had messed up their plans again. Now they wouldn't have the time to relax before they boarded their plane; they needed to reconfigure their mission to account for Jude's absence. Their orders were detailed and lengthy, filled with topographical maps, secret destinations, and acronyms that only military staffers could decipher.

As the team descended on the Congo, Jane wondered what they'd uncover during this mission. She always learned something new. Jane didn't realize it at the time, but she would learn some of her greatest life's lessons from the insight of an eight-year-old Congolese girl.

The team drove to the compound with their emissary, Benjamin, to drop their gear. He assigned his daughter Ula to be Jane's servitor, or maidservant. Ula was stick thin and black as night. Her skin resembled black onyx—so black it had a blue hue. She often stood as still as a proud stone sculpture, her posture correct in every way. Jane later discovered Ula was a formative thinker and a profound listener.

Benjamin also had a son named Ulu, one of the hundreds of children "recruited" by the newly formed LRA. Jane knew its numbers would grow quickly into the thousands if her team was unsuccessful. They were the first to be sent in to assess the LRA developing in the area and to handle it, hopefully, without formal military intervention. They came to the Congo specifically to combat this group.

The child–recruits were taken into the jungle after they witnessed their parents and elders being slaughtered, dismembered, and beheaded. Some of the children survived the brutal initiations to become LRA soldiers. Those who did not were thrown into mass graves. Very few were able to escape and hide successfully. Somewhere in the tumultuous, deadly Congo, young boys and girls were praying for a savior. These were the children Orion sought.

Ula brought Jane some *matoke* (mashed banana gruel) to eat while Jane cleaned her weapons and sharpened her machete.

"Good God, Jane! Don't eat that! You'll be sick before we get out of here," warned Tom. He never ate the local food; he opted for C rations, which tasted like cereal box tops.

"I'm not gonna eat MREs. They have, like, four thousand calories and a gazillion grams of sodium," Jane replied. The military rations were disgusting. Even the US federal prison system wouldn't serve them because they were so unhealthy. Jane turned to Ula and spoke to her using a serious tone.

"Ula, I'm sorry about your brother. I understand how hard it must be for you." Ulu and Ula were twins, so Jane assumed Ulu's status as an LRA soldier and the team's presence made the situation even more difficult for Ula.

"Hatari," responded Ula, calling Jane by the name ascribed to her by the village, which in Swahili means "danger," "you cannot know. You cannot understand. I haff dese eyes dat see unlike you. I haff dis mind dat tinks unlike you. I haff my black skin dat feels unlike you. My soul has seen much dat you haff not. So, Hatari, you can only pretend you know, but you will never know."

"Get that, Jane? You were just trumped by a child!" crowed Pilot, who had been listening.

Screech, who had also heard the conversation, knelt down next to Ula and asked rhetorically, "Where in the world does an eight-year-old child gain the knowledge of a renowned philosopher?" Ula's body movements stilled and her eyes grew wide and scared.

"Oh, *do* take a guess, Professor," Pilot quipped while polishing his magazines. However, he did appear interested in where Screech was going with his statement. Sometimes Screech sprinkled useful information into his random rants.

"In 'What Is It Like to Be a Bat,' by American philosopher Tomas Nagel, Nagel wrote something like: 'To understand something from a completely true fact we must have all the similar qualities of that organism.' So, just imagine you have webbed wings, fly at night using sonar to determine your location and that of others, and eat piles of flying insects. This tells you what a bat looks like and does, but we cannot truly know what it's like to be a bat," Screech lectured.

"Did you seriously study that?" Pilot asked, irritated. "Did some yuppie-fuck college kid get a grant to sit around eating flies to try to figure out what it feels like to be a *fucking bat?* All so the Professor here could use it thirty years later in a quirky antidote? Un-fucking-believable waste of American education."

"You evidently missed the point, jack-hole," smirked Screech. "You're jealous of my superior intellect, you barf-noggin."

"Easy with the language, boys. There's a child here," Butch admonished.

"I suppose Ula is making a clear point," Jane said. "I can guess at what she feels, but it's virtually impossible for me to truly realize her pain. Lesson learned."

"And for the Professor to imagine what it's like walking around every day with my huge cock, he can never really understand what that's like until he first grows into his five-year-old kindergarten cock!" Pilot explained.

"Come on, you dipshit!" Jane yelled. "There's a fucking *child* in the room! Watch your goddamn language, you cockbag!"

"Jane," Screech said condescendingly, shaking his head, "it's a cock thing. You wouldn't understand."

Jane knew the squabbling and the swearing was a way for the team to try and lighten the mood. They all had an idea of what they were in for. Some things in life are meant to be seen; some things are meant to be buried so deep within the bowels of human defenses that only God could retrieve them. Jane hadn't yet decided which of the two she would attribute to their work in the Congo.

Night had fallen while gear was being stowed and their servitors were being introduced. Benjamin then presented their MONUC representatives and Godlove, their UN Security Council officer. Rather than whisking the team directly to the safety of a compound and spending hours dissecting maps and plans, as most American military officers did, the team members and their liaisons climbed into Jeeps an hour after arriving and drove 130 kilometers to see firsthand why Orion's help had been requested.

After driving over washboard roads deep into the jungle, the vehicles slowed as they approached a pit. The stench of decay—thick, acrid, nauseating, and foul—overtook them. When Jane closed her eyes momentarily, she felt as if she was suffocating and standing on the rotting forest floor of the Amazon. But she was far from there. Before them was a mass grave that contained hundreds of Congolese citizens. Most of the smell came from coagulated blood and melted flesh. Butch lit up the site with halogens and the team members adjusted their vision.

They stood there, looking into a deep hole filled with dismembered children laying in the arms of their mothers, whose heads had been severed. Twisted and torn corpses were piled one on top of another. Some of the faces were frozen in terror; others appeared as solemn as stone casts. Jane's initial impulse was to vomit, but she held back in the hope that her intense emotions would abate. Butch hurled his dinner into a bush. He usually had a high threshold for death pits; but, when there were children involved, his emotions got the better of him. Many of the bodies were shot a dozen times or more. Most of the killing, however, had been done with blades—machetes, most likely.

Jane turned to speak to Godlove, but she couldn't voice her thoughts. There were no words to describe what she felt. He turned from the scene and walked back toward their vehicles. His face was devoid of hope. He was wearing the same ghost expression Orion soldiers saw on countless people in Uganda and the Congo.

"Oh God," whispered Tom as he dropped to his knees. "God, have mercy and bless these women, children, and fathers. They are innocent and should be welcomed into your flock."

Tom continued to pray quietly all the way back to camp; the rest of the team remained silent. Part of Jane wanted to drop down on her knees and pray with Tom, to show him support, but she couldn't do it. Jane didn't believe in a God that could let this happen. She wanted to scream out loud and curse his god for letting this carnage unfold. Instead, she chose to say nothing and fought back her tears.

Jane wondered briefly if she would find her friend D'Narambi in that pile of death—and nearly choked at the thought. The last time she saw her, they were fifteen years old. Jane called D'Narambi's father Tshopo, which wasn't his real name. Tshopo was the name of the province from which he hailed. His real name was a bewildering amalgam of tones and tongue clicks she could never master. The rare friendship that blossomed between Jane and D'Narambi began when father and daughter brought Jane to their home to tend to a broken leg she sustained during a covert op. Jane really hoped D'Narambi was safe and not in that death hole.

When they returned to the compound, the team members went their separate ways. Jane found Ula straightening her tent and pulling uniforms from her rucksack. Jane sat at her desk and held her head in her hands. It was moments like these when Jane wished she could rush into Tom's arms, to have him hold her and reassure her that everything would be okay. She knew that could never happen. Although they were married, Howser mandated strict codes of behavior: no public displays of affection, and separate quarters while deployed.

"Did you see de grave?" Ula asked Jane, knowing she had. "No ting heavenly about dat, is dere, Hatari?" Her deep brown eyes stared directly into Jane's. Jane was taken aback by the way Ula spoke to her like a grown woman.

"Have you been there, Ula?" Jane questioned, afraid to hear her answer.

"Yes. For two days I searched de bodies, looking for Ulu. When de soldiers come to add more bodies, I lie myself down to look dead until dey go." Again Jane felt the urge to vomit. She couldn't imagine a child of eight years risking her life to search through hundreds of rotting corpses, looking for her brother.

"I got scared dat de soldiers knew I was alive, because sometimes dey would shoot and shoot into de pile, making everyone dead again," Ula said calmly.

Well, that explains all the gunshot wounds, Jane thought. The LRA would fire into the pits to shoot looters and people looking for their families.

Ula lay down to sleep on her reed mat, but Jane scooped her up and tucked her into her rack. Looking down at Ula, Jane thought about the children in America. They had no idea what the world was really like. *Should* they? Would they work harder and respect their parents and teachers more if they knew what children like Ula had to endure every day? But that was one of the reasons Orion existed—so they'd never *have* to know. Jane covered Ula with a light blanket and went out to find Butch.

"Hey, Little Joe!" Butch greeted her, using another nickname he had for her.

"How about 'ma'am' or 'general' or anything that sounds like you respect me?" Jane asked, irritated.

"Easy there, General, ma'am. Your Holiness. No disrespect, but you look like you need a break from soldiering," he said, cocking his head to one side and squinting at her. "Come here, kid. What's the matter?" Butch was only four years older than Jane, but at twenty-one he seemed to know things she didn't about how the real world worked.

"Butch, what's wrong with our *children*?"

"Whoa, there! Last time I checked, *we* did not have children. What children are you talking about?"

"You know what I mean! American children in general. They have no idea what the world is really like. They're sheltered from it by their white-collar, dysfunctional parents, who push television and Big Macs down their throats. So many rich, egotistical, rude children talk back to their teachers, vandalize their schools, and whine about not getting a Porsche for their sixteenth birthday. I think about those mall-crawling, marijuana-smoking jobless rats, chowing down on fast food and stealing clothes and fancy purses from stores and I wanna *puke*!"

Butch interrupted Jane's rant. "And the PTA of Pine Valley, Utah, would like to nominate Elizabeth Finn as this year's Mother of the Year!" he exclaimed in his best Bob Barker impersonation.

"You know, *you* are the reason abortion clinics are so popular, you bastard!" Jane yelled as she stomped back to her tent.

"Hey, Jane! Aren't you gonna kiss me goodbye, sweetie?" Butch shouted.

As she clomped into her tent, her expression softened when she saw Ula's little black stone face glowing in the night, expressionless. Jane knew Ula had the heart and courage of a lioness.

Jane tossed and turned most of the night. It usually took her about a week to acclimate completely to the Congo. The nights were alive with thousands of insects clicking, whirring, buzzing, and biting. While predators and scavengers roared and snarled, Jane lay on Ula's floor mat and began to put together a plan.

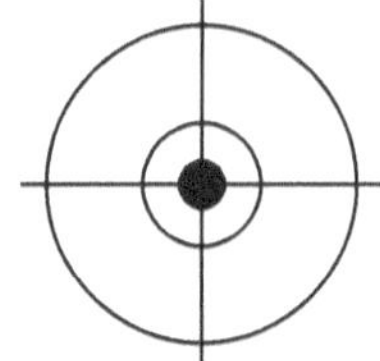

CHAPTER TWENTY-ONE

As dawn broke, its golden rays crawled slowly through the barbed wire surrounding their camp and infiltrated each crevice and seam of the canvas tents that sheltered the team. Jane woke up, lurched off the floor mat, and plopped onto her rack to begin looking through her orders for the MONUC team, which she needed to train. Already awake, Ula had assembled Jane's supplies and now brought her precious coffee to her. At seventeen years old, Jane had no other vices. No drugs, alcohol, or cigarettes—just good ol' caffeine. And Jane had discovered that the compound had no coffee. The one bag she brought with her wouldn't last very long and she needed her daily caffeine fix.

She stared blankly out of the opening of her tent, thinking how much she regretted having to order the local men in their camp to do *anything*, let alone get her coffee. They had been terrorized for years—intimidated, traumatized, and tortured. She wished she could load them onto a bus and send them to the heart of Uganda, to a safe haven with clean water and healthy food. However, Jane knew that if she could even make this offer, none of them would go. This was their war. They had each been affected by it. Most of the men in the compound had lost their wives, parents, and siblings, and the majority had children who had either been kidnapped and conscripted forcibly to the LRA or killed.

Joseph Kony, an Acholi man—who was more "boy" than "man"—was the seventeen-year-old leader of these brutalities. Many rebel groups had sprung up after Idi Amin was removed from power in Uganda. Kony was involved in one group called The Holy Spirit. After their defeat, Kony himself began to amass power. In 1979, he recruited many of his own soldiers from the disassembled Holy Spirit. Kony believed he was a religious savior. He planned to overthrow the government and rule according to the Ten Commandments, although he was violating every one of those Ten Commandments during his reign.

Kony started his violent coup by raiding villages and massacring anyone he thought opposed him. He abducted children and brain-washed them—using drugs and alcohol—into becoming soldiers in his newly established army. He told these young children that the drugs were infused with magical powers to make them bulletproof. The children ran eagerly and directly into the line of fire because they thought they were immune to gunshots. He made them believe that when they went into battle, rocks would turn into grenades and sticks into swords. He even resorted to some of the tactics used by The Holy Spirit, such as smearing oil on the children's bodies and telling them it was a protective forcefield that made them bulletproof.

He convinced nonconformists of his might through brutal displays, such as standing resistant children in front of other kids and chopping off their arms with machetes. He sliced off their noses, their ears, and their lips, then let them run off into the bush. If they survived, their disfigurement was a clear message to villagers that the LRA was a power to be feared.

Often, a child–soldier was forced to mutilate a fellow peer to demonstrate obedience. Many children became so brainwashed that they readily rushed into their own villages and hacked their own parents to death. Upon return to the LRA camps, they were rewarded with Coca Cola, alcohol, and heroin. Any child who escaped and survived became a ghost child—never the same and emotionally untouchable.

"Hey! G.I. Junior!" Butch yelled as he blasted into Jane's tent.

"Don't you knock?"

"What the hell am I supposed to knock on? The canvas? What're you doing?"

"I am considering my thoughts." Jane paused for a moment and looked at Butch with a straight face. "Butch, in America, how many fathers do you think are devoted to protecting their children from all harm?" she asked, trying to sound mature.

"Seriously, Jane? '*Considering your thoughts?*' You're *thinking*, Jane. It's called *thinking*. What is it with you and America? We're fighting a war *here*!" Butch started rummaging through her bags. She had no idea what he was looking for, but she let him search.

"I *know* that, but look at these fathers. They're willing to die for their children. Most American fathers don't even know how their kids are doing in school or who their friends are or where they were the night before. Most of them know more about their boss than their own kids!"

"General, you are generalizing. Or is that what generals do?"

"Most American dads hit the bars with their friends after work, go home, and collapse on the couch in front of the TV," Jane continued. "Then they get up the next morning and do it all over again." She knew she was generalizing, just like Butch said. Jane really had no idea what most American dads did. She hadn't been around any. This was just stuff she read in magazines or overheard on airplanes.

"Jane, darling, I think you have some daddy issues. Not all American dads are like that. Didn't you ever watch *My Three Sons* or *Father Knows Best*? How about *Leave It to Beaver*?"

"Not here, though," Jane went on, ignoring Butch's questions. "These men are beyond fathers. They're philosophers, teachers, and doctors to their children. Every day they teach their children to hunt, to read, to survive. Every night they cradle them and tell them stories of their fathers, and their fathers before them. Their stories are so exact, so descriptive, that throughout history they remain unchanged."

"Jane, I think you need to get a mosquito net that doesn't have holes in it. You may be suffering from malaria," joked Butch as he sat next to her on her rack. "What's gotten into you? Why're you so emotional? We really can't afford to be emotional. Are you okay? Dammit, Jane, come here!" Butch put his arm around Jane and pulled her into an awkward hug. "I need you to slow down for a minute. You need to realize you can't save the planet from every wrong-doer. You have to know that you have feelings and emotions, and sometimes it's okay to let them out and be real, especially here with your brothers. I'm not going to tell anyone," he whispered.

"Ugh. Whatever, cockbag! There! Is that better?" Jane asked, pushing his arms away. "I *feel* like you are an asshole trying to get into my face. We *are* here to save the planet and we don't have time for emotions—although what that little girl is witnessing will bother her for a *long* time."

"For God's sake! You sound like Howser! What's *really* bothering you? I think I know you pretty well—better than most—and you're acting really weird, Jane. So drop the tough-girl crap and shoot straight. What's up? You know I have an obligation to you as your brother."

"Okaaaay. You're right, Butch. Something is bothering me."

Butch began to rifle through Jane's duffle bag again. He pulled out a few empty magazines and began loading them for her. "See? I *knew* it! You have that cute little pouty look on your face." Butch made a sad puppy face and then smiled.

"Stop it or I'm not gonna tell you—or, I mean, I'm not gonna *ask* you."

Butch heard her serious tone, so he set down the magazines.

"What is it, kid? You sick or something?"

"No, I'm . . . I'm married."

"I know that, Jane. I was at the 'ceremony,' remember? But don't worry. That doesn't mean we can't keep having this thing between us. I see how you look at me." Butch gave her a playful nudge accompanied by a wink. "Of course you're married, silly, and that's swell. So what's the matter?"

"Butch . . . you're older than me."

"Yeah. Not by much, though."

"What comes next?" Jane finally asked.

"What do you mean, what comes next? Like a house? Bills? What? I don't know what you're asking."

"Never mind. You're right. It's dumb." *God*, Jane thought, *doesn't anyone know about sex?* Howser must have wanted them to be so preoccupied with training and wars and governments that they forgot to be human.

"We gotta go. Let's get out of here, Butch. We have a meeting." Jane got up and stepped out of her tent, trying to refocus on the tasks at hand, starting with a team meeting.

"Gentlemen, the first order of business is to sort out the bodies from the grave and bury them properly," Jane announced. She looked at Tom and could see in his face that he was happy with her decision. He had been troubled since they left the mass grave, although she knew the others would protest her decision.

"Hatari, it is not possible. Den we haff to go to *all* de places for *all* de people," Godlove replied. He clearly thought it impossible and unfair to sort out and bury three hundred people without finding and burying the other three hundred *thousand* that had also died in that region. Although Jane understood Godlove's concern, she was dead set on her decision.

"We *will* do this. I am ordering that *every single body* your team comes across in the future be identified and buried. The LRA *thrives* on leaving behind exposed, mutilated corpses to instill fear. It's right to respect our fallen brothers and sisters," she said bluntly, then walked back into her tent.

Jane instantly thought of a story she once read of Vlad the Impaler. He killed his enemies by running a huge, sharpened pole up their assholes, then planted their bodies around the grounds of his castle as a warning to his enemies. The world had always been full of sick people. This was another reason why she struggled so hard to comprehend Tom's devotion to God and Jesus.

At fifteen, Jane went to see the Shroud of Turin, a linen cloth imprinted with the faint image of a man said to be Christ. Believers thought his disciples wrapped him in this cloth after his crucifixion. Mesmerized by the image, Jane struggled to make out the man's face. She stared at the bloodstains where he supposedly wore his crown of thorns. Jane examined the faint marks of crimson along the image's side that might have come from the sword wielded by Pontius Pilate. Deep inside, Jane felt so much pain and sadness to think of how this man, whoever he was, had been beaten, tortured, cut, and bruised. Jane simply couldn't comprehend how a human being could crucify another. If it *were* Jesus, as the story goes, he did this willingly, sacrificing himself.

Jane began to weep as she stood motionless before the cloth, experiencing the empathy she felt for this man. Howser stood beside her the whole time. When he noticed her tears, he grabbed her by the shirt and led her to a corner of the room.

"What in the hell's come over you? Are you sick?"

"Why did he *do* that?" Jane asked, tears rolling down her face. "If he thought dying like that was going to stop all the bad stuff in the world, and all the torture and killing . . . he was so *wrong*," Jane sobbed.

"Oh stop this shit! That piece of cloth over there is just some elaborate hoax to sway the minds of feeble people like you. Would you look at yourself? You're a mess!" Howser barked. "Come on. I have business with the archbishop."

The image of the shroud continued to haunt Jane for years. Seeing evidence of such brutality made her question Jesus' sacrifice. *Why did he die? It didn't change anything.*

Tom wandered into Jane's tent and watched as Ula helped Jane sort through her *chambo*, or tools. He picked up a knife that looked like its purpose was to cut steak.

"I see the camp isn't quite up to par on resources. It looks like most of the weapons are kitchen knives, machetes, and a handful of AK-47s," he remarked.

"We have two trucks coming from Kampala. We should be getting some M-16s with modified reflex sights. Hopefully, these makeshift soldiers will be able to fire them—and the trucks can handle the rough terrain and get the weapons to us on time."

"And with any luck, they won't be carried off by *wachawi*," Tom said. "This is a very superstitious group we're dealing with. Did you know they're calling you Baba Yaga? That means old witch." Tom laughed deeply. He had a big, hearty laugh that Jane loved.

"I know what Baba Yaga means! I'm so proud of you for learning a new language. It's about time you exercised your fat brain, you big knuckle-dragger," she replied, smiling at him.

"Ooooo! Darling! You're starting to turn me on! Keep insulting me!" he said, pushing her gently. "I think we should change your call sign. Baba Yaga! Come in, Baba Yaga! This is Spread Eagle twenty. Copy," Tom rasped as spit flew from his mouth.

"You *ass*. I love you." Jane pushed him back—hard. In any other place, they might have started an all-out fistfight. They loved to fight each other; it helped to keep their skills sharp.

Most people didn't understand their behavior. Once, when they were at the beach on vacation, they made a ring in the sand and started fighting. They were pile-driving each other, throwing and landing hooks and jabs. Deeply concentrated on their fight, they hadn't noticed the people who had formed a circle around them. The crowd didn't know they were playing. Some of the other vacationing soldiers from Fort Bragg were probably tempted to jump in and break up the fight. Tom's size must have intimidated them, however, because instead of intervening, they called the cops. When they spotted the police, Jane and Tom stopped the fight immediately and started kissing and waving in an attempt to disperse the onlookers, most of whom decided to move on, taking their towels and beach umbrellas as far away from Jane and Tom as possible.

The sound of Ula polishing Jane's machete interrupted her daydream. She watched as the little girl ran a tattered rag meticulously over the surface while holding the machete across her skinny legs.

"Ula? It bothers me that you think I don't feel your pain and that I don't understand what is happening to you and your people."

"Why does dat trouble you, Hatari? Why do you tink I am helped by you haffing my pain?" Ula continued to sit at Jane's feet, turning the machete over in her hands and looking at her reflection in the blade.

"Let me try to explain why I think I know how you feel. When your brother was taken, did you cry?"

"Yes, yes! Of *course* I cried! I *did*! So many tears dat de Nile burst its banks!" Ula replied passionately.

"Did you throw yourself down on the ground and hit it with your fists? Did you feel emptiness inside, as if part of your own soul was missing?"

"Hatari, you are a silly woman." Ula said, moving closer to Jane.

"Then did you curse the sky and feel your blood boil? Did you vow to find your brother with all the energy in your body?"

"I am here, aren't I?" Ula asked, taking Jane's hand.

"Ula, we are human and we react the same to similar situations. I think it's fair to say that I understand how you feel. I'm not assuming anything and I'm not pretending to feel something

I do not. Why would I come here to help if I didn't know your suffering?" Jane held up Ula's chin lightly with her fingers and looked into her dark eyes.

Ula pushed Jane's hand away as she stood up and replied fiercely, "For big American dollars is why you are here!" She raced out of the tent, passing Pilot on the way out.

"Whoa, whoa, little one! What's the hurry?" he asked as Ula blazed past him. "Well, I see you're fit to raise children," he teased Jane, shooting her a dazzling white smile.

"Oh for God's sake! Sit down." Jane grabbed Pilot's hand and forced him to sit. "Ula thinks we're here for 'big American dollars.' I really hurt her feelings."

"Big American dollars? Oh, fuck! There you go, showing off your paycheck, you high roller! Does she realize we can't even afford our own uniforms? That I was captured twice last month and tortured? Then I was shot, stabbed, and had my car blown up? Hell! I made a whopping thirty-five hundred bucks for all of that! Are you making more money than me?" Pilot asked, trying to make a joke of the encounter.

"Yeah, yeah. I think the government's busy buying toilet seats and gold hammers. I didn't get paid at *all* last month!" ranted Jane. "It's just sad that this is the view people have of us here. I wish I never left South Africa. We may not have been paid any better, but the people are kinder and the climate is nicer. Ula left before I could tell her we aren't getting paid to be here."

"She's a kid, Jane. She wouldn't understand anyway."

"I don't know about that. She seems pretty damn smart." Jane paused. "I'm gonna prepare the MONUC tonight. Do you think you can handle the boys?" Jane asked, switching the subject.

"If you're referring to Screech, then no. *No one* can deal with Screech. But Butch and Tom, I think I got it handled. G'night, Jane," Pilot said as he got up to leave.

"Thanks. See you in a few hours," Jane replied, suddenly feeling an upswing in her adrenaline level as she thought about what they were about to do. Pilot hesitated at the doorway to her tent, turned back, and sat on Jane's rack.

"Hey. Congratulations, by the way, on you and Tom getting hitched. I think that's cool. I hope it goes well."

"Thanks. I think it will. We've known each other forever."

"Yeah, but being married is different. My parents knew each other forever too, but they didn't get along."

"Funny, I never really thought of you having parents. I mean, I know you *do*, but you never talk about them. I guess I just think all of us are family now."

"I never 'got' my mom. She was weird. She always bragged about all my stuff to her friends, but when we were home, just the two of us, she was a horrible mom."

"Horrible? Like she beat you or something?"

"No, not like that. She was always just . . . She was a big ol' alcoholic. She was just drunk all the time. Or passed out."

"Oh, yuck. I hate that. You had a mom and she wasn't stable. I wanted to know my real mom so bad. Then I got stuck with Dr. Reid."

"Who?"

"Reid, you dummy! Mary Reid, the sociopath."

"Jane, are you still seeing her? I thought we talked about that. You gotta let that go, man."

"I don't have a choice, Pilot. I see her all the time. She's always there when I get back."

"Just tell her to go away, Jane."

"Don't you see her too?"

"No, Jane. I don't see her. Neither does Screech. Or Butch. Or Jude. Or Tom. Tell her to back off." Pilot brushed Jane's shoulder as he stood, then stooped to kiss the top of her head. "Love you, Jane."

"I love you too, Pilot. Thanks."

Jane left the tent and gathered her five MONUC comrades. Uruzandokiko, the lead officer for the MONUC, was a lean and very serious twenty-eight-year-old. Jane had trained him in Cuba a year earlier for this particular mission, along with his second-in-command, Narotu. Jane called Narotu "Buzz" because of his speech impediment when he spoke Kiswahili. His s's sounded like bees buzzing. The other three soldiers were fathers of recruited LRA kids. The level of tension in the air that night could have been cut with a butter knife. They dissected their plan as they waited for nightfall. This op was to be the first of many night assaults they had planned for the LRA.

As the camp grew darker, Jane packed her thermal lenses, an XM8 future assault rifle, and the blade she coveted the most. She knew the mission might end with brutal hand-to-hand combat, which happened to be her area of expertise. At that moment, she wished for her Katana sword.

All soldiers prepare for battle differently. Jane put herself through a rigorous routine of push-ups, sit-ups, stretching, and Kendo swordfighting moves. She limbered up and visualized the impending battle. Buzz sat quietly in the corner, cleaning his weapon, talking to it, and caring for it—as it cared for him. Watching him reminded Jane of her own rifle creed.

"This is my rifle. There are many like it, but this one is mine. My rifle is my life. Without it, I am nothing," she said under her breath.

Kiko, a Muslim, prostrated himself and prayed to Allah. Some Americans assumed that all Muslims were terrorists. Jane knew some terrorists happened to be Muslim. Just like some Irish liked to fight and some French people smoked. *Well, actually*, she thought, *all French people smoke*. Jane respected Kiko for his devotion. He reminded her of Tom. But after all she'd seen thus far in her short life, she didn't have it in her to pray to a god in whom she wasn't sure she believed. Jane needed evidence that God existed in something good. All she ever saw were evil and death.

Charley, a Baluba father, sat quietly, clutching a photo of his son while Sunni, the last member of her team, listened to his Walkman. Each of them prepared individually, waiting on night to settle in.

Outside her tent, the other MONUC gathered for evening rice. They sang as they ate.

"Kiko, why are they singing?" Jane asked, her voice breaking the silence in her tent.

"Dey believe deir songs will infiltrate the deep forest and land on de ears of deir sons. Maybe deir songs will remove deir sons from de drug-induced brainwashing and bring dem home. I am not relying on song to bring dem home." He picked up his machete and raised it above his head. "Eh, Baba?"

Buzz touched Jane's shoulder and pointed outside the tent. "Baba, it izz time."

The MONUC soldiers and Jane lined up in ranking order and emerged from the tent. Jane's Orion team members exited their tents as well. The soldiers who were not going on the mission lined the path through their tents. Jane's combined team walked through the gauntlet, like football players rushing onto the field before a game, only they walked in what looked like slow motion.

The soldiers surrounded them and touched their hearts, then their foreheads, which symbolized the transfer of courage from them to the team. Jane thought it may have been more of a gesture of saying, "Goodbye, my brothers. We won't be having dinner together tonight."

At the end of the line, they were offered a rice alcohol shot. Jane hated this part of the leave-taking. The liquor burned its way down her throat and instantly made her gag. She couldn't stand alcohol. Screech slugged down two shots as Jane choked down one.

Ula sat on a table, watching them. She barely acknowledged Jane. *Big American dollars*, Jane thought.

The team followed a river for four miles before breaking off from its winding path. As they walked deeper into the thick jungle, they heard their enemies. The LRA didn't bother to be quiet or covert. Before that night, no one had been a threat.

Jane wasn't afraid. To her, the LRA was like a big gang of Crips. They recruited—and intimidated—the same way. They were not highly trained soldiers; they were drugged-up thugs.

When the team reached the LRA camp, they were not surprised at what they saw. Multiple bonfires were ringed by drunken men, many of whom had passed out. A few men played cards as American heavy-metal music blared from the tents. What *did* catch Jane by surprise were the Kalashnikov rifles strapped to the backs of what looked to be seven-year-old boys. At one table, boys who were not much older sat shooting each other up with heroin, presumably supplied by Joseph Kony. The team circled the fringes of the camp, trying to locate Motu—the big dog of that particular LRA faction.

Not for long, Jane thought.

Eventually, she spied Motu sitting at a card table. His eyes were bloodshot and sweat dripped from his scowling face. He adjusted his dark-green beret on his head, tilting it to the left. A belt of ammunition crisscrossed his chest and back, and a dark sweat stain soiled the back of his shirt. A young girl sat at his feet, visibly incoherent; she stared at the ground utterly motionless. Motu suddenly rose to his feet, grabbed the child, and dragged her through the dirt toward one of the tents. Jane slung her rifle across her back, spit into her hands, and grabbed her machete.

"Don't wait up, boys." Jane signaled the engagement to her team, and they began their silent assault on the camp. She made her way to the back of Motu's tent and peered through the crack in the canvas. He dosed the child with heroin and she slumped onto the bed like a rag doll. *Piece of shit*, Jane thought as she felt her guts churn. She reminded herself that in about three minutes, Motu would be dead. Jane could smell his sour sweat, and she had an idea of what he was about to do. She watched her team members fall silently into place.

Jane waited for the girl to pass out entirely and for Motu to drop his pants. He took a swig of alcohol and let the bottle fall to the floor. Jane was sure he had no idea she was watching. When she gave the GO signal to her awaiting team, Jane moved to the front of the tent and straight through the front opening, slashing Motu's throat before he could even yell for help. The blade cut with precision and his blood sprayed across the tent wall. Jane felt the oozing sludge on her hand, which was still gripping Motu tightly. There was no big Hollywood brawl or exchange of dialogue between good and evil, followed by a final death scene. Her team members were trained to kill quickly. Jane remembered Howser saying once that if they found themselves in a fair fight, their tactics sucked.

Motu's hot, thick blood drained rapidly from the deep wound in his neck, soaking the floor of the tent. She sloshed through it fast;

grabbed the young, waifish girl; and threw her over her shoulder with ease. Jane carried her outside and hid her in the brush, where she slumped, still unconscious.

That night was not only about bringing all the children out; they also aimed to kill all the adult soldiers in the camp. The disoriented children were easy to round up. Buzz collected Motu's victim and all the other children the team had gathered.

As Jane turned to storm another tent, Buzz whispered, "Thankzzz, Hatari. If only one child izz free, den we haff won tonight."

"No worries, Buzz. I'll get them all." Jane turned to go back to work.

Tom engaged four men at once, using only his blade to keep the attack as silent as possible. He disemboweled the LRA members quickly and then slit their throats. He prayed to himself that the children wouldn't be affected even more by witnessing his actions, yet reality sunk in as he watched one child try to put a man's guts back inside him. Tom dragged the child toward Buzz, with the man's guts trailing behind them. The child refused to let them go.

"What the fuck?" Screech looked at the child as Tom handed him off to Buzz. "That kid is worse than me! Is he taking a trophy?"

"Shut up, Screech! Get back in there!" Tom ordered.

"Fuck! I took care of my guys! They're all sleeping with Satan tonight. You need some help?" Tom looked at Screech more closely and gagged at the sight of Screech's blood-soaked beard and neck. "Don't worry, man. I didn't *eat* the guy, if that's what you're thinking. I just tore off his face with my teeth. Had to. No other choice." Tom wasn't certain about that.

One by one, the entire team eliminated the LRA members quickly and quietly. Like ballet dancers, they moved with rhythm and grace, silently cutting down their enemies. Pilot lurked behind his targets as they went into the brush to piss, then he broke their necks or plunged a dagger into a kidney. He was a stealth hunter; he enjoyed stalking his victims.

Butch made deliberate, subtle noises to lure his targets to check an area. In one instance he drove his machete into a soldier's bowels as he shoved his fingers into the man's throat. Butch uttered a deep, low growl as he tore out the man's esophagus.

In the aftermath, ghostly moans from the dying men filled the LRA camp, coupled with the sounds of sobbing children. The cries of the children were ones that no one on her team would be able to hear without reliving that nightmare.

They killed twenty LRA soldiers that night. As the sun rose, another MONUC unit rolled into the outskirts of the LRA site. They helped round up about thirty child–soldiers, scooping up the drunk and drugged kids, disarming them easily. They also rescued more than one hundred enslaved Congolese children awaiting recruitment. The Jeeps headed back to the Orion/MONUC compound while the trucks bearing the children continued on to hospitals.

Jane was glad no mirrors existed in their compound. The horrified look on Ula's face when she saw Jane made it all too clear to Jane what she looked like. She could feel the dried blood cracking on her face and congealing in her hair. Her boots still sloshed with blood as she approached her tent. Thankfully, her blood-saturated BDUs were black. Jane's MONUC comrades wore green uniforms, so their clothing showed the night's carnage more clearly. From the blood splatters and slices in their uniforms, they had obviously fought courageously.

Jane scanned the camp quickly for Tom. He had not returned with her in her Jeep. They spotted each other at the same time, and he looked as relieved to see her as she was to see him.

"I love you," he mouthed.

Jane smiled back and whispered, "I love you too."

"Hatari!" Ula shouted at her. "How de hell am I supposed to clean you?!" It never occurred to Jane that Ula was going to clean her. "Get de damn bloody rags off!" she scolded, as if she were Jane's mother.

"Nice to see you too, Ula."

"It is not nice to see Hatari. You are gross and you stink like dung!"

"All in a night's work, Ula. All in a night's work," Jane replied exhaustedly as the adrenaline rush wore off.

Ula warmed some water that appeared to be just as dirty as Jane was. She scrubbed Jane's face and hands, even though Jane insisted she could do it herself.

"I can do nothing about your hair. There is not enough water in de whole Nile to clean it," Ula said, fussing over Jane and trying to hide her relief that Jane made it back to camp safely.

"Ula, why do you keep talking about the Nile? The Nile is a river in Egypt. Why not talk about the Congo River instead?"

"Because de Nile is de birth of all life, stupid. Did you not go to school?"

Ula spoke like Screech; she was blunt and showed no respect. Ula had a stonelike manner only in the presence of her father. Around Jane, however, she behaved like a little feral cat. Jane understood this was Ula's way of hiding her fear; it was mostly an act.

"I thought all American soldiers had to cut their hair slick, like the Eagle," Ula said, motioning to Butch. She called him "the Eagle" because of the Nazi eagle tattoo on the back of his neck. She didn't understand that its meaning was offensive. The tattoo protected Butch while he was deep undercover with white supremacists.

"I do other jobs that I have to have long hair for, Ula," Jane said softly.

"Pssh! Den let me braid it for you!" she said excitedly.

"As you wish, Ula." Jane ached everywhere and was worn out from fighting. She wasn't about to argue with an eight-year-old girl.

The next morning they were fed a banquet to celebrate their victory. When Jane emerged from her tent for breakfast, she forgot her hair was still in long braids

"Well look, Pa! It's Laura Ingalls come over for grub," Screech chortled, pointing at her.

"Shut up, ass! I like them!" Jane did rather prefer the braids to the tight bun she wore every day.

"Here, General." Tom approached her and secured a red paper carnation on her breast pocket. The whole team sported them—a token and thank-you from the native soldiers. As the men sang loudly, Jane noticed a Jeep approaching the compound.

"Crap! Attention boys! Howser's on the horizon!" They quickly scrambled around the camp and removed the carnations, shoving them in their pockets. They didn't want to look as if they were getting too comfortable.

"Screech! For fuck's sake! Wipe off your beard! You have at least three meals on that disgusting mop of fur!"

"It's a survival thing, Jane. What if I get lost? See? I'd be able to eat for a couple days," he quipped as he pulled bits of scrambled egg from his beard and put them into his mouth.

The Jeep tore into their shoddy, makeshift FOB. Howser stepped out of the rickety vehicle and wiped the dust from his BDUs. It was nice to see him in combat gear. At fifty years old, he was as muscular and fit as he was at thirty.

"At ease, gentlemen, Widowmaker." Howser glanced over at Jane. She swore she saw him smile, but couldn't tell for sure because she was blinded by the sun reflecting off his oversized aviator glasses.

"I thought those shades were supposed to be mirrored on the inside so you can see yourself in them," Jane chuckled.

"Sit down, smart-ass." That time, she *did* see him smile.

"So I hear we were successful in taking out eighteen LRA soldiers and two LRA commanders last night. I look forward to the after-action report." Howser had been briefed before he was driven to the compound, so he knew exactly what had transpired.

"Oh really, sir?" Tom strode over to Howser and patted him on the shoulder. "And how many children did *we* bring back?" he asked, pointing out the irritatingly obvious fact that every time the team accomplished something, Command took all the credit.

"Shut the fuck up, Marine! Go get me a drink. It's hot as hell here! I'm sweating like a whore in church," Howser bellowed as he took out a cloth and wiped his brow. He then tossed the sweaty rag at Butch and said, "Souvenir for you, son. Wipe your ass with it, you mongrel." Howser let out a hearty laugh. "You did good, kids, but get me that damn drink."

The team's laughter broke the tension.

"Yeah, lass, and bring me a Twisted Sour. On the rocks!" Pilot ordered, tossing his CamelBak to Tom. "Or just some more muddy, putrid water."

"I brought you kids some toys," Howser continued. He motioned to the truck that stood parked behind his Jeep. "We got in some pretty cool PEK-4s for the MONUC. Get those mounted on their M4s. That laser should help 'em engage targets at night. Anything helps, I imagine," he said, wiping his brow again.

Screech and Pilot raced to the truck like kids on Christmas morning. They also discovered Howser had brought in some M2s. The .50 cals had been in US Army use for almost seventy years.

"*Ma deuce!*" Screech shouted gleefully, affectionately stroking an M2.

"You sound like that little fucked-up frog guy from that Frodo book when you stroke that machine gun! 'My Precious! My Precious!'" teased Pilot as he mimicked Gollum.

The two of them also uncovered MK19 grenade launchers that worked like a machine gun and a plethora of M240 machine guns.

"Oldies but goodies!" Pilot crowed, grateful the cavalry had finally arrived.

Screech had already begun thinking of ways to modify the weapons and started to discuss them excitedly with Pilot. "We can add rails here. Maybe strip this one down and combine it with that AK over there. Let's add some bayonets too!"

Jane escorted Howser to his tent and helped him lug his gear onto his rack.

"Elizabeth, I'm glad you're all right." He put his hand on her shoulder. And with that simple act, Jane realized her father was planning to have a serious discussion with her, which Jane avoided at all costs. In her eyes, it was too late for her father to act like a *father* toward her.

"Thanks . . . *Dad.*" The sarcasm just slipped out of Jane's mouth. She was usually more stoic around her father, but her emotions were heightened from what she had witnessed the night before. "Can I have a drink?" Jane asked facetiously. "This sounds like a Catholic come-to-Jesus meeting and I don't know if I have the strength to listen to your sins without backup."

Howser turned toward her with a straight face. "Look, I need you to listen. It's about your mother," Howser explained, dismissing her joke. Howser had been feeling unusually exhausted the past several weeks, although he was good at hiding it from those around him. He had begun to worry about his health—he was even thinking of seeing a doctor—which prompted his desire to speak frankly to Jane about her past.

"Oh, Jeezuz! Excuse me, sir. I apologize for calling you 'Dad.' I don't know what came over me. I'm a little outside myself right now." Jane's immaturity began to seep out. "Did you see what's happening here? Have you *seen* those kids with their mouths hacked off? Did you stand in that rotting grave? Oh, *noooo*! You sit back in some comfortable chair, shooting the shit with other UN fucks, talking about how to gain financial leverage over small countries. I, however, have a duty to serve my country, to protect the nation's security, and, above all else, to sacrifice my very existence for the office of the presidency and the entire cabinet of losers!" Jane yelled. The horror of what she had witnessed came spilling out of her, making her oblivious to anything Howser had to say.

"Elizabeth, I am approaching you as your father. Now shut up and listen to me," Howser said as he tried to move closer to her.

Jane didn't want to hear what Howser had to say. He'd never approached her as a father figure before, so why should he do it now?

"You're not a *father*!" Jane raged. "Fathers read stories to their daughters. They tuck them in at night and make them feel safe. They fill their heads with ridiculous ideas that, one day, they'll walk them down the aisle to be wed." Jane looked down and shook her head.

"Howser, fathers don't bring their daughters on their first covert op for their tenth birthday. They don't teach them close quarters combat before they can ride a bicycle. Hell, I don't even know if I *can* ride a bike. They don't send them to secret military school and buy them topographical maps of Arab countries. They make sure their English is good before they teach them to speak Russian! Real fathers are proud of their daughters when they win the spelling bee, not when they are awarded a pistol sharpshooter badge at age nine!

"The only time I ever got *close* to a Christmas tree with you was when we were looking at it through thermal night-vision goggles. I was nine years old, dammit! Instead of chasing boys in high school, I spent four years tracking Soviets on a Navy sub!"

"Are you finished with your dissertation about your miserable childhood?" he asked calmly.

"Yes!"

"About your mother, then—"

"Holy Christ!" Jane couldn't believe he kept bringing up her mother.

Howser suddenly grabbed her by the throat and slammed her into the wall of the tent, nearly knocking it down.

"Listen, young lady, your mother damn near lost her life in Argentina because she wasn't properly trained. They ripped her to *shreds*. Who do you think invented the Killing Circle? *I* did. And I did it to save your sorry, miserable ass from the same fate. You killed someone who meant more to me than my own life! And you can *never* give her back. Part of me will despise you until I rot in hell. I would just as soon slit your throat than listen to you disrespect her. You'd better get that giant chip off your shoulder before I knock it off! *Do you understand me?* She survived *unspeakable* horrors and yet one fucking child killed her! A child! You *will* show her some respect."

Jane was suffocating in Howser's grasp. Her chest heaved and she struggled to breathe after he released her. She wasn't going to let him shake her, though.

"Is that an *order*, sir?" Jane spit out.

"You ungrateful bitch!"

"Sir, yes sir!" she shouted in defiance, endeavoring not to lose *all* her dignity.

"Screw this! Prepare for duty. Your orders are in that case," he said, pointing to a black briefcase. What Jane didn't realize until later was that Howser had slipped her mother's journal in the case beneath the orders.

Jane stormed out of Howser's tent with the case and headed toward her own, where Ula was waiting for her.

"Did you find Ulu, Hatari?"

After taking one look at Ula's face, Jane was able to calm down. "I don't know, Ula. All the children were taken to Modan. If he was at that camp, we probably found him. If not, we *will* find him. I have to sleep now, Ula. Just for a while."

"Don't sleep, Hatari. Pray first."

"I don't pray, Ula. I don't have a god."

Ula looked utterly stunned. "What?! We all haff God! Who made you?" she asked, perplexed.

"My parents did, Ula. Not God."

"We will haff to talk about dis when you are not so crazy," she said, waving her hand at Jane, sounding just like Tom.

Jane curled up on her rack, holding her knees. As she drifted off to sleep, she almost said a silent prayer to herself that no one else could hear.

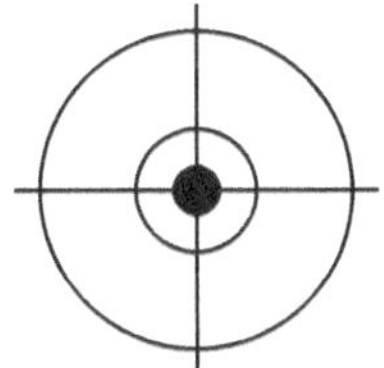

CHAPTER TWENTY-TWO

Jane tossed and turned in her rack on that hot night in the Congo, thinking about a commercial flight she had taken with Tom when they were about sixteen years old. She had certainly questioned Tom's religion over the years because she saw so much hypocrisy in it. During the flight, Jane noticed a Bible nestled in the seatback and she pulled it out.

"Someone must've forgotten this," said Jane as she held it up to show Tom. "Or maybe it's like the Gideon Bibles stuffed in every hotel bedside drawer. Huh. Maybe someone is stuffing them in airplanes now." Jane opened the book and set it on her lap. "Let's see what ye ol' book of crap has to say," Jane continued. "Oh wow! Exodus 11:5: 'God kills all first-born children.' Why would he do that, Tom? Oh, let's see . . . 13:8." Jane continued reading, "'This is because of what the Lord did for me when I came out of Egypt.'"

"Stop it, Jane! You're totally misinterpreting that," Tom said defensively.

Jane continued to flip the pages. "Hmmmm, 14:28: 'He killed them all because they didn't believe in him.' Hey! Wait a darn second! If I remember correctly, God killed the Egyptians for enslaving the Jews. That was a great scene! Charlton Heston, I think."

Jane scratched her chin and looked over at Tom. He grabbed her leg and gave it a hard, painful squeeze.

"Jane, stop it right now or I'll take you to the back of the plane and beat the crap out of you," threatened Tom, refusing to let go of her thigh.

"I can't, Tom! Didn't God tell Moses it was okay to have slaves? Yes! Here it is in Exodus 21: 'Hey, Moses! Have some slaves!' Oh, man! I thought *I* killed a lot of people!" Tom sat there, red-faced, gritting his teeth. He said nothing so Jane pressed on. "Oh, yes. 21:16: 'Kidnappers . . . killed'! 21:17: 'Curse your mother and father . . . killed'!" Jane continued. "21:21: 'Strike a man a mortal blow . . . killed'! Oh, this is interesting. Kill a slave and you're only punished, not killed! Ahhh! Let my people go!" Jane said as she threw her head back and shook it vigorously.

Tom had had enough. He stood up and walked to the back of the plane. Jane supposed she didn't fully understand his self-torment regarding what he did, despite what he believed. He truly thought he would go to hell for doing his job.

Jane kept reading in silent astonishment. According to the rules Jane read in that book, God had already killed her three times. She was batting a thousand. Deuteronomy 22:21 read: "If a girl marries a man and she is not a virgin, she shall be taken to her father's house and stoned to death." Jane could just imagine that conversation.

Hello, Dad. About that virgin thing? There's something I need to tell you. Oh yes, Jane could see how she could have misinterpreted that. And who was this Deuteronomy dude anyway? Deuteronomy 23:2 read: "No one whose testicles have been crushed or penis cut off may be admitted into the community of the Lord." *Wow! Sorry, boys. Blown up in the war? Is your junk gone? You're outta here! Can't have you messing up heaven.* Jane couldn't believe the messages the Bible contained. Leviticus 20:13 shockingly noted: "If a man lies with another man they shall be killed."

Jane stood up from her seat and shouted to Tom at the back of the plane. "So if the Bible is the word of God, and God determines morality, then executing homosexuals is morally sanctioned? Get the *fuck* out, Tom! That's blind obedience to an arbitrary authority! You're a son of a bitch!"

The passengers looked at Jane as if she were either drunk or crazy. Or both. The flight attendants immediately rushed down the aisle in her direction.

One man, however, stood up. Jane thought he was going to throw a punch at her. Instead, he said, "It's about time *someone* said something! *Thank* you, lady!"

Jane lay in her rack, agitated from the memory. How could Tom live, breathe, and walk on this planet when everything he did was a violation of his religion? She got up and stormed over to Tom's tent. As Jane burst in, he jumped up, ready to fight.

"Easy, there. It's just me." Jane put her hands in the air.

"What the hell time is it? Are you okay?"

"Leviticus 19:28 says, 'Do not tattoo yourself . . . I am the Lord.'" Jane ripped open his shirt to reveal the huge image of Jesus surrounded by glowing light tattooed on his chest. "What about *that?* Do you think having a tattoo is okay just because it's of Jesus? You're such a hypocrite!"

Jane kept her hand on his chest as her gaze drifted up to meet his. Their eyes locked. Jane then dropped her stare to Tom's chest and the image of Christ looking back at her. She wondered why he held on to his god. She felt so confused. She had gone to bed that evening saying a silent prayer to herself—and she wasn't sure why. She didn't really believe that if God existed, he—or she—would allow the atrocities they had all witnessed. She pressed her hand harder against Tom's chest in anger and sadness. He took her hand, then he tucked her hair gently behind her ear. Her tension eased as she looked back up into Tom's eyes.

"Jane, does it really matter? We have to believe in something. I can't endure a day if I don't believe there's a beautiful place waiting for me. Just let it go," he said softly. He then held her face lightly with his hands and pulled her into him as their lips met.

"Oh God, Tom!" Jane was shocked as she realized they were man and wife and they hadn't done anything more than kiss. She looked back down at his chest. His skin was damp with sweat and Jane could hear his heart beating.

"Do you . . . do you want to lie down with me for a while?" Tom asked nervously.

"I don't know. I mean, should we? I mean, we should. We can. And we're married." Jane lay down on Tom's rack, then quickly sat back up. "Would you like me to take off my clothes? I should probably do that, right?"

"Yeah, I think there'd be more room if we do that. These racks are so small." Tom answered, just as nervous as Jane.

"Tom?"

"Yeah?"

"I don't know what to do," Jane admitted.

"Me neither." Tom leaned closer to her and kissed her more gently than he ever had before, in places that had never been kissed before. His lips grazed across her neck, her ears, and down her chest. As he reached her nipples, Jane felt a rush of warmth through her body and she melted into him.

As her hand brushed between his thighs, Jane sat up quickly. "Oh no!" she whispered urgently, utterly stunned.

"What's wrong?" Tom looked down at his erection and moaned.

"That's not gonna work. That's *way* too big. There's *no* way *that's* gonna fit in me," Jane insisted.

"Jane, it's supposed to be that big."

"It wasn't like that when we started! You're making it bigger!"

"No, *you're* making it get bigger," he laughed.

"Stop it."

"Oh, it's gonna get huge now," he smiled and pulled her in closer. Jane pushed him away slightly so she could look at his erection.

"That is so *cool*! How do you *do* that?" Jane asked, fascinated. She gripped his penis with her hand.

"Oh my God, Jane! You can't touch him like that or he'll go off too soon. Try and put him inside you, okay? *Please*, for God's sake."

Jane didn't understand his urgency. She had never been with any boy before. Completely enthralled, Jane just kept rubbing his dick, watching it get bigger.

"Jane! Shit!" Tom said, as all the muscles in his body tightened visibly.

"*Aggh*! Oh my *God*!" Jane yelped.

"Oh my God," Tom moaned, tilting his head back.

"Oh good *God*! Crap! Why didn't you tell me *that* was gonna happen?" Jane whispered, looking at the warm liquid running down her hand.

"I tried." Tom lay back on the rack, motionless.

"Well, I think I can put him in me now," she giggled. He's *much* smaller."

"You're an asshole. Lie down here with me."

Jane tried to memorize the contours of his body. She tasted his sweat, trying to savor the rare moment of closeness between them. They buried their faces in each other's neck and breathed in deeply, knowing they had to let go soon. Tom stroked her face and stared into her eyes. Jane wished she could climb inside him and stay in his heart forever. Tom laid his ear to her chest and counted her heartbeats.

"I'm gonna play your heartbeat like a song in my mind when we're apart. I'm gonna close my eyes and remember the way you smell. I love you with every thread of my being," Tom said as he pulled her hips against his. Jane felt his erection against her thigh. He moved on top of her and slowly, gently slipped inside her for the first time.

Although it hurt slightly, Jane didn't care. She sunk her teeth into his shoulder to muffle the sound rising inside her as he pressed his hips into hers. She had ached for this moment every day she was with him. Now that it was here, Jane wanted to stay forever. As they made their eternal memory, Jane knew that at least she could always relive this moment in her mind. She wrapped her arms around his back tightly, feeling every defined muscle working as her body held the weight of his.

Afterward, Jane snuck back to her tent, crawled under the thick mosquito netting, and fell fast asleep. Ula woke her when she ran into the tent, yelling.

"Hatari! Dey are killing people in Kampala! Wake up!" she shouted frantically, motioning for Jane to get up.

"What? Kampala? I was just there."

"I know! You haff to use dat box to read de news, please." Ula was worried because her grandmother was a schoolteacher in Kampala.

Jane took Ula's claim seriously and immediately went to look up her Ugandan newsfeed on the Xenix box via Telnet.

"Rioters sweep through Kampala. Ten are dead," Jane read at first glance. Ula stood by anxiously, awaiting information. Jane censored a lot of it as she read aloud, omitting anything about burned-out schools.

"It's nothing, Ula. Just some boys rioting over the King. This stuff happens all the time."

Jane went back to sleep despite Ula's protestations and was only awakened when Howser gathered them for a briefing of their next mission. They were embarking deep into the region between the Central African Republic and the Democratic Republic of Congo.

"Here, soldiers," Howser addressed them, pointing at a map, "is where we'll attempt to capture the LRA leader, Kony." Howser made it sound as if he was going to be at their side during the battle. He never was. "This army is much more skilled and is considered a high threat. These aren't a bunch of gangbanger punks."

Jane looked at the Ugandan and Congolese soldiers in her group. They probably didn't understand the phrase "gangbanger punks," but they nodded in agreement. There were only about twenty-five hundred LRA members, but getting to them through the practically impenetrable jungle posed their biggest problem.

Jane and Kiko began the long process of inventory for their assault on the Central African Republic. That night, their French team would join them. Operational Control occasionally chopped units together for short-term missions. Jane was relieved to have their French brothers fighting with them. She loved her MONUC team, but many of them were so personally involved that they could jeopardize the mission by committing spontaneous acts of vengeance, rather than following mission protocol.

Jane and Kiko conducted the inventory in the dark so Kiko could grow more accustomed to wearing night-vision goggles. As they sorted and stacked, Jane felt a sudden, sharp, stabbing pain in her leg.

"Fuck! What was that?" She scanned the tent floor, but saw nothing.

Kiko grabbed his 1911, a .45-caliber pistol, and moved to her side. "I do not see a ting, Baba."

Jane leaned on the table, "Lift up your lenses. I'm gonna light the place up." She felt like her whole leg was on fire as she untied her gaiters and kicked off her boot. Jane tried to get her pants off but forgot they were tied at the ankle. "Good God," she groaned in pain.

Kiko untied the bottom of her BDU and examined her leg. "A snake, Baba! You haff been bitten by a snake!"

"Shit! Where is it? A viper or a mamba?" Jane hated snakes, especially the black mamba. If that was what bit her, Jane would be dead in minutes.

"No, Baba. Dis is no viper bite. It is too small, see?" Kiko's face wore a look of concern, as if he were disguising the truth.

Tom had heard Jane's shouting and he ran into the tent to find out what was wrong. "Search the camp!" he ordered. "I want to know what kind of snake this was." He grabbed a snakebite kit and sanitized the wound surface. Next, he pulled back the plunger of the snakebite extractor.

"I feel fine, Tom, but my fucking leg is swelling out of its skin. It's tight and on fire," explained Jane, trying to minimize her injury. She never wanted to appear weak.

"Just stay calm. If a mamba bit you, you'd be dead by now." He looked toward her hand as if he wanted to take hold of it, but he didn't. He just kept extracting the poison. "Fuck, fuck, fuck! How you holdin' up, Jane? You stay with me, okay? Think about that red door, Jane. Who's going to paint that God-awful door? You gotta stay with me 'cause I'm not painting that thing by myself!" Tom kept talking as sweat ran off his forehead. Jane could tell he really was worried that the bite was from a mamba. As she watched him try to cover up his emotions, Jane started to get scared.

"Sweetie," Tom said as he took her face in his hands, "you're a fucking Marine and you are *not* going to die." He whispered inches away from her face, "I would *die* before I ever let anything ever happen to you. I'll do everything in my power to save your life *at all costs*. Do not doubt me. *Ever. Or* my love for you."

Jane relaxed and quieted her breathing. Her body let go of some of the tension she was holding as Tom drew out more of the poison with the extractor.

Kiko returned, without the snake. "Baba, we could get you to de hospital but I tink you do better just to have de kava." He left the tent quickly to whip up his magical brew. Jane watched her leg continue to swell.

Ula entered the tent. "Oh, Hatari! You are needing to pray! See? Dat is a sign. Just like Eve, you are bad and bitten by the Satan snake."

Tom sensed what Jane would say in response to that statement, so he quickly interjected, "Ula, Eve was not bitten by the Satan snake.

Eve bit into the forbidden fruit *offered* to her by the snake," he said in a calm and comforting voice.

"Oh, for fuck's sake, you two! Eve didn't exist!" Jane yelled.

"Oh, Hatari. You secretly love God, don't you?" Ula whispered her question, as if she didn't want God to hear the answer.

"You pesky tsetse fly! Go on! Go braid Screech's beard!" Jane motioned for her to leave the tent.

"Amen!" she yelled and ran out of the tent laughing.

Meanwhile, Kiko had brewed his kava and brought it to Jane.

"Baba, drink dis all while it is still hot," he said handing her a clay cup.

"I've never seen miraculous healing with kava, Kiko," Jane said as she reluctantly took the cup.

"Drink it, you damn fool!" Kiko snapped. Jane could see Tom agreed with him as he nodded at her.

"Tom! You won't eat their food, yet you insist I drink some witchy, magical—"

Before Jane could finish her sentence, Tom forced her head back and poured the hot liquid right down her throat.

"There, you stubborn woman!" Tom yelled. Jane could hear Kiko laughing as he patted Tom on the back, then everything went dark.

The next thing she knew, Jane felt tapping on her forehead. "Wake up, Hatari. It is time to wash and go," Ula commanded.

"What the *hell?* Why are you hitting me with a *branch?*" Ula stood in the far corner of her tent and was using a very long stick to wake her.

"Because you wake up like de ninja and I am too little to fight you."

Jane put her hand to her pounding head and forced herself to sit up. She immediately became nauseated and ran out of the tent to throw up. Every soldier in the FOB stopped and turned to look at her.

"Ah! See, Baba, witchy-poo? The poison is on its way out!" Screech's wide white-toothed grin blinded her. "Want to see your enemy?"

Jane looked over and saw him turning a spit over the fire. On it was a narrow string of meat. She gagged and hurled again into the brown, dusty dirt.

During the next few days, Jane worked in utter agony. She felt like she had a dagger in her belly. She couldn't bend or sit without wincing in pain. She assumed the kava was more the culprit than the snake.

Howser had ignored her for days, even through the snakebite incident. When she finally approached him in his temporary base of operations, where he was going over plans with Tom and the leader of the MONUC for yet another op, he shooed her away. The night missions continued while she recovered.

"Your head isn't right yet. You still have poison moving through you. We got it for now," he said curtly as he chewed his cigar.

When Jane's health finally returned, the entire team gathered in the center of the administration tent and were given their instructions to engage in their next mission. They drove into the steaming jungle for hours, until the vegetation became too dense for the Jeeps to penetrate. They stopped the vehicles, gathered their weapons, and continued in on foot. The captain of DAOS, Feraud, served as the joint command leader on this op. Jane never wanted to get on his bad side. He was rugged and very tough on his men.

"I watched Feraud stomp a man to death once," Screech said in admiration. Then continued with a fake French accent. "Eee was twice Feraud's size, but Feraud, eee just jumped on 'eem and stomped away at 'is 'ead until it looked like zee platter of ratatouille." Jane had never heard anyone kill a French accent more brutally.

"He is a force to reckon with, little buddy. I'm sure *you* could take him, though," Jane replied. Because Screech was absolutely insane, he probably *could* take the Frenchman.

They split their twenty-man team into two groups and proceeded to maneuver through the dense terrain. Jane hugged her rifle close as they approached their destination.

Pilot and Jane lay side by side in the thick, moist vegetation, overlooking a crude road. Jane was comforted having Pilot next to her, and she patted his shoulder to express her feelings.

"Nice place for an ambush, eh, Jane?" he asked. She agreed. Their intel indicated that within a few hours, a Land Rover would be coming through carrying Kony, which surprised them. He wasn't usually far from the innermost protected regions of the Congo. It would be a nice prize to eliminate the leader of the LRA earlier than planned. So they waited patiently.

Jane could discern easily which of the MONUC had lost their children to the LRA, because they were nearly salivating at the thought of killing Kony. At that moment, the men believed they'd be bringing their children home soon, but Jane knew all too well that they weren't children anymore. They were the walking dead.

Tom crawled up on her left flank.

"Look at them, Tom," Jane said, pointing to the soldiers. "They're uneasy."

"I know. I worry about their disappointment. You know, we've seen these kids and have brought 'em home by the truckload. Most are just ghosts—tiny shells of their former selves." He softened when he spoke about the children.

"Yeah, I think their spirit leaves their little bodies during those horrific moments of extreme torture," Pilot said in agreement.

"Doesn't yours? Mine sure does." Jane tried not to think about that too deeply.

"But at least we survive and come back with our sanity," Tom replied.

"Are you sure about that?" Jane asked. After a mission, Tom was always deeply affected.

Once again, Jane wondered why they did what they did. She was under orders to kill Joseph Kony and as many LRA leaders as possible, and to find out in which areas of the Congo they were drilling for oil, then report to the United Nations. Above all, Orion was there to stop the killing of innocent Congolese civilians.

"Widowmaker, copy your location." Feraud's voice broke the silence.

"Two, twenty, thirty-six on top of target, Captain."

"Roger that. Engage."

As the vehicles entered the clearing, the team began strafing the LRA soldiers from both sides. Jane took out the driver with her XM8; the DAOS team took out the second vehicle. The MONUC fired on the soldiers who tried to scatter. Feraud's team took out multiple vehicles with an RPG. Some of the LRA soldiers caught on fire as they bailed out of the flaming vehicles that had been hit with the RPG. The team laid down more suppressing fire and eliminated the remaining vehicles in the convoy. Game over. Just like that.

The transports stood torched and smoldering as the joint team grabbed anything they could find that might give them information on other camps and LRA movements.

"Nice work, Feraud," complimented Jane. "I think that was over a little too fast. I didn't even break a sweat."

"I think that's how we want it to happen. I'm not a fan of fancy takedowns. The simpler the better."

Her team regrouped quickly and returned to their vehicles. Feraud followed with three captives and they all headed back to the command post.

Howser led the after-action report as they debriefed. "We weren't entirely successful," he said, looking right at Jane, "although we did apprehend Kony's bodyguard." Jane laughed to herself as Howser spoke, as if he had personally aided them. "He's no one of any real importance. However, we did establish the location of a concentration camp thirty-two kilometers away. Nice work," he said, then dismissed them.

Jane headed to her kingdom for a bath. Her swollen leg ached and, somehow, Jane had broken a finger. She hadn't realized it until hours after returning to the FOB. After years of sustaining broken bones and multiple injuries, her brain dismissed a broken finger as a nonthreat.

When Jane entered her tent, she found Ula sitting on the floor, carving a wooden giraffe. "Here, Hatari. This is for your daughter."

"Ula, I don't have a daughter."

"You are a mother. I know you are. You have a mother way about you dat I like very much. So dis is for her. She is a good girl," she said confidently. Jane gave in without a fight, knowing she could never convince Ula she didn't have any children. However, if Jane had, she wished they'd turn out like Ula. Jane was growing very fond of the little girl. At times, she even loved her.

The three different tribes among them—the Baluba, the Bantu, and the Kwa—planned to treat the entire team to entertainment that night. Each was to sing and perform a dance for them around the fire.

Tom popped his head into her tent. "Hey, Janie! Who're you taking to the big dance tonight?"

"You dork! I'm going stag. I couldn't find a date."

"Awww, come on! A pretty little thing like yourself? I bet the boys back home are just dying to get your number!" He inched toward her, and Jane couldn't resist him.

"Come here, lover," she said as she grabbed him, stealing a quick kiss. "I'll see you in a few."

"Hurry up. They're starting to sing." Before he closed the flaps of her tent, he reached back in and smacked her ass. "Nice! I love it!" he said with a lustful look on his face.

Jane emerged from her tent to a colorful sight of painted warriors gathered around the fire. Some had elaborate headdresses and wore strings of beads and shells. Others had stripped naked and covered their bodies with soot from the coals. All of them wore masks or painted their faces with the colors of their respective tribes.

Kiko looked fierce, with his black-rimmed eyes and red stripes across his forehead, but he stood stern and still, as though he had slipped into a trance. As the herbalist among the tribes, Jane knew Kiko was responsible for brewing the drinks. Her stomach turned as she thought about the kava she drank days earlier.

Uruzandokiko performed a warrior spirit dance. He crawled on the ground like a lion, mimicking the feline moves so precisely that it was just like watching a wildcat prowl through the savannah. He made throaty growls and clawed at their faces, then he shape-shifted from beast to warrior, pounding his chest as he jumped over the fire and spun in circles, stomping the ground.

Narotu performed a peace offering. He shed tears and wiped dirt across his chest as he spit into the fire. Clearly distressed, he asked the gods to bring the children home. Jane found the Bwola dance to be the most impressive performance of all. The men moved fiercely, springing, stomping, and shaking their bodies in unison. It seemed as if a force held them—and the entire team—in a tight grip. The noise from the clapping, stomping, and singing could surely be heard all the way to the LRA camps. And that was the intent.

When the dances were over, the performers turned to the team to reciprocate. They all looked at each other awkwardly. What did Marines and Rangers do in a situation like this? Feraud managed to sing the French National Anthem without being stoned to death for his horrible rendition. The tribesmen laughed and patted him on the back.

Pilot closed his eyes and began to sing while he tapped his foot. "Heeeere come old flat-top, he come groovin' up slowly. He got ju-ju eyeball; he's one holy roller."

Screech piped in, trying to remember the lyrics. "He got dreads . . . down . . . to his knees."

Butch, Tom, and Jane got up and started dancing around the fire and singing with them, "Come together! Right now . . . over me!"

Although they were a hit among the tribes, they were definitely not ready for prime time. Jane couldn't believe how much fun she had making a fool of herself with a bunch of fellow soldiers honoring a blood battle with a favored hippie, pot-smoking song from the Vietnam era.

The celebration lasted for hours. The guys drank rice liquor and Jane, Ula, and the rest of the team all fell asleep on the ground by the fire, which was probably not the thing to do in the Congo. Hours later, Jane awoke and opened one eye just in time to see a black mamba slither along the ground between her and Ula. She was close enough to count the scales around its eye. Jane remained completely frozen and hoped no one moved in his sleep. She didn't even blink. She watched the glistening serpent slither over Butch's leg and on into the darkness surrounding the camp. She scooped up Ula quickly and tucked her into her rack. Jane scoured the grounds for the remainder of the night, looking for that snake. As she rounded the corner behind one of the tents, she heard Kiko's voice.

"You haff to look in de trees, Baba," Kiko instructed, looking up at the trees. Sure enough, he had spotted the snake. He threw rocks at it, knocking it to the ground, where he beat it to death with his walking stick. "We haff to bury dis deep in de ground. Years after de mamba is dead, you can still be poisoned by stepping on its bones."

Jane wasn't sure about that, but she still dug a deep hole. Jane hacked off its head, secretly hoping it was the snake that bit her. Sweet revenge.

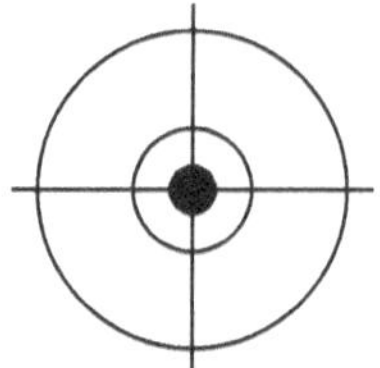

CHAPTER TWENTY-THREE

Tom accompanied Ula and Jane to the outskirts of the Central African Republic to look for Ula's brother in one of the camps. The Kanyazee Achati Camp, named after the eldest surviving chief there, contained some estimated fifty thousand Acholi and other Ugandan peoples. Jane thought the actual number had to be more like a hundred thousand. Maybe more. When they arrived, tents stretched as far as they could see. The blue plastic shelters surrounded tightly packed mud-and-cinderblock huts. Armed soldiers patrolled the border. It wasn't unusual for camps like these to spring up in warring regions. Citizens were willing to travel hundreds of miles to gather together for safety, hoping the large population would protect them and perhaps bring their plight into the open, raising awareness and garnering government assistance.

The northernmost region of Uganda experienced the most vicious of the wars and attacks, and Jane, Tom, and Ula saw the agony in the faces of the people who survived. As they entered the refugee camp, Jane felt as if she were walking through a dark veil of misery. There were people all around them, but they all moved in a zombielike trance. Some cooked or hung laundry, but most looked through them with lifeless eyes.

Girls stood in long lines, waiting for USAID trucks to arrive with supplies. Younger children clustered around these girls, who had become mothers to the many orphaned children in the camp, as they walked back to their tents and huts with supplies.

Ula set off alone to search for her brother while Jane and Tom searched together. Several minutes later, Jane saw Ula running toward her.

"Hatari! Come! Come!" Ula tugged at Jane's hand, pulling her into a mud house. "This is my friend Fina!" The two girls embraced each other and began to cry, stroking each other's hair and wiping the tears from each other's cheeks. Ula buried her face into Fina's dress and began wailing. Jane caught a glimpse of the young, vulnerable girl that Ula really was.

"Oh Fina, Fina, Fina! I love you, my sista!"

Jane was overcome by emotion and leaned instinctively into Tom and took his hand. He put his arm around her and kissed the top of her head. The girls danced in a circle, squeezing each other's hands, then hugged and cried some more.

"It's okay, Jane. We aren't Marines here. Just people," said Tom as he kissed her again. They never showed their affection in public, but Tom knew Jane needed it that day.

Fina was ten years old, but roughly the same height as Ula. She had two brothers, ages nine and six; and two sisters, ages two and four. Fina began tugging on Tom's belt loop to get his attention. Tom sat down. To their surprise, Fina immediately climbed into his lap and pressed her head into his chest. Tears welled up in Tom's eyes as he rocked and comforted her. At that moment, Jane wished desperately that they had conceived a child when they made love in his tent. This was the first time Jane let herself acknowledge that she wanted a family with Tom. Jane touched her belly, then she quickly dismissed the thought and hoped Tom didn't notice the look on her face. They both knew having a family would never be an option for them.

Fina began to speak, weeping as she did so.

"De rebels come down to de village in de night. Dey drug all dem outside and tol' dem to lay in de dirt. De babies and me were tol' if we looked at dem dey would be shot. Dey took my mamma and my dadee and both my older brothers out into de bush," Fina said, weeping as she spoke.

Tom sat quietly and rocked Fina. Riveted by her story, Jane almost forgot to breathe. When Jane became light-headed, she finally took in a deep breath. Her vision cleared and Jane felt pins and needles in her hands and feet. Tom's pale face looked almost translucent; he'd forgotten to breathe during the retelling as well. Jane nudged him and he immediately filled his chest with air. Fina then went on to tell them how afraid she was that the rebels would come back and kill the children in their village, so she jumped up and led them, as fast as she could, into the bush to hide.

"We hid dere all night. In de morning, I ran to de village to look for my mamma." Jane saw the fear in Fina's face as she told her story. Fina could not find her parents in the village, so she went into the bush where the weeds had been trampled. She recounted that she found body parts strewn across the grass; they were covered with flies and ants. Then Fina described how she looked down and saw her mother's severed head by her feet. She told them how she picked it up, held it, and sobbed. Fina spent the entire day picking up the arms, legs, and any other identifiable pieces of her parents to bury them. As she sat on Tom's lap, Fina balled up her dress and mimicked the way she had rocked her mother's head in her arms. Her story was almost too much to bear; tears began to stream down Tom's cheeks. He kissed Fina's head and continued to rock her to calm her.

"*No* child should suffer like this," he whispered. "This is *heartbreaking.*" Jane had never seen Tom so emotional. She took his hand and they sat for a moment, rocking the girls together.

Fina had become the mother of her younger siblings. She believed her brothers were recruited into the LRA.

"I could not find my brothers. Unless a lion took dem, I tink dey are now with de bad soldiers. De rebels keep dem to be deir own children."

Most of the boys in the camp that Jane, Tom, and Ula had seen thus far had had their lips and ears cut off. The children's mutilation horrified Tom and Jane. Ula refused to speak to any of the boys.

"Dey were rebels too. Dey killed farmers." Whenever a boy passed, she looked at him suspiciously.

"Ula, the rebels *made* them do that. They threatened them and told them they would be killed if they didn't do as ordered," explained Jane, trying to inform Ula and comfort her at the same time.

"Den dey should haff given deir own life. No one should kill. It is in de Bible." Ula looked into the sky, possibly expecting some god to shine down on her for her willingness to be sacrificed.

"Ula, I kill people when I have to. Do you hate me? No, you don't, because it's my job." Jane turned Ula's face toward her and looked her in the eyes. "Ula, if you have a belief that you use to judge, then that belief must be so strong and so absolute you would die for it. You can't say something as absolute as 'Don't kill because God says so.'" Jane paused for a moment and thought.

What if it was okay to kill if it supported one's mission? If they believed this was what they *had* to do? That was what the LRA did. Jane continued, "Why is it okay for me to kill for my mission and cause but not for the LRA to kill for its mission and cause? I struggle with these questions every day. I would love for your god to appear and answer them for me. For now, you have to understand that those boys made a choice to live—a difficult choice for them to make. I imagine they feel pain in their heart every day because of their choice. Thankfully, the boys in this camp are alive and not with the LRA. I think you should try to accept them like you accept me."

Ula looked down at the ground. Jane lifted her chin up to look at her and asked, "Remember 'To Be a Bat'? Remember what Screech told you?"

"Yes, Hatari. The only way I would know exactly what dat terrible boy did is if I *was* dat terrible boy." Ula patted Jane's shoulder and went to go wash up.

Tom and Jane got two buckets of dirty water and poured them over their heads. They had been invited to separate huts for a cultural dinner. Jane's host family consisted of a woman, who had renamed herself Mary, and her six nieces and nephews. Her dinner was pulverized grain boiled in water. As Jane expected, there were no vegetables, no bread, no coffee. Jane was surprised people could survive eating this food for any period of time, with no nutritional balance to their diet.

As they sat and ate together, Mary told Jane the rebels killed her sister and brother-in-law while they were farming. All four of her sons were abducted.

"I tought dey would not take my sons because dey were very small babies, but dey did."

"You are lucky to haff a daughter," Mary said to Jane. "Dey won't take de girls." Puzzled by the daughter reference, Jane assumed Mary thought Jane had adopted Ula. Part of her wished she *could* adopt Ula. But Jane knew, first, that Howser would never let her adopt her and, second, Ula was on a mission. Jane could tell she was planning her destiny in Africa—to save the children somehow. Ula sought to learn as much as she could as fast as she could.

Jane, Tom, and Ula left the tent village at first light. Their driver raced over the dirt roads at the usual 160 kilometers per hour. Jane felt sick from the jarring of the truck as it flew across the washboard road and careered around corners, spewing red dirt from its tires. At this point, she was more concerned about a rollover than the LRA. She held on to Tom, choking from the dust kicked up by the vehicle in front of them.

As they neared the FOB, Tom and Jane instinctively pulled away from each other and sat up straight in preparation for their meeting with Howser. As soon as they arrived, Jane and Tom sought him out.

"We have intel that an LRA training ground is located only one hundred kilometers north. We believe this is where they are holding the five hundred boys who were abducted from Eugene Territory earlier this month," Jane explained to Howser.

As soon as their meeting ended, they began the process of cleaning their weapons and performing their private warrior rituals. Jane skipped the push-ups this time because of her broken finger. Instead, she took time to visualize what she called "going down the rabbit hole." During her warrior meditation, she connected herself to her enemy. She looked into the intricate web of the universe and then focused on killing her intended targets. She imagined coming home with the five hundred rescued boys. She did this to allow herself to work backward. If she felt she had already accomplished her mission successfully, then she only had to fast-forward. When their assault preparations were complete, they began the long trek into the jungle. The journey took time and endurance. Ironically, it allowed them the luxury of appreciating the beauty that surrounded them. It was a cathartic walk into chaos.

When they reached the outskirts of the LRA camp in the middle of the night, they waited. The earliest hours of the morning were the best time to attack. The soldiers would be in their deepest sleep, and their bodies would be distracted by urges to pee and eat. Also, their eyes would not be accustomed to the light. The team continued to wait for an opportune moment to strike. Jane listened as a few nesting birds started to chirp and shuffle in the trees. A cold fly landed on her cheek looking for body heat, which broke her silent concentration. A few of her soldiers were so still they looked like sculptures in a museum display. So focused were they on their targets, they barely blinked. Even as nervous sweat beaded up and ran into their eyes, they did not flinch. They never moved until they were ready to strike.

As the sun crested the horizon, the team begin to spread out. Each of them moved closer to their intended targets. Jane's were in a three-walled tent, which made her killing task efficient; her targets were readily accessible. She peered quietly into the tent and saw that all ten men were asleep. She gave her team a silent GO signal and they moved in, again using blades for a silent attack.

The first three targets were always easy to take down—a quick and lethal slice across the throat. However, as the others began to hear their comrades drowning in their own blood, they awoke. This was when everyone had to work swiftly.

Jane had to stomp vigorously on the fourth man's skull. As it shattered, she thought about how Feraud had once done the same thing. Jane used her Ka-Bar on her fifth target—a jarring strike straight to the chest, which punctured his heart. Jane's aim had to be very precise so that she missed bone. The blade sunk in deeply and she twisted it to ensure his immediate death. Jane then shot the rest of the group. Gunfire began to be heard throughout the camp almost simultaneously, which meant they were all in sync on their mission. She heard LRA soldiers yell for help, then their voices were silenced. Some were able to run a few steps before they were gunned down. The MONUC took no prisoners. Their anger and lust for revenge was apparent as Jane watched them hack LRA members to death. Kiko burned the tents as he walked through the camp. Some of the LRA soldiers were set ablaze by his flamethrower.

The commotion ended as quickly as it began. The sounds of moaning and gurgling, mixed with the crackling of burning tents, echoed throughout the jungle. Jane hated these sounds, but she wasn't about to put any of those wretched men out of their misery.

This is for Mary and Fina, Jane thought. These men deserved to suffer. She watched as life left the body of the man who lay at her feet. His eyes were wide with fear. Jane imagined the hundreds of children who wore that same look as he murdered them. Visualizing this scene allowed her the separation she needed to do her job effectively.

Feraud located the boys. They had been packed into a chain-link box. Some were bloody. All were traumatized. They were willing to leave, yet they moved like the undead. Not one of them spoke to the team or looked anyone in the eye. A few appeared relieved when they saw Jane, Feraud, and the other white soldiers, because they realized they were not LRA soldiers. A few of them began to cry, knowing they were saved.

The team radioed for trucks, and Jane asked a few of the boys if they knew Ulu, although she thought he wouldn't be so far from his home. Still, Jane promised Ula she'd ask. No one knew him.

It had been nearly a year since Jane and her team began their work in the Congo. She started to feel like a surrogate parent of the children they found. She grew fond of them. She had learned about many of them from her earlier meetings with their families. She recognized the children's names and hoped to reunite them with their parents. Years would pass, yet the parents still clung to the hope that their child still lived. Despite evidence to the contrary, they never gave up unless they saw the body of their child with their own eyes.

The trucks finally arrived and took the Orion and MONUC teams back to the refugee camp. Jane commanded them to stop outside the barbed-wire perimeter.

"Send five of the cleanest men we have into the camp to get water. We're all gonna wash up before we go in there. These people have seen enough of this," Jane ordered, as she looked around at her team members, who were covered in dried blood and caked with dirt. Some of them had brain matter and bone on their jackets and in their hair.

The trucks containing the boys continued on to a hospital. There they would be cleaned, treated, identified, and then moved to smaller camps, where the process of healing and deprogramming would begin. Many would die either from heroin withdrawal or from infection of the wounds they had incurred. But some would make it. A few might even fully recover in body *and* spirit.

As the team neared the camp, nearby villagers swarmed around them, asking whether their children had been found. The soldiers gently pushed them back and gathered in an abandoned school to rest.

The next day, Jane awoke as the sun crested the horizon. She walked the perimeter of the barbed-wire camp. It saddened her to think the villagers were forced to live this way. All the huts were forlorn and there was no clean water at all. There was no traditional dancing and singing or playing. They could not even farm their own food. There simply wasn't the room to do so. In the distance, Jane saw a child of about four years old picking up single pieces of dry corn from the dirt path and putting them in her pocket. Jane looked beyond the fence and saw so much potential for agriculture, but it was too dangerous to move outside the camp and farm the land.

"Hey, Hatari! Wait for me!" Ula ran toward Jane.

"Hey, little sunshine!" Jane replied, glad to see this bright child. Jane had started to get depressed as she realized the hopelessness these people faced; Ula lightened her spirit. They walked around the camp together for a while in silence before they entered a hut that had been assigned to them. Ula's face beamed with joy as they approached the stark, sparse hut. Jane figured Ula was up to something. When Jane entered, she saw that Ula had placed a mat on the dirt floor. On it were coffee and biscuits.

"It is a tea party, Hatari! Only with your favorite drink! Coffee! Do you love it?" Ula asked, her face glowing with pride. Jane *loved* it, perhaps more than she had ever loved anything ever before. In the middle of nothing, Ula had found coffee and biscuits for her, and presented them with flair. Jane thought Ula might faint from excitement.

"Oh, *Ula*! I love it so *much*! How did you *do* it?"

"Dere is more! Dere is so much more! Sit down. Drink coffee before it is too cold." Ula fussed with the cups and smoothed the mat. She watched Jane as Jane lifted a cup to her lips.

The coffee tasted like burnt cardboard. It was absolutely the worst-tasting coffee Jane had ever consumed. She had to choke back her reflex to gag so Ula wouldn't see.

"Oh, Ula! Wow! This is wonderful! Where did you get coffee?" It sure didn't taste like coffee. Plus, they hadn't had coffee since they had first arrived at the compound.

"De captain had de coffee in his bag, so I borrowed some."

"Ula, did you ask Feraud if you could have this?" Jane had asked Feraud for coffee several days earlier and he said he didn't have any.

Ula ignored the question. "Okay, Hatari. Give me your arm." Jane extended her arm and Ula began to tie strands of red beads around her wrist.

"What is the special occasion, Ula?" Jane asked, noticing Ula fastening the bracelets tightly so Jane couldn't slip them off. Jane remembered that her friend D'Narambi had done this to her the last time Jane saw her. The friendship bracelets are never meant to be taken off. Jane wore the ones D'Narambi gave her until they finally disintegrated.

"You can't forget me, see? When you leave here today, you won't forget," Ula said, shaking Jane's hand to prove how snug the strands fit her wrist. Ula's smile lit up the whole hut.

"Ula, I will remember you until all my memory is wiped clean. I promise that the last thought I ever have in this life will be of this very moment." Then Jane took off her dog tags and hung them around Ula's neck. "Keep these for me, okay?"

"Oh yes! Yes, I will!" Ula threw her bony little black arms around Jane and cried. "You are like my mother, Hatari, and I love you—even though you have no god." Ula just had to get in one last dig.

Jane rocked Ula and drank bad coffee for an hour before she left the hut to load the trucks for the drive back to the compound, where they would make preparations for their return to the States. En route, Jane told Feraud she'd replace his coffee when they returned to the FOB.

"Coffee? I have no coffee," he stated, puzzled.

"The tin in your bag?" Jane asked. Feraud burst into laughter, spewing French gibberish, then tossed her the contents of his bag.

"Widowmaker, that's tobacco in that tin. You put it in your goddamn American mouth and spit it on the ground!" Feraud roared as he spit a wad of chew onto her boot. The guys burst out laughing.

"Oh, shit! I think I just pissed myself! That's fucked up!" laughed Jane as she wiped the wad of masticated tobacco off her boot with her opposite boot.

Jane would certainly never forget Ula *or* their tea party. The team spent the remainder of the week packing vehicles with gear and breaking camp. Although Jane never found Ulu—or D'Narambi—she knew Ula would never give up her search.

As Jane watched Africa disappear beneath her as they soared into the sky, she wondered if she was going home or leaving home. She realized she never again needed to ask herself, *What am I doing?* She simply needed to look down at her friendship bracelets for the answer.

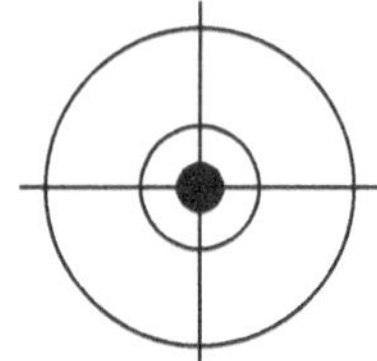

CHAPTER TWENTY-FOUR

As Jane sat on the porch at the Stapelton farm, drinking real coffee, she thought about Ula. She felt a pang in her gut and realized how much she missed her. Her "little Ula" was in her midforties now and had turned out to be quite a remarkable woman. She was a schoolteacher and a leader of a resistance army from Uganda against the LRA. She saved thousands of children by hiding them in the cellar of her schoolhouse. She then smuggled them out of the region when she saw an opportunity to do so. Ula continued her education at a university in Botswana and received a PhD in Global Human Rights. She felt that furthering her education was the only true path to freeing the people from the wrath of the LRA. African women with an education were few and far between. Many people who live in a region where men are educated and hold most of the power view a woman with a university degree as a threat. Ula sought to defy all that.

Jane smiled and let out a deep sigh. Images of the orange African sky at sunset slowly faded into a clear, deep-blue hue as her eyes refocused on her surroundings. Jane looked across the yard and saw Sam painting a fence. He rarely sat still. He always seemed to be doing something around the farm, whether it was tending to the horses, the yard, or the house. In her peripheral vision, Jane saw Marlene peer around the corner of the porch as she leaned against the wooden doorframe. Jane turned her head toward her and their eyes met. Marlene smiled at Jane and gave her a nod. Jane smiled back, knowing they were okay.

"Alright! Come on, kids! Let's get some food! I'm starving!" Eugene yelled from behind Marlene.

As Sam joined Jane on the porch, he smiled at her and rifled through his paint-splattered pocket. He pulled out a small cylindrical package wrapped in Christmas paper and tied with a red bow. Jane laughed to herself and thought, *Christmas in August?*

"This is something I picked up for you to try," Sam explained as he handed her the present.

Jane took it from him hesitantly. "Uh, what is this, Sam?" Jane asked as she started to unwrap the gift. Even after she had unwrapped it completely, she had no idea what it was.

Sam beamed. "It's an electronic cigarette. See?" He took it from her and turned it over. "It smokes like a real cigarette, but it doesn't make real smoke—just vapor, like theatrical smoke. You'll *feel* like you're smoking, but you won't be killing yourself with all the bad crap in tobacco."

"Uh, Sam? Why would I *want* this? I already have cigarettes and I love to smoke." Jane knew Sam wanted her to stop smoking, but this sounded ridiculous.

"I think this'll help you stop. I have a friend who uses them and they worked. They have nicotine in them. You still get some kind of high or something, but you don't have all the other stuff. Would you at least try it?" he asked, waiting for her to take a drag.

"Maybe after we eat. I don't feel like smoking right now anyway." Jane put the object in her pocket. She liked the feel of a real cigarette, not a fake ceramic one. She did, however, appreciate the effort on his part. "Thank you, Sam. That was sweet." Jane patted his shoulder like she would a five-year-old. Sam sensed her dismissal.

"You don't feel like *smoking*? You smoke like a *chimney*!"

"Good God! It's almost as if you want me around for a while!" Jane laughed. "Let's get some food in you, mister. You're getting *way* too attached to me. Don't be thinking just because I'm telling all sorts of personal stories that I'm getting all maternal with *you*, young man. I'll kick your butt!" Jane said jokingly and, swiping her boot toward Sam, kicked him lightly. He shoved her a bit and put his arm around her shoulders as they walked toward the kitchen. Jane was touched that Sam cared about her health. No one else in her life really had. Nearly everyone who surrounded her up until that point also had bad health habits.

"Dammit, Sam. I'm lucky to have you," Jane said, reluctantly admitting her newly discovered attachment to him.

Sam was becoming equally attached to Jane. He felt like he finally had someone to talk to and mentor him. He was far too concerned about his grandparents' happiness to bother them with the deeper feelings he was harboring. He was beginning to realize just how hurt—and angry—he was over the loss of his parents. He thought Jane might understand.

During dinner, Eugene asked what Jane thought about her new electronic cigarette. Earl, who had joined them for yet another meal, sat next to Eugene and appeared to focus more on his food than the conversation.

"Isn't it somethin', what they can do these days? They make a cigarette that has all the stuff you like in it, but it won't kill you," remarked Eugene as he held out his hand for the electronic cigarette so he could examine it. Jane pulled it from her pocket and placed it in his paw, hoping he would keep it for Marlene.

"Now that *is* something," Earl said, with a furrowed brow, barely looking up from his plate. Jane sensed he was unimpressed.

Jane turned to Eugene and whispered, "Let me ask you something, Eugene. If they made electronic bacon and electronic pancakes, would you eat them just because someone told you they won't kill you?" He almost spit out his mouthful of mashed potatoes and gravy as he started to laugh.

"What's so funny, you two? You're like two conspirators over there. Is there somethin' wrong with the food?" Marlene asked as she stood at the head of the table and looked to see if she'd forgotten to put anything out.

"Relax, young lady." Eugene motioned to Marlene to sit down. "The general was just saying how she was going to pick up a carton of electronic cigarettes tomorrow and a carton of electronic eggs," he chuckled.

"Hey! Can you hand me one of those electric pork chops, Eugene?" Jane quipped. "I may just be able to eat solid food again, now that it's all gone electronic." Eugene and Jane laughed so hard, tears seeped out of their eyes. Sam, Earl, and Marlene just looked at them with blank stares. No one else seemed to get the joke.

"Shit, General! My damn electric food bill will be through the roof! You know how many watts of beef I can eat in a day?" Eugene had a contagious laugh. Jane could see Earl was struggling not to laugh as he ate.

"Stop playing with your food. You two are acting like a couple of kids." Marlene giggled and everyone relaxed.

"Go ahead. I want to see *you* use this thing," Eugene demanded, holding the cigarette out toward Marlene.

"Let me see it," Marlene insisted. Eugene handed the cigarette to Marlene, who sat and turned it over in her hands a few times.

"I think it looks nice," Marlene commented. "How do you plug it in?"

"Grandma! You don't plug it *in*. It doesn't have a cord like a vacuum cleaner," Sam said, laughing.

"Well, you said it was electric. I just thought it was like a toaster or something." Marlene held the gift up to the light and examined it again, squinting her eyes. "Oh, Lord, I need my glasses."

"You just take a drag on it like a regular cigarette, Grandma. Well, if you knew how to do that—"

Before Sam could finish his sentence, Marlene had taken a long drag on the electronic cigarette and French-inhaled it. She blew the smoke out her nose.

"Mmmmm. That's actually pretty smooth," she noted, taking another drag. "Try this, Eugene." Sam watched stunned as Marlene handed the cigarette to Eugene, who had been leaning into her and holding her arm mesmerized, watching his pretty wife smoking like a French film actress from the 1960s.

Eugene took the cigarette from her and took a long draw. "Gosh darn! That's just like a real smoke." He turned toward Jane and asked, "Have you tried this yet?"

Jane wasn't even planning to *try* the thing until she saw Marlene make such a stink over it.

"I really haven't tried it yet," Jane said, looking away. She didn't want to be disloyal to her trusty American Spirits.

"Here! Smoke it," demanded Eugene as he handed it to her. "Go on! Try it." Jane took it from him reluctantly and took a deep drag. She was just about to exhale when Eugene said, "Now if they made a goddamn electric apple fritter that was that good I'd eat the damn thing!" Jane burst out laughing and nearly choked on the fake smoke.

"Well now, *that's* a damn authentic smoker's cough!" Eugene joked.

After dinner they all retired to their customary spots on the porch to enjoy coffee and the purple evening sky. This time, Jane cozied up with her new electronic cigarette instead of her usual American Spirits. She was willing to give it a shot. Sam gave her a wink of approval and Jane let him have his moment. There was a question she had wanted to ask the entire time she had been at the farm, but she'd forgotten about it until now.

"Eugene, why doesn't Mackey eat with us? I never see him at all."

"Oh, he's been at the Lowden farm. It's down the way a bit. He's workin' on a project in their barn. A surprise for Sam, I think. He isn't buildin' any pipe bombs or anythin' weird like that. I had Wayne Lowden go in there and check. You read about that kind of thing—kids goin' off on their own, hidin' out in a friend's garage, and the next thing you know they're blowin' somethin' up. You have to keep an eye on teenagers." Eugene nodded at Jane and tapped his forefinger next to his right eye to validate his point further.

"For goodness sake, Eugene! Do you really think we raised a child to build a bomb and blow things up?" asked Marlene.

"Well, you two," Jane remarked, "I suppose you better hope you *did*. They both want to be Marines, so let's *hope* they can build a bomb and blow something up."

As the family sat on the porch, Deputy Sheriff Bill Lightner's truck rumbled down the driveway. It coasted to a stop, then Bill stepped out of his vehicle. Donning his black cowboy hat, he grabbed a brown paper bag from the backseat and headed toward the porch. Marlene was the first to greet him, and Jane could see she was nervous; she was strangling her apron.

"Bill! Hello! Come on up here and sit a spell! It's nice to have you out to visit. Let me get you some coffee."

"Eugene, would you hurry up and die so I can steal this pretty wife of yours? Marlene, I swear you're gonna give me a heart attack with those eyes." Marlene blushed.

"Easy there, Bill. I'm sittin' right here. Don't make me take you down on the lawn and fight you for her like when we were boys. I won her fair and square."

"Jane, these two have been fighting over me since they were kids. It's all in fun, of course," explained Marlene as the color on her cheeks deepened.

"Well, General," said Bill, "I came out here to talk about those bloody clothes of yours and what we found out."

Jane was glad the deputy got right to the point. He handed her the bag and she peeked inside. There were her clothes; however, when she withdrew them, she discovered they'd been laundered and pressed. There wasn't a trace of blood on them.

"Bill? Where's the blood? My clothes are clean! What's going on?"

"Oh, my sister took care of those for you. Did you know that hydrogen peroxide is the best thing to get blood out of clothing? She uses that on my hunting clothes." Bill was still staring at Marlene, who nodded in agreement.

"I'm not following you, Bill. Why'd you have my clothes washed? Where'd the blood come from?"

"It seems you hit a deer out on County Road 16."

"A deer? I didn't see any damage to my truck. I looked."

"Well, I said you hit a deer. I didn't say you used your truck to do it. It seems you actually attacked a deer and beat it to death." Sam's eyes practically bulged out of his head. Bill continued, "We found it that night and brought it in to examine it. I have to say, General, that was one of the strangest things we've seen around here." He pushed his hat back and scratched his forehead.

Jane drew in a deep breath, then exhaled slowly. "Well, at least I didn't hurt anyone."

"Except for that deer," he remarked seriously. "I do have to write you a citation. I imagine you don't have a hunting license and it certainly isn't deer season."

"Come on, Bill! Are you *serious*? We hit deer all the time! You gonna go runnin' around writing us tickets for that?" Eugene stood up; he was getting angry.

"Calm down there, Eugene. I was only kidding." He started to chuckle. "Shit. You think I'm stupid enough to write a ticket to a hundred-pound mean son of a bitch who can bludgeon a full-grown deer to death with her bare hands? Shit no! I want to live long enough to see you die so I can steal me your lovely wife and provide her with some good golden years." He winked at Marlene.

"Awww, shut the hell up, you old fool," Eugene laughed.

Bill stayed for another cup of coffee and a piece of pecan pie with vanilla ice cream. Eventually, duty called and he drove away.

The night was quiet. Any sound carried across the still desert was amplified. Jane flinched when she heard rifle fire in the distance. *Maybe someone else hates snakes just as much as I do*, she thought. Eugene noticed her movement and sought to distract her.

"General, how'd you come back to life after you got shot dead?"

"How do *you* know about that?" The information was fairly top secret and Jane wondered whether Earl had disclosed it to Eugene. He *was* former CIA, after all. She looked over at Earl, but he kept quiet. "It's not often you hear a story about a resurrection. That's fairly profound, don't you think, Sam?"

Sam looked at Jane in disbelief. "Aunt Jane, is that true? I *gotta* hear this." He moved in closer to Jane.

Eugene really had a way of getting Jane to open up. He meant a lot to her—and so did Sam—so she indulged them.

"Alright, but this information doesn't leave this farm," she stated as she shook her head and gave Earl a not-too-subtle glare. "I was back in Virginia. Robert and I had a very on again/off again relationship at that time. I guess at that point we were on again. I must've been about twenty-eight or so. I'd just finished talking to Robert on the phone when I got a call from Jude. I knew he was working on a Saudi terrorism mission for Orion. Because it was his case, I hadn't pressed him for any information, but I was jealous that he was gonna be the one to get to kill Sharik Arsama—a guy who'd been at the top of the FBI's Most Wanted List since the Gulf War. I was surprised Jude had called me while he was working. *That* was unusual."

Sam moved in even closer to Jane as she began her story.

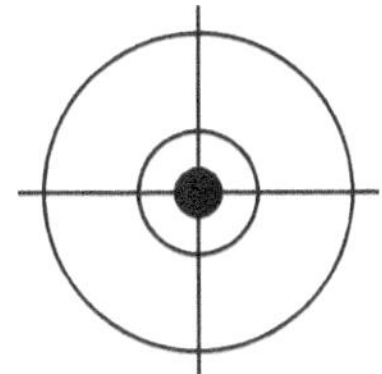

CHAPTER TWENTY-FIVE

"Speak to me, Bulldog. What's up? Are you already calling in for backup?" asked Jane sarcastically. She knew Jude was on an important mission, and she hadn't expected him to reach out to her at all. When her phone had rung and she saw that Jude was calling, she felt oddly upbeat, thinking he may have already failed on his first big solo mission.

Jane had just agreed to have dinner with Robert before receiving Jude's call. She hoped Jude needed her help so she could bail on dinner. Ever since the incident with her team, Jane carried a lot of anxiety when she was around Robert. She had even begun to regret her relationship with him, after he discovered her dual life. He seemed to leverage his newfound knowledge of her to get her to spend more time with him. He would give her a look as if to say: *You do know I could go to the press with this.* These days, Jane felt paranoid and uneasy around him. She also became more withdrawn and less caring. The softer woman that existed at the beginning of their relationship had vanished. She was a secret agent to him now.

"Hot one, Jane. Sorry to say, but I do need your help," Jude said, confirming Jane's assumption. "It'll be like shooting fish in a barrel. I promise. I just need to make the shot count and I'm afraid I'm second seat to you. You still hold the record," he noted, referring to her 1280-meter sniper shot in Iran.

"I have to say, I've never known you to give up so easily, Jude. I suppose I could take a few shots for you. I'll bring my H&K so you can sight me in on that. Where do you need me to go?" Jane's adrenaline started to surge at the thought of killing Sharik.

"Meet me at the eastern port as soon as possible." Jude hung up and Jane quickly grabbed her gear and jumped on her motorcycle. She relished the unrestrained feeling she got from riding it. It was the best purchase she ever made. Because she weighed only 110 pounds, the little CBR600 engine was enough to make her fly.

Jane arrived at the port, slightly north of Langley, in Curtis Bay, where she met up with Jude.

"Wow! You look *gooood* tonight! Dressed to kill!" Jude looked at her admiringly as she straddled her bike in her black suit. After all, Jane had been ready to go to dinner with Robert when Jude called. She'd at least made a point to slip on her combat boots on her way out the door.

Jane stared right back at Jude.

"What's with the duds?" she asked, surprised to see him wearing a white button-down shirt and Dockers. He wasn't dressed in TAC gear. At first, Jane thought he must've left the house in a hurry, as she had, but she dismissed the thought.

"I like to make a good impression. What can I say? Target in T-thirty," Jude said as he hopped on his bike and revved the engine. "Think you can keep up?"

Jude punched it and disappeared as fast as a flash of lightning. He hugged the corners, practically dragging his knee. Jane stayed with him, weaving through traffic, dropping gears, and occasionally swerving to miss hitting him. Despite the fact that she was not as skilled a rider as Jude, she still had no problem cranking up to an exhilarating 130 miles per hour.

They slowed as they pulled into the dark shipyard, then parked their bikes and carried their gear a few hundred yards to begin setting up.

"Why're you so dressed up?" Jane asked. "Do you have a date after this?" She couldn't resist asking; Jude really did look nice. On the rare occasion Jane saw him out of his tactical gear, he usually wore a T-shirt and jeans.

Jude took out his equipment and began to dial in as he eyed the tanker across the water. "As a matter of fact, I do have a date after this. Does that bother you, Jane?"

At first, Jane thought he was kidding, but then she noticed Jude had stopped what he was doing and was looking right at her. Jane could tell he wanted an answer to his ridiculous question. *Why should he care what I think? We work together. That's it*, she thought.

"Are you *serious*? We're about to kill Sharik and you're asking me if I care whether you have a *date*? *Jude*, you are my *partner*. Come on. We don't talk about stuff like this; we talk about work and we horse around. Whatever advice you want on your personal life, you're gonna have to get it somewhere else. I'm not good with relationships," Jane replied coldly.

"Jane, there are a few things I need to get off my chest. This is important to me. Can you just listen to me for once?" Jude moved in front of her and looked her in the eyes. "Jane, I've known you nearly *all* my life. I know I haven't been the easiest partner to work with. I need you to know that, without you, I wouldn't be here today. You've saved my life countless times. You pulled me out of mud holes in the middle of the jungle all shot to hell, rescued me from the desert with half my body broken, you even paid my rent to keep me from getting evicted. You sat by my side for *hours* while I sweated that *shit* out of my system. You've never left my side. I can't *believe* you've never left my *side*. I don't think I ever thanked you for those times," he said softly.

"Jude, what the hell is going on with you? Look, none of that was a big deal. I'd do that a thousand times over for you. You're my best friend and my partner. Hell, we can't function without each other. I mean, *look* at us. Here we are, about to execute a huge mission, assembling our equipment, setting up and ready to engage, all while having a casual conversation about your girly emotions." Jane ragged him on purpose. She really needed to break the tension, and she figured a slight jab might snap Jude out of his desire to talk about their "relationship."

"Yeah, well, did you hear what I said? It's important that you hear me. I'm sorry. And Jane? Thank you." Jude leaned over and kissed Jane on the cheek before he grabbed the rest of his gear.

They spread out a hundred yards from each other and switched to their headset communicators.

"Distance to sights, Bulldog? Give me a range," Jane commanded.

Jude *was* an excellent partner. His attention to detail and his accurate sighting made them an elite team. Together they had more kill shots than any other team in Orion. That night was really going to give them an even higher elite status among their members because their mark had been sought for *years* and *they* were the ones about to take the shot.

Jane thought about what Jude had said. Those were painful nights they had spent together when he was in rehab. She wasn't sure he'd survive any of his stints. She never left his side, except for brief moments, because she was afraid he might die while she was gone. She'd race to use the bathroom to make sure she was always near him as much as possible. No one should have to die alone. Jane had always tried to picture what dying would be like. She'd certainly come close to dying, but she'd never had any out-of-body experiences like other people she'd talked to. Jane had never heard a voice telling her to walk toward the light, like you see in the movies. She thought that when you die, you just die. The lights go out. That's it.

Jane spoke to Jude through the headset. "Bulldog, I need that range. What's the distance to your target?"

"Thirty yards. Target locked on."

"Locked *on*? What the *fuck* are you talking about? You haven't even given me the coordinates yet! I'm not dialed in! Who's doing the shooting here?" This was supposed to be her shot, not his.

Suddenly, Jane's gut told her something was wrong. She felt her blood surge through her veins and her heart raced. Jane stopped toggling her weapon and swung around to look at Jude. She saw a red beam aimed at her forehead. Jude stood in her direct line of vision with his weapon pointed right at her.

Jane heard a pop and felt an instant burning sensation in her eye, then she went numb. She opened her mouth to yell but couldn't make a sound. The dock seemed to disappear from beneath her as she fell backward onto it. She couldn't move her body. She couldn't scream. She couldn't feel any pain. She lay on her back completely frozen, looking through one eye up at the night sky as the lights went out.

This can't be right. I can't be dead, she thought. *Oh my God! This is what being dead is like—trapped in eternal darkness with your thoughts. I'm in fucking hell. I can't move. I can't feel my body breathing. I can't hear anything but myself yelling inside of me.*

Jude walked over to her body and bent down to check her pulse.

"Oh dear God, Jane. I'm sorry. Forgive me. I don't know what I'm doing. I just have to—"

Jude stood up quickly and ran to the side of the dock and threw up. He then turned his communicator back on and began speaking in Arabic over his headset. A few minutes later, rotor blades cut through the night sky and the wind began to pick up and swirl around them. Jude grabbed his gear as a helicopter hovered over him and dropped a rope ladder. He held it as the chopper hoisted him off the pier. Jane was sure he looked back to see her laying on the ground. Her eyes were wide open, as if she were staring right back at him. She imagined him shutting his own eyes tightly to avoid imprinting what he'd just done.

Judas, she thought. *We should have called him Judas.*

The helicopter transported Jude only several hundred yards across the bay, to the Arab trade ship that awaited him. Jude dropped onto the deck of the ship and walked forward to shake hands with Sharik.

Back in Jane's hometown, alarms sounded throughout the usually calm, quiet municipal fire department, alerting the guys to posse up. In the middle of the night, the firefighters donned their uniforms, loaded into the trucks, and headed toward a four-alarm blaze in the center of town. The captain wriggled in his seat as he attempted to secure both his seat belt and headset as they sped through the streets.

As their truck rounded a corner, the captain let out a gasp.

"Sweet Jesus! That's a goddamn inferno!"

An entire apartment complex was engulfed in flames and spewing black smoke. Residents shouted as they fled into the street. Some stood in shock while others ran to grab their camcorders. The firefighters got to work securing hoses while the captain radioed for backup.

Twenty miles across town, Howser walked slowly through Jane's home, examining her things. He opened her closet gingerly and then ran his hands across her clothes. He pulled a sweater off a shelf and held it close to inhale her scent. He dropped it on the bed and walked over to the nightstand, where he found Amelia's journal. He picked it up, looked at the cover, and sunk into a bedside chair. Agent Cope entered the room to speak to Howser.

"They have nearly everything boxed up, sir, and ready to go, except for this room. Do you need more time?" He wasn't certain how to proceed; he'd never seen Howser act this way.

"What's the status update on Robert Locke?" asked Howser, clearing his throat.

"I'll find out, sir."

An hour earlier, Robert performed his usual nightly routine in his apartment. He laid his uniform on his bed, ensuring there were no creases. His shirt was perfectly pressed and the buttons on his jacket shone brightly. As he brushed his teeth, he planned out the story he would tell to the guys the next day regarding his adventures. He enjoyed keeping his buddies on the edge of their seats regarding Jane. They asked about her constantly, and he was becoming an expert at fabricating stories to mislead them. Robert squeezed more toothpaste onto his new blue toothbrush and scrubbed at his teeth, stopping occasionally to watch as he flexed his arms in the bathroom mirror. As he spit, he considered hitting the gym more often. He wished they would let him beef up a little. He thought Jane might like him more if he looked like he *was* with Special Forces.

Robert's dog entered the bathroom and began to whine.

"What is it, Sadie? Do you have to go outside?"

Robert patted Sadie on the head, then put on sweatpants so he could take her for a walk. As he was hooking up her leash, he heard something at the front door. He moved toward it and saw the knob turn. He stepped backward slowly toward the kitchen to find a weapon when the door swung in. Suddenly, he was blinded by bright lights and the room filled with uniformed men.

"Engage three-nine! Target in sight!"

Before Robert could even reach for a weapon, the tactical team had crossed the room and pinned Robert to the ground at gunpoint.

Across town, Agent Cope received the news and returned to Jane's room to report to Howser.

"Locke has been secured, sir."

"Get me the team leader."

Agent Cope stood silently in the bedroom while Howser waited to be connected to the team leader holding Robert.

"Torch the place," Howser ordered. "Burn the body to cinders. I don't care *what* you do with the fucking dog. Give it to your goddamn kid for Christmas. Just get the fuck out of there. There's a plane waiting. Get your ass on it."

Howser placed the phone in his pocket and slumped in the chair. Quill Gordon tried to curl up on his lap, but Howser pushed him off.

The admiral was oblivious to the agents rummaging through Jane's things, stuffing them into boxes. He simply sat there with his memories.

What have I done? Howser struggled with his own orders to have Jane shot and Robert's apartment torched.

Agent Cope had been standing in the room for nearly ten minutes when he finally spoke.

"Sir? Due respect, sir, but I need to ask you a question."

"What is it, Agent Cope?"

"It doesn't seem logical to take out Agent Locke like this. For all the years Jane was with him, he kept a tight lid on his cover regarding the general. She never suspected a thing. He played the Opie role to a T, sir, and hated every minute of it, I can assure you. No disrespect, sir. I mean, I'm sure he liked the general and all. I just mean he was a real badass agent, but his cover . . . well, it was less than macho. To go in with a B team like that full force . . . shouldn't they have just kept a lid on it? Sent in Mr. Dobbs, the private assassin, or something to clean up the scene? Keep the whole thing quiet?"

"Come *on*, Cope! Are you an *idiot*? You think I'm gonna take out one of my best agents? Robert is loading up for Afghanistan by now. He has another job to do. And so do you. Get moving."

"But the body, sir. You said to torch the body. Didn't you mean . . . Oh. You're planting another body at the scene. Sorry, sir. I *am* an idiot. You must think it's my first damn day on the job. I apologize."

"Yeah, well, you might want to reevaluate some of those meds you've been taking. See if some of them are stupid pills."

"Yes, sir."

Howser stood up abruptly and marched into the living room. "Pack this place up!" he barked, even though the agents were nearly finished. "I want everything delivered to Quantico. And take that fucking door off! We're taking that with us." Howser pointed to Jane's red front door, which was propped open as agents came and went.

It was well into the morning before three departments were able to contain the catastrophic blaze that engulfed Robert's apartment building.

"Captain, is it true that this was the residence of one of the city's very own firefighters? Was he inside at the time of the blaze? Can you tell us if he's alive?" The reporter shoved her microphone into the face of the clearly exhausted captain.

"That information is unavailable at this time. A full investigation needs to be conducted. Thank you." The captain sighed. He knew the building housed Robert's apartment, but it was too early to discern the number of survivors. He had a gut feeling Robert was inside and that they had been unable to reach him in time.

"Captain, they found Robert's dog," said one of the firefighters as she led Sadie toward the captain. Her leash was attached and she was covered in ash. The captain bent down and patted her. "That's a good girl, Sadie. Where's your dad, huh?" He crouched next to the dog and looked solemnly at the burned building. A minute later he stood up abruptly with the dog in his arms. "Alright. Let's move out."

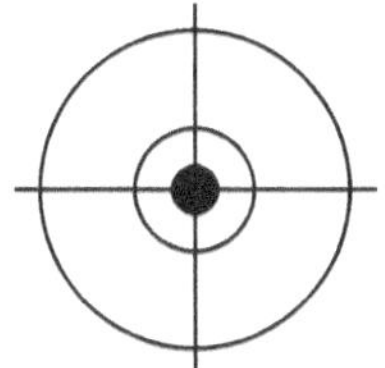

CHAPTER TWENTY-SIX

"Obviously, you're not dead," Sam observed as Jane approached him in the barn, where he was feeding the horses their breakfast. She'd gotten fatigued the night before and went to bed, leaving everyone wondering what happened after Jude shot her. In part, she wanted to hold the suspense for at least one night. She liked feeling in control.

"Let's go for a walk," suggested Jane, putting her arm around Sam's waist. She was getting just as comfortable with Sam as he was with her. "You think your grandpa wants to hear the end of this? He's over on the porch having breakfast." Sam gave her a reassuring nod and they made their way across the lawn to Eugene.

"Mornin', you two," said Eugene around a mouthful of pancakes.

"Morning, Grandpa. Aunt Jane was just about to finish telling us her story from last night." Sam motioned for Jane to sit beside Eugene. She slowly pulled up a chair and smiled at Eugene without saying a word.

"Well, I was up all night thinkin' about that. You sure left us hangin', and I gotta hear from the horse's mouth what really went on. If you'd care to oblige . . ." Eugene scooted his chair closer to Jane. Marlene came out and placed a steaming cup of coffee directly in front of Jane.

"You're gonna need this," she advised in her Texas twang. Before Jane could thank her, Marlene swatted the air and said, "Don't mention it, honey," as she pulled up a chair next to Eugene.

"Alright. Well, I was left there on the ground, alone in my head, in complete darkness, with my own thoughts."

After she was shot, Jane had remained a captive in that black, paralyzing pit, without any concept of time. Eventually, limb by limb, she began to feel pins and needles throughout her body. Her hearing also began to return; she heard the muffled sound of her own breath, as if she were underwater. She came to slowly, but her mind was subject to a plethora of fleeting images. Brief flashes of the Killing Circle passed. Then Jane remembered seeing a blurred outline of Jude's face, the laser beam on her forehead, and the projectile coming toward her. Her breathing grew rapid and she began to panic. Her heart raced faster as more memories returned.

"Were you aware of your surroundings at all?" asked Sam.

"Well, I knew I wasn't dead, but I didn't know where I was. I thought I'd been taken hostage and was being held for some type of interrogation and that I had a hood over my head. I thought of all the times I'd been interrogated. I'd just invite those assholes to take the damn hood off and face me. I knew I could take them."

Jane didn't tell Sam that she had actually focused her mind on the video sent to her of Tom in Baghdad. *His* captors didn't take off his hood. After the terrorists had made the exchange, her for Tom, they took him into a room and sat him in front of a camera. Four men wearing ski masks forced him down. She could tell he had been beaten so badly that he was barely alive. His nearly lifeless body slumped in the chair. He appeared to have no fight left in him at all. As Jane silently remembered the details of the video, she tried to shake them off. She couldn't allow herself to start reliving that memory at that moment. She needed to collect herself and find a way out of the situation in which she found herself. Jane wondered if her captors were also videotaping her.

"Wow! That must have been *really* scary," Sam responded, his jaw practically hitting the floor.

"Yeah. It was. Luckily, our training taught us to solve problems with caution. So, when I realized my hands weren't bound, I moved them discreetly in case someone was watching me. I began to run over my escape scenario in my head: In three seconds, I'd grab the hood from my face. I expected up to ten armed men to be in the room with me, with one standing at the entrance. More than likely they had placed my back to the door. I told myself to prepare for battle in three, two . . ." Jane crouched on the ground to simulate her next moves.

"I jumped up and reached for my face, but there was no hood to remove. The whole time I assumed my head was covered, I was actually blind. I had to compensate quickly, so I felt around the room as fast as I could. I found a metal bar and began to swing it. A man came into the room and yelled for help. *First target*, I thought, and then I locked on to his voice. I felt a direct hit travel up the bar as I swung it."

Jane continued to explain that she moved in the direction where she heard the person enter the room, and she ran for it. She stayed low and hugged the concrete walls. Then she heard two more people coming toward her. She counted their footsteps as their shoes hit the tile floor. She felt for the edge of a doorway and slipped in. As the men approached, she moved out and attacked them with the metal bar.

"Oh my God! You didn't have your *sight* but you still took those guys *out*?!" Sam was clearly impressed. Jane crouched down again as she narrated what happened next.

"I felt the floor around the two men I'd laid out, searching for weapons. I didn't find any, which I thought was odd. I felt their bodies and realized they were wearing badges and stethoscopes. They were doctors! I slipped back into another doorway and felt around—sink, toilet, bed, rails, person. Person! I started to shake the body that lay in the bed, telling it to wake up. I didn't know if the patient was sleeping or dead. Apparently, he was alive, because he woke up and started yelling at me and asking why I was in his room, waking him up. I demanded he tell me his name. Bear in mind, I was still holding the metal bar. He said, 'I'm Major General Briggs! Now put down that bar before I shove it up your ass!' Well, Sam, he was rightfully upset."

"So, you *were* in a hospital, right?"

"Yep. What I *didn't* know was that I'd been taken to Fort Bragg in North Carolina, to the military hospital there. I was really confused when I realized my 'captors' weren't out to get me. I asked to use his phone."

Sam pushed his cowboy hat up to scratch at his head. "I'm still trying to wrap my mind around all this."

"Patience, young Jedi. It'll all come together," Jane said, patting his back. "So, the major general asked me who *I* was, turning my question back on me. I wasn't planning to answer him, but then he asked if I was General Stapelton."

"No way! How'd he know who you were?"

"Believe me, I was just as stunned as you are now."

Although Briggs had called her by name, Jane still didn't answer him. How could she trust someone she couldn't see? His irritated tone indicated his frustration at her lack of cooperation. He had no clue Jane had no vision. Briggs didn't just hand over his phone at Jane's request, and she couldn't blame him for questioning her semipsychotic behavior. Jane would have hesitated too, if their roles had been reversed. Instead of giving the phone to her, he offered to dial the number for her.

When Jane told him to call the White House, he said, "Right. From your hospital bed?"

That's when Jane fully realized she *was* in a hospital. It wasn't until she demanded he hand his phone to her that he complied. She felt the phone pads and entered her code. When Jane heard Tully's voice on the other end, she felt tremendous relief.

"Delta fox scepter."

"Outland A-T twenty dash nine. Jude Common Ice. Forty-four, ninety-nine, forty-four," responded Jane in one fast exhale. Jane thought she might have said the code incorrectly, but she knew Tully would know her voice. Tully asked her what she was doing calling in, which affirmed for Jane that she was supposed to be in the hospital. Jane ordered Tully to get Howser on the phone and to alert him to her level 3 situation; she may have killed her doctors. Tully told her not to worry because his staff was already posted outside her door.

Jane told him she wasn't in her own room, she had no visual, and she didn't think anyone was actually there. She explained how Jude had shot her and that she had *no visual whatsoever*—that she was blind and she thought she was going to be tortured. Then Jane burst into tears and insisted she needed backup.

Tully calmed her down by saying, "I'm on it, Jane. We're sending someone to you."

Jane shivered at the memory of what Jude did to her. And it finally penetrated that she was really *blind*. Then she felt someone gently take her hand.

With great empathy, Briggs said, "I'm here, Special Ops."

Jane removed her hand angrily from his and yelled, "I don't need you, sir!" Then she felt for the walls of the room, made her way back into the hallway, and yelled, "I need medical!"

Jane paused in her retelling to gather her composure.

"You don't like to feel vulnerable, do you, Aunt Jane?"

Jane gave Sam a half smile. "Yeah, I think you're catching on to me." For some reason, Jane didn't mind Sam knowing what she considered to be a fault—one of *her* faults. She wanted Sam to realize that one day he may need to fall back on some of the same survival tactics she used.

"Go on!" urged Eugene. "We're on the edge of our seats here!"

"Well, after I yelled, I heard a swarm of people dragging carts down the hall toward me. They sedated me immediately. When I woke up, I was restrained in a surgical chair. A doctor was holding my head back and using a laser on my eyes. I couldn't feel or see anything, but because I could hear the equipment and I smelled a burning odor, I knew what was going on. I'd gone through the same procedure years before when my eyes were injured in a flash-bang explosion.

The family leaned forward in the porch chairs as Jane told them the rest of the story.

"Jane," the surgeon said softly. Jane was surprised to hear a female voice. "I'm Dr. Horne. We're going to remove the restraints that are keeping your eyelids open. I want you to close your eyes and keep them shut. Don't open them for two minutes; I'll tell you when two minutes have passed. When you open your eyes, I want you to do it slowly to let them adjust to the natural light in the room. We have the light fixtures turned off, so don't panic if you still can't see well. You'll have full vision in thirty minutes."

Jane detected a slight hesitation in the doctor's last statement, as if she wasn't really sure if what she said was true.

"Roger that, ma'am," replied Jane, trying to remain calm and professional.

"No formalities here, Jane. I'm just a doctor." Then she laughed and recited a line from *Star Trek*. 'Damn it, Jim! I'm only a doctor!' Although it was a cheesy joke, Jane laughed too. "Try to relax," the surgeon said as she placed a hand on Jane's shoulder.

Jane couldn't tell if her eyes were open or closed. She felt nothing and realized it was probably the anesthetic. Suddenly, she heard a familiar voice in the room and her body tensed immediately.

"Jane?" Jude asked.

Jane's respiration increased and her blood pressure skyrocketed. She began pulling at her restraints, and she wanted desperately to open her eyes.

"What the fuck? Help!" Jane shouted. "Dr. Horne! Don't let him in! That's the guy who shot me! Call Howser!"

The doctor tried to calm her. "Don't open your eyes, Jane. It's okay. I'm right here."

"What the fuck is going on? Release me! You don't understand! He tried to kill me!" Jane continued to struggle to free herself. "Don't let him in! Guards!"

"Look, Jane. It's not what it seems. Those were my orders." Jude's voice became louder as he neared her. He spoke in a calm, reassuring tone, but Jane didn't buy it for a second. "Howser *ordered* me to do that. Calm down."

"Jude, you *shot* me! You tried to *kill* me! What the fuck? Howser? Why? Help! Guards!"

"Listen, Jane. You were thirty yards from me. If I wanted to kill you, you'd be dead!"

"I don't *understand*. Why would you *shoot* me? Jude! I'm fucking *blind*! What orders?"

"You never were the brightest crayon in the box. I never did understand how you pulled your rank with such a low IQ." Jude's joking made Jane even more livid.

The doctor's voice broke the tension. "Jude, I'm going to have to ask you to leave if you continue to upset her. This procedure has to be done right if we want her to regain her eyesight." Dr. Horne put her hand on Jane's. "Okay, Jane. I want you to open your eyes *slowly*. Remember, your vision will be slightly cloudy, but in about thirty minutes your eyes should be as good as new." Jane could've sworn the doctor murmured "hopefully" at the end of her statement.

"Jane, when we get back to Quantico, I'll explain everything to you. I'll show you my orders. You need to rest now," Jude whispered in her ear.

Jane turned toward the doctor and was pleased to see she could make out her form slightly. "Doctor, can something be done about these restraints?" Jane asked in a soft, submissive tone. "You're right. I need to be calm. I understand there has to be a good reason behind what happened. We have to follow orders." Jane pretended to ease up so Dr. Horne would remove the restraints.

Jane's eyesight was still too bad for her to see the doctor look to Jude for permission. If Jane knew *Jude* was responsible for her freedom, her head would've probably exploded.

"Okay," replied Dr. Horne, "but go slow. Don't stand up."

Jude unbuckled the first restraint, then moved to the second. In a soft, warm voice to coax Jude closer to her, Jane asked, "Jude?" She needed him within arm's reach. "Jude? Did you mean all that stuff you said on the dock that night? And were you really following orders?"

"What? What did you say? I can't hear you," responded Jude as he leaned in toward Jane's face.

Jane grabbed Jude swiftly by the throat and smashed the bridge of his nose repeatedly into her forehead. "I am your *CO*! Don't you *ever* fucking shoot me again, you motherfucker! I will tear off your balls and mail them to your father!"

Jane needed to attack Jude to begin healing emotionally. She didn't *care* about Jude's motivation. Jane wanted him to feel pain for what she'd undergone.

Jude fell to the floor, writhing in agony as blood spurted from his nose. Jane could taste his blood in her mouth and she was satisfied that she had made her point.

"You asshole!" Jude shouted, holding his nose as the doctor tried to help him. Jude reached out to punch Jane, but Dr. Horne placed herself between them.

"Get out! Get out right now!" ordered Dr. Horne.

Jane just smiled as she regained her sight, slowly recognizing more shapes around the room.

Later that evening, Jane was packing up her stuff to leave the hospital when Jude knocked on her door. He had a bandage over his nose and his face was bruised.

"Let's get out of here, Jane. I hate hospitals," he said, keeping a safe distance from her, in case she attacked him again.

"I'll meet you outside. There's something I have to do first."

"Suit yourself, asshole!" Jude touched his nose, as if to remind Jane of what she'd done. Jane waved her hands back and forth in front of her eyes.

"Uh, remember this, *dumb ass*? You blinded me!"

"Fine!"

"Fine!"

They sounded like a couple of kids fighting over a toy.

As Jane exited her room, she closed her eyes and swept the walls with her hands until she reached the doorway of Major General Briggs' room. She had to retrace her steps blindly because she had no idea which room she had stumbled into that day.

"What the *hell* are you doing?" Briggs shouted at her when he saw her standing in his doorway with her eyes closed.

"Just making sure I had the right room, sir." Jane entered the room and approached the bed. She didn't know he had been burned and scarred from head to toe—that is, if he had toes. He was missing both of his legs. In addition, he had a series of tubes running out of his bandaged body and a sling hung from a pole attached to the bed, which suspended one of his arms.

"Sir, I was rude to you earlier. I came to apologize," Jane said, ashamed by the way she had treated him.

"Was that before or after you knew I looked like this? Are you apologizing because you feel sorry for me or sorry for your lack of respect?" he asked bitterly.

"Sir—"

"I don't give a shit, Marine!" he barked, then he suddenly softened. "I know who you are. When they told me they were bringing you in, I tried to will myself a new set of damn legs so I could walk into your room. I wanted to see the President's little watchdog. The Ghost. I don't know how you do what you do. Hell! I don't know whether half of what I've heard about you is truth or legend. It's too far-fetched. Even Chesty himself couldn't pull that shit off." Jane was honored that Briggs would compare her with Chesty Puller, the most decorated Marine in the history of the Corps.

"However, I can tell you this rush of independence won't last—not if you don't have faith in your band of brothers. You aren't a one-person Marine Corps. Don't let this be you," Briggs lectured as he motioned to his missing limbs. "Your partner said you're a real asshole and think you run the show alone. Well, you don't. You're part of a team, part of the Corps. Do you love the Corps?"

"Yes, sir!" Jane replied, feeling even more ashamed that she'd disgraced him.

"Listen to me," he continued. "If enemies get ahold of you and torture you, if they cut off your legs and throw gasoline on you and light you on fire, and if you still manage to fight your way out . . ." Briggs hesitated as he struggled to give voice to what he was feeling. "Dammit! You kill yourself right there. Die on that battlefield in honor, not in some fucked-up hospital without your brothers!" He looked down at his missing limbs and shook his head. "Now get out of here! Make me proud!" Clearly Briggs had finished his pep talk and wanted no more of her, so Jane turned and walked out.

"Holy crap!" Sam said as he jumped down from the porch rafters, where he had hoisted himself while Jane spoke. "You must've been scared, pissed, and really confused!"

"I was. I still didn't know why Jude had shot me and I had *no* idea why I wasn't dead. But I was most pissed at Howser."

"Why were you so pissed at *him*?"

"Shit, Sam! Your aunt was probably pissed that she woke up in a hospital, blind and terrified, and her own father wasn't there by her side," Eugene said. "He wasn't there worried about her or waiting for her to wake up. Her meet-up with Briggs wouldn't have happened if he'd been there for her like a real, caring father." Even at that moment, all those years later, the thought still made Jane sad. Eugene was right.

"Well, did you think it was your dad who ordered Jude to shoot you? Maybe he couldn't face what he'd done," said Sam, playing the devil's advocate.

"I didn't know," replied Jane. "I didn't believe it, at least. I hadn't read the orders. Jude could've been lying to me." Back then, Jane just knew her dad wasn't there for her once again.

"How'd you find out about losing Robert in the fire? That must have been awful, especially after losing Tom." Sam plopped down next to her.

"Sam, I'm gonna be truthful with you."

"That's what I want. Honesty," Sam told Jane with sincerity.

"I believe, looking back on the whole experience, that was the moment when I really began to transform with regard to relationships. I was in love with Tom, beyond all words and measure. Then I let Robert in a little bit and had started to feel serious about him. We'd spent five years together, and I *liked* spending time with him. I even allowed myself to soften up a little. But Robert didn't die in the fire, Sam. Jude told me that Robert was an agent, performing his duty to Howser. After that, I just shut down. I never opened my heart again."

In reality, Jane was extraordinarily upset over Robert's betrayal. She had let herself be vulnerable and even feminine around him. Yet she assumed that, in his mind, he was only on a mission. Jane thought he used her—and she fell for it. She was angry when she thought about how Robert feigned surprise and fear in "discovering" her status, tricking her into buying even more into his deception for a number of years afterward. And she felt humiliated and violated by Howser.

Jane looked at Sam, who stared back at her, stunned at her revelation.

"I can't believe Robert was an *agent*! You must have felt *so* betrayed. Oh, Aunt Jane," he said, rubbing his head.

"Yes, Sam, but the other half of me praised myself for my strict and rigid discipline. I had a duty to perform. I knew unquestionably, in all those years, I never violated the Code of Orion. I never discussed my participation in it or its existence with Robert. He never had *anything* to report to Howser. From that moment forward, I reminded myself constantly that my life was a test. Remember that. You're always under constant scrutiny." Jane looked Sam dead in the eyes. "I mean this, Sam. Remember what I just said. You'll *always* be tested. Just remain true to your beliefs and hold yourself to a high standard.

"I took every memory of Robert that I had and stuffed each one mentally into tiny boxes and sealed them behind a brick wall. I never wanted to access those memories or those feelings again. But while doing that, I also packed away the compassionate, loving, empathetic, caring parts of myself and replaced them with anger and, well—to be truthful—stronger, darker, violent emotions.

"For a while, it felt like a refreshing change. Yeah, I was angry. *All* the time. But I also felt *strong*. I knew there was *no way* I'd ever be vulnerable to serious relationships and loving partnerships. I could remain in control at all times. The problem is that I still live like that. I still carry *so* much anger. I can't *stand* relationships. I can't *stand* the thought of being tethered to someone else. When I see a man's weakness, I slowly begin to rip him apart. When he doesn't 'man up' and grow stronger, it makes me sick to my stomach and I send him packin'. It usually only takes about two weeks for a guy to retreat with his tail between his legs."

"Okay, okay, hold on! Ma'am, you can't go through life like that! You sound like a jerk."

"Sam, for the record, I *am* a jerk." Jane took out her electronic cigarette, which made Sam smile.

"So what happened after Jude told you about Robert?"

"Well, then Jude told me that Howser had been the one who ordered him to shoot me. He didn't elaborate and said he'd tell me all about it when we got back to Quantico. I was left hanging, and that added even more fuel to the fire regarding my feelings toward Howser."

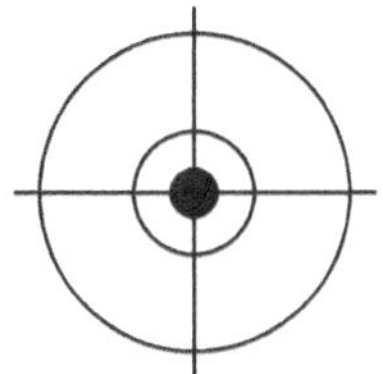

CHAPTER TWENTY-SEVEN

Jane practically blended in with the Secret Service agents who surrounded her as she crossed the tarmac on her way to *Air Force One*. Dressed in black from head to toe, her heels hit the ground with determination in every step. The sun reflected off her black aviators, which protected her eyes and covered her eyepatch.

As Jane stepped onto the plane, Howser greeted her with more enthusiasm than usual.

"Elizabeth!" he said, almost smiling. He seemed truly grateful to see her—more so than Jane to see him.

"Hey, Dad," Jane replied curtly. At that point, Jane no longer cared about formalities. After all, aside from the pilots, only the two of them were on the plane. Jane didn't even bother to look at him. She brushed right past him as he tried to hug her.

"Easy there, Elizabeth. We're on the same side here," Howser countered softly.

"I don't know *what* has come over me!" Jane snarked. "Let's see, maybe it's knowing that you gave orders to my subordinate to shoot me in the *face*. Oh! And I thought I was *dead*. I guess I'm a little outside myself right now."

Jane walked to the bar and stood there for a moment, contemplating the bottle of whiskey. Jane unscrewed the cap and poured herself a drink, then sat down with it and stared at the liquor clinging to the sides of the glass as Jane swirled it. In her peripheral vision, she could see Howser glaring at her. Jane shot back the drink and tried not to choke.

"Now what'd you go and do *that* for?" Howser asked as he sat in the seat facing her.

"I'm thinking about taking up smoking too, you bastard. What're you gonna do about *that*?" Jane got up, walked back to the bar, and poured herself another drink.

"Smoking, huh? Well here, then. Let's see if you're any good at it." Howser joined her at the wet bar and opened the cupboard. Inside were a few packs of cigarettes. He tossed one to Jane.

"Fine. This saves me from having to buy a pack when we land." Jane didn't intend to buy a pack of cigarettes nor did she want to smoke one. She'd worked hard all her life to keep her body in perfect shape so she could do all the physical things she had to do to survive. She hated smokers. But at that moment, she hated Howser even more.

Howser lit the cigarette, handed it to her, and Jane began to smoke it.

"No. See? You're not even inhaling the smoke. You're just sucking on it like you're trying to siphon gas from a gas tank. Really *draw* the smoke into your lungs, then exhale slowly." Howser took the cigarette from her and demonstrated. As a longtime cigar smoker, the smoke didn't bother him at all.

Jane tried to do the same but the smoke burned her lungs. It reminded her of when they had to remove their masks during tear gas training. She felt the same instant urge to vomit. Her eyes began to water and she started coughing uncontrollably.

"Don't worry. You'll get the hang of it. I'm actually glad you've picked up a vice. It might relax you a little. I'll have a carton sent to your room at Quantico and you can practice." Howser turned to get himself a drink. "By the way, there's a case there with your orders."

Jane picked up the briefcase and cuffed it to her wrist. She sat down by the window with her back toward Howser. Again, Howser took the seat across from her. As he stared out the window, he kept darting glances at her as if he was about to say something. Jane tried not to look at him. She didn't have the energy to fight with him anymore that day, and she felt sick from the alcohol and cigarettes. She put her head back against the seat and didn't utter another word for the rest of the flight.

She arrived at Quantico to find her team preparing for a big deployment. She forced herself to focus and began to prepare their briefing. Eventually, she'd get to read the supposed orders to which Jude referred—and learn the how and why of it all.

Jane walked into the conference room and looked at her team, appalled. They looked like inner city, gangbanger high school students confined to detention. Paper airplanes flew around the room. Screech sat on the table cross-legged in a stained Hawaiian shirt that smelled like stale beer. He looked like he hadn't combed his hair in a week, and his thick beard was encrusted with dried bits of food. Butch slept with his head on the table, snoring like a freight train. Drool seeped from the corner of his mouth, and the guys had drawn stars on his forehead with markers. At least Jane hoped they used markers and that the stars were not new, really bad, tattoos. Pilot drew pole dancers on the chalkboard, most of whom were in nasty poses doing vulgar things to themselves with pieces of fruit. Jude looked high. His eyes were bloodshot and, clearly, he hadn't slept in days.

"Okay, gentlemen . . . and ladies," Jane said, looking straight at Jude with one eye.

When Jude spotted her eyepatch, he spouted, "Arrggghhh, Captain! What're we plunderin'? Avast, me hearties!" The team busted up with laughter.

"Yeah, Bulldog. Funny. You *do* know that pirates were gay?" Jane informed him, then she realized she'd been distracted. "Listen up, ball lickers. We're going south—"

"You're going down south, Jane? Me first!" Butch lit a cigarette and leaned back in his chair, motioning for a blow job.

"God!" yelled Jane in frustration.

"You can call me Bulldog here," quipped Jude. "Only my people call me God."

"What did they put in your dog dish, Bulldog? Crack? At least you'll be able to identify it when we seize it." Jane paused for a moment. She thought the comment might have crossed a line. Jude wasn't that far out from rehab. Again.

"Oh, man!" wailed Butch. This is a *drug bust*? Fuck that shit! That is *not* our shit anymore, Jane!"

"Yeah, well, just say no." Jane knew Butch hated handling dealers. He'd infiltrated many SOS bike rallies over the years and had also killed a slew of Columbian cartel members. "You guys are on fuckin' fire today, boy. Like I haven't heard any of *this* before. Get some new material! Now listen up! The mission is this target." Jane brought up a photograph on the projector screen, then felt her jaw tighten slightly while she checked a deep sigh that threatened to escape.

"Jeezuz, Jane! That's Lance Broad!" said Screech as he jumped off the table and moved closer to the screen to get a better look. "Guys like that don't go missing, Jane."

Screech was right. When Jane opened the orders, she was equally amazed to learn that Agent Lance Broad, a twenty-year CIA operative, had been apprehended and was being allegedly held in a compound in South America.

"Broad is the guy I want to be when I grow up! Are you *kidding* me?" Screech asked, stunned. "I heard he cut himself free from the belly of a croc that was eating him alive, then roasted the bastard on a spit."

"I'm not sure about all *that*, but—let's face it—this guy is *cool*. He was my instructor in the Middle East on covert improvised explosives. Broad could make a bomb from a shoestring, toothpaste, and a dead rat," Butch exaggerated.

"Is that how you practically lost half the skin on your arm, shitbag?" Jude wasn't impressed. "If he's such a hot shit, then how'd he end up in *this* fucked-up mess?"

Lance Broad certainly was the hot shit the guys made him out to be. He was brusque, gnarly, tough, and mean. Yet instead of being a knuckle-dragger, his home library would make any professor salivate. Jane discussed a wide range of topics with Broad and was always impressed with his extensive knowledge of literature, philosophy, mathematics, politics, religion, and science. He nailed the cool factor even further with his mastery of martial arts and weapons marksmanship, not to mention military hand-to-hand combat skills that were out of this world. Nearly old enough to be her father, Jane thought it was stellar that an "old dude" could still be a badass. At almost thirty, Jane considered fifty-six to be ancient.

Jane brought up several more images on the projector screen.

"Broad is believed to be out here somewhere," said Jane pointing, "in this region of Kieon. Although he's been missing for twenty-seven months, he was presumed dead until Command received an ambiguous, coded radio message. We believe that message was sent by Broad."

"What the hell? We're supposed to go find someone based on an ambiguous coded message that may or may not be from Broad?" Pilot asked, sitting up in his chair, finally chiming into the conversation. "We don't really have a clue where to begin, except for this huge region of dense jungle the size of Texas! I'm gonna need more greasepaint than this," he noted, motioning to the black smudges under his eyes.

"Oh! Hey! Don't forget the part about the armed militias that will try to kill us *and* Broad," Jude added. The guys groaned.

"Jude's right. There'll be about forty-three militias, the FARC, and maybe three or four cartels searching for him. It appears he pissed off the wrong people and has got a hefty bounty on his head. I imagine they'd just as likely chop off our heads as well," Jane continued. "It looks like the only advantage we have is that of surprise."

"That makes their odds about three hundred to six—maybe five, if they don't get Broad," calculated Jude.

In Jane's eyes, Jude was the perfect killer. He always looked at the dark side of things. However, as leader, she needed to get her team pumped up about any situation they might encounter. Jude would never be ready to lead a team.

"Don't forget, we don't know the terrain. And there's monsoons and alligators and rats. I *hate* rats," Screech sneered. He was lying.

Jane knew how much he loved the jungle. He was just complaining for the sheer fun of it.

"Fuck you, Screech. There are no alligators in Kieon and the monsoon was over months ago. What are you, a bunch of infants? This is paradise, boys—warm weather, great waterfalls, and sunshine." Jane said, trying to sell them.

"What's our timeline?" Jude asked.

"Twenty-six hours, so let's move it."

Jane left the conference room and headed to her quarters at Quantico. She hadn't been to her room since her arrival. When she rounded the corner, her legs almost went out from under her. She thought she was hallucinating. She closed her good eye tightly, then opened it. Facing her was the red front door from her old house. It hung at the entrance to her quarters. Jane felt her pulse quicken.

"What the *fuck*? Is this some kind of sick joke?" Jane asked the empty corridor. What she didn't know was that Howser had it brought with them and installed, thinking it might bring her comfort.

Jane reached for the handle and turned it, but it wouldn't open. Jane swiped her badge on the wall-mounted card reader and the door popped open. She touched the wood and pressed her face to it. She could practically smell Tom and hear him laughing as they argued over who would paint the door. Jane traced the crevices of the wood with her hand and remembered the nights she had run her hand over his chest. Jane felt tears begin to well up in her eyes, and her throat started to close.

Three things, Jane. Find three things. This was a technique she learned to stay focused when she felt overwhelmed. *Card reader, gray carpet . . .* Jane scanned the cement corridor for a third item and found it: *security camera*. When she regained control, Jane turned to the security camera and looked directly at it. She gave it the finger and went into her room, slamming the door behind her.

That son of a bitch! Jane thought. *What the hell was he thinking?* She ran into the bathroom to throw up.

Jane could hear the haunting voice of Dr. Reid in her head. "Look at you, Jane. Do you need a refresher course in self-control? I could send you away for a while if you'd like. Maybe you're getting too soft."

"Fuck you, Reid! Get the fuck away from me!" Jane yelled out loud, remembering Pilot's advice.

As Jane sat on the bed, Jude entered her room without knocking.

"I'm not going to get the fuck away. I need to use your bathroom." Jude squirmed nervously and fidgeted with her things, just like Butch did, which Jane found equally ballsy. Jude didn't mention the door because he knew it upset her. "Look, Jane, you didn't have to break my nose. I had my orders. I was working the Arabs. Sharik was my target and, to prove my credibility, I had to kill you while he watched."

"Why wasn't I informed of the mission?"

"It had to appear real. The less you knew, the better. Plus, we were being videotaped by Sharik. Jane, you're just not that good of an actress."

"Goddamn it, Jude. You shot me in the face."

"He'd have known I was bullshitting him if I'd shot you anywhere else. Then he would've sent his men to check and they would've killed you for sure!"

"I don't get it. How'd you shoot me and not kill me?"

"We developed a special weapon for the mission. I shot you with a paralyzing agent. It short-circuits the central nervous system. It has to enter through your cornea. That's why you went blind. I had to do it quick. I couldn't give you time to sight in. Once you dropped your goggles, I would've been screwed," he explained. Jane actually thought it was a cool op—if someone *else* on the team had been the target.

"Did you know it was going to work? Did you test it first? What if I hadn't regained my sight?" Jane asked, upset that she was used as a guinea pig in an op she knew nothing about, and with Jude as the leader.

"Jane, we're all about sacrifice. Briggs reminded you we're not a one-man Corps, didn't he? We're a team, with bigger responsibilities than any one of us. Quit yer whinin'. It worked, didn't it?" Jude asked, putting his hand on her shoulder.

"Yeah, and I just about killed three innocent doctors!" Jane brushed his hand off and thought about the poor men she nearly slaughtered.

"Are you slackin', Chuck Norris? Why'd you let them live? If that had been a real hostage situation, you'd have been screwed!

"Fuck *you*, man!" Jane said and got up from the bed.

"Am I right? I'm right." Jude stripped off his clothes. His body was lean, muscular, and covered with scarred tattoos. He walked toward the shower and turned it on.

"Jane, I'm showering here. Screech left a steaming present in my bathroom and I'm fumigating the place."

Jane joined him in the bathroom, unscrewed the top of her tube of toothpaste, and began to brush her teeth methodically as Jude stepped into the shower.

"Look, Jane. You have to knock this shit off with Howser," he said as he soaped his body.

"What shit?" Jane mumbled through her mouthful of toothpaste.

"I'm getting disgusted by your lack of respect for our leader. You march around here like a spoiled brat, undermining his decisions whenever you get a chance."

"What the hell are you talking about?" Jane spit into the sink and rinsed her mouth.

"Jesus Christ, Jane. He's a brilliant man and you treat him like crap! You should be kissing his ass for your position. We all know how you got it." Jude's voice trailed off as he shut off the water. It may have been easier for Jude to understand Jane's attitude if he, or any other member of her team, was allowed to know that Howser was her father.

Jane yanked open the curtain. "Just what the *hell* is that supposed to mean? Do you think I'm like Howser?"

"No, you asshole!" Jude reached for his towel and shoved her out of the way. "You'd never be where you are if Tom didn't die trying to save your pretty ass. You and I both know Howser sacrificed Tom to save you. And how do you repay him? By shitting all over him. You're a disgrace."

"What are you *talking* about? Fuck you! That is *not* what happened. Howser would *never* sacrifice Tom for me. He hates me." Deep down, Jane believed this to be true.

"Trust me, Jane. For the life of me, I'll never figure that one out."

Jane had had enough. She was beyond angry and losing control. She grabbed Jude by the throat but he pulled a tactical move and held her head forcefully against the sink.

"You're gonna have to learn to trust me, Jane. Trust the Corps. This isn't just about you." Jude let her up and turned her around to face him. For a moment, he considered kissing her.

Jane felt defeated. She thought, *I don't know who to trust. I don't even trust myself.*

"Jane, I meant what I said." Jude's tone softened slightly.

"What? That I'm a spoiled fucking bitch?"

"Shut up. I meant what I said on the dock that night. You've always been there for me. Can't you soften up a *little* bit with me? I care about you, Jane. You just have some messed-up shit going on in your head, that's all. I know my shooting you didn't help."

As soon as Jude reminded her he shot her, Jane felt searing pain in her eye, and her anger returned.

"Go fuck yourself, cowboy! We have less than twenty-three hours to prepare for hell. Now, get the fuck out of here!"

Jude grabbed his clothes and shouted as he left, "Trust the Corps, Jane! This isn't about you!"

As Jane watched Jude leave, she tried to shove down what had just transpired between them. *I don't have time for this crap*, she thought. Jane attempted to rinse away the negative residue further by taking a shower, then she crawled into bed.

"Bravo, Janie! That was beeeeoooootiful!"

"Jeezuz!" Jane shot out of bed and turned toward the speaker, who was scrunched down in the corner of her room, hiding in the shadows. "What the *hell* are you doin' in my room?"

"The usual. Nothin'." Screech remained crouched down on the floor as he cupped his knotty, scraggly beard with both hands. A muffled whistle escaped the confines of tangled hair. Jane watched Screech as he appeared to speak into his beard. "Ssssh. Shut up! She's gonna see you!"

"What're you doin', you bastard?"

"Nothin'." Screech continued to press his fingers into his ratty beard. To Jane's amazement, a feathered head popped out of the matted mound of whiskers.

"Is that a fuckin' *bird*?!"

"Maybe."

"What the hell are you doing with a bird? Hey! That's *my* bird!"

"It was in my room. There's a cat in there too."

"Quill Gordon?"

"Shit, I don't know. It's not like he introduced himself. I'll go get him. But can I keep the bird? I think he kind of likes it in here."

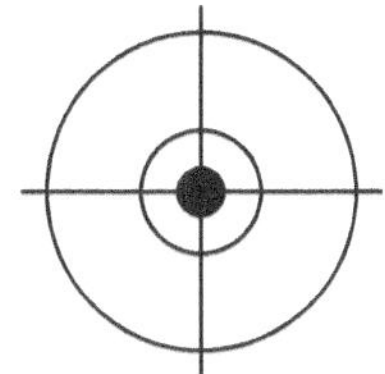

CHAPTER TWENTY-EIGHT

"Aunt Jane? I don't understand what happened to the rest of your team. You said they were all dead or crazy now." Sam handed Jane some lemonade as he took a seat next to her.

"I don't want to talk about that Sam. I can't."

"Is it a secret?"

"No. Well, sort of. It's just too hard to talk about. I don't trust myself not to lose it again."

"I understand. I'm gonna go up and start packing." As Sam started to walk away, he turned back toward Jane. "I'm really honored to have you accompany me to boot camp. Thank you for being here for me."

"That's what salespeople call an 'assumptive close,'" laughed Jane. "Of *course* I'll go with you. It'll be *my* honor."

Jane liked being needed. She thought of herself as a leader; mentorship, however, was a little new to her. She had grown genuinely fond of Sam. He worked hard, he loved his family, he had heart. Also, as driven and competitive as she was by nature, she wanted to contribute to his success in any way she possibly could. As Sam walked away, she thought about what he had asked and what *did* happen to her team.

Although all of them had done a night drop into the jungle at least once, Jane always had a sense of foreboding beforehand. As she gazed out the window of the plane, she thought about her fellow team members. A few of the Rangers hadn't done a night drop since Ranger training, which required them to survive in the jungle for several weeks with only a knife. As part of that training, they had to navigate their way through the dense, dangerous environment to a designated pickup zone. This time would be different. They wouldn't have choppers available to extract them seventy-two hours after their drop. There would be no search and rescue if they didn't return, and no close air support.

Howser had deemed the mission highly classified and withheld most of the details from The Brass. None of them had any idea how long they'd be in Kieon. They suspected it would take several months to recover Agent Broad. Their survival, and Broad's, depended on their skill and training. There was the distinct possibility that they'd encounter more than three hundred armed men who they'd either need to kill or outmaneuver. This was when the team's training in Orion's jungle facility would be put to the ultimate test.

From what Jane knew about Broad, Beyond Badass should be his middle name. Had it not been for an altercation between him and his supervisor, they might be taking orders from Agent Broad as Orion's second-in-command. However, Howser thought Broad's insubordination was enough to discount him from the program. Certainly there had to be more to it than that. After all, her entire team was made up of insubordinate assholes. Despite that fact, they only acted that way toward each other, not Howser. Broad must have pushed Howser's buttons in a bad way. A twenty-year CIA operative, combat instructor, interrogation specialist, hostage negotiator, forensics specialist, linguist, explosives specialist, weapons instructor, technical advisor, and communications specialist, Broad was overqualified for his position. Even by Howser's standards, his determination and dedication to duty was admirable.

Agent Broad sacrificed years of his life moving covertly between extremes—from jungles to deserts—gathering intel to formalize and affirm the associations between Sharik and Ascrazada, the drug lord supplying weapons to the Middle East. Basically, Broad tied Middle Eastern terrorists to large South American drug cartels, and confirmed a highway of drugs, money, and weapons between them. Broad believed it was his duty to stop secret associations like these from forming. He admitted that his life's mission was to curb these cells before they got radically out of control. Jane admired Broad's perseverance and intellect. And, as with any brother-in-arms, it was their joyful duty to do everything they could to facilitate his safe return.

"Hey, kids, I have something special on the menu for tonight," said Howser over the communicator.

Jane moved to the front of the plane so she could hear him better. "Repeat that, please."

"Check under the front hatch. I sent you kids something special. I figured it would be a while before you got a decent meal again."

Jane turned to Screech, "Hey, pop-tard, open the front hatch and see what's in it. Howser said he sent us a care package."

"Fuck no! You do it, Butch. Knowing Howser it's probably a lion that hasn't eaten for three days. I'm not looking in there."

"Howser, is this a joke? Is there something deadly in there?" Jane asked over the communicator.

"Just open the damn hatch! Oh, I don't care. Starve to death. I was just doing something thoughtful." Howser shut off communications from his side.

"Open the fucking hatch, Butch! What's in there?" yelled Screech.

Butch opened the hatch lid reluctantly. "Holy shit!" he exclaimed as he slammed the lid shut.

"What *is* it? What's inside there? Do I need my gun?" Pilot asked.

"You are not going to believe this." Butch reached in and began pulling out food. Scrumptious cheesecake, covered plates of spaghetti, loaves of bread, and their favorite: chocolate milk. Pilot spread out the food and they began digging in. He tossed slices of garlic bread at Jude, who tried to catch them in his mouth. As Jane slurped her spaghetti, Screech tried to pull a *Lady and the Tramp* moment with her.

"Here, Jane. Suck my noodle with me." He held one end of spaghetti in his mouth and wiggled the other toward Jane.

"Yuck. That totally didn't come out right, Screech." Jane laughed as she moved on to the cheesecake.

Pilot wiped cheesecake on Jude's jacket, which began the food fight that ensued. Before long, the team and the hull of the craft were covered in food. Screech licked some sauce off the window of the plane. "Look, Jane! I'm a window licker." They finished out the flight with full stomachs, which made their travel time seem shorter.

"Should we call Howser and thank him?" Jane asked.

"Nah. We'll see him soon enough. We'll get Broad right away, then thank Howser in person," commented Butch. They were able to log a few hours of sleep before it was time to jump.

"Okay. Screech and Butch on deck first. Pilot, you're next. Bulldog and I'll bring up the rear, then we'll switch to silent mode until further notice. Make your way to the coordinates. You have twenty-five minutes to reach the check-in location. Anyone not at check-in will be left out of the mission. We won't wait for you," warned Jane. This was a lie, but she wanted them to internalize the time constraints.

"Break your balls, boys!" she shouted as a whopping dose of supercharged adrenaline flooded her body as she prepared mentally for the jump. "In three, two, one . . ."

"Welcome to the Jungle" by Guns N' Roses blared in her head as Jane sailed through the night air, thinking how much she hated to fly in planes but how much she loved to jump out of them.

The team regrouped on the ground according to plan. Every time they executed a mission it reminded Jane just how good her team was. In silent mode, they forced their way through the thick, dripping vegetation to a safer zone. Jude took the lead in navigating them. As soon as Jane knew they were in a better area, she ordered her team through her multiband tactical radio to resume transmissions.

"Goddamn! Someone turn down the heat!" Screech wrenched off his helmet to reveal his long ponytail soaked with sweat.

"Yeah, yeah. You'll get used to it. Maybe you'll lose a few more pounds," Jane joked, rather surprised by how much smaller Screech appeared in his tight-fitting tactical gear than he did in blousy Hawaiian garb. Jane wouldn't be surprised if he *was* wearing a tropical-themed shirt under his jacket.

"My balls are chaffed already!" Screech complained. "I thought if I wore wool underpants, my 'nads would have a layer of protection." They watched him as he had a quiet discussion with his gonads, looking down at them and splaying his hands out in disbelief. "Geez, guys! That's where lanolin comes from—sheep sweat. I'm so sorry. I just thought if I sweat, you'd have a nice little wooly lanolin sauna down there," he murmured as he readjusted and patted his package.

"You know, Professor, you're kind of cute all scrunched into that tight-ass suit with your big, furry marmot head. You look like one of those creatures in *Star Wars*," Butch teased. His comment was meant to be an insult, yet Screech took it as a compliment.

"I *do*? Which one? If I were a *Star Wars* guy, I'd have six hidden arms that retracted inside my body and then, if someone tried to hug me or something, I'd whip out my arms and shred them."

"Of course you would," added Jude.

"Except if I ran into that Leia chick. I'd definitely use my six arms for something else," he said as he began groaning while ogling his hands. "Hey, Jude, can you come stand over here and bend over a bit? I need to see if this could work." Screech approached Jude, waving his arms like an octopus.

"Fuck you, Professor Perv! You'd stand a better chance with that eight-foot-tall furry bastard than Princess Leia," Jude said, pushing Screech away.

"Hmmmm," pondered Screech. "That could be interesting."

"Oh, Jeezuz!" Jane snorted as she slapped her forehead.

"Come on, Jane! If anyone was gonna do the furry dude, it'd be you. You're always so frickin' cold that you need to wear a goddamn fur blanket. That would translate into literally hot sex!" Screech laughed.

"Christ, can we get back to work here?" Pilot asked as he linked the team back to Command.

"Alright, ladies! Let's move!" Jane ordered, realizing how much time they were wasting.

"Hold on a sec; I gotta pee," announced Pilot as he rushed up the hillside, grabbing his crotch.

"Wait for me, scrotum! You know I can't pee without support," Butch said, running after Pilot.

"*Now* look what you made me do! I tinkled a little just thinking about it." Screech winked at Jane and slithered away to join the guys, only in an attempt to delay work.

"Christ! I forgot to ask everyone to go potty before they left! Fine! Take five. I'll be over here powdering my nose, ass munches! I've been sent to the jungle with a bunch of kids," Jane griped, shaking her head.

She walked down the hill, took out her spotting scope, and began to scan the horizon. She reached into her jacket pocket and took out a piece of garlic bread she had stashed there.

"Wait up!" Jude hollered as he ran after her. "I peed my pants during the jump, so I'm good." Jude spotted the bread. "Hey, give me some of that." Jane broke off a piece of the bread and handed it to Jude.

"That was so not like Howser to do that, but it was kind of awesome," Jane noted.

Just as Jude opened his mouth to answer, rockets ripped through the sky and slammed into the team's soon-to-be-makeshift head-quarters. Jane turned and saw a giant explosion as another rocket tore through the camp. The two of them scrambled to search for a depression in the landscape that they could use for protection from direct fire. Jane watched as an explosion launched Screech and Pilot thirty feet into the air and over the hill. Missiles continued to pound the area as Jane screamed at her team.

"What the fuck?" yelled Jane as dirt flew into her mouth and over her face. Turning toward Jude she hollered, "Bulldog! Are you okay? Bootleg sixty yards left, continue five kilometers, then circle right. I'll meet you at these coordinates. Go!"

Explosions continued to rip the earth. Jane scanned the area where they were standing just five minutes earlier; it was completely destroyed. Minutes later, Jane heard a vehicle pull into the clearing, so she jumped into a large bush to hide. Uniformed men erupted from the Jeep, looking for survivors to execute. Headlights illuminated the area. Nothing remained but shredded vegetation.

As Jane watched them patrol, one of the soldiers walked into the clearing holding a severed arm. It was Butch's. Jane recognized his tattoos through the blood and dirt. The man left the site for a second, then reappeared, dragging Butch's body by his foot. Jane collapsed into the bush and covered her mouth to suppress the noise that was trying to escape, along with the vomit that was forcing its way up into her throat. She tried to swallow both, but failed. Vomit spewed onto her boots. She froze, looking down at the regurgitated food.

The image seared itself into her brain. She was unable to look away. She thought of Screech, just hours earlier, playing around with the spaghetti; Pilot was holding up the cheesecake. Now they'd been flung over a cliff.

Jane, get your shit together and move. Now! she told herself. Instinctively, Jane rose and bolted without another thought. She had to run. Her legs were almost numb but she rocketed through the jungle anyway, moving her head from side to side in an attempt to spot enemy fire. She tried to inhale fresh, brisk air, yet she tasted only humid, hot jungle stench mingled with sour vomit. She had to keep moving and clear the haunting image of her brothers getting killed. She wiped away sweat and tears constantly as she ripped through the thick vegetation. She ran for miles before she finally scaled a tree to survey the area. She spotted the zone where she told Jude to meet her, jumped down from the tree, and headed out to locate him.

She finally exhaled when she found Jude at the meeting point, looking just as cashed out and shocked as she did. He took off his helmet as sweat dripped from his face.

"I thought we had the element of *surprise*! Dammit, Jane!" he growled as he threw his helmet to the ground.

"Yeah, me too. And now we have no communication with Command."

"Unless you count the giant thermal explosion that's given away our location on command center satellites."

"Let's move out!" ordered Jane abruptly. Jude looked at her in surprise.

"Wait a minute! You can't be *serious*. There may be only two of us left. We have no communication with Command and only a few weapons. Need I remind you that our enemy hasn't changed and we no longer have the element of surprise? All we *need* to do is go find our fallen brothers. Jane, I *need* to find them!"

"They're dead, Jude. Well, I know Butch is. I saw him." Jane squatted on the ground as she put her hands on her head, trying to hold it together. "Oh, God! Jesus Christ! They're fucking dead, man! I saw Butch's body." Jane sat in the dirt at Jude's feet, staring off into the jungle.

"Oh, shit. Just Butch? Did you see Pilot? How about Screech? Jane, we *have* to go back and get them!" Jude crouched down next to her.

"I know. We will. We won't go home without them." She stood up and started pacing. "If they're alive, I guarantee they're following orders and regrouping as we speak. You always tell me to 'trust the Corps.' Well, I have to do that now. We have to move out. Agent Broad is counting on us. Jude, we're the best. Butch was the greatest. If I don't keep moving forward right now, I'll start internalizing what I just saw and I'm afraid I may seize up and never move again. I can't let that take hold of me. *Please*, Jude. We have to keep going."

Jane held Jude's face in her hands, feeling the warmth of his skin. His silence indicated his agreement. Jane's entire body blazed with fury and she heard her heartbeat pounding in her ears. She tasted her own blood where she'd bit down on the inside of her cheek. It felt as if all the vessels in her body were swelling and tightening, and her limbs twitched sporadically. Outwardly, she didn't understand how to react to their situation other than with callousness, for fear she'd have a complete meltdown. The only world she knew had just been annihilated. She could barely breathe. She scrambled mentally to stuff every one of her feelings, images, and emotions into jars and shelve them. Fast. And by the look on Jude's face, he'd started the same process based on their similar training.

"Okay. We have a mission to complete. Let's get going! That's an order!" Jane barked.

"Whoa, whoa, whoa. We will, but let's just bring it down a notch for a minute, okay? Look, Jane, I got it. You're the general here and I'm just the lowly ol' colonel. Neither one of us, under normal military protocol, would be in a combat situation like this. We'd be safe and sound behind some computer thousands of miles from any direct action. You and I are different. We're a team and part of Orion. Screech and Pilot, those guys are out there regrouping too. Let's just slow down, make a plan, breathe, and find Agent Broad, okay? No more shouting orders as if you're the only one in the game." He patted her shoulder.

"Okay. Move out, Colonel Fucker." Jane forced a smile, still battling against her anguish over losing Butch.

"Aye, aye, General Jerk-off." Jude put his arm around her.

They only managed to travel several hundred yards into the dense jungle before the same thought hit them like a bolt of lightning. They both stopped abruptly in their tracks and turned to face each other at the same time.

"Jude, I have to know. I have to go back there and look for the guys. At least some sign that maybe they made it out of there." Jane began backtracking as she spoke.

"I know. Me too. I can't think straight. They might even be right around the site waiting for us. We have to go back."

The two of them scoped out the wreckage for several hours, from many vantage points, to ensure the enemy had dispersed, then approached carefully to search the site. Jane purposefully steered clear of the area where she knew Butch's body lay—or at least what was left of him. She wasn't ready to see that yet. As they combed the area, they discovered only blasted craters, shrapnel, and burned-out divots, along with shredded jungle debris.

"Oh Christ! Jane! Shit! Help me!" Jude hollered from across the way. "Jane! Fuck! Help me!"

Jane ran as fast as she could with her weapon drawn, believing Jude was under attack. However, she discovered him on the ground, embracing Pilot around his chest as he lay limp on the burned-out jungle floor. Both of Pilot's legs were missing at the thigh, and he'd been shot between the eyes. Tears streamed down Jude's face. Jane was in shock as she moved toward Pilot in what seemed like slow motion. She bent down and removed the blood-soaked boots he clutched in his lifeless arms. Widowmaker, they read, in black Magic Marker.

"Jude," stammered Jane, "these are Screech's boots. You wrote my name on them. *You wrote my name on Screech's boots.*" Her voice began to elevate. "Jude? *These are his boots!* Where the fuck is Screech?" Jude didn't seem to hear her as he rocked Pilot's body. She had to go find Screech.

Jane tore through the area, ripping up logs and pushing over rocks, shouting for Screech. She scoured the ground for footprints, blood—*any* trace of him. Then something colorful caught her eye about twenty yards from the worst of the destruction in another large, bombed-out crater. She ran quickly to examine it. She recognized the piece of colorful fabric immediately. Barely protruding from deep beneath the rubble, she saw a remnant of Screech's Hawaiian shirt. He must have been blown up in the explosion that took Pilot's legs. Her mind flashed back quickly to the sight of them being blown over the hill together.

How did Pilot end up with Screech's boots? Maybe those assholes handed them to him before they shot him, to show Pilot that Screech was dead, Jane thought.

Once again, Jane stood as if she was frozen, completely unable to move, and stared at the scrap of Screech's dirty shirt. She could almost hear him in every leaf that moved around her: "Holy fucking shit, Jane! What a goddamn rush it was to be blown to shit like that! A million fucking pieces of me spewed across the fucking jungle and no one around to see it! Such a fucking waste, Jane. I didn't want to die like that. I wanted to get eaten alive by a tiger. Remember that, Jane? I love you, Jane. I fucking love you, Jane."

"Oh, Jesus. I love you too, Screech. You're my best friend. I can't *do* this life without your crazy ass in it. What the hell? Butch is dead, Pilot is dead, and now you're scattered in a million pieces in this jungle. *Shiiiiit!*" Jane yelled, not caring who might hear her.

After nearly twenty-four hours of immobility and grieving, Jude and Jane managed to bury Butch and Pilot; they figured Screech was buried enough for the time being. They planned on retrieving the bodies for transport to the States after they completed their mission. Moving forward and focusing on the op now felt like an enormous task. It seemed impossible.

"Jude, I don't know—"

"Yeah, me neither."

"No. I am *not* giving up. Let me finish. I don't know how we can possibly grant our brothers the respect and honor they deserve, other than find Agent Broad quickly, bring him home, and complete this mission. We have to get our shit together. Broad has something Howser and America desperately need. It's our duty to get this information into the right hands. You and I are unstoppable," reassured Jane.

"I agree, Jane," Jude said, as he stood up to start moving. While they geared up, Jane heard Jude mutter under his breath, "I just wish you and Howser would've recognized that earlier." Jane pretended she didn't hear it and kept loading her equipment; she didn't want to flood her mind with any more negative thoughts.

The two of them moved through the jungle for weeks before Jude spotted something mysterious. His voice rasped as he called out to

Jane to get her attention. Jane realized days had passed without them speaking to each other.

"Jane, take a look at this," Jude said, handing her his binoculars. "I can't be certain with this piece-of-shit spotting scope, but I think there's a man by the river." Jane looked through the lenses and agreed.

"Maybe it's Broad. We did leave a pretty big fireball. Maybe he saw it and is making his way toward it to check it out. Let's split up and get a vantage," Jane suggested, feeling suddenly optimistic.

"Split up? Why don't we just signal him? He's an agent. He should be able to handle that," Jude cracked with a smart-ass tone.

"*Signal* him? With what? Did you forget that we lost all our equipment in the explosions, MacGyver?"

"Piece of cake." Jude maneuvered up a hill fifty yards from her, cutting a few branches with his machete along the way as Jane kept an eye on the man by the river. By this time she felt certain the person was Lance Broad. Her spirits rose again. The man had an unmistakable giant eagle tattooed across his back. Broad's nickname was Thunderbird, and there it was—a large, black tribal eagle glistening with sweat. Relief poured over her as she turned to Jude to confirm her findings, and got distracted by a bright, shiny signal blinking through the jungle toward Broad. Jane quickly turned her scope toward the agent to see if he registered the signal. Within seconds, Broad ducked instinctively under some bushes for cover, seemingly uncertain of whether to trust his eyes.

Jude scooted down the hillside and made his way back toward Jane.

"How the fuck did you *do* that?" asked Jane, shocked that Jude had figured out a way to signal Broad so quickly—without most of their equipment.

"Wouldn't you like to know?"

"Yeah, I really would, just in case you get waxed out here and I need to do that. So tell me, dipshit."

"Okay, okay. It's a combination of the reflection and the secretion of some kind of snail. It leaves a trail that's almost ninety percent mica. It actually deters birds from seeing them when they're exposed. It acts like a mirror to blind them. Add a little sunshine and voila!" Jude's last comment sounded like something Screech would've said. Jane shuddered at the thought of Screech for a minute and then quickly shoved it out of her head.

"Show-off," replied Jane. She was actually impressed, but wondered if Jude had picked up that trick from watching Animal Planet rather than from training.

Jane continued to monitor Agent Broad through the scope. He removed the heel of his boot to take out a lens that appeared to be fashioned from a bottle. He then sent a crude signal back to them.

"Oh, how cute! He must be a Boy Scout! Did you see that lame-ass signal?" Jude mocked.

"You're jealous of Agent Broad? Why?" Jude had been acting a little weird. "Is it because he's handsome and all beefcake for an old dude? Or that he's a badass agent superhero?" asked Jane, intention-ally trying to get Jude's goat.

"Look, let's just go get the guy, okay? If he's such a badass, then why're we rescuing him? *We're* the badasses. Come on."

When the two of them reached the river, however, Broad had disappeared. They'd signaled for him to sit tight.

"Where'd he go?" Jude asked, pissed.

"Circle around," ordered Jane, motioning Jude to go left.

Jude walked into the thick jungle, navigating through dense foliage, and slipped right past the well-camouflaged agent, who was hidden and waiting to pounce. Broad grabbed Jude from behind and choked him out, taking him down easily, then landed several brutal blows to Jude's face. The agent then moved on in search of Jane, who'd grown uneasy when she couldn't spot Jude. Broad should've recognized the signal and simply sat tight. Too much time had elapsed; Jane should've crossed paths with Jude by now. She suddenly sensed Broad approaching her from behind. He grabbed her, which is exactly what she wanted. Without hesitation, she reverse head-butted him and grabbed his arms while bending forward. She then threw her butt into his pelvis, sidestepped, reached between her legs, grabbed his right leg, and lifted it quickly. Broad was thrown to the ground on his back. Jane held his leg up while nearly sitting down on his knee, demonstrating that she could hyperextend it easily.

"Wait! Wait!" he shouted.

"Yeah, wait! Broad! What the hell! It's me, General Stapelton."

Broad's glazed eyes studied her for a moment, then relief washed over his face, which appeared older than ever. He had deep worry lines between his eyes, a gray beard, and long, greasy salt-and-pepper hair that hung down in front of his eyes. He looked like he'd been through hell, but his body was as chiseled as a twenty-year-old's—lean and muscular.

"What the fuck is wrong with you? We're here to save you, man. Where's Colonel Aikens?" Jane was growing more and more concerned for Jude, especially because Broad seemed intent on killing her—and he actually *knew* her. Jane wasn't so certain about how Broad felt about Jude; they'd never met.

"Colonel Aikens? That was a *colonel?* He's one of *us?*" Broad looked at Jane in utter confusion. "But, he . . . General, I *saw* him—"

Jude blasted through the jungle and into the clearing, his face battered and bleeding. He beelined directly toward Broad and punched him square in the face, knocking him unconscious, then hammered at the agent repeatedly with his fists as Jane tried to stop him.

"You saw him *what*? You motherfucker!" yelled Jude as he continued to punch Broad.

"Jude! Stop!" Jane grabbed Jude and threw him to the ground.

"He tried to *kill* me, Jane. He jumped me and then tried to *kill* me."

Jane crouched down next to Broad to ascertain the damages Jude inflicted, then noticed something astonishing.

"Jude! Look at this! This is how Broad must've gotten that signal to Command." Jane held up an old handheld communicator. "Maybe we can work on this a bit and get a better signal. Shit yeah! I'd kiss you both if you weren't covered in blood! You look like crap," noted Jane. "Not bad for a Boy Scout, huh? He kicked your ass."

Jude was not amused and he bared his teeth like an attacking wolf. He had an unusually wild look in his eyes, which jarred her. Jane decided to back off.

"I'm sorry. Hey! That signal was awesome, by the way," commented Jane as she took a few steps back from Jude.

"Yeah," he sighed and walked off.

Jane proceeded to work on the communicator. After a while, she had some success. Although the transmissions were broken, she was able to ascertain two very distinct lines of communication. Neither one was secure, which meant they had to act fast if they hoped to be picked up. Jane determined coordinates that were feasible for them to reach, then radioed them on a line she knew Broad used to reach Command. They needed to get Broad up and moving as quickly as possible.

"Jude, can you grab one side of him and I'll get the other? I got a comm out to Command. We've gotta get to these coordinates before nightfall."

"Grab a side?" Jude smirked. "Move aside, Minnie Mouse. This calls for Dudley Do-Right." He heaved Agent Broad onto his shoulder in a firefighter's carry and they proceeded to move out.

"Jude, Dudley Do-Right was a massive dork. You know that, right? I think you meant to say something like the Incredible Hulk or Andre the Giant. Dudley Do-Right was like this wimpy Canadian Mountie from *The Rocky and Bullwinkle Show*. He wasn't tough at all." Jane poked Jude's side repeatedly while he carried Broad.

"Okay! I get your point! I thought he was a muscle guy."

"No, come to think of it, I think even Underdog was stronger and more badass than Dudley Do-Right. So, even if you'd said, 'This looks like a job for Underdog,' I'd have taken you more seriously."

"I got it, asshole. Underdog. Either way, you couldn't do this if you wanted to. You're a twerp. You have always been."

"You called me a twerp the first day you met me at school."

"I know! And I was right. Underdog and Twerp."

"Shut up."

"*You* shut up."

"I fucking loved those guys."

"Who? Underdog?"

"No. Screech, Pilot, Butch . . ."

"Jane, don't. Not now."

"Okay."

They walked for several hours, without Broad regaining consciousness. Jane thought it wise to pause for a few moments and check his status, but Jude said the agent was fine.

"I'm sure he's exhausted, plus he probably wants a free ride on my back. He's most likely been faking it this whole time."

Broad certainly had to be exhausted from living on the run for twenty-seven months in a jungle, but the blows Jude administered to him were unusually harsh—almost intentionally lethal.

"Put him down, Jude. I need to check him," ordered Jane, grabbing at Broad's legs to pull him down.

"Shut the fuck up, Jane. He isn't a baby. We're almost there. The site's just up that hill. He'll be fine." Jude kept walking, brushing her aside.

Jane stood in front of Jude, blocked his path, and ordered, "Put. Him. Down!"

Reluctantly, Jude sat Broad on the ground, slumped over. Jane moved the agent gently onto his back to examine him. He had an obvious concussion and appeared to be in a semiconscious, dazed state. Jane held his head and attempted to wet his lips with her canteen water, hoping to rouse him.

"Damn, I wish we had a medical kit," muttered Jane as she checked his eyes.

Broad came to and seemed to recognize her. A slight smile began to crest his face, but as he looked beyond her and saw Jude, his look of peace turned to disdain. Broad reached up and grabbed the back of her head and whispered, "General! That guy! Don't trust him! I know that guy. I've seen that guy."

Before Jane could pry more out of him, Jude put his arms around Broad's chest to lift him back into a firefighter's carry.

"See there, Jane? He's perfectly fine." Jane wondered if Jude caught on that Broad had spoken to her before he lost consciousness again. She felt an urgent need to understand what he was trying to tell her. They had to get to that hill—and their extraction team—quickly.

"We're within five kilometers of the extraction point," Jude assured her.

"We have a thirty-minute window after the cavalry arrives; otherwise, we're basically dead out here."

"Not dead, Jane. Just a little lost. Might take a few years, but we could probably work our way back. Or hell, we could just Swiss Family Robinson it out here. Build a nice little treehouse, start a family, swing from vines, and eat snakes for dinner. Sounds good to me," he said as he trudged through the jungle, looking straight ahead. Jane couldn't tell if he was serious or not. Either way, the thought grossed her out.

"No thanks. I miss Quantico. And shitty snakeless food."

Although they were close to the extraction point, Jane wanted to ensure they didn't miss the rendezvous. She risked using the radio communicator a second time to affirm their pickup, which proved to be a mistake.

Jude saw a signal in the distance. "Holy mother of God. They're here!" He dropped Broad and started to walk out into the open. They watched the light for a moment, not realizing Broad had woken up. He stood and grabbed Jude's shoulder and pulled him back.

"Something's not right. Get down," Broad murmured quietly.

"He's right. He's right," whispered Jane, taking out her scope. She squatted next to Broad, who had sat back on the ground as he tried to collect himself. "What was the first number in that sequence?" she asked.

"That's just it, General. It wasn't a number; it was a letter. Those are Sharik's men. This is an ambush," Broad said as he lay back and

put his hands to his head. "Aikens just walked us into an ambush."
Broad attempted to grab Jude's shirt.

"Oh, shit," Jane said, missing—or perhaps dismissing—his
accusations toward Jude. Just as she started to think about kissing
their asses goodbye, three Apaches swarmed in above them, lighting
up the countryside with explosions from cannon fire. Jane signaled
to Jude to take Broad and make a break for the extraction point. She
followed from the rear and circled around looking for enemy soldiers.
She managed to shoot a few stragglers who charged toward her.

By the time Jane reached the helicopters, Jude and Broad were
already inside. Jude had a strange look on his face. "What's the
matter? We did it! We're going home," shouted Jane over the din of
the choppers.

"I'm sorry, Jane. Broad didn't make it. He took some fire as I was
getting him out." Jude motioned toward the agent's lifeless body.

"What? What the fuck! How? Goddammit!" Jane slammed her
fist into the side of the metal bird, furious. "Our brothers died for
nothing!" Jane also knew she'd never know what Broad had tried to
tell her. "Shit! Goddamn this life!"

She considered sulking, but that feeling lasted mere seconds as
rage sank in. She demanded a headset from the pilot. She wanted to
talk to Howser.

"Get me Admiral Howard immediately," ordered Jane.

"No can do, ma'am."

"Is that any way to address your CO? Get me the president of
Orion, you cocksucker!"

The pilot replied, "Ma'am, Admiral Howard is incapacitated.
We have higher chain-of-command orders to deliver you directly to
him, ma'am."

"Incapacitated? What the *hell* does that mean? No! I'm not going to Command. Agent Broad is dead. There's no reason to go straight there. First we need to go back and retrieve the bodies of our fallen brothers. We aren't leaving them. That's an order!"

Jane swore that if he wasn't flying the chopper, she would've choked him out right then and there she was so fuming mad.

"Ma'am, I assure you that your team members will be extracted immediately and delivered safely to their homeland."

"Safely?! You asshole! They're *dead*! Turn this son of a bitch around right now or I'll slit your throat! *I'll* be the one to bring my brothers home! DO YOU READ ME?"

Jude tossed her a Ka-Bar, gave her a wink for confidence, and told the pilot, "You know, this bitch eats Cap'n Crunch for breakfast. I'd listen to her."

"I'll radio in the change orders, ma'am," the pilot replied with no hesitation.

Jude and Jane watched as the Marines carefully searched the site where the explosion took place, looking for remains she and Jude may have missed. Several times Jane felt like her legs would give way, especially as she heard the zipper opening on the plastic body bags.

"Oh, Jeezuz, Jude." Jane clutched his jacket.

"Yeah," he said, cringing at the metallic rattle. He then marched over to the Marines and said, "Nuh-uh. Not for these guys. Get some blankets for now." He motioned for the empty body bags to be taken out of their sight. Returning to Jane, Jude explained, "I can't do that to them yet. We have to make them comfortable." They followed the securely wrapped bodies to the chopper and demanded they accompany them inside.

"Jude, I think they should probably—I don't know." Jane couldn't think of anything to say as she looked at her brothers' wrapped bodies laying in the chopper. Jude crawled into the back and lifted Pilot onto his lap. He held him and cried the entire flight. Jane rocked back and forth, nearly shredding the soft, dirty scrap of Screech's Hawaiian shirt that she had recovered earlier from near the crater. She knew someone might want to bury that remnant along with his boots when they returned, but she had to keep it.

When they finally approached familiar territory, the pilot noted, "Your stop, ma'am."

"I'm going with her," responded Jude.

"No can do, sir. You're to report to the Commandant."

"Yeah, well I think Orion'll write me a pass," Jude shouted as he followed Jane out of the aircraft.

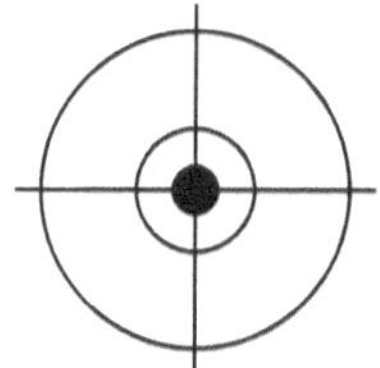

CHAPTER TWENTY-NINE

Jane walked into the Stapeltons' kitchen to find Marlene in a pink ruffled apron, bending over to remove a glistening, steaming peach pie from the oven. Sam sat at the wooden kitchen table and watched the pie like a hawk. Jane wished she could indulge in a slice or two, but she knew she couldn't. Her peach pie–eating days were long gone.

Since the incident in Kieon, whenever Jane thought about food, her mind went straight to the moment her team was blown apart. She couldn't choke down food without it coming right back up—a reminder of that day. Marlene placed a slice of pie in front of Sam, who didn't hesitate to dig in. Jane was sure he would have eaten it with his fingers if Marlene hadn't handed him a fork. Jane silently hoped that when Sam reached her age, he could still eat solid food.

"Now *that* was just what the doctor ordered! I'm ready for round two." Sam smiled, rejuvenated by the sugar high. Marlene laughed and cut another large piece of pie and placed it on Sam's plate. "Aunt Jane? You mentioned Howser was incapacitated. What happened to him? Was he sick?" he asked through a mouthful of peaches.

"He died. That's it, Sam."

"Oh, *come on*, Aunt Jane! I know there's more to it than that. Even though you may not have been close, he was still your dad. You must've gone to see him."

"You really want to know, huh? Fine. Okay, there is more to it than that. You're a smart kid." She ruffled his hair and he swatted her hand away. "Bring your plate and let's go out and sit on the porch. I'll tell you all about it."

Jane began her story as they left the kitchen. "When Jude and I landed, the Secret Service guys took us to a hospital, which surprised me. I was even more surprised to find out that Howser was a patient there. When we got to his room, we saw that he had tubes connecting him to all kinds of machines. Seeing him like that, well, he seemed small and weak. I'd never seen him that way before."

"Wow. How did he end up in the hospital in the first place?" asked Sam.

"I don't know. I guess he'd been feeling shitty for months, but he never told anyone. We just got home and there he was in this crappy hospital, dying."

For Jane, entering a hospital room was like walking into a Catholic church. As an Orion general, she saw and experienced indescribable horrors. She felt betrayed by God and the church every single day. How could there be a god that would allow so much pain and suffering to occur? Jane had the urge to search for a basin of holy water at Howser's hospital door and dip her finger in it, then trace a cross on her chest. The same silence of the church hung over Howser's room. And a feeling of hopelessness. Jane felt guilty for being alive. She almost said aloud: "Forgive me, Father, for I have sinned. Why am *I* not nailed on that cross? Why am *I* not lying in that hospital bed?" It angered her that some people prayed in the hospital—when they thought prayer was *needed*—rather than prayed every day. Again, hypocrisy.

"God doesn't keep people from entering the hospital, so why would he break 'em out?" Jane asked as she looked at Sam. He had stopped midbite to listen to her opinions on God. She knew full well Sam thought differently. She had his undivided attention as she took him back to that day.

"Elizabeth! You're alive!" Howser exclaimed as he extended his hand out to her. He didn't have the strength to hold it up; it lay on the hospital bed. His paper-thin arms were weighed down by tubes.

"Of course I am. What about you?" Jane looked at his sunken face and noted his sallow eyes and skin. She could almost see the blood coursing through his veins. Jane couldn't believe all this had happened in the six months since she saw him last.

"Not for long," he said deliberately. He feared nothing, not even death.

"Howser, tell me a story. Tell me about my mother." Jane wanted to take them away from that hospital room, even if it was figuratively. She knew he wanted to tell her the story of Amelia and that he didn't have much time. He'd given Jane her mother's journal and he had tried to approach her several times in the past to talk about her mom, but Jane's anger always pushed him away.

"Not today, little Marine. I'm on my way out. You had your chance to hear that story," he said coldly. "You're as stubborn as she was. I thought you got that from me, but I think it came from your mother."

"Tell me the damn story! I need to know about her!" Jane burst into tears. She lay her head on his chest. "Tell me about Mom, Dad." Jane sobbed, silently pleading with him to hold on. She didn't know why she held on to this man. She'd always waited for this day with pleasure because she despised him for hurting her and for abandoning her every time she needed him. Now that his death was near, she clung to him, willing him to stay with her.

"Awww, come on now. It's okay. I'm right here," Howser whispered, stroking her hair. Jane suddenly remembered the last time Howser held her in his arms, comforting her. Tom had just died.

Jane had thought it best to withhold from Sam the details of the horrific trauma of Tom's death, which replayed in her mind countless times. She and her team considered it from every angle to see what they could have done differently to save him. Sam didn't need to hear about that. Just that he died was enough pain for him. However, Jane's thoughts drifted back and she froze when faced with that memory yet again.

Jane was just twenty-one years old. It was March 31, 1983. Her entire team was together that day, except for Tom, and they clustered around a TV screen, helpless, as they watched terrorists brandish their blades, raise them in the air, and shout "Allahu Akbar!" They then moved around Tom's slumped body. One of them grabbed his hooded head from behind, tilted it back, and sliced his throat.

Jane screamed at the top of her lungs as the scene unfolded before them. She saw the terrorist continue to hack back and forth at Tom's throat as he tried to decapitate him. Jane lost it. Jude and Screech grabbed her, and they yelled at Pilot to stop the feed.

"Stop the tape! Stop the fucking tape!"

"Oh my *God! Tom! No! Oh my God! Help—help him!*" Jane shouted as she tried to punch the screen. Screech held her in a bear hug from behind as she fought against him to destroy the TV.

The room had erupted into chaos. Everyone was yelling in panic and didn't know what to do. They had been expecting a negotiation, not an execution.

"Get her out of here!" Howser barked. "Get her into my quarters and get a medic! She needs sedation!" Howser tried to establish order in the room while Jude, Pilot, and Butch yelled in outrage and disbelief.

Screech carried Jane to Howser's room, where she collapsed in a pile on the floor, sobbing hysterically. At times she cried so hard she barely made a sound. Her mouth hung open, slobber ran down her chin, and no sound came out. She could barely breathe.

"Breathe, Jane!" Screech yelled as he grabbed her face and held it between his hands.

Jane took in a breath and felt a violent swirl of noise erupt inside her and she wailed like a banshee. "*Ayeeeeeee! Oooooohhhh, God!*" She fell into Screech's arms. Soon Butch, Pilot, and Jude joined them.

"Jane, oh sister," sobbed Pilot. They huddled together on the floor, tears streaming down their faces.

"Fuck! Fuck! Oh my God! Tom!" Butch cried as he rocked back and forth.

Medics came in to give Jane a sedative. She refused it, but Howser overruled her.

"Give it to her, then put her in my bed," he ordered. "I'll stay here with her."

Jane was limp when the medics placed her in Howser's bed. She had no use of her legs and she was barely coherent as her system went into shock.

Howser turned to the men. "I want you boys to stay together tonight in Jude's room. I'm sending medical in for you and I'll come check on you."

"Sir! We have to *do* something!" Butch pleaded as he tried to rise to his feet. His voice cracked. "Sir, *please! Oh my God! This can't be happening!*"

"We'll regroup and attack this situation in the morning. There's nothing we can do tonight. I'll assign B team to start looking over the tape to see if they can make out any useful identifiers. I don't need you kids watching that right now."

Howser sent them out and turned to Jane. She lay on her back and was staring up at the ceiling. Tears flowed uncontrollably from her eyes and onto the stark-white sheets.

"Come here, sweetheart." Howser propped up a pillow next to her and lay down. He wrapped his arms around her. Jane wrapped her arms around his big barrel chest and buried her face in it as she sobbed. Howser stroked her hair and cried. He'd never done that since she'd known him. Howser cried so hard Jane could feel his chest rise and fall with each painful release.

"*Why,* Dad? *Why* did they do that?"

"Oh, God, honey. I'm so sorry. I loved him *so* much. You know that, don't you? I love you both *so much.* A bunch of goddamn dirty animals! That's what they are!" shouted Howser. He released Jane and got out of the bed. "*A bunch of fucking animals!*" he yelled and abruptly left the room. Jane rolled onto her stomach and let her arm hang over the bed as she looked at the empty doorway. She felt the sedative start to blur her vision and everything went black.

✛

"Aunt Jane? You alright? Where'd you go?" Sam asked worriedly as he watched the emotions play on Jane's face.

"Sorry, Sam. I was just thinking about something."

"It's okay. If you really don't want to talk about Howser, that's cool."

"No, it's okay. Where were we? Right. Howser was in the hospital. I remember listening to the beeping of the monitors, some of which matched the beat of his heart. I must've dozed off for a while because I woke up slowly and could feel him stroking my hair."

Sitting next to Howser's hospital bed as he lay dying, Jane realized she had a chance to share the father–daughter bond they experienced when Tom was killed. Jane squeezed Howser's arm, then sat up when he began talking.

"She was just like you, your mother. Strong and damn stubborn. She gave her life so you could live. Elizabeth, I loved her so much. I'm going to her, but I'm leaving you." Howser looked at Jane longingly as he spoke. "Elizabeth . . ." Howser struggled to express his thoughts and feelings.

"I'll be okay, Dad." At that moment, there was a part of her that wanted to walk out on him like he had done to her the day Tom died, but she couldn't do it. She felt his anger that day—and it mirrored hers. She also knew it was too late for him to change. She had to let it all go.

"I know you will. I love you, Elizabeth. I know I've been a shitty father. I don't know any other way."

Jane didn't believe his last claim, because she saw a glimpse of a loving father the day Tom died. She wondered why he hadn't been able to share that side of himself with her as she grew up. She couldn't let her father die thinking she hated him. For some reason, she wanted to make him happy for this short time they had left.

"Hey, Dad, for God's sake! What other kids got to track Santa Claus on multibillion-dollar satellite equipment?" she joked, trying to lighten the mood and not really knowing how to do it.

Howser smiled at the memory. "I'm tired now, Elizabeth. I'm going to sleep for a while."

"I'll be here when you wake up, Dad."

"Elizabeth, there's something I want you to do."

"Anything! Anything at all," promised Jane. She took his hand and squeezed it gently.

"I want you to get a damn bicycle and see if you can ride it. I remember you telling me we forgot to cover that when you were younger." Howser tried to laugh, but started coughing and hacking.

"Yeah, good idea, Dad, you old ass. I'll do that." Jane kissed him on the forehead and walked toward the doorway, where Jude was standing. He put his hand on her shoulder. She could tell he'd been touched by the exchange between father and daughter.

"Jane, I need to talk to Howser." She watched Jude walk into the room and bend slowly over Jane's father. He whispered something in Howser's ear and then kissed him on the cheek. Jane's brow furrowed at the gesture. It seemed "off" to her. Howser grabbed Jude's hand and squeezed it so tightly that Jude had to pry it loose. He walked past Jane, catching her wrist as he did so, and urged her to follow him.

They found an empty room and went into it. Jude took hold of Jane's shoulders. "I'm so sorry, Jane. I didn't know Howser was your father."

"None of you could ever know that, Jude." Jude pulled her into a hug and she felt tears spill from her eyes. Jane pushed away from him. "Orders. I had my damn orders. You know what that's like."

"Come on, Jane, let me do this." Jude held her close while Jane cried for the father she never really had.

After several minutes they both let go and the reality of the loss of Butch, Screech, and Pilot set in. Searing emotions ripped through them as they realized their lives had just been torn apart. This was it. They were all they had left.

Howser never awoke.

Back in her room at Quantico, Jane sat on her bed holding Amelia's journal. Her door buzzed and Jude entered.

"I brought you a bedtime snack and thought I might tuck you in." Jude carried a tray with milk, cookies, and two sleeping pills.

"You aren't obligated to wait on me just because I cried on your shoulder, you know." Jane struggled to smile as she grabbed the pills. She didn't swallow them, but she did drink the milk. She couldn't bear to eat the cookies, though.

"Just lie down and play along." Jude tucked her in, kissed her on the head, and began to walk out of the room.

"Jude?"

"Yeah?" Jude turned around to see Jane laying on her side with her back to him. She raised her arm and gestured for him to come back. He lifted the covers, crawled in next to her, and wrapped his arms around her.

"Jane," Jude said softly, "I'm sorry for all this pain."

"It's not your fault."

"I just don't understand. I was the first kid at the Orion school. Why didn't Howser let me lead? He gave it all to Tom and then to you. What did I do wrong?"

Jane pushed back into him slightly. "He was just cruel like that, Jude. You know how he could be."

"What about you? Why didn't you ever give me a chance? We were partners. Even after Tom died, you never let me in, no matter what I did."

"Stop it, Jude. We aren't like that and you know it." Jane rolled over to look Jude in the eyes.

"I just think everything would've turned out so different if Howser had given me more command. I could've shown him I was capable, but he gave it all to you and Tom."

"You act like we had control over Tom's death, and now Howser's. This is just life and we have to deal with it." Jane closed her eyes as Jude fell asleep next to her.

Five days later, Jane walked across the grass and climbed the steps to the platform to stand next to Jude. She was wearing her black suit, her hair was pulled back into a tight bun, and her swollen eyes were covered by dark sunglasses.

"We had to watch the funeral service from a distance," Jane told Sam as he rocked the porch swing.

"Why?" Sam asked.

"So the media wouldn't inadvertently capture us on film. No one can ever know what exists behind the Corps. Howser's coffin was blanketed by the American flag. The major general I had met in the hospital was wheeled in behind it to pay his respects. Howser's casket was followed by three more. I knew Screech's was empty, but each one was shrouded in the American flag: Major Bryan 'Butch' Wright, Sergeant Major Wilson 'Screech' Jared, and Lieutenant Greg 'Pilot' Walker. I remember reaching for Jude's hand, then we turned and walked across the grounds to the chopper that was waiting to take us back to Africa."

"Man, that's tough, Aunt Jane. I'm so sorry," said Sam. He saw Jane's eyes begin to water so he scooted a little closer to her. Although he was young, he had a nurturing way about him. He wanted to comfort Jane; he knew she needed his support.

"Oh, Sam, it is what it is. Can't change it now." Jane rested her head on his shoulder. After Tom died, she hadn't shared her thoughts and emotions with anyone—until she let Sam in.

"Come on, Aunt Jane. Let's talk a walk."

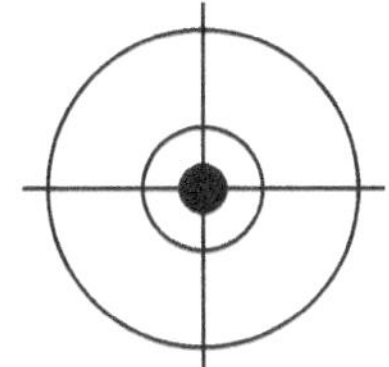

CHAPTER THIRTY

"Sam! Jane! Come on in! Dinner's on the table!" chirped Marlene from the porch. Sam had wanted to walk off his dessert before dinner, or so he had said to Jane. What he really wanted was for Jane to get some fresh air. He didn't want her to be alone. They had wandered past the barn when they heard Marlene calling for them.

"Doesn't it seem like we're always eating around here?" asked Jane, turning to Sam.

"Yep!" Sam grinned. "And her timing's remarkable." Sam's face grew serious. "Thank you for sharing all those things with me. I'm guessin' it wasn't easy to do."

"Actually, it wasn't hard to share those stories with you, Sam. You're the first person I've been able to open up to in a *long* time. Not many people know about my life." Jane was surprised to realize that she meant what she said. In that moment, she felt cleansed of her past.

"Maybe Jude?" asked Sam. "Maybe I could be like Jude was for you."

"No, I don't think you want to be Jude." Jane thought about Jude. He was still out there somewhere and she was going to find him.

"You know, Sam, telling you these things about my life is meant to benefit both of us. I want you to see what it's like on the inside. I can't send a naive schoolboy off to boot camp. You need to know the dirt."

"Ma'am, I appreciate that more than you know. I picked up a lot of insights—for a farm boy." Sam winked at her.

"Hey now! Don't make fun of the farm boy. He can saddle a horse in no time!" Jane placed her hand on his shoulder and pushed. Sam's feet stayed firmly in place. "*Good*, Sam! Good." He stood straighter and smiled.

"See? I'm learning."

"I know you are. But now I'm thinking it might be your turn," Jane said as they crossed the grass toward the house.

"What do you mean?"

"Well, tell me about this girl of yours. Why doesn't she ever come out here? When're you going to ask her to marry you?"

Sam stopped dead in his tracks. "Oh, come on. You don't want to hear about that," he replied, looking down at his cowboy boots.

"Oh yes I do! It's only fair. You made me talk about the men in my life. Now *I* want to know about this girl. I need to know if she's good enough for a Marine."

"Oh, she's good enough! Probably *too* good. We could go see her if you want to. Maybe after supper." Sam's eyes lit up.

"Okay, sure. I promise not to embarrass you. I won't break out any baby pictures because I don't have any. Hey, I could go upstairs to your grandma's room and grab a few dozen!" Jane started running toward the house as if she was going to do just that. Sam started to chase her.

"Don't you dare or I'll—"

"You'll *what*, Sam? Kick my ass? Ha! That's a good one! I'm getting them!" Jane ran faster toward the porch, where Marlene was still standing.

"Alright, you two! I swear I have two teenagers here. General, how old are you?" Marlene asked, patting Jane's cheek.

"Fifty-five. But most days I act like I'm thirty." Jane gave Marlene a quick kiss on the cheek.

"Must be all that clean livin'," commented Marlene. "Now wash up for dinner!"

"Ma'am, yes ma'am!" saluted Jane.

When Jane opened the screen door, Maxine came bounding toward her and jumped up onto her leg, nearly knocking Jane's knee out from under her. Shep followed closely behind.

"Easy there, Maxine! You're like an expert in Dog Maga. Get it, Max? Dog Maga? Like Krav Maga? Oh, never mind. I thought it was funny." Jane was happy and surprised to see Maxine scampering around like a puppy—and so soon after receiving her injuries.

"Thank God!" exclaimed Eugene as he walked into the room. "Now maybe Shep'll go back to guarding the goats and chickens. I think we lost two chickens to coyotes since that little dog got hurt."

"I don't know, Eugene. Shep looks ruined to me. Looks like he found a good woman and just wants to play all day," said Marlene.

"Well, if he wants to keep her, he better know he's gonna have to work his fingers to the bone every goddamn day of his life until he finally drops dead of a heart attack in the middle of a hot, dry field somewhere. A pretty girl is expensive as hell to maintain."

"Hush up and eat your electric chicken and dumplings before you get too thin and blow away in the breeze," Marlene said, handing him a plate. They didn't even try to contain their laughter.

After dinner, Sam and Jane ambled toward Sam's beat-up truck. They were headed into town to see his girlfriend. He wore a white long-sleeved, sharply pressed shirt and a new Stetson. Jane noticed Sam's jeans were a little more snug than usual. He had polished his cowboy boots so thoroughly, she could practically see her own reflection in them. And the glare coming off his big silver belt buckle could be used to land a plane in the dark.

"Good heavens, Sam! You look like you're going to prom! Maybe I should change?" Jane looked down at her jeans, ratty T-shirt, and Converse Marine boots.

"No, it's like that saying, 'The bridesmaid can never look better than the bride,'" he remarked. Then Sam smiled and sprayed breath freshener into his mouth.

"Oh my God! You're a *shit*. Where'd you hear that? From your grandmother? You're such a Grandma's Boy," she teased.

"Get in the truck," he ordered as he opened her door.

They drove into town, which was just as small and quaint as Jane remembered. Most of the buildings still sported their original stucco, but she could see places where it had been patched repeatedly. There were a few, slightly newer, one-story brick buildings that were whitewashed. They seemed out of place among the adobe. The majority of the roads were hard-packed dirt, with the exception of Main Street, which ran through the middle of town.

Sam parked in front of the largest building, which was the grocery store. He turned off the truck, pulled the rear-view mirror toward him, and checked his reflection.

"Okay. You ready?" Sam asked nervously.

"Are *you* ready, pretty boy?" Jane laughed as she opened her truck door.

They headed to the front door of the grocery store. Sam moved to the far right side of the wide automatic doors and signaled Jane to join him.

"Come on!" he ordered as he waved her in quickly. "Come on, hurry," he motioned to her, as if they were getting ready to rob the place. "Okay," he whispered. "We're gonna slip in unnoticed and then move left to the produce department. We'll meet at the bananas. Now move!" Sam dove in through the double doors and strode quickly to the left of the store. Jane was tight on his six.

"Why're we whispering?" she asked. He ignored her and kept moving. He leapt behind the freestanding cucumber bin, walked sideways covertly, then hunkered down behind the bananas, where he stared at the checkout lanes.

Jane grabbed a plastic produce bag and tried to open it while she pretended to be interested in the grapes in the bin directly across from Sam.

"What're you *doing?*" Sam hissed. "I told you to come to the bananas!" In his attempt to conceal himself, he actually drew more attention to the two of them.

"Sam, you're being obvious. I, however, am being inconspicuous. Now what's going on? Where's your girlfriend?" Jane asked, still struggling to open the thin bag. "These fucking bags! Look at this shit! I just put a hole in it." She waved the punctured bag at Sam.

"Don't! Don't look at me! She might *see* us!" Sam hadn't taken his eyes off the checkout lanes, so Jane assumed his girlfriend was one of the cashiers.

"Sam! Are you *kidding* me? I thought you said she was your *girlfriend* and that you were going to ask her to *marry* you! You haven't even asked her out on a *date*?" Sam cowered behind the fruit.

"Well, these things take time," he said as he started to walk discretely toward the back of the store, motioning for her to follow him.

"*Time*? Sam, how much *time* do you think you have? You're leaving tomorrow! You'd better go ask her out or I'll ask her for you." Jane turned around and headed for the front of the store.

Sam ran after her and ducked behind the grapes while Jane stopped in front of the bananas. There, she pulled one of his baby pictures from her pocket. She'd grabbed it off Marlene's dresser before they left. "Look what *I haaaave*," she sang and waved the picture at Sam.

Oh, God! You *wouldn't*!" Sam lunged at her from across the grape display, then rounded it and reached out to grab the picture. Jane jumped out of the way, but Sam's abrupt movement had caused bunches of red grapes to spill onto the floor. Sam's arms cartwheeled as he slipped and slid on the grapes. Nearby customers let out a collective gasp. Every eye was on them, including his future girlfriend. Jane noticed that a pretty dark-haired girl with stunning blue eyes was taking an avid interest in their antics.

Jane ran around the banana display toward Sam and slipped on the slick crushed-grape mess. Her legs went out from under her and she collided with Sam. They both went down, with Jane landing on top of Sam, who was facedown on the floor. His beautiful white shirt was stained purple. He looked like he just took a grenade to the chest.

A freckle-faced teenager was laughing and using his phone to video the show. Jane was sure it'd end up on YouTube within minutes. Sam stood up, shook his head, and ran out of the store. Jane rose and walked after him slowly. As she passed the check stands, she made sure to look at the young girl and smile. She smiled back at Jane.

Jane found Sam sitting in his truck staring out into the parking lot. As she climbed onto the passenger seat, she said, "Sam, I'm so sorry. I know I said I wasn't going to embarrass—"

"Did you *see* that?" He turned to her and he was grinning. His face was covered in so much purple grape juice that his smile seemed even brighter than usual.

"Uh, what? That we made a total fool out of you in front of your dream girl? That we wrecked the produce section of the only grocery store in town?"

"No, no! Did you see the way she *smiled* at me when I went by her? She *noticed* me!" His face beamed at the thought of that girl's smile.

Jane sat there with her mouth hanging open, looking at Sam. She'd forgotten what it felt like to be swept away by the very thought of someone. "Sooooo, I guess my plan worked?"

"Come on. Let's go home," said Sam as he started the truck.

"Shouldn't we go back in there and offer to clean up that mess?"

"*Hell* no! *I'm* not going back in there. I'm not pushing my luck."

They were just about to back out of the parking spot when the girl with the long dark hair ran out of the grocery store waving Sam's white Stetson.

"Sam! You almost forgot your hat!" She flashed him a wide smile as she leaned into the truck and handed him his hat. Her turquoise eyes seemed to stare right through him. She gave him a quick kiss on the cheek, then turned and ran back into the store.

"Well! I guess my plan *did* work!" Jane exclaimed as she smiled at Sam. He didn't respond. His hands gripped the steering wheel of the truck as he stared after his "girlfriend." Jane finally had to offer to drive them home.

At that exact moment, Jane knew she loved this kid. He was funny, free spirited, and yet he still held on to those strong family values Eugene and Marlene had instilled in him. He was kind and easygoing. He was just the type of boy she'd imagined Tom and she would've had as a son. He made her proud.

When they got back to the house, Mackey joined them at the kitchen table for an evening snack. Surprisingly, he wasn't glued to his phone. Sam sat next to his brother and the two boys whispered furiously.

"What're you two talking about over there?" Marlene asked curiously. "This is a family table and there aren't any secrets here."

"Mackey was just telling me he had a surprise for me after we finish our dessert. He's just excited about it, that's all," Sam said coyly.

"Yep, we all want to know what he's been up to for the past few months. Lowden and I couldn't bribe it out of him," Eugene griped, taking a big bite of strawberry shortcake.

Mackey shoved a heaping forkful of chocolate cake into his mouth and said, "Yeah, well Grandpa, you can't keep anything quiet, so I couldn't tell you. This is special." Then he rested both elbows on the table while he chewed.

"Mackey, honey? Could you try and act like you weren't raised by monkeys?" Marlene swept his elbows off the table and motioned for him to eat with his mouth shut.

Mackey made monkey sounds at her and smiled. "Sorry, Grandma."

"Well, if everybody's done, let's just leave these dishes for later and go see this surprise, shall we?" Marlene suggested as she stood up.

"*Seriously*? We can go *now*?" Mackey jumped up. "Come *on*, Sam!" Sam had already stood and was wiping his mouth with his blue-checked cloth napkin.

"Come on, General. Hopefully it's not a giant party cake with one of those girls that jumps out at us." Eugene winked and paused for a moment. "Well, maybe if she were in one of those German chocolate cakes, it'd be okay. I like *that* kind of cake!"

"Oh, Eugene!" chided Marlene as she smacked him playfully with her napkin.

They all piled into Sam's truck and drove a mile down to the Lowden farm. Mackey had Sam pull his vehicle right up to the barn doors.

"Okay," Mackey instructed, "now just wait for a second. I have to go in and set it up. Don't come in and *don't* look." Mackey jogged around to the side door and flipped on the lights. They could hear him rummaging around.

"I think I just want Sam to come in alone first for a second, okay?" Mackey yelled from inside the barn.

"Okay," Sam yelled back. "You want me to open the big door or come in the side door?"

"The side door. Then, when I say so, the rest of you guys can open the big door," Mackey responded, still clanking around in the barn.

"Is this like a magic show or something, Mackey? You know you aren't any good at magic, son," Eugene hollered through the door.

"Eugene, stop that." Marlene tugged him away from the door.

Jane watched Sam walk through the side door, then they all stood outside for what seemed like an unusually long time. After about three minutes, Eugene shouted, "You boys okay in there?"

"Uh, yeah. Don't come in yet, okay?" Sam said.

Another minute passed. "Boys, now what's going on in there?" Eugene yanked the door open impatiently. Sam had his arm around Mackey; their eyes were shining while they looked at what stood before them.

"Oh my God! Eugene!" Marlene stepped inside slowly, as if she were sleepwalking. She moved forward, held out her hand, and lightly swept the hood of the 1956 Ford F-100. Moonlight shone into the barn and helped reveal the dazzling fresh coat of root beer–colored paint. The truck looked like it had just rolled off the showroom floor. No one spoke a word.

Eugene stood in front of the vehicle with his head down and placed both hands on the hood, then he lifted his head with his eyes closed. Sam and Mackey stood together, their arms around each other, wiping away tears.

Finally, Mackey spoke softly, "Do you like it, Grandpa? I mean, if you don't, I . . . I can, well, Sam said he won't drive it." Mackey looked at Sam for a little help.

"Grandpa, Mackey redid everything. It's all brand new. It's really not the same truck. Look how he restored the interior. He did everything from the ground up. I promise; it's not the same truck. He was trying to do something great. Don't be mad." Sam walked closer to Eugene and put his hand on his grandpa's shoulder.

Eugene turned to Sam and grabbed him. He pulled him in tight and began to cry softly. "Oh God I love you boys. Get over here, Mackey." He held both boys in a tight embrace. "I love both you boys so damn much. Sam, you better come home from boot camp and take her for a ride, you hear?"

Sam hesitated for a moment, remembering his parents. He had told himself he'd never drive that truck, but he wasn't one to let his grandfather down. He'd have to begin to let go. He thought about Jane and all the traumatic events she'd seen and lived through. She was still standing and very much alive to tell her tales. It suddenly dawned on him that he had his own trauma to deal with. Maybe getting behind that driver's seat would help him heal. Like Jane, he had to press on.

"Yes, sir. I will. Thank you, Grandpa," Sam smiled. Then he opened the driver-side door and reached in to pop the hood. Excited, Mackey began to tell Eugene about the motor and the undercarriage.

"Alright, you three. We have to get back. Sam has to leave in less than eight hours. Start wrapping it up." Marlene and Jane stepped outside. "They died in that truck," Marlene whispered as she drew in a deep breath. "Good Lord. This is gonna take some gettin' used to."

Mackey had worked so hard to restore the truck in which his parents had been killed. A fifteen-year-old might not understand that what was significant to *him* could have an entirely different meaning to someone else.

"He didn't know what he was doin'. He was just trying to be a good boy," Marlene convinced herself.

"Do you want to walk back, Marlene?" Jane opened her jacket and showed her the pack of American Spirits she'd stuck in her inside coat pocket.

"Yes, I do," smiled Marlene as she took the cigarette Jane offered to her. They walked home, mostly in silence, and chain-smoked the entire mile. Marlene didn't open up to Jane about the accident that killed her son and his wife, and Jane didn't press her.

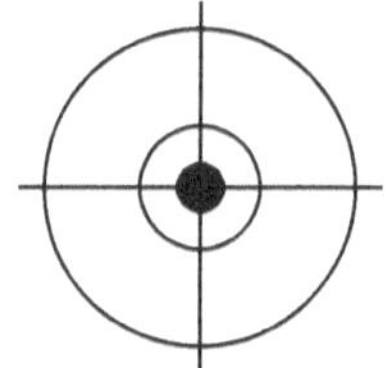

CHAPTER THIRTY-ONE

Sam and Jane drove together to Albuquerque to catch their flight to California. They were leaving at 0400 sharp. There wasn't much time for breakfast, let alone long goodbyes. After seeing Sam off, Jane planned to return to Marlene and Eugene's to pry Maxine away from Shep, then make her way back home. The family all kissed and embraced one last time, and watched as Jane and Sam drove away.

"You ready for this, Sam?"

"Am I?" he questioned.

They didn't talk for most of the drive and they spent the duration of the flight sleeping. When the flight attendant announced they were about to make their descent, Sam shot straight upright from a dead sleep. He twisted his seat belt strap nervously. As they disembarked, Jane reassured Sam.

"Hey, just relax. This is the easy part. All you have to worry about now is some drill instructor pissing down your neck. Just stay focused and don't get any injuries in boot camp. And remember the 'special bus.'" Jane nudged him as she smiled.

Gunnery Sergeant Patrick Stammers met them at the airport. He was wearing full dress blues and sported a chest full of medals, including the Silver Star. He wore a patch over a missing eye, and half of his left ear was shredded. Under his crisp, blue dress pants, Jane knew he wore a prosthetic, which gave him a very slight limp. He looked gruff and beat to hell, yet he stood tall. It was obvious he was still proud to serve his country.

"Sam, see that?" Jane asked as she pointed to the sergeant's sleeve. "Three up, two down, cross rifles in the center," referring to Stammers' rank insignia. "Gunnery sergeant. These guys know their shit." Sam stood mesmerized by his first Marine contact on their journey. Jane wondered what Stammers was doing at the airport. What she didn't realize was that a lieutenant colonel was at the base waiting for her. He was her biggest fan and wanted to acknowledge her importance by catering to her in an unconventional manner.

"General Howard, ma'am, Gunnery Sergeant Patrick Stammers." He stood at attention. "I have an escort waiting for you, ma'am."

"An escort? I don't recall bringing my arrival to anyone's attention."

"Pardon me, ma'am. We received a call from Sheriff Earl Nez about your arrival. It's not often that a general of your caliber comes out here. It's an honor to meet you, ma'am," Stammers continued, still standing at attention.

"At ease. Thank you, Gunny. I assure you this isn't necessary."

When the three of them reached the curb, Jane and Sam were ushered into a black Lincoln Town Car. Two Marine Corps flags flew from the front headlights.

"So much for delivering you under the radar, Sam. I have a feeling you can expect a little more hazing than usual when you get to camp. These boys may think you got preferential treatment."

"Didn't I?" Sam patted her knee.

When they arrived at the recruiting depot and stepped from the vehicle, they were escorted down a red carpet lined with Marines in full dress uniform—a far cry from the yellow footsteps Jane had warned Sam about. Jane was glad she decided to wear her black business suit on the trip rather than her T-shirt and cargo pants.

Lieutenant Colonel Justin Briggs met them at the end of the carpet. He was a smart-looking Marine who, at around forty-five years old, appeared to be too young to hold such a high rank. He saluted her and said with a cheeky smile, "I've been waiting most of my life to meet you, General. I never thought I would. Welcome to Camp Pendleton," he said and shook her hand firmly.

"Hello, Lieutenant Colonel Briggs. This is Sam Stapelton. He's a new recruit and he's family. I expect you'll treat him well."

"Of course, General. My grandfather spoke of you all the time. You became a legend in our home. You're one of the reasons I became a Marine," he explained, glowing.

"Your grandfather? Briggs? *Major General* Briggs? He was your *grandfather*?" Jane stuck out her hand to shake his again. "Did you hear that, Sam? This is Major General Briggs' grandson! I'll be damned!"

"I did," smiled Sam.

Briggs looked at Jane a bit uncomfortably and said, "General, you know I have to do this, don't you?"

"Affirmative," replied Jane, and she gave Sam a quick pat on the back.

Briggs bellowed, "Gunnery Sergeant Stammers!"

The gunnery sergeant reappeared and Briggs winked at Jane. She knew this performance was at Sam's expense. Briggs would never call out his gunny like this. Clearly, he was having some fun with Jane. And Sam.

"Sir, yes sir!"

"What is this slimy little maggot doing messing up my fine Persian carpet and disgracing my perfect Marines? Did he escape and run wild like a monkey out of the zoo, shitting on my boots? ANSWER ME, GUNNERY SERGEANT! Why did this happen on your watch?" Briggs' neck veins were throbbing. Jane knew the display was meant to test Sam.

Stammers took over, yelling at Sam, "Did you hear what the lieutenant colonel just asked, you maggot? Did you escape and go shitting your little monkey ass all over his boots?"

Sam didn't answer. He clearly didn't know what to say.

"DID YOU SHIT ON THE LIEUTENANT COLONEL'S BOOTS, RECRUIT?"

"No sir, I did not." Sam stood firm, his eyes focused straight ahead.

"YOU *WILL* ANSWER: 'THIS RECRUIT DID NOT SHIT ON THE LIEUTENANT COLONEL'S BOOTS, SIR'!" Spit flew from Stammers' mouth as he screamed in Sam's face.

Jane looked at Sam as he stood tall and did not flinch. She knew then he'd be just fine.

Jane remained in San Diego with Lieutenant Colonel Briggs for the evening before flying back to Albuquerque. When she returned to the farm, she gathered the few things she had brought with her. Jane reassured Eugene and Marlene that Sam was going to be a wonderful Marine and she promised to watch over him. Jane thought she had come to teach Sam the lessons of a Marine's life. It turned out Sam had taught her a few things as well—about loyalty. He had reconnected her to this family, and they had once again become a deep part of her life. She hugged Eugene and Marlene, and quickly said goodbye, confident she would see them again soon.

"Come on, Maxine! We have another adventure ahead of us." Maxine cocked her head to look at Jane in loving approval. They drove several hundred uneventful miles through the golden wheat fields of the western plains. Jane spent many of those miles wondering how many rattlesnakes lay hidden among the tall, deep rows. She hoped the combines would do a sufficient job of shredding them during harvest.

"Fucking snakes. They're everywhere," she said aloud. "Well, Max, where we're going next, there'll certainly be snakes more dangerous than these rattlers."

Jane arrived at a private airport on time. She kept Max on her lap for the entire flight. Jane barely moved for the twelve hours it took to reach the landing strip at the small village of Komodeen, in southern Africa.

"Here's a perk for being a former general of Orion, eh, Max? No commercial flights and no Customs to deal with. You'd be quarantined if it weren't for me." Max reached up and gave Jane a couple thankful kisses as Jane watched the ground approach over Orion's airstrip.

After they touched down, Maxine jumped off Jane's lap and stretched her cramped legs. The plane door opened, ushering in the familiar, welcoming African heat. Max followed Jane to their awaiting Jeep, where Jane loaded her gear and placed Max in the seat next to her. Jane paused for a moment to drink in the warmth and gaze across the exquisite red sand. She then stepped on the gas and began navigating the road's familiar twists and turns. Her heart began to race as she realized she was home. *This* was where her body craved to be. In Africa, Jane felt whole and healed.

She turned a corner and came to a stop before a small tan house surrounded by tall trees. A quaint front porch beckoned her. Jane's energy surged even more as she spied scruffy hornbills perched on a tree branch and a stunning lilac-breasted roller diving for grasshoppers.

As she pulled into the familiar, hard-packed clay driveway, Jane asked, "You ready for this, Maxine?" Max pawed at the door and wagged her tail feverishly. Maxine also knew and loved this place, although she was probably missing Shep by now.

As Jane approached the front porch, she saw a young woman in an upstairs window. She was gyrating to blaring hip-hop music and was oblivious to Jane's arrival. Jane studied her for a moment and realized the young girl was kickboxing, not dancing.

Jane shook her head and chuckled under her breath as she mounted the steps, "Oh, Murphy. You're so silly."

Jane had just raised her slightly shaking hand to knock on the screen door when she noticed a torrent of red dust roiling out from behind a fast-moving vehicle in the distance. For a moment, she was reminded of Sam and the way he would tear up the country roads in his truck, causing dust to swirl behind him like a tornado.

The car approached the house at excessive speed, especially for a 1965 El Camino. Behind the wheel, a wild-haired lady sang her heart out to Metallica, which blared from the car windows. "Give me fuel, give me fire . . ."

Jane laughed out loud as the car barreled into the drive. Quinn jumped out and ran up the long drive toward her.

Jane turned back to knock but the door had opened. A striking onyx-skinned woman stood before her. Her long, black hair hung in dreadlocks that were braided at her shoulders. The woman's eyes swelled immediately with tears when she recognized Jane.

Although she looked older, the woman appeared more sophisticated than she used to, but she still cast that glowing blue hue. Ula reached out to hug Jane. Her bony arms were wrapped with thick, beaded bands of friendship bracelets she made each time Jane returned. She never took them off. As they hugged excitedly, Jane's hair became entangled in the dog tags Jane had given to Ula thirty-seven years earlier. Ula still wore them around her neck.

Ula burst with joy as she hugged and kissed Jane, and jumped up and down with excitement.

"Oh, Hatari! *Look* at you! You look *horrible*. I must fix your hair. *What* has happened to you? You are like a *child*."

Jane protested Ula's usual fussing and yelled through her tears, "Girls! Girls! Come quickly! Murphy! Quinn! Your mother's home!"

THE END

GLOSSARY

Actual a form of address, usually used during transmissions to denote the person in charge, on the ground

A team first team to go on the offensive

BDU Battle Dress Uniform

burst mission a short recon mission with very little planning

cal caliber

Cal Force calibrated force

CamelBak water container, portable hydration pack worn strapped to a person's back

CO commanding officer

CQB close quarters battle

CT op covert tactical operation

DAOS French Special Operations team

deuce gear standard Marine Corps–issued gear that contains a helmet, pistol belt, magazine pouches, first-aid kit, and an entrenching tool, or E-tool, among other things

Elevator 23 the steel elevator used to transport trainees to subject them to torture

FARC The Revolutionary Armed Forces of Columbia, The People's Army

FOB forward operating base

FORECON US Marine Corps Force Reconnaissance

FSX French Special Assassins

H&K Heckler & Koch

HALO High Altitude–Low Opening

IED improvised explosive device

intel military intelligence

Ka-Bar military fighting knife

Krav Maga military self-defense and fighting system

LRA Lord's Resistance Army

MANPAD Man-Portable Air-Defense System

MI6 British Secret Intelligence Service

MOLLE Modular Lightweight Load-Carrying Equipment

MONUC United Nations Mission in the Democratic Republic of Congo

MRE meal ready to eat

NORAD North American Aerospace Defense Command

pdr pounder

PTSD posttraumatic stress disorder

rack military cot

range days days spent at the shooting range

recon reconnaissance

RPG rocket-propelled grenade

ruck rucksack

SAM surface-to-air missile

skaggers large camel spiders notorious for their nasty, venomous bites

SOS Sons of Silence motorcycle gang

split the goose divide the team to launch a counterattack

TAC tactical

"the cow's gone dry" "there's no sign of the target"

"tight on his six" "right behind him"

thermal mini monocular military-grade thermal imaging device

The Room where soldiers were subject to torture

tiger-stripe to apply greasepaint to the face in a striped pattern

wachawi witches

warrior tactical belt, worn around the waist, loaded by soldiers' personal weaponry

waterboarding an interrogation technique that simulates the experience of drowning; large quantities of water are poured over a cloth that covers the mouth and nose of an immobilized captive

WHCA White House Correspondence Agency

yellow signal that means "Stand by!"

ABOUT THE AUTHOR

When I was six years old, a neighbor boy shot me in the knuckle with a pellet gun. I thought that was pretty damn cool. Surprisingly, that was not my first injury. Farm living was risky for an adventurous girl. I had already seen the inside of the ER earlier that year when my brother launched a large dirt clod down a hill into my small body. Diagnosis: blood clot in my leg. The following year I thought I was Evel Knievel. I finished building my BMX bike, set up several five-gallon buckets, and built a ramp out of plywood. I then proceeded to break three ribs after slamming into my handle bars in an attempt to jump the buckets.

In the fourth grade I single-handedly fought an eighth-grade boy who had been tormenting some of my friends. The fight lasted two hours. I won. The next evening, the kid's dad came to the door to chew out my parents. Then the dad saw me—a twerpy girl. He looked at his *son* and apologized to my parents. I still got a spanking, but at school I was a hero.

When I was eleven, I was the cool kid that fell down some stairs, broke my leg, and had a cast. The following spring, I broke my fingers (all of them) playing football in middle school (but I caught the ball and scored a touchdown). I proceeded to tear ligaments in volleyball, break my tailbone in basketball, get stitches dozens of times, and nearly drowned. (I'm still prone to recurring skateboarding accidents at nearly fifty years old. My poor parents. They just bought me a helmet.) The list kept growing and so did I as my life of adventure continued. Broken arms, hernias, herniated disks—wahoo! Chemical burns, more blood clots, West Nile encephalitis, dengue fever, seizures, cot spider bites, and snakebites. Shit! All these injuries are linked to some great adventures, intriguing countries, deep physical scarring, and brutal emotional damage that led to this unique story.

I am traumatized. I am scarred. I am littered with imperfections. I suffer from PTSD. Yet I rejoice in every experience I have endured. I am inspired that one day we will commit to ending violence against women and children, and care adequately for veterans suffering from PTSD. Enjoy this book and the ones to follow.

With gratitude,

E. D. Erker

* 9 7 8 1 7 3 3 0 4 8 7 0 5 *